SF Books by

DOOM S
Star
Bio
Battle Pod
Cyborg Assault
Planet Wrecker
Star Fortress

EXTINCTION WARS SERIES
Assault Troopers
Planet Strike

INVASION AMERICA SERIES
Invasion: Alaska
Invasion: California
Invasion: Colorado
Invasion: New York

OTHER SF NOVELS
Alien Honor
Accelerated
Strotium-90
I, Weapon

Visit www.Vaughnheppner.com for more information.

Star Fortress

(Doom Star 6)

by
Vaughn Heppner

Copyright © 2012 by the author.

This book is a work of fiction. Names, characters, places and incidents are either products of the author's imagination or used fictitiously. Any resemblance to actual events, locales or persons, living or dead, is entirely coincidental. All rights reserved. No part of this publication can be reproduced or transmitted in any form or by any means, without permission in writing from the author.

ISBN-13: 978-1496194244
ISBN-10: 1496194241
BISAC: Fiction / Science Fiction / Military

Part I: The Beginning

-1-

Defensive satellites ringed the Red Planet in geosynchronous orbit. A few of the satellites were armored with particle shields. Most were half-built structures still under construction. Three were battered wrecks, masses of junk from damage sustained during the Third Battle for Mars.

Station Santa Anna presently orbited the night-side. It boasted an operational laser, a completed hull and a full array of sensors. Inside the satellite on the bridge, an alarm sounded.

"What's going on?" the commander asked. He sat up from where he'd been dozing.

A warrant officer checked his screen. "It appears the computer has picked up an anomaly, sir."

"Where?" the commander asked as he buttoned his uniform. He was a one-armed man, which might have made the buttoning difficult, but he deftly completed the task. "Give me specifics."

The frowning warrant officer bent over his sensor equipment, making swift adjustments. "I'm putting the image on the main screen, sir."

The commander shoved a cap onto his gray hair as he looked up at the screen. Something black and round plunged through the Martian atmosphere. Even as he watched, the object deployed massive chutes.

"Give me an—"

"Sir!" the warrant officer said. "The capsule is composed of an anti-radar polymer, and those are stealth-chutes we're witnessing. Computer analysis gives it a ninety-three percent probability of being a cyborg vessel of unknown design. It's obviously attempting a landing."

"This is a code eleven emergency," the commander said, his voice steely. "Activate our laser."

"I'm tracking," the warrant office said. "Sir, the object is headed for a sandstorm."

"Weapons!" the commander shouted.

"Just a minute, sir," the weapons officer said nervously. "There seems to be a glitch in the system."

The commander leaned forward as he stared at the main screen. "Is this their first infiltration or simply the latest of an ongoing effort?"

People stared at him in horror. Several years ago, there had been a cyborg converter in Olympus Mons. The volcano was Mars and the Solar System's largest.

"The object is entering the sandstorm!" the warrant officer shouted.

"Fire the laser!" the commander roared.

The stricken weapons officer looked up, shaking his head.

The commander's eyes widened as two red spots appeared on his pale cheeks. "Prepare a Chavez Seven missile."

"Sir," the weapons officer whispered. "Those are nuclear-tipped missiles."

"Don't you think I know that?" the commander asked in a harsh voice.

During the Third Battle for Mars, the Highborn had exploded a Hellburner on Olympus Mons. The missile's devastating effect had turned the idea of nuclear bombardment into a taboo subject. The fractured moon Phobos had also rained chunks onto the planet, killing even more millions.

"We dare not let the cyborgs get another foothold on Mars," the commander said. "Launch now before it's too late."

The weapons officer's forehead was shiny with sweat as he tapped his screen.

Through camera five, the bridge personnel watched the missile expel from its tube. In seconds, an orange contrail made it the brightest object against the planet's dark surface.

"It needs to accelerate faster," the commander whispered.

The seconds ticked away as the race absorbed everyone's attention. The warrant officer tapped a command. A split-screen appeared, showing the sandstorm that had swallowed the capsule and beside it, the missile headed down.

"Give me a radar fix," the commander said.

The warrant officer shook his head. "Cyborg stealth technology is better than our sensors, sir."

Five minutes and forty-three seconds later, the missile entered the sandstorm.

"They could have landed by now," the commander groaned.

Thirty-eight seconds later, there was an explosion, hopefully, detonated by a proximity detector. In any case, cheers erupted on the station.

"We got it!" the weapons officer shouted.

"Can you confirm that?" the commander asked.

The warrant officer hunched over his screen, finally looking up. "No, sir. I cannot confirm a kill, although it seems likely."

The commander cursed under his breath. He'd lost his wife and grandchildren to the cyborgs during the Third Battle for Mars. "Maybe this secret vessel launched escape pods, scattering cyborgs before the missiles hit."

"That seems highly unlikely, sir," the warrant officer said.

The commander took off his cap, setting it on an armrest. As he agonized over his choices, he scratched his scalp. "We must saturate the possible landing zones with nuclear weapons."

Three seconds of stunned silence ensued.

"Respectfully, sir," the warrant officer said, "that's a High Command decision."

Fitting the cap onto his head, the commander scowled. "Then let's hope they make the right decision. Patch me through to Satellite Defense HQ. Time is critical."

-2-

Two days later, Captain Ricardo Sandoval of the Martian Commandos struggled through a sandstorm. The storm was the worst *red-out* in memory, with millions of particles of iron-oxide dust howling around him.

The cyborgs are dead. What could possibly survive a nuclear holocaust? Ricardo snorted, his disgust growing. *This is stupid. Why am I even here?*

He knew that one of the reasons was a nervous High Command. A few generals had wanted to carpet bomb the surface with nukes. Cooler heads had prevailed. To keep the others happy, however, they had sent for him, the leader of the Martian Commandos. Unfortunately, they had placed the most frightened general in charge of the search operation.

The man had told him, "We could be sending you into something worse than death, Captain. If this was a reinforcement landing and the cyborgs have already built a converter…" The general had insisted on a suicidal procedure. "If you're captured, the enemy might run you through a converter, changing you into a meld of machine and flesh. For your sake, we can never allow that to happen."

Yeah, right, for my sake.

Through his suit, Ricardo rubbed his gut. For the mission, he had swallowed intestinal explosives that would detonate if he failed to tap in the needed code every half hour. Because of the explosives, every Commando was on stims to keep him awake for the duration of the mission.

The only danger is these gut-bombs. What a deranged idea.

Ricardo had thought about declining the assignment. The reason he hadn't was that he was one of the privileged: a steroid-pumped Martian with a normal caloric intake. On Mars, privilege definitely meant responsibilities. For Ricardo, it was risking his guts in this storm.

Knowing the general would check his radio-log later, Ricardo clicked on his suit-com. "See anything?" he asked.

There were four other Commandos out here with him. The rest were in the APC laager or checking out different coordinates.

"Negative, sir," Max radioed. A few seconds later, he added, "What's your Geiger counter say?"

"That we're in a radiation-streaked storm," Ricardo said. "Keep your eyes open. It would be just our luck that one of those things made it onto the surface."

Max laughed, letting Ricardo know the sergeant understood the joke.

Checking a gauge, Ricardo found that wind-speed had risen to seventy-three km/h. It kept threatening to lift him airborne. Worse, visibility had dwindled so all he could see was several meters ahead. The swirling particles, they were like a living wall, a red shroud, an avalanche ready to bury him on the surface. The only thing worse was the noise. The shrieks were like vibrating spikes driving into his skull.

Like his men, Ricardo wore a bodysuit and a rebreather. His eyes felt gritty and his breathing was harsh. He had thin features and a spacer's tan, with a mustache hiding his lips. Despite the polymer visor, hundreds of tiny lines were etched across it. If the particles abraded *through* the mask, he would choke to death on sand—or would die from a lack of oxygen.

Ricardo snarled as the suit's air-conditioner unit whined, trying to cool his overheated body. He clutched a waist-high rock and glanced behind. The others struggled through the sandstorm. Like him, each gripped a gyroc rifle.

"How much farther are we walking, Captain?" Max radioed.

"Another two kilometers at least," Ricardo said.

The answering oaths and curses made him nod. What a meaningless assignment. He ought to—

A warning tone beeped in his helmet. Ricardo frowned. *That can't be anything serious.* He swiveled his head, watching on his HUD. Another tone sounded. His sensors had picked up something moving out here, something that was heavier than a man. All Ricardo saw was red rocks and swirling sand.

"Captain," crackled in his comlink. "I'm picking up something. Could it be a cyborg?"

The idea intensified Ricardo's frown. This was a lousy spot for a showdown. Worse, the red-out made it impossible to radio for backup or to warn High Command if it proved they had been right. Who would have believed that?

"We need to set up a perimeter," Ricardo said. "Max, take the south. Rodriguez, you have east. Carlos is west and Bandores is in the center to provide a quick-reaction force."

The men radioed in, and they took up their positions. As they did, Ricardo recalled Osadar Di, Marten Kluge's cyborg. He had seen the things she could do: the bounding leaps, the exhibitions of inhuman strength and worst of all, the insect-like speed. He had trained with Osadar and he had listened to Kluge's combat maxims, which had broadened his thinking. After Kluge's departure, Ricardo had become the trainer of advanced tactics. His blog had become famous on Mars because of his retelling of his time with Marten Kluge.

Using the rock as a shield, Ricardo lay on his stomach, letting the storm howl above him. Swirling dust-clouds blew over other rocks and boulders, and created ghost images on his sensors. Tiny particles of iron oxide continuously struck his visor, causing a steady clicking noise.

Then he saw movement. Was it a rolling rock or was it a cyborg?

He curled his lips. Kluge had taught them: *You don't win by defending. You attack.*

"I see something," he radioed.

"Is it a cyborg?" Max asked. The sergeant sounded nervous.

"I'm going to find out," Ricardo said gruffly. "I don't want anyone panicking. We do this by the numbers."

"Roger," Max said, and the others radioed likewise.

Breathing deeply, Ricardo crawled out of the rock's protection into the fury of the sandstorm. The wind slammed against his helmet and almost tore away his gyroc.

Ricardo gripped his rifle more tightly. Cyborgs moved with incredible speed. They had armored brainpans, graphite bones and reinforced muscles. Computer enhancements gave them speeded rationality to assess in nanoseconds what a man needed seconds or even a minute to decide.

The howling storm rattled pebbles against his suit. Ricardo looked up. He saw it then. The sight thinned his lips. The cyborg was a dark blot in the sandstorm, and it moved like a jittering fly.

"It's here!" Ricardo shouted, with the sound reverberating in his helmet. "Grid seven-B-eight." He raised his rifle and pulled the trigger. The gyroc fired a .75 caliber spin-stabilized rocket-shell. The rifle was effectively recoilless, meaning the butt didn't slam against his shoulder after each shot. The shell popped out of the rifle-tube as its mini-rocket-engine ignited. He shot an APEX-round: Armor-Piercing Explosive. The super-hard penetrator used a big motor and a bigger explosive packet.

Ricardo heard the hisses of other APEX-rounds firing into the storm and whooshing past his head. Unfortunately, the rounds went in a variety of directions, blown off-course by the violent wind.

"Cease fire!" Ricardo shouted. "We'll never hit it at a distance. We have to get close."

At that moment, the cyborg rose up before him. It wore a metallic-fiber suit, and it seemed unaffected by the wind. With its mechanical-melded parts, it must weigh enough to ignore the lifting power of the storm.

Ricardo froze. He might have stayed frozen longer, but he had trained endless hours since Marten Kluge taught Martians how to fight. A portion of his training had been in acting fast and then faster yet, to increase his reaction time when surprised.

Ricardo frantically rolled left as the cyborg kicked a spiked boot at his head. He saved himself, as the cyborg bounded at someone else. It sounded like Bandores screaming over the comlink. Using his booted toes, Ricardo swiveled on his belly. Then he raised his head.

The thing's arm was a blur of motion as it hurled a rock, smashing Rodriguez's helmet. Ricardo swore. The cyborg was too fast for them, especially in this environment. Had it lost its weapons? Is that why it used primitive means to fight?

"Kill it!" Ricardo shouted, as he surged to his feet. A rocket-shell whooshed past him, a blur of darkness and an orange contrail. It missed his head by centimeters. He couldn't worry about that now.

The cyborg reached Max. Something dark moved in its hand as the hand made contact with Max. The third Commando crumpled onto the rocky soil.

Hatred boiled in Ricardo as he leaped at the thing. The wind lifted him, shoving him fast at the cyborg. Ricardo landed, and he staggered, almost slamming down onto his belly. Like a dancer, Ricardo moved his feet, maintaining balance as the wind blew him.

The cyborg whirled around.

In a microsecond of time, Ricardo saw the inhuman eyes, the plasti-flesh face. The cyborg held a dark blade, a wet one—bloody! Without thinking and as he moved into close range, Ricardo shoved the muzzle of the gyroc against the cyborg's stomach. As soon as he felt the pressure of contact, he pulled the trigger. Just as fast, a knife swiped at him. Ricardo shouted and he twisted. The tip of the blade slashed open his environmental suit. At the same time, the APEX shell in the cyborg's combat-armor exploded. That knocked the abomination off its feet.

Ricardo landed on his side, but he scrambled up faster than the injured monster. At the same time, the auto-sealants fixed the breach in his environmental suit. Somehow, Ricardo had kept hold of his gyroc. He shot the cyborg at pointblank range. The shell broke into the cyborg's helmet. A half-second later, another explosion occurred, ripping away the monster's faceplate. The thing tumbled back and thudded onto the ground.

Ricardo tried to fire again, but the creature kicked its leg, smashing the rifle. Then the cyborg attempted to rise.

By fallen Phobos, I have to kill it before it kills me!

As the wind howled and threatened to lift Ricardo airborne once again, he drew a bayonet. As the cyborg climbed to its feet, Ricardo lunged and thrust the bayonet into the thing from Neptune. He stabbed it seventeen times before it died squirming on the sands of Mars. Seventeen times before a red light vanished somewhere behind its eyes.

Only then did Captain Ricardo Sandoval think about hunting for the surviving member of his squad.

-3-

In Far Mars Orbit, a cyborg *Lurker*-class Assault-ship—L7R325—stopped receiving signals from the surface. The large vessel was composed of black, radar-resistant polymers, built at odd curves, angles and planes to lessen sensor identification. It was not technically a warship, although it possessed a load of stealth-drones.

It drifted at far orbit, having sailed through the void on built-up velocity and braking with low-signature thrusters. Its design and tactical application was predicated on proven cyborg superiority. It was a troop ship: stealthily approaching the target in order to insert cyborgs and capture it. The Web-Mind in charge of operations presently ran through options as it computed known data on the Red Planet.

The missile launched from Station Santa Anna told it much about the defensive satellites ringing Mars. It was surprised the stealth-capsule had reached the surface at all. Martian defenses were much weaker than it had anticipated. Yes, the Web-Mind now knew how the Homo sapiens communicated with each other, how they reacted to an insertion invasion and the location of their primary defensive stations. Conquest of Mars…there was a sixty-two percent probability of victory.

Eighteen minutes after the analysis, the Web-Mind pulsed orders: *Load five stealth-capsules with soldiers and the sixth with a converter unit*. Once launched, it would fire three black-ice pods, one for each of the key satellites. It would hold five other stealth-capsules in reserve and the second converter as it continued its cloaked orbit.

The Mars Assault would be run along different parameters than any of the former campaigns. That would confuse the Homo sapiens, who reacted predictably and would expect similar moves from their opponent.

As the Web-Mind reconfigured the optimal strategy, the Lurker's rail-gun ejected the first stealth-capsule at the distant Red Planet. It would take the capsules eight weeks to reach an insertion orbit. By then, the Homo sapiens would begin to relax, expecting that the worst was over.

-4-

Three days after killing the cyborg, Captain Sandoval hung onto the insides of a shaking Comet 9 strike-jet. After the sandstorm fight, he had been badly injured and was now on a ton of painkillers and half out of his mind.

The strike-jet was an old military plane, a two-seater, having survived countless hits and patch-jobs. Ricardo had already endured hours in it and now found himself on the other side of Mars.

Below, red dust-clouds billowed across the surface. It was a global storm, covering most of the planet. Although Mars was smaller than Earth, its landmass was a little more than all Earth's continents combined. The surface of Mars consisted of a worldwide desert. As dust entered the atmosphere, sunlight heated it, increasing the temperature, sometimes as much as thirty degrees Centigrade. That caused winds to rush to colder areas, picking up yet more dust and adding to the situation. On Earth, water vapor was the main heating agent instead of dust. And on Earth, deserts were limited in area and therefore unable to feed a global storm. Dust clouds often grew in the Gobi desert of Mongolia Sector, for instance, but when they blew over the Pacific Ocean, the storm soon died from the lack of new fueling dust.

Looking down through the billowing iron-oxide particles, Ricardo spied volcanoes and deep valleys.

"Hang on," the pilot said. "It will get rough for a few minutes."

As the plane blanked, it shivered hard into the wind. Something metal dislodged from the console in front of Ricardo. The part struck his foot, and sparks shot from the console.

"There's an extinguisher to your left!" the pilot shouted.

"What?" Ricardo shouted back.

The sparks caught fire, and a burnt electrical smell assaulted Ricardo's nose. The flames before him flickered with bitter purpose. To add injury to the emergency, the rattling and shaking around him increased.

"Put out the fire, amigo!" the pilot shouted. "Do it before it shorts something important and we crash."

The words finally penetrated Ricardo's hazy thoughts. He spotted the extinguisher, tore it from the holder and studied it for a half-second. The burnt electrical smell was worse now and the flames bigger. He aimed the nozzle at the flames and pressed the switch. Foam hissed, coating the console. Some of it sprayed back onto Ricardo. A fleck landed on his lips. It tasted awful. He leaned forward in his seat, pulling against the restraints and pressed the button again, putting out the electrical fire.

By this time, the jet plunged out of the bottom of the dust storm and entered one of the long Martian valleys that crisscrossed the planet. The shaking and rattling quit. Now Ricardo heard the laboring jet engine. At the same time, he noticed the sharp decrease of illumination. They were at the bottom of the dust cloud and had huge canyon walls on either side of them. He glanced right and left, and estimated each wall as about a kilometer away.

"Where are we?" Ricardo shouted.

"We're nearing Salvador Dome, amigo."

Ricardo blinked several times, until he grew aware of the extinguisher in his hands. He shoved it back into its holder so it the locks snapped.

Like this jet, just about everything was old and aging on Mars. Ricardo wouldn't have been surprised if the extinguisher had lacked foam. Salvador Dome was a grim reminder of the luck and disrepair here.

After the Third Battle for Mars, everyone had died in the dome. Against odds, a boulder-sized piece of Phobos had flashed into the valley, streaked the half kilometer to the bottom and shattered the main structure. The moon-meteor had proceeded to smash through every level of Salvador Dome. No one survived the impact. To save time and effort—critical commodities on Mars—workers had dumped the corpses down the meteor-made hole. It was a sealed mass grave now and a ghost-haunted dome.

Why take me halfway across the planet to bring me here? It made no sense in terms of jet-fuel and use of the aging Comet 9.

The pilot's radio crackled into life. "You have ten seconds to identify yourself," a female operator told them.

Ricardo frowned. Ten seconds? That would imply a military capacity to do something about non-compliance. That made even less sense. Large-scale defensive equipment was among the rarest of commodities on Mars. Why station anti-air missiles down here at a dead dome?

A constant whine sounded from the pilot's console.

"Ground control has lock-on," the pilot informed Ricardo. "I guess I'd better answer." The pilot clicked a switch, saying, "This is an Omi Operational flight."

Omi? That was the name of Marten Kluge's best friend. That couldn't be a coincidence, could it?

"I'm bringing Captain Ricardo Sandoval to the site," the pilot said. "Those are per the orders of Secretary-General Gomez."

Ricardo looked up in wonder. No one had said anything about the Secretary-General. "What's going on?" he asked.

"You have permission to land," the operator said. "But if you deviate from the flight corridor, you will be targeted and shot down."

"They want us to feel welcome," the pilot said over his shoulder.

"Salvador Dome is defended?" Ricardo asked.

The pilot laughed. "They're targeting us with Veracruz SAMs."

Ricardo knew those were the highest-grade Surface to Air Missiles the Mars Planetary Union possessed. What he couldn't fathom is why they ringed Salvador Dome, a dead city.

"Do you know what's going on?" Ricardo asked.

"Yes I do, amigo. The SAMs have lock-on and the operator means exactly what she says. We stay in the flight corridor all the way down. With your permission, Captain, I will concentrate on that."

"Yes, please do," Ricardo said. He leaned near the canopy as the jet banked slightly. Below was a great dome, with a jagged hole to the left of center. He spied the SAM sites flanking the dark dome. What did they guard down there? He supposed he would find out soon enough.

The rest of the flight proved uneventful. They soon taxied down a runaway, put on their masks, climbed out and entered an APC. The military vehicle took them to a large garage separate from the dome.

There Ricardo parted company from the pilot and soon found himself alone on a chair in an empty room. It was more of a large box with a metal floor and walls. There was a faint drone coming from somewhere and the slightest vibration against his feet. Ricardo was used to this: move here, go there, hurry up and wait. It surprised him High Command hadn't kept him on the ground searching for more cyborgs. Had the generals decided the capsule was a first landing attempt?

Ricardo's stomach growled, but then it often did. He was always hungry, even though he ate sumptuously according to Martian standards. Before it could growl again, one of the doors opened.

To his amazement, Secretary-General Gomez entered. He recognized her from the news blogs, particularly as she wore her customary green uniform. She was a tall woman with darker-than-average skin. She had tight curls, wore sunglasses and moved stiffly, using a cane as she dragged her left foot. Long ago, she had been a gunman in the Resistance. Nine, Political Harmony Corps guards had died on Martian streets due to Gomez's firing. The tenth PHC guard had worn the latest body-armor and returned fire, sending three explosive slugs into Gomez's frame. Reconstructive surgery had saved her life, but she lived with constant pain these days.

"Captain Sandoval," she said in a strong voice.

Ricardo lurched to his feet at attention as he saluted crisply.

"You recognize me, do you?"

He nodded.

The faintest of smiles appeared on Gomez's thin face. "You are Mars's great Cyborg Slayer, are you not?"

"I killed one in a sandstorm."

"And thereby saved one of your Commandos," Gomez said. "I read the report. You bayoneted it to death. From what they tell me about cyborgs, that is most impressive."

"The cyborg was already damaged and lacked modern weaponry," Ricardo said.

"It also slaughtered your men as if they were children," Gomez said. "Under the circumstances, your feat was amazing."

Ricardo nodded brusquely.

Gomez tapped the floor with her cane. "Tell me, Captain. What is your estimate of the war?"

"I'm not certain I follow you."

"Then you are not the man I need and this entire situation was a costly waste of time."

"You mean the wider war, the one against the cyborgs."

"At the moment, it is the only war that matters."

"I agree," Ricardo said.

"How gratifying," Secretary-General Gomez said dryly.

Ricardo refused to let that bother him. "We are losing the war," he said.

Gomez became alert. "What is the probable outcome?"

"The maxim is simple," he said. "To win, one must attack. We do not attack. Therefore, we will lose until we successfully take the offensive."

"And we should attack where do you think?"

"The heart of the cyborgs lies in Neptune. You must attack there. I thought Social Unity and the Highborn planned exactly that."

"Not Social Unity, Captain," Gomez said. "Social Unity is merely one component of our allied front. The Jovians,

Martians and Earthmen have formed an alliance of regular men, don't you remember?"

"The Highborn, Social Unity and the Jovians have warships. We do not."

Gomez leaned on her cane toward him. "Does our lack of a fleet bother you?"

Ricardo grew puzzled. If seemed as if his answer was important to her. What possible reason…his face grew slack. "We're building warships," he whispered. "Is that what this is about?"

Pain creased her features, and the fist holding the cane knotted. "Where did you gain this information? You will tell me, Captain. We have learned from our enemies and will resort to whatever means necessary to find what we must."

"I fail to…" Ricardo saw it then—the reason why they had put SAMs here. Yes, the reason they had chosen Salvador Dome for a secret project.

"Secretary-General Gomez," he said, "no one has informed me of anything. I merely added two and two together. Your line of questioning, the defensive perimeter erected here and the operator's willingness to destroy a Martian jet all points to some highly secret project. Your last question points to the nature of the secret."

"Go on," Gomez said.

"Both Inner Planets and the Jovians have warships. Mars has none. The war for survival is *the* critical action now if humanity is to survive the next few years."

Gomez lifted the cane, pointing it at Ricardo. "I have read your blog, Captain. You thrive on this war, on your association with Marten Kluge. You have a quick and agile mind. I seek those needed qualities. Even more, as you often point out in your blog, potential means nothing. The man of action who has *proven* himself capable should lead others into combat against the enemy."

"You're talking about my advancement because I killed the cyborg?"

"Exactly," Gomez said. "You fulfilled Kluge's maxims to a nicety. In the face of danger, you took a simple tool—your bayonet—and finished killing the meld. Mars needs men of your caliber, men who take what they have instead of complaining they lack the proper equipment. With the tools at hand, you achieved the needed goal. Mars has little to add to the armada. In many ways, I believe both Social Unity and the Highborn would torpedo our attempt to act the part of soldiers." Gomez shook her head. "Mars will not be denied its place in the Sun. We will join hands with the others, helping kill the common enemy. Captain, you will come with me."

Gomez turned around and limped out the door. Ricardo hurried after her. They moved down a steel corridor, toward the sound of humming and increasing vibration. Entering an elevator, they went down, the noise increasing the entire time.

The elevator stopped, the doors swished open and the two of them walked onto a balcony with a railing. Beyond was a cavernous area. Ricardo gripped the rail and carefully peered over. It was a good three hundred meters to the floor. Cables snaked everywhere and carts hurried here and there.

Ricardo swallowed as he gazed at a huge missile-shaped vessel. Metal scaffolding encompassed it. Most of the vessel was girders and fierce welding sparks. Workers crawled everywhere over it.

"The planet's resources are badly stretched," Gomez shouted into his ear. "Many of our people starve. The satellite defense is incomplete—the reason the cyborgs could slip their capsule through our net. Nearly every piece of military hardware on Mars is old and decaying. We should do everything else *except* build a warship. As we know, those are built in space, the best ones at the Sun-Works Factory."

Ricardo tore his gaze from the skeletal vessel, staring into those dark sunglasses. "Mars will join the attack?"

"Many of the Local Bosses are against this," Gomez said. "If the cyborgs launch a stealth fleet against us…"

"I understand," Ricardo said. "I also know that to win you must attack. The cyborgs are winning. Humanity is going down to defeat unless we can turn this war around. We won't turn it around building defensive satellites."

"You speak the truth," Gomez said.

Ricardo heard the fatigue in her voice. He saw the lines in her face. The Secretary-General was taking a risk, risking an entire planet on the edge of collapse. She likely risked her political career as well.

"What can I do to help you?" Ricardo asked.

Gomez limped to the railing, putting one hand on it. "You are a man of action, Captain. You are not a political infighter. There is little you can do to help me."

"Granted," he said. "Ah, I know. I'll write on my blog—"

"You will do nothing of the kind," Gomez said sternly. "Your blogging days are over."

He glanced at her. Then he nodded. "Our vessel will need Commandos, will it not?"

"There will be little room for them, but a complement of Martian Commandos will board the vessel once the time comes."

"I want a berth," Ricardo said. He dared clutch the Secretary-General's wrist. "You just said a few minutes ago that you agree with me that a proven man should lead. I killed a cyborg. Therefore, I should lead the Commandos."

"No," Gomez said.

Ricardo's fingers slipped off her wrist. He blinked in confusion. "Why did you bring me here then and show me all this? Who is a better Commando?"

"No one is better," she said, "at least in terms of killing cyborgs."

"Then why not let me go?"

"I won't let you go as the leader of the Commandos," she said.

"Then—"

"I want you to *captain* the sole Martian warship," Gomez said.

"What?"

"You will take orders directly from Marten Kluge, when and if we discover his whereabouts. Otherwise, you will make your decisions as the sole representative of the Mars Planetary Union Fleet."

"A fleet composed of one ship?" Ricardo asked.

"It is all we can launch in time, if we can even manage that. What do you say, Captain Sandoval? Do you accept the commission? Are you willing to journey to Neptune in a cramped warship?"

Ricardo studied the skeletal vessel-in-building. The thrill in his heart—"I accept with everything in me. Even if it means my death, I want to attack the cyborgs. We must attack."

Secretary-General Gomez nodded as a grim smile stretched into place. "You comfort me, Captain."

"Why is that?"

"Because I want a man in command of our ship who will draw a bayonet and stab a cyborg seventeen times. I want a man who is willing to fight to the bitter end."

"You want Marten Kluge."

She laughed. It was a short, sharp sound. "Either that," she said, "or the Martian version of him."

Pride swelled in Ricardo's chest. That was the greatest compliment of his life. Here and now, he vowed to do everything in his power to live up to the reputation. Mars must be free and humanity must survive the cyborgs!

Part II: The Build Up

-1-

Supreme Commander James Hawthorne sat before a screen as he spoke with Grand Admiral Cassius. The coiled ferocity of the Highborn never failed to impress him. It was like looking into the eyes of a psychopath. The sharp facial angles, the stark whiteness of the skin and the short hair like a panther's pelt…at heart, Cassius was a killer. It was good to remember that.

Hawthorne sat in his office in New Baghdad. The years had worn him down. He was stooped and thin, with bags under his eyes. Massive crop failures and a strain of poisonous bacteria in the algae had caused grim malnutrition or outright starvation among eighty-three percent of the SU population. There were constant food riots and battalions of riot-control militia now. Misery abounded as extinction stared humanity in the face. He felt old and used up. The nuclear destruction of the Soviets last year—

Hawthorne forced himself to concentrate on Cassius. It was hard looking into those eyes. He yearned to turn away, but the Highborn would view that as a sign of weakness.

How are we supposed to destroy the cyborgs? I can't even trust my allies.

By all reports, the Grand Admiral was aboard the *Julius Caesar*. Each of the three Doom Stars had collapsium shielding now. Hawthorne had asked for collapsium to shield some of the SU battleships. Cassius had agreed, provided such warships came under the authority of Highborn commanders. Hawthorne couldn't agree to that.

"Don't you wish to save your species?" Cassius had asked.

Hawthorne could have told Cassius you don't turn your back on a psychopath. However, he was too careful about what he told the *Master Race* to say such a thing. Highborn were proud and as ready to battle as dogs bred for the fighting pits. According to reports, the Highborn had been busy these last several weeks rearranging command slots. That was a surprise. Highborn usually made those changes immediately after a battle, not a year later. Scipio now commanded the *Genghis Khan*. The reports said that strengthened Cassius's position. Analysis suggested Cassius might have ordered the old commander's murder. That didn't strike Hawthorne as Cassius's way. The supreme Highborn was a soldier, not an assassin. It was one of the reasons Hawthorne could trust the Grand Admiral to the minimal extent he did.

"If you could give me some gesture," Cassius was saying onscreen. "It would help me thwart Admiral Sulla's position."

Hawthorne knew about Sulla. The Highborn was an Ultraist. Military Intelligence had learned about them. Ultraists spoke about purity to the Race and an elimination of the *premen infestation*. Ultraists worried about the possible seepage of the weak emotions of mercy, kindness and humility from too much contact with the premen, with normal men.

"I thought Sulla was an officer aboard your ship," Hawthorne said. He knew very well that Sulla had gained rank. He wanted to see how Cassius answered.

Onscreen, Cassius stiffened. "He is *Admiral* Sulla to you. He is Highborn and worthy of the proper respect."

"Of course," Hawthorne said.

"Admiral Sulla has gained a following and managed to oust the previous commander of the *Napoleon Bonaparte*."

"I see," Hawthorne said. That fit with his information. "What seems to be the problem then? Does Admiral Sulla not approve of our planned attack into the Neptune System?"

Cassius stared at him.

Hawthorne kept a poker face throughout the silence. Did the Grand Admiral know about the secret communication with Sulla? The new Highborn commander might be an Ultraist, but Sulla wanted the Grand Admiral's chair more than purity to his theories—at least in the short term. According to reports, Sulla was *concerned* about Cassius. If was difficult and in most cases impossible for a Highborn to admit to fear. Apparently, concern was the most they could feel. Intelligence believed there was a power-struggle going on among the Highborn. Well, there was an *intensification* to the constant power-struggle. The Highborn lived like a pack of beasts, constantly jockeying for position.

Hawthorne decided that Cassius knew about the communication with Sulla. It would be a foolish mistake to underestimate the Grand Admiral.

"What sort of gesture are we talking about?" Hawthorne asked.

"Perhaps you should return North American Sector to Highborn control," Cassius said, his eyes oily dark.

"I thought you and I had agreed to a freeze on territorial changes," Hawthorne said. "The cyborgs would rejoice if we reopened hostilities against each other."

"IImm," Cassius said. "Admiral Sulla has rightly pointed out that you broke the original agreement, taking North American Sector during the planet-wreckers' approach. By the terms of our initial truce, you must return North American Sector to us."

Hawthorne cleared his throat. This was a delicate topic. "Grand Admiral, I would like to speak frankly. Beginning in 2349 you bombarded Geneva and invaded—"

"Supreme Commander, I am not interested in listening to objections that originate from preman moral philosophies. We attacked Social Unity because we are the stronger species and were in subjection to a lesser race. The situation was unnatural, as the only true imperative is survival of the fittest. The laws of Nature are immutable, particularity in this regard. We have stopped attacking because the cyborgs represent a unique threat to both of us. What use is our victory in Inner Planets if the cyborgs swallow us afterward? You originally thought to use the cyborgs against us and realized the error of your strategy only after they had turned on you. Now at last you have turned to us for aid. We both understand that it is in our combined interests to work together. This unity cannot function, however, if you will not abide by the agreed-upon terms."

"We did not *take* North American Sector from you," Hawthorne said. "You abandoned Earth during the cyborg attack from Saturn, leaving the Free Earth Corps behind as garrison. Some of them claimed independence from you and later asked for admittance into Social Unity."

"You should have refused them."

"On what grounds?"

"To keep the continued alliance with us," Cassius said.

"But if you willingly abandon territory—"

Onscreen, Cassius leaned near. "Enough! I am simply relating to you Admiral Sulla's argument. I understand your logic. Because I do, there is a different way for you to redeem yourself with me."

"Grand Admiral?"

"The Ultraists represent a grave threat to premen—excuse me, to *humanity's* continued existence. In your thinking, why trade one threat for a similar threat several years down the corridors of time?"

"It is true I dislike Ultraist creed," Hawthorne said. "But the cyborg menace represents an immediate—"

"I dislike Admiral Sulla as he is a thorn in my side." Cassius showed his teeth in what he might have thought was a smile. "You and I have certain similarities, Supreme Commander. Our fellow soldiers waste time and effort attempting to pull us from power. Tell me, haven't you faced coup attempts against your authority?"

"I have," Hawthorne admitted, wondering where Cassius was taking this.

"Be assured there are similar attempts among the Highborn against me. In that regard, Admiral Sulla represents a problem to our alliance. By protocol and custom, however, there are only several avenues I am allowed to react concerning his objections. In other words, I could use your help."

Hawthorne raised his eyebrows. This was unprecedented: the Grand Admiral asking for human help. Despite the Highborn's arrogant way of talking, this gave Hawthorne hope. He had an ongoing debate with Security Specialist Cone. He believed Highborn could feel gratitude. Cone said the super-soldiers thought of humans as dogs. One could not feel gratitude toward a dog. Hawthorne disagreed. As food continued to disappear from the stores, many people had found it difficult butchering their dogs for the table, having a deep sense of loyalty toward the animals. If he helped Cassius now, the Grand Admiral would likely feel honor-bound to him later.

"We have several common enemies," the Grand Admiral was saying. "The first are the cyborgs. We are banding together with you to destroy them before they can convert us into abominations. The second is Admiral Sulla and his Ultraists. I do not *fear* him or them, although I know humans view their competitors in that light. The admiral's sin is that he weakens our united attempt to destroy the cyborgs. That is why I am asking you to help me send a message to the Ultraists."

"How can I do this?"

"The first way would be by ceding North American Sector to us." Onscreen, Cassius held up a hand. "You have already admitted your reluctance and probably your inability to making such a gesture. I understand. It is good for you to realize that my understanding is unique among Highborn. The reason is that I am unique in my ability to think along premen lines. It is one of my strengths."

Hawthorne nodded, impressed once again with a Highborn's innate arrogance. Sometimes he wondered how two million hyper-ambitious super-soldiers could agree to do anything together. They would never be able to survive their victory—if they could achieve it. A Solar System filled with Highborn was inconceivable. They would war against each other long before that happened. It would be constant civil war.

"There is a second way?" Hawthorne asked.

"There are two other ways. I choose the easier option because I am considering your limited capabilities. Simply stated, I ask you to meet with me as we discuss strategy together."

"We are meeting together," Hawthorne said.

"I am talking about a face-to-face meeting, a physical greeting between you and me. This will surprise you, but I have long wanted to speak with you, Supreme Commander. You have waged war relentlessly against a superior foe—us—and shown great tenacity in—"

"How would such a meeting help you against Admiral Sulla?"

Cassius scowled. No Highborn liked being interrupted. Hawthorne had done it on purpose to test the Grand Admiral's resolve.

With his right hand, Cassius wiped away the scowl. "Our meeting will show the Ultraists that I consider premen—excuse me. That I consider *humans* as worthy allies."

"Before I could agree," Hawthorne said, "I would need to speak with my people about this."

"Time is our enemy."

"I'm afraid your proposal will create a stir of distrust among my councilors. I will need to mollify the distrust."

Cassius sat back, showing surprise. "I offer this gesture in order to heighten trust among us. We are soon to begin the fateful journey, heading for the Neptune System. Our two fleets must learn to act as one. How can we achieve this unless the two supreme leaders act in concert?"

"We lack unity of command, I agree with you there," Hawthorne said.

Cassius's eyes narrowed. Then he showed his teeth in another predatory smile. "You have rare genius, Supreme Commander."

Hawthorne nodded, deciding he didn't like such praise from a Highborn.

"Hmm," Cassius said, "this distrust you mentioned, how could I help you dampen it?"

"I can think of several ways," Hawthorne said. "Firstly, I would have to bring a security detail."

"Security against Highborn?" Cassius asked, attempting a rare jest.

"We would ask you to bring a correspondingly smaller team."

"Done."

Hawthorne became thoughtful. The Grand Admiral was trying to be appealing. What lay behind it?

"I would like to meet soon," Cassius said.

"I understand. You still have not said where."

"In Low Earth Orbit, on a station in sight of your Eurasian beams and my Doom Star."

Hawthorne drummed his fingers on the desk. The idea of meeting Cassius face-to-face… "Let me talk with my councilors."

"I would appreciate an answer in three hours."

"I'm sure it will not take us long to decide. I am curious about one thing, however. How will a meeting between us help you versus Admiral Sulla and the Ultraists?"

"Ah," Cassius said. "That is one of the subjects you and I must speak of alone."

Hawthorne's heart rate quickened. "I understand. I will call the meeting at once."

"Excellent. I await your reply."

-2-

At 4:11 PM, a meeting began on Level Three of New Baghdad. It was held in the Supreme Commander's quarters. Director Juba-Ryder of Egyptian Sector joined Security Specialist Cone and Force-Leader Marten Kluge, the Jovian Representative.

***

From the Supreme Commander's biocomp transcriptions, File #13:

HAWTHORNE: That's the situation. Now Cassius wants to meet me face-to-face in Low Earth Orbit. I would like your thoughts or observations concerning his proposal.

CONE: I don't like it, sir. Why does Cassius need to speak to you alone? He has an ulterior motive.

JUBA-RYDER: His motive is clear. He wishes the Supreme Commander's help in removing Sulla from command.

CONE: I don't believe that.

JUBA-RYDER: Motives are not always complex or devious, Security Specialist. The Highborn are soldiers—

CONE: They are genetic racists first and foremost.

JUBA-RYDER: What bearing does their racism have on the situation? Sulla impedes the Grand Admiral. For that reason, Cassius wishes the commander's removal. We can help him. Therefore, Cassius attempts to use us. That sounds like perfect Highborn reasoning to me.

CONE: I'll tell you my objection. The Highborn don't know how to treat us as equals.

JUBA-RYDER: Again, I must ask: What does that have to do—?

CONE: Your logic implies that Cassius sees us as equals, or near-equals. That is contrary to everything we know about the Highborn. That being so, I question the Highborn's motives.

HAWTHORNE: You're awfully quiet, Force-Leader Kluge. You've had more direct experience with the Highborn than any of us. Do you think Cassius needs our help eliminating Sulla?

MARTEN: There's only one way to speak with a Highborn—with a gun aimed at his belly. The minute the cyborgs are dead, the Highborn will turn on us.

HAWTHORNE: How does that relate with Cassius's proposal?

MARTEN: She's right. (Points his thumb at Cone.) To them we're animals to collar, geld, experiment on or insert in missiles as a biological weapon. They're only a little better than the cyborgs because you can revolt against Highborn more easily.

JUBA-RYDER: It is impossible to revolt once a person is altered into a cyborg.

MARTEN: Osadar Di would disagree with you.

HAWTHORNE: If I understand your point, Force-Leader, you don't think I should meet with Cassius.

MARTEN: (Shakes his head). The Highborn don't know how to work with people. You can ask the Martians what they think about the super-soldiers. Before the Third Battle for Mars, Planetary Union personnel worked with Highborn. They learned to hate them to the same degree they hated Political Harmony Corps. The best way to deal with Highborn is from a distance as we did during the Cyborg Assault in the Jupiter System.

JUBA-RYDER: I cannot agree. A principle of cooperation is learning by experience about the other. The more you know from personal contact, the closer you become to that person or people group. This is a priceless opportunity to learn more about the Grand Admiral.

MARTEN: You weren't listening. The more contact you have with some people—like Highborn—the more you hate them. Too much contact with the Highborn will make us forget the cyborgs until it is too late.

JUBA-RYDER: That is an extremely negative view.

MARTEN: (Laughs sourly).

JUBA-RYDER: Did I say something humorous?

MARTEN: My negative view has kept me alive in more than one situation.

HAWTHORNE: To say your biography is remarkable is an understatement. And I accept your premise, Force-Leader. Yet these are tragic times that demand the unusual from all of us. Admiral Sulla and the Ultraists represent a grave threat to humanity. If Cassius will help us eliminate the Ultraist position among the Highborn—

MARTEN: The Grand Admiral will not do anything for our good, at least not willingly.

HAWTHORNE: I understand.

MARTEN: Supreme Commander, I distrust Cassius's motives because I do not know what they are. You should take as a given that he works counter to your position unless you have a concrete reason to believe otherwise. Even then, I wouldn't trust him.

JUBA-RYDER: No, I cannot accept such thinking. My proof is that he already helps us. Cassius desires the elimination of the cyborgs as much as we do. He acts in concert with us and thereby wishes a strong Social Unity, at least for now. Your advice is born from your fear of the Grand Admiral. He has personally threatened you. Oh yes, we know all about that transmission. There are many things we know about you, Force-Leader.

HAWTHORNE: That's enough, Director. Marten Kluge is here by my invitation.

JUBA-RYDER: He was a Free Earth Corps soldier once, a traitor to Social Unity. I've been studying his file, including Hall Leader Reports concerning his profile. The man doesn't have the first idea about loyalty. Wherever he goes, he brings disunion and death.

HAWTHORNE: These past years we have all done things that we're not proud of. Now we find ourselves allies against a hopeless future. The critical fact concerning Marten Kluge is that he has slain both Highborn and cyborgs. I applaud such deadliness and desire his advice concerning our common enemies.

JUBA-RYDER: I'm afraid that I don't know how to trust a traitor.

HAWTHORNE: Your language is too strong. Curb it at once.

JUBA-RYDER: I am at your orders, sir. But I wonder, has the Force-Leader taken a new oath yet to Social Unity?

HAWTHORNE: He is here as a representative of the Jovians. No oath is needed.

JUBA-RYDER: Has he at least *denounced* his former actions against Social Unity? He was a hero of the Japan Campaign, winning Highborn medals for murdering our soldiers. If he sits here with you, sir, I think the least he could do was foreswear his former actions and awards in Japan.

HAWTHORNE: We have not spoken about such things. There has been no time.

JUBA-RYDER: (to Marten) Do you denounce your FEC affiliation and awards?

MARTEN: Do you denounce sending people to the slime pits or allowing some to enter punishment tubes where they drowned to death because they failed to pump fast enough?

HAWTHORNE: Please, let there be peace among us. (Looking at Juba-Ryder.) I appreciate your zeal for Social Unity. You are to be commended for it and you are a true guide to the masses. However, at this time there is no reason to stir up old memories. We are attempting to save humanity from annihilation. Nothing else matters. If we must work hand-in-hand with murdering Highborn to defeat the cyborgs, I will do it.

JUBA-RYDER: I am at your orders, sir. You are the guiding hand of Social Unity and no one else could do as you've done these past years. Some have questioned your zeal, but they were wrong to do so. I know your heart, and it beats strongly, pumping true socialist blood. As for the Grand Admiral, I would like to speak in his defense for a moment. Despite what has been said here concerning Highborn, we should remember that Cassius agreed to work with us against the planet-wreckers. Without his actions and those of other Highborn, human life on Earth would be extinct. We must never forget that. And logically, what Cassius and the Highborn have done once, surely, we can expect them to do again.

CONE: I agree with much of what you say, particularly that without the Highborn, Earth would be a dead planet.

MARTEN: If the Highborn had never attacked you, Social Unity would have possessed enough warships to destroy the planet-wreckers on their own.

CONE: Hypotheticals don't interest me. The Highborn saved human life by their assault on the planet-wreckers. They might help save humanity by attacking the cyborgs in the Neptune System.

JUBA-RYDER: You agree with me then that the Supreme Commander should meet with Cassius?

CONE: (Shakes her head). Cassius's motives may have changed since the planet-wreckers a year ago. In fact, I believe they have changed.

JUBA-RYDER: On what do you base this assumption?

CONE: My communication with Admiral Sulla.

JUBA-RYDER: This is an amazing statement. You have spoken with the chief Ultraist?

HAWTHORNE: At my orders, she has.

JUBA-RYDER: (Glancing from Hawthorne to Cone). What does Sulla say?

CONE: There is a fierce battle going on between the Highborn. Cassius has been losing political ground as new commanders rise up. Then several weeks ago, things began to change. Sulla believes Cassius resorted to assassination in order to place one of his people in high command, namely, the newly promoted Admiral Scipio.

JUBA-RYDER: Is assassination unusual among them?

CONE: Apparently, it is. It means the Grand Admiral has possibly changed his feelings about murder and now willingly employs it as a tactic. I find that troubling.

JUBA-RYDER: I find your admission of communication with Sulla troubling. We've spoken here about our distrust of Cassius. Sulla is an Ultraist. Yet apparently we have no problem speaking with him. Sulla's view about us is even harsher than the Grand Admiral's. For what possible reason could Sulla be speaking with us, and why do you seem to trust him?

CONE: (Looks at the Supreme Commander).

HAWTHORNE: (Nods).

CONE: Our *trust* comes because Sulla is in an inferior position compared to the Grand Admiral. In addition, Sulla wishes our help in assassinating Cassius.

JUBA-RYDER: (Sits up). Sir, this communication with the Ultraist could be a trap. Sulla—it seems obvious what is happening. This is a loyalty test by them. The two Highborn work against us, they are testing to see if *we* are trustworthy.

HAWTHORNE: The citizens of Social Unity are not their subjects.

JUBA-RYDER: If we take the Force-Leader's words at face value, the Highborn believe we are animals. An Ultraist would have an even lower opinion about us. We must tread with caution and keep out of their political battles.

CONE: The Director's unease mirrors my own feelings. I find myself at a loss in this situation. I distrust both Sulla and Cassius. If I had to choose, I would believe the Grand Admiral before the Ultraist. But I would not want to make the choice. Therefore, in this instance, I must agree with Force-Leader Kluge. Sir, do not meet with the Grand Admiral.

JUBA-RYDER: As long as we refrain from entering into their political maneuverings, I do not see what we can lose from your meeting with Cassius.

MARTEN: (to Juba-Ryder) Have you ever been in combat with a Highborn?

JUBA-RYDER: Obviously not. I am a political representative of the people, not a soldier.

MARTEN: Then you have no idea what you're talking about. Even without weapons, Highborn are extremely dangerous.

JUBA-RYDER: (Slaps the conference table and opens her mouth to retort).

HAWTHORNE: (speaking quickly) Could you elaborate, Force-Leader?

MARTEN: The Highborn are amazing soldiers, and they are daring to an intense degree. I wouldn't discount the idea that they are trying to assassinate you, sir.

JUBA-RYDER: Why would they want to kill our Supreme Commander? It would shatter the alliance. The cyborgs would win then and we would all lose. Humanity would die.

MARTEN: That's just it. Realizing humanity would die, wouldn't you still work with the Highborn even after they killed the Supreme Commander? The stakes would be too high to face the cyborgs alone.

JUBA-RYDER: There would be no more trust.

MARTEN: Is there any now?

CONE: Not much, Force-Leader, but a little, yes.

MARTEN: That's your first mistake. Never trust a Highborn.

CONE: We trusted them to help us with the planet-wreckers, and we were right to do so.

HAWTHORNE: Suppose I do go to Low Earth Orbit, Force-Leader? What would you suggest?

MARTEN: Take a gun.

HAWTHORNE: The Grand Admiral stipulated that neither of us go armed.

MARTEN: Then carried a concealed weapon.

HAWTHORNE: They have detectors for that sort of thing.

MARTEN: Use an implant. Those are nearly impossible to detect.

JUBA-RYDER: That is preposterous. You wish to alter the Supreme Commander of Social Unity with a bionic part?

MARTEN: These are unusual times and call for unusual actions.

JUBA-RYDER: You dare to hurl that in the Supreme Commander's face. I find that offensive. Pray that nothing happens to our leader, Marten Kluge.

HAWTHORNE: You will desist at once with threats, Director!

JUBA-RYDER: Yes, sir. I'm sorry, Force-Leader. I wish you a long and socially useful life.

MARTEN: That's great.

HAWTHORNE: As usual, we have had a spirited meeting. I appreciate the candor. Know that I have decided. I will meet with Grand Admiral Cassius.

MARTEN: Good luck. You're going to need it.

HAWTHORNE: The meeting is adjourned. Security Specialist Cone, if you would remain a moment longer, please…

End of File #13

-3-

Several hours later, Grand Admiral Cassius piloted an armored shuttle toward an old command station in geosynchronous orbit above the Earth. Three other Highborn rode in back as his security team. The *Vladimir Lenin*, a SU battleship with particle shielding, was interposed between the station and the *Julius Caesar* ten-thousand kilometers away. In Cassius's opinion, letting the premen have a protective battleship was an excellent method of lulling the enemy.

The Earth hung below and masses of heavy clouds hid the majority of the surface. The cloud-cover was thick enough that surface-based lasers would prove ineffectual against the station. The proton beams were another matter. Cassius respected them. They could punch through the clouds and annihilate the station. Nevertheless, he had a plan for that and for the battleship. Checking his chronometer, he saw that he had nineteen minutes to kill Social Unity's Supreme Commander James Hawthorne. With him out of the way, chaos would result. In the chaos, the Highborn would achieve in weeks what they had been unable to do in years: complete conquest of Earth. Once he possessed unity of command in Inner Planets, he would be ready to destroy the cyborgs.

It would be enjoyable to interview the preman. One of Cassius's fantasies was to go back in time to speak with Alexander the Great. Another fantasy he mentally indulged in was the idea of what he could have done with one hundred Highborn during Ancient Times. He would have conquered the

Earth, swinging an axe and leading an army of subservient premen.

Cassius decided that conquering the Solar System would have to do. He chuckled. The heavy lifting of his plan had already been achieved. James Hawthorne walked…floated to his death at the station. A video cam recorded it and a chemical sniffer had made its analysis: the preman was unarmed.

"Thirty premen security people are on the station," he told his guards.

"Thirty cattle," the chief guard said. The Highborn wore combat-armor and had bristly white hair.

Cassius frowned. "Listen to me. You must avoid overconfidence. We are superior, but arrogance holds a trap for the unwary.

"Yes, Commander."

"This is a delicate mission and we must perform at the height of our powers. The preman are soldiers, and they have held us at bay for years. We will not underestimate them, especially with the *Vladimir Lenin* nearby."

"We hear you, sir."

"At my signal, you will draw your weapons and ruthlessly destroy all thirty guards. Those of you who fail to enter the shuttle in time will die. The premen will surely destroy the station in retaliation for the Supreme Commander's death and we must be gone by then."

"Those of us who fail to enter the shuttle deserve to die," the chief guard said.

"I have longed for this day," Cassius said. "The clever preman has played his last card against me. Now is the hour of the Highborn as we consolidate our power."

Cassius clicked the shuttle's controls. Seconds later, thrusters blasted, slowing the armored spaceship as they began docking procedures.

***

James Hawthorne floated before the chamber's viewing port of ballistic glass. It had been a long time since he'd been in space. He felt queasy floating here. It felt as if he was constantly falling. Because of that, his stomach roiled and he was afraid he would vomit.

He wore a silver vacc-suit. The helmet hung behind his head and he'd taken off the magnetically-sealed gloves. The chamber was spacious, a former carbon-scrubbing station. Some time ago, workers had removed the wrecked filters and patched the breached bulkheads. Outside, the view was spectacular. The stars shined brightly and the grim bulk of the *Vladimir Lenin* orbited nearby. Commodore Blackstone was the commanding officer, back at last from Mars. 600-meters of particle mass provided the warship's main shielding. The oblong-shape of the warship showed it was a man-made construct and not just stray matter. It had been a long time since SU warships had been parked in Earth orbit. Beyond the battleship and out of visual range was the *Julius Caesar*.

Hawthorne had seen Cassius's shuttle, at least he had seen its intense exhaust. Now he heard loud clangs from outside and vibrations against the floor.

I'm finally going to meet Grand Admiral Cassius. This was a historic moment. After all these years, all the enemy's strategic plans…he was going to meet their author. As a student of military history, he understood the value of a genius. Frederick II of Prussia had once simultaneously fought France, Austria, Russia, the Holy Roman Empire, Saxony and Sweden. Collectively that represented a coalition of 70,000,000 people against 4,500,000 Prussians, fought in an era of flintlocks, cavalry and cannons. Napoleon had said of the king: "It is not the Prussian army which for seven years defended Prussia against the three most powerful nations in Europe, but Frederick the Great." The Highborn were incomparable as soldiers. The Grand Admiral made them even greater.

Hawthorne swallowed in a dry throat, and he flexed his fingers. Had he guessed correctly or was Marten Kluge right? Infighting among humans and Highborn with the cyborgs threatening everyone, it would be suicidal madness. Surely, Cassius couldn't be *that* arrogant.

The stars shined so brightly up here. It was beautiful and serene. Hawthorne frowned as he studied the stars. It came to him that he was more than weary of leading Social Unity. The weight of responsibility was crushing. The deaths of so many soldiers that he had ordered into hopeless situations…

It is time I risked my life against the cyborgs instead of just ordering others to their deaths.

The combined Highborn-Human Fleet would soon begin the long journey to Neptune. It would take over eight months to reach the enemy system.

I must go with them. The stooped Supreme Commander nodded, and he took a deep breath. Who would lead Earth in his absence? Who had the fire, the cunning and desire to match wits against the—

Behind him, the door swished open. Hawthorne turned his head. His eyes widened.

A nine-foot-tall super-soldier filled the entrance. The Highborn wore combat-armor, which was against their agreement. With a clang of magnetized boots, the Highborn walked into the chamber. Behind him, the door swished shut.

"Grand Admiral Cassius, I presume."

The visor rotated open, and a wide face filled the helmet. The eyes with their oily film and the slash for a mouth, combined with the sharp planes of the face...Hawthorne understood Kluge's objections better now.

"This is a pleasure," the Highborn said.

Hawthorne tightened his slack muscles in order to suppress a shudder. The voice was inhumanly deep and rich with authority. This was a soldier born to command. He felt inadequate standing in the Highborn's presence.

"I am Grand Admiral Cassius. You are James Hawthorne?"

Hawthorne nodded as the feeling of inadequacy grew. The sheer vibrancy of the Highborn awed him, the coiled intensity of the soldier...

"I am glad we can finally meet," Hawthorne managed to say.

"You have come unarmed?"

"I have," Hawthorne said.

"Excellent. I knew you were an honorable man. You have fought a good fight, preman. You held us at bay from Eurasia longer than I believed possible. It is the reason we are in this fix."

"You wanted to speak about Admiral Sulla, I believe."

Cassius checked a chronometer on his armored wrist. "We have little time, which is a pity. Never fear, Sulla's days are numbered. He would eliminate you premen, a strategic piece of folly that I cannot allow. As a species, you are too needed in order to work the factories, at least until the cyborgs are destroyed."

The direction of the conversation…it made Hawthorne sick. He had guessed wrong, it seemed. Marten Kluge had been right. He should have listened to the expert on Highborn. With a gentle shove, the Supreme Commander of Social Unity pushed himself off the ballistic glass toward Cassius.

"You understand what must happen," Cassius said. "I see the knowledge in your eyes. With you gone, Social Unity will split into factions. In their fear of death and dishonor, the weaker factions will turn to us for help. Using that, I shall easily occupy Eurasia and Africa, completing my conquest of Earth."

Hawthorne shuddered. The Highborn were killers. It was their genetic heritage.

"Even as you attempt to be brave, you show your fear," Cassius said. "It is the great preman weakness."

"What about my security team? You can't hope to fight past them?"

"Thirty premen against three Highborn?" Cassius asked. "Bah. The odds are stacked in our favor. We cannot lose such an encounter."

"With the cyborgs ready to destroy us," Hawthorne said, "killing me is a mistake."

"The cyborgs are the reason I *must* kill you. To defeat them, I need unity of command."

"We're already allied."

"Loosely," Cassius said. "I need obedience in order for my genius to flower. You made your greatest strategic error today in coming here. Otherwise, you fought brilliantly."

"Are you armed?" Hawthorne asked.

"I have my hands," Cassius said, lifting them. "They will be more than enough to twist your neck. For a preman, you fought better than anyone could have believed. However, I will take pleasure in this. My genetic imperative and greatness relentlessly leads me to the ultimate prize—victory!"

Hawthorne took a deep breath as he drifted near Cassius. The Supreme Commander raised his left arm and pointed his index finger at the Highborn's face.

"Do not beg, preman, and do not preach to me concerning preman morals. Fight me and go down to death as a soldier should—struggle until the last breath leaves your pathetic frame."

With his middle finger, Hawthorne pressed the pad embedded within the skin of his palm. He had undergone emergency surgery. The left index finger was a functional prosthesis. The tip of skin blew away as a dum-dum bullet fired from the finger mount.

Cassius might have shown surprise. It happened so quickly, however, that Hawthorne couldn't tell if the Highborn knew what was happening. The dum-dum slug entered the Grand Admiral's face under the right eye. As that occurred, the piece of mercury in the hollow part of the slug was flung against the lead. That caused the slug to fragment like a grenade as it entered the Highborn's face. The slug exploded, instantly killing the soldier.

A hidden transmitter in the palm pad trigger also alerted the security team outside. They were not ordinary humans, but bionic soldiers. This was another clear violation of the agreement they had made. The bionic soldiers attacked the three Highborn, who proved themselves marvelous fighters. Cassius's three guards killed fourteen soldiers before they died, but die they did.

Afterward, the surviving members of the security team entered a pod and dropped for Earth. James Hawthorne strapped a propulsion pack to his shoulders, sealed his vacc-suit, entered a lock, waited until the chamber rotated into space and launched for the *Vladimir Lenin*.

***

Aboard the *Vladimir Lenin*, Commodore Blackstone stood at the command module as the chamber was bathed in red light. He watched the pod drop toward the heavy cloud cover. A tiny blip on the screen showed him Hawthorne's position.

"Propulsion," Blackstone said, "give me bearing seven mark ten. Put us between the *Julius Caesar* and the Supreme Commander."

There was a lurch aboard the battleship as subsystems fractionally moved the multi-million-ton vessel.

How much time will they give us? Blackstone asked himself. The answer came almost right away.

"Highborn weapons systems are hot," Commissar Kursk said. She monitored the situation from her part of the module as she stood near him. "I think they know what happened to their Grand Admiral."

Blackstone gripped the module's sides. "Are they targeting us?"

"They're not responding to our calls," Kursk said.

Blackstone flinched as he watched the module's screen. A laser on the *Julius Caesar* activated. It was a stab of brilliant light that caused the small vessel to wink out of existence, killing the bionic soldiers aboard. Then a floating, and up until this point, invisible stealth-missile appeared on the module's screen. The missile's exhaust brought it to glaring notice.

"Should I intercept?" Kursk asked. "The missile is heading for the station."

"Leave it," Blackstone said. "Let the Highborn think they're getting revenge."

"There's a probability that an exploding fragment from the station will kill the Supreme Commander."

"It's a risk he'll have to take," Blackstone said.

He had received a communication from Hawthorne an hour ago. The orders had been sketchy, but Commissar Kursk had helped the Commodore fill in the gaps. Blackstone knew what he needed to do now. If the Doom Star targeted the *Vladimir Lenin*, they were all dead. It was madness fighting another warship at such close range, especially a warship with collapsium shielding. Collapsium was an incredible advantage.

"Sir," Kursk said. "An officer on the *Julius Caesar* is hailing us."

Blackstone tapped his screen, putting the picture onto his portion of the module. It showed an angry Highborn. They all looked alike to him, big and volatile. This one had a scar on his forehead that disappeared into his hairline. Had this Highborn *died* before?

"I am Tribune Vulpus. You will lower your particle-shielding or face an immediate attack."

"I'm sorry to report that Supreme Commander James Hawthorne is dead and so is Grand Admiral Cassius," Blackstone said. "I suggest we call an immediate ceasefire until we can figure out why this happened."

"You have broken the truce and caused the death of the greatest Highborn ever," Vulpus said. "The penalty is death."

"I have not broken any truce," Blackstone said, struggling for a calm voice. "You have already fired a laser, killing men, and you have activated a missile, destroying an orbital station. I ask that you refrain from further destruction."

"Highborn always act with swift assurance," the tribune said. "We are unstoppable. You will immediately surrender your ship to me, preman."

"No sir, I will not," Blackstone said.

"Then you will die."

"Yes, you have the capacity to destroy my ship," Blackstone said. "Or we can continue to work together under the terms of our agreement. United, we can destroy the cyborgs. Divided, we fall. The choice is yours, sir. Do you speak for all Highborn?"

Tribune Vulpus glanced at someone off-screen. When he faced Blackstone again, he said, "You have acted treacherously, preman. You must surrender immediately or face annihilation."

"May I remind you, sir, that you are in range of our proton beams from Eurasia," Blackstone said. "I am in command of a *Zhukov*-class Battleship. It will last long enough to allow our lasers and missiles to fire. Combined with the Earth's proton beams, we can severely damage your ship. Maybe we can even destroy it. The destruction of the *Julius Caesar*, one third of your Doom Stars, will likely ensure a cyborg victory. Do you wish to risk that?"

"You treacherously killed the Grand Admiral."

"You have monitored us throughout the proceedings," Blackstone said. "We have done nothing of the kind. I think our two leaders killed each other. Now we're both in disarray. Maybe now it is time for soldiers like us to forget our differences as we band together to destroy the cyborgs."

Tribune Vulpus stared at Blackstone. Then he glanced off-screen again.

"The cyborgs are the greater enemy," some unseen Highborn said.

Vulpus glared at Blackstone. "I will maintain the temporary truce. The commanders will decide our next course of action. You have been spared."

The screen flickered off.

Blackstone sagged as he leaned against the module.

"The Supreme Commander has activated his thruster-pack again," Kursk said, as she watched the monitor.

"Radio him—" Blackstone said.

"That would be a mistake," Kursk said. "Until he's aboard, we must maintain radio silence with him. Let's hope he does the same. Otherwise, the *Julius Caesar* will open hostilities with us."

Blackstone nodded. What a mess. He was beginning to wonder if he should have gone back to Mars instead of returning to Earth.

-4-

"It was a mistake our landing on Earth," Marten whispered to Nadia.

They walked through the second level of New Baghdad, hoping to speak personally with a transportation minister. From above sunlamps poured heat and light on them. Communal buildings towered seven stories high and small shops sold coffee and biscuits, provided one showed his ration card to the worker.

The sidewalks were full of pedestrians wearing the new severe cut of jacket and slacks. Everyone looked undernourished. They weren't as thin as Martians, but they were much too thin for people living in the capital of Social Unity. Most of the passing crowd glanced sidelong at Nadia and frowned at Marten.

He wore a gun and leather jacket, and there was something feral about Marten Kluge. The card-holding people of Social Unity must have sensed the difference, realizing that he wasn't tame like them. He had bristly blond hair and gaunt cheeks, and there was something compelling about the way he held his shoulders. Nadia wore a cap, with long hair spilling out of it. Her slacks showed her trim figure and the cut of her blouse heightened the fullness of her breasts.

Behind them followed two peacekeepers in helmet and dark visor. The peacekeepers wore body-armor but lacked combat weapons. Shock-rods dangled from their belts.

"I wish they'd leave us alone," Nadia said.

Marten glanced back and grunted. Hawthorne hadn't returned from orbit. It made his—Marten's—standing on Earth more problematic. He needed to get his space marines back, tell Omi to hurry here and then find passage back up to space to the patrol boats. He never should have let the marines go to Athens. His Jovians were crazy interested about ancient Greek ruins.

Marten scowled. He didn't like the feel of the crowds. The two peacekeepers paced them. There was something going on. He—

"There he is!" a woman shouted.

Marten almost drew his gun, but he hesitated.

"You!" the woman shouted. She was hidden but nearby. "Push those people back. You, make sure to use zoom. I want close-ups of his face."

Police whistles began to blast.

"What's going on?" Nadia whispered.

Before Marten could answer, several dozen new peacekeepers in red riot-control uniforms stepped through the crowd. They wielded shock-rods as the weapons sizzled with electric power. People screamed, shoving and pushing one another to get away from the red-suited thugs.

"Stand back!" a peacekeeper shouted through his voice amplifier. "Make room for the Information Advisor."

As the red-uniformed peacekeepers drove the crowd apart, a woman with glossy lips and a stylish pantsuit approached Marten and Nadia.

Nadia sidled closer to Marten, gripping his left arm with both of hers.

Behind the woman—Nancy Vance by the crowd's whispers—came several men with video devices, followed by thick-limbed security personnel wearing black armor.

"I'm speaking today with Jovian Representative, Marten Kluge," Nancy said toward the cameras. She smiled. It was a radiant thing. She had sparkles in her hair and wore a shimmering blouse.

Marten pried his fingers from the butt of his holstered gun.

"Hello, Marten Kluge," Nancy said, turning to him.

"Try to smile," Nadia whispered.

Marten did try. The hundreds of people staring at him, however, made his scalp prickle. The curious knot of humanity pressed toward the guarding peacekeepers and the busy cameramen.

"Have you enjoyed your stay on Earth?" Nancy asked.

Marten nodded.

"The Jovians are a taciturn people," Nancy explained to the cameras. "They ponder philosophic insights as they struggle to engage themselves with the regular world."

"You think I'm a philosopher?" Marten asked, bemused.

Nancy made an elaborate bow. "I do not wish to presume, sir. On Earth, social justice and a fair distribution of the wealth supersede airy notions of archetype and forms."

"Both political systems are useless these days," he said.

Nancy Vance's eyebrows rose. "You do not believe in an equal distribution of wealth?"

"Be careful, Marten," Nadia whispered.

Marten scanned the crowd, noticing how people listened for his answer. Years ago, he had endured the hall leaders prattling about their empty slogans. How he'd longed to speak his mind then.

"You should ask yourself a question," Marten said.

Nancy nodded politely.

"Do the directors live as simply as apartment dwellers? You know the answer. Directors, hall leaders and other functionaries go to high-class parties, dine at the best eateries and receive top-grade medical procedures. Apparently, not even the lords of Social Unity believe their own slogans."

Nancy turned to the crowd. "Notice the craft which Jovians frame a question, which they then answer. It is diabolically clever. Notice, too, the effort our Jovian Representative has gone to learning our norms. It shows great intellect and the belief in hard study." Nancy turned back to Marten. "On Jupiter the philosopher-kings possess incredible mansions. There—"

"On Jupiter?" Marten asked.

Nancy Vance smiled more brightly. "You are the Jovian Representative, correct?"

"I am."

"Then Jupiter—"

"Jupiter is the gas giant," Marten said. "No one can live on it. The people of the Jupiter System live on Europa and Ganymede, the moons orbiting—"

Nancy laughed in a delightful manner as she turned to the cameras. "Jovians are logicians, known for their lack of humor and rigorous attention to detail. It appears that Marten Kluge is no exception. I ask you," Nancy said, turning back to Marten, "do all Jovians go armed as you do?"

"Don't say anything else," Nadia whispered.

Marten stared at the cameras, at Nancy Vance and then at Nadia.

"I apologize if I have touched upon a taboo subject," Nancy said. She turned to the cameras. "Life is strange and unordered on the fringes of the Solar System. There, men and women must go armed to protect themselves from lawless behavior."

"It's not like that," Marten said. "People should go armed so the government fears them more than the people fear the government."

Silence swept over the crowd. Nancy Vance turned back to him, frowning in disbelief.

Nadia's arms tightened around Marten's bicep.

"We go armed so we can be free," Marten said. "We have guns in case thugs in red-armor try to march us to the slime pits. We refuse to live beneath others who would attempt to tell us exactly what we can and cannot do."

People in the front of the crowd began to murmur.

The tip of Nancy's tongue touched her glossy lower lip. "Representative Kluge—"

"Once they take your guns, you're no longer free," Marten said. "Once you fail to speak your mind, you're a slave to the system. I know. I once stood up for—"

"Marten," Nadia whispered in his ear.

Nancy's eyes brightened. "Please, be free with us, Marten Kluge. Tell us what we were about to say."

Marten's desire evaporated as he studied the crowd. People glared at him, some muttering angrily. His fingers twitched, and he longed to draw his gun.

"Give us your Jovian wisdom," Nancy Vance said in a sugary voice.

"I'm late!" Marten declared. "I have an appointment with the Transportation Minister. Our two systems are working together so we may destroy the cyborgs and bring wealth and prosperity to Earth. If you will excuse me…"

Nancy Vance nodded. "Thank you, Mr. Kluge." She turned to the crowd. "Make way for the Jovian Representative. He brings aid to our battered world."

People glared at Marten, but they listened to Nancy Vance and slowly parted.

Nancy indicated several peacekeepers. "Escort the representative to the elevators. We don't want the people to mob him."

Marten glanced at her. Then he grabbed Nadia's hand. Together they hurried for the elevators. It was time to get off the streets.

-5-

Half a world away in Australian Sector, a small man with narrow shoulders and thinning hair watched a holoset. He lived in Highborn territory and presently watched an illegal channel. He did so with impunity, however, because he was the Chief Monitor of Sydney.

The small man with vigilant eyes and a down-turned mouth fiddled with a tiny piece of paper, which sat on the glass table in front of the holoset. On the paper was the barest amount of *dust*, a highly addictive and illegal drug. Even though he was the Chief Monitor, he lacked immunity from the drug laws. Possession of dust brought an immediate death sentence.

Chief Monitor Quirn stared at the holoset, watching Nancy Vance interview the so-called Jovian. Quirn remembered Marten Kluge all right. Even these days, Molly spoke about him fondly. Quirn made a face as his right index finger hovered over the dust. He longed to snort the drug and let his fears vanish in a hazy dream.

He was sick of Molly and her complaining. The woman had become too sharp-tongued lately. The sex had been adequate in the beginning. Now it was horrible and she had become fat. Quirn shrugged, trying to tell himself it didn't matter. Using his powers as Chief Monitor, he had found another woman, a better sex partner. She was small and Chinese, Ah Chen, a brilliant woman. In the beginning, he had enjoyed mounting Marten Kluge's former girlfriend. Then she had spoken about him one night. Her tone had revealed much, and that had angered Quirn. Marten Kluge had plagued his life from the beginning and continued to do so.

What had happened several years ago? Yes, yes, there had been the ponderous Major Orlov. She had drawn a stunner and shot Marten Kluge for striking him. It had occurred at a Social Unity hum-a-long. Quirn grinned at the memory. He had been a hall leader in those days. That was before the Highborn had come, and before he'd switched his allegiance.

His gaze strayed back to the holoset, and he frowned. Listen to Kluge spout his nonsense. Quirn shook his head and wondered how Marten of all people could be mistaken for a Jovian philosopher. What did SU propaganda wish to achieve with this little hit piece?

What do the Highborn have on file concerning Marten Kluge? It might be interesting finding out.

Quirn licked his lips. He was supposed to meet Ah Chen tonight. The thought of her supple little body twisting under his—Quirn's hands shook with anticipation. He banged his knuckles on the glass in his haste to pick up the small piece of paper with dust.

The Controllers would kill him if they knew the Chief Monitor of Sydney was a dust addict. Thus, he went to great lengths to make sure they never learned.

He carefully folded the paper over the dust. It would be a joy to inhale the drug and hold his breath. He shivered in delight just thinking about it. Then he would lie back on his sofa. His eyelids would flutter as he began to dream in a dust haze.

If he did that, however, he would miss the sex and conversation with Ah Chen tonight. He wished she loved him. He shrugged. Sometimes it paid to be Chief Monitor as he collected dirt on everyone in Sydney. Ah Chen needed him to keep quiet about her past, and about certain activities she engaged in now. Imagine rebelling against the Highborn. What folly.

Quirn shook his head. As long as she pleased him, she would be allowed to live and to perform her duties in the deep-core mine. No. He wouldn't miss his chance of using her tonight. He imagined her pleading with him to be gentler. He imagined her squirming under him. With a grunt, Quirn stood and limped for the door.

Outside, the sunlamps were dim, simulating twilight. It would be dark soon, and then the curfew would be enforced by immediate execution for those who lacked a special pass like him. After all these years, the Highborn still practiced martial law.

Quirn noticed that several of the big lamp-sockets up in the ceiling were empty. Work-crews unscrewed broken or damaged bulbs but none of them had replaced any yet. Sydney had fallen into disrepair since the conquest several years ago when the Highborn had invaded. Labor crews cleaned wreckage, swept the streets or removed broken pipes but they seldom built or installed anything new. Even worse than the disintegrating city were the recruitment raids for military and labor personnel. The pressgangs stopped people on the streets and demanded to see their cards. Those below a certain category were tested on the spot. If they passed, they entered a van, which roared away, taking them to their new life. Most went to the labor battalions. The best people went to the Free Earth Corps and the rest became farm workers. That was a nice way to say they went down to the slime pits to harvest algae.

The raids had emptied Sydney, but not enough to assuage the hunger, the borderline starvation. Quirn knew that certain rumors were very true. Useless mouths went to the bottom levels, there to die a lingering, painful death, as they were no longer given rations. Down there, people practiced cannibalism to eke out a few more months of life.

The Chief Monitor shivered as he shoved his hands in his coat pockets. It was better not to think about such things. He didn't make the rules. He just enforced the ones that kept him alive and kept him in the Highborn's graces.

Quirn held the packet of dust in his clenched palm. His bad leg hurt tonight. Maybe he should have stayed home and enjoyed his dreams. He could use Ah Chen later.

He scowled. It was hard work ferreting out people's secrets. He had few joys with a harpy wife. Who would have ever suspected that Molly would get fat and argumentative? He would have sent her out into the streets long ago, but her job was in the Records Department. It would be easy for her to alter critical pieces of his biographical data and help bring it to the attention of the Controllers. Molly was good at altering records. He had taught her his secrets, learned many years ago as a hall leader for Social Unity. No. he would endure Molly for a little while longer. In the meantime, he would inhale the precious dust and punctuate those glory moments by blackmailed sex. These days, it was hard for him to enjoy any other kind.

I've become a deviant.

His scowl intensified. He needed help. He would like help with his problems. He didn't like the person that he'd become. Sometimes he used to wonder what small choice in his early years had led him down this path. He had a theory about that. He now believed that a person made small choices in their youth. Those choices set a person onto various paths. One path didn't seem very different from the other in those early years. But later, as one walked down the chosen path, it took him far, far away from what he had envisioned as good or proper.

Where can I get help?

That was the problem. He had no idea. He was the Chief Monitor of Sydney. If he showed weakness, people would use that against him. He knew that to be true because that's how he operated.

His fist tightened around the packet as he limped onto Ah Chen's street. He entered a lift and rode up to her floor. The hallway was carpeted, and her door was number A342.

Knocking would imply a choice on her part. The little minx had no choice. He pulled out a key, unlocked the door and let himself inside.

It was a tidy apartment, as one would expect from a deep-core engineer, and it was quiet. A light flashed from the living room. There was darkness, and another flash.

Curious, Quirn investigated, moving quietly. He spotted Ah Chen on her sofa, with her pretty legs curled up under her. She held a clicker, wore loose clothing and she had cut her black hair into a bob around her elfin head. A holo-unit sat on the floor, with a holo-image of the Sun above it. There were

Chinese symbols on the wall, a few paper-made art pieces and a half-full glass of liquor on a stand beside the sofa.

Three things about the situation angered Quirn. The nights he visited, Ah Chen was supposed to paste sequins on her body in erotic swirls. He had told her to buy extensions and wear her hair long. Lately, he wanted music playing as he entered the apartment. He did not want her to be working on something.

"What are you doing?" he said in a querulous tone.

She screamed, twisting around as terror contorted her features.

That mollified him a little, as he limped toward the sofa.

"What…?" she whispered. She stared at the holo-unit and clicked it off so the Sun disappeared. Another click and the living room's lights came on.

Until that moment, Quirn wasn't curious about what she was studying. He stopped, and he blinked at Ah Chen and frowned at the holo-unit.

"Was that the Sun?" he asked.

"It's nothing."

"That isn't what I asked," he said, his professional senses alerted. "Why do you have a holograph of the Sun?"

"Would you like a drink? Are you thirsty?"

"Why are you nervous?" he asked.

She shook her head, her lips firming.

"Put the hologram back on," he said.

Something he hadn't seen before swirled in Ah Chen's eyes. It looked like determination or stubbornness. Just as quickly as it came, however, it disappeared. Demurely, she lowered her head. If she had been wearing sequins and nothing else, the motion would have been very erotic.

As it was, Quirn licked his lips in an obscene manner. "Hurry," he said, in a husky voice. "Put it up. Let me see what you were looking at."

Ah Chen weighed the clicker in her tiny hand. Everything about her was petite and pretty. She glanced up at Quirn. It was so artfully done. She bobbed her head in acquiesce and pressed a button.

The living room's lights dimmed. The Sun hologram returned.

Quirn frowned as he examined it. "I don't see—" No, wait. There was a dot, several dots in fact in front of the Sun. "Give me greater magnification."

Reluctantly, Ah Chen pressed the clicker several times. Each click produced a larger Sun hologram. Soon, it encompassed the entire living room. Now the dots had become mirrors. Since they appeared to be very close to the Sun, the mirrors must be gigantic.

"What am I looking at?" Quirn asked.

"That is what I am attempting to learn," Ah Chen said.

He stared at her, at the blank look on her face. "You're lying," he said. "Tell me what I'm seeing."

She hesitated a moment longer. Then she said, "It is a prototype, I believe."

"Of what?" asked Quirn. "What are you trying to hide?"

She lowered the clicker. "I am being reassigned in several weeks."

Quirn hid his dismay. It wouldn't do to let her know how much he needed these times with her. That could possibly give her an advantage over him. "Where—" He studied one of the mirrors. "Are you going there?"

She nodded.

"I don't understand," he said. "You're a deep-core engineer. You work with magnetic forces…" He turned back to the Sun mirror. His gaze tightened. Without looking at her, he said, "You work with the great temperatures of the core." He pointed at the dot, the mirror. "What is that exactly?"

"I believe it is a weapon," she said.

Quirn shook his head. He didn't understand.

"What if one could focus the Sun's energy into a single coherent beam?" asked Ah Chen.

"Those mirrors can do that?"

"I cannot see how. Yet I think the Highborn are setting up mirrors to focus some of the Sun's heat and energy. Perhaps such a beam could reach the Earth."

"Tell me why that matters," Quirn said.

"I am not a military person."

"Neither am I," Quirn said. "But you are an engineer. I think you have an idea of why it's important. In fact, I'm certain you do."

"I have an idea, yes."

"What?"

"We've all read news-blog releases of the incredible range of the Doom Stars."

"One million kilometers," Quirn said. He'd watched an illegal Social Unity show on it, and the incredible victory at Mars. The show had highlighted the impossibility of facing the Highborn and surviving.

"The Sunbeam should easily be able to outrange a million kilometers," she said.

"By how much?" asked Quirn.

"That is what I'm trying to determine."

"I still don't understand why you're taking such an interest in it."

Ah Chen dropped the clicker and let a smile appear. "I'm tired, Quirn. I need to go to bed early tonight."

He laughed. It was an ugly sound. As he advanced upon her, he said, "I have a different idea. Take off your clothing, and be quick about it."

She hesitated a moment. Then she began to strip. Their couching was short and vigorous, at least Quirn's part of it was. He became red-faced and shouted at the end, his hands clutching her smooth skin.

Afterward, as they lay on the sofa, Quirn began to talk. He rambled after his sessions with Ah Chen. Sleepy-eyed, he complained about Molly, going on and on about her many faults. He even told Ah Chen how he hated Molly speaking about Marten Kluge. Then Quirn lapsed into a moody silence.

"Would you like a drink?" Ah Chen asked. "I have brandy."

He nodded. She got up. He loved looking at her slinkiness. She was so trim and fit. He could spend hours devouring her with his eyes. She poured brown brandy into a snifter and returned with the glass.

"Make yourself one," he said. "Tonight, you will drink with me."

She nodded, returning with brandy for herself.

They drank for two hours as Quirn steadily became drunker. He failed to notice that Ah Chen only took the tiniest of sips from her glass. He began to ramble about Marten Kluge, telling Ah Chen what he'd seen on the holo.

"Marten Kluge is on Earth?" she asked.

"He's in the enemy capital," Quirn said. "Nancy Vance was giving him a live interview. Can you believe that they're calling him the Jovian Representative?"

She blinked at him.

"I was monitoring the Nancy Vance Show for my superiors," Quirn muttered. "It is one of my duties."

Ah Chen waved that aside. "What does it mean that Marten is a Jovian Representative?"

"I guess that he has his own spaceship. Our Marten Kluge has gone a long way since leaving Sydney."

"That is very interesting," Ah Chen said.

"Why?" Quirn asked, his small eyes shining with malice. "Why do you find that interesting?"

She laughed easily. "It shows how foolish the other side is. We have made the right choice in following the Highborn."

"Yes," Quirn said with a sharp nod. "You're a smart girl," and he slapped her butt.

He left the apartment ninety minutes later. She helped him get his coat on. Then he staggered home, showing his pass three different times to curfew guards.

He went to his bedroom and found Molly snoring on the cot. In disgust, he retreated to his den. He sank into his favorite chair and put his hand in his coat pocket. With a frown, he withdrew his packet of dust.

His fingertips were very sensitive. It was one of the reasons he enjoyed Ah Chen's smooth skin so much and found Molly's lumpiness so disgusting. It felt as if someone had tampered with the paper.

Carefully, and with a critical eye, he unfolded it and examined the dust. He had expected some to be missing. Instead, it almost seemed as if there was more. Maybe if he'd been sober…he was still drunk and still desiring a dust-dream.

One of the wonderful things about dust was that it was just as powerful when taken sober as when drunk.

With a slobbery grin, Quirn brought the dust to his nose and inhaled deeply. Then he sank back into his chair. Before he entered the dream haze, however, the poison so recently added to the dust began its nefarious task of murdering Chief Monitor Quirn. He went into seizures nine minutes later and cardiac arrest three minutes after that. His days of monitoring for the Highborn and enjoying women like Ah Chen were over.

***

That morning at first lamplight, Ah Chen left her apartment. She carried several money cards, but otherwise went empty-handed. She was on a mission, certain that she had learned various technological secrets for a reason. That the last piece of the puzzle had come from Quirn…it made the many nights in his disgusting embrace less shameful.

At this point in her life, she had to take what she could get.

-6-

Marten seethed inwardly as he pulled Nadia away from a cybertank. The hulking vehicle threatening them was one hundred tons of lethal destruction, with six warfare pods. An anti-personnel turret presently aimed at him. The giant tank blocked the arched brick entrance to the Supreme Commander's Mansion, where Osadar was presently under house arrest.

"I can't see anyone on the grounds," Nadia said, craning to look past the huge tracked vehicle.

There was an ominous clack from the warfare pod aimed at them.

"We're leaving!" Marten shouted at the cybertank. He yanked Nadia beside him.

"I have logged your attempt to gain access to a restricted area," the cybertank said in its mechanical voice. "Now I am radioing the authorities. Do not make such an attempt again or I shall take immediate action."

Marten turned away from the giant tank. Nadia and he were in the Governmental Area of New Baghdad, the third level. Here there were monumental buildings set along wide plazas and avenues, while the sunlamps blazed at twice the normal ceiling height.

In the distance was the octagonal Directors House where debates raged. Hawthorne hadn't returned from orbit and his "disappearance" had thrown the highest levels of government into disarray.

Marten and Nadia hurried away from the Supreme Commander's Mansion. It was an imitation of the ancient Palace of Versailles near Paris. They passed artifacts meant to celebrate various facets of human history: fountains, statues and various plinths and arches. At the end of one promenade, there was even a Sphinx.

The Nancy Vance interview had shaken Marten from what he now considered as his complacency. He didn't belong on Earth, not an Earth ruled by Social Unity. He had come down to the surface as the Jovian Representative, hoping to drum up greater support for a united war against the cyborgs. With Hawthorne's disappearance…

Marten's few SU friends were in space with the fleet. His plan was simple now. He would free Osadar, get his space marines at Athens and find Omi. Then he would return to his patrol boats in orbit and join the fleet before it set out for Neptune.

"Why is Osadar a prisoner?" Nadia asked.

"That's a good question," Marten said. The idea of leaving Osadar behind—he didn't like it. "We have to get her out of there."

"How?"

Marten strode to a set of fountains, sliding his butt onto the lip of a smaller one. The air was cooler here, although the sounds of tinkling water did nothing to soothe his anxiety. He had to come up with a plan. He needed a way past the cybertank.

"Oh-oh," Nadia said. "I think someone took the cybertank's report seriously."

Looking up, Marten spied a tall woman wearing a bright orange, flowing robe of African design. The woman also wore an orange turban, and there seemed to be something familiar about her. She had long, purposeful strides.

"Director Juba-Ryder," Marten said, snapping his fingers. "She must have hurried out of the Director's House. Yes, I think you're right. She received the cybertank's report."

Behind Juba-Ryder followed three strange humans wearing heavy body-armor. They were big men, with outsized handguns holstered on their belts. The way they walked and the ease with which they carried the armor—

"Bionic guards," Marten whispered.

He slid off the fountain. Social Unity Military altered a very few of its best soldiers, turning them into a super elite. They were all loyal to the Supreme Commander, however.

"I've heard rumors of this," Nadia said.

Marten glanced at his wife.

"Osadar told me about it," Nadia said, "illegal modifications to select bodyguards. It's supposedly done in secret."

"Cyborg agents would know how to help alter bodyguards," Marten said.

"If cyborgs are on Earth, then we've already lost."

Marten shook his head. "You only lose when you're dead." His hand dropped onto the butt of his holstered slugthrower. The bullets might not penetrate body-armor, but they would smash though skull-bone. Only cyborgs had armored brainpans.

"Juba-Ryder has never liked me," Marten said. "If she thinks I'm a traitor to Social Unity—" Marten scowled. "I'm done being anyone's prisoner. Get behind me."

"Marten—"

"Let's not argue," he said. "Just do as I say."

Nadia moved behind him as Marten took a wider stance. He hated fancy maneuvers, so he kept his hand on the butt of his weapon. If Omi was here with him or better yet Osadar—he shook his head. This was his play, and if he did it wrong, it could be the end of him and his wife. He rolled his right shoulder, trying to loosen it for quick-draw firing.

Juba-Ryder smiled triumphantly as she strode near. Each of the bodyguards had hard features and cold eyes. Their armor clattered. They wore dark helmets, with forehead and cheek protectors. They watched him closely, intently—predatorily.

It made the hairs on the back of Marten's neck bristle. These three meant to kill him or to pulverize his flesh with their fists.

"Marten Kluge," Director Juba-Ryder said. "I am here to inform you—"

Marten drew his .38. The three bodyguards had holstered guns, with flaps over the weapons. Despite their size and the bulk of their muscles, they moved with bionic speed. As Marten aimed at Juba-Ryder, the three guards aimed .55 caliber hand-cannons at him.

"They can blow me away," Marten said tightly, "but I'll still riddle your body with bullets."

"I am a director," Juba-Ryder said, outraged. "I have immunity against violence."

"Yeah? Then you shouldn't have made this tactical error. You should have just sent them, not come yourself."

Juba-Ryder stiffened. "Lay down your weapon and submit to my authority."

"Not a chance," Marten said.

"You will die."

"Yeah, but so will you."

"I can fire at his gun-hand," one of the bodyguards said. "I will destroy it before he can shoot."

Before Juba-Ryder could answer, Nadia gasped.

"What is it?" Marten asked, refusing to take his eyes off the director.

"A fighting robot," Nadia said, "a floating one."

"Those are illegal here," Juba-Ryder said. "Is this your doing?"

"Right," Marten said, feeling a sense of helplessness. Three bionic bodyguards and now a fighting robot—he debated killing Juba-Ryder while he still had a chance. He could get off one shot, maybe two, but no more than that. The .55 caliber bullets would knock him flying.

Juba-Ryder moistened her lips.

"We can destroy the robot," one of the bodyguards said.

"I wouldn't try," the robot said.

Marten saw it now out of the corner of his right eye. The robot floated, probably propelling itself through magnetic lifters, using the city grid. The robot looked like an elongated metal egg the size of a man. If he looked closer, Marten was sure he would make out sealed ports. Those could open for a laser nozzle or the tip of a machine gun barrel. The fighting robots belonged to the Cybernetic Corps, presently under Manteuffel's control.

A large upper port opened then, revealing a screen. The face of Security Specialist Cone appeared on the screen. She had a sharp beauty and wore dark sunglasses.

"What is the meaning of this?" Juba-Ryder demanded.

"Before I answer," Cone said onscreen, "I prefer to learn your intentions."

"They are simple," Juba-Ryder said with an imperious gesture. "I am here to arrest Marten Kluge. As you can see, he is resisting arrest. I demand that you assist me with that machine of yours."

"I would be glad to assist," Cone said. "However, he is the Jovian Representative and has diplomatic immunity."

"He was born under Social Unity and thus remains subject to our laws and customs," Juba-Ryder said. "Just as important, he is a traitor to the People."

"Possibly true," Cone said.

"Possibly?" asked Juba-Ryder. "How can you doubt it?"

"I don't so much doubt it as I don't think it warrants any action at this time. Despite his SU birthplace, he has become a Jovian and he is their representative to us. This is the critical factor."

"I cannot agree," Juba-Ryder said. "As my first order of business, I plan to make a clean sweep of traitors."

"Could you elaborate please on what you mean by: my first order of business?"

Juba-Ryder eyed Marten and then the robot. "The Supreme Commander is gone."

"Gone," Cone said, "but we both know he is alive."

The director shook her turbaned head. "That is inconsequential. You have read his resignation."

"He is tired and weary," Cone said. "Give him several weeks rest and then he will—"

"You think to honor him by this...*loyalty*?" Juba-Ryder asked. "No. You are disobeying his last command. James Hawthorne has stepped down from power and—"

"Hawthorne will lead the Human Fleet to the Neptune System," Cone said.

"You are incorrect on several counts," Juba-Ryder said. "Firstly, it is Social Unity's Fleet, not the *Human* Fleet. Secondly, he cannot lead. If the Highborn learn he is alive, they will annul our alliance or demand his death. Therefore, he must remain incognito. Frankly, in the interest of cementing our alliance, James Hawthorne should surrender himself to the Highborn."

"You are a political animal," Cone said. "To cement your power, you would willingly give up a human to the genetic freaks. And not just any human, but the military genius who had kept us free from the Highborn."

"Those 'freaks' you refer to will help us defeat the cyborgs and thus save humanity," Juba-Ryder said. "This is a harsh world, Security Specialist. Or didn't the planet-wrecker teach you anything?"

Through the robot's screen, Cone stared at the director. Then the floating machine rotated slightly so the screen aimed at Marten. "Why were you attempting to gain admittance to the Supreme Commander's Mansion?"

"I want to free Osadar," Marten said.

"He means the cyborg," Juba-Ryder said.

"I can arrange that," Cone told Marten.

"Didn't you hear me earlier?" Juba-Ryder asked loudly. "This traitor will speak with no one, certainly not with a cyborg. He is coming with me."

"In case you've forgotten," Marten said. "I have a gun pointed at you."

Juba-Ryder spread her hands in the robot's direction. "His words betray him. He is a traitor, eager to shed our blood."

"You plan to shed *his* blood," Cone said.

"I am the new legal representative for Social Unity," Juba-Ryder said. "In me resides the authority of billions of socially responsible people." She faced Marten. "By what authority do you dare to threaten my life?"

"The right of self-preservation," Marten said.

"In the face of billions of people?"

A grin tightened Marten's lips. "Your time is running out. If you believe in any deities, I suggest you make your peace with them now."

"If you kill me," Juba-Ryder said, "my guards will kill you and your wife."

"The minute I drop my gun, I'm dead anyway," Marten said.

Juba-Ryder grew thoughtful. "I will bargain with you. Spare my life and she can walk away."

Marten stared into the director's eyes. He couldn't trust her. He knew that, and yet...

"One moment," Cone said. "I have a solution to our dilemma."

"Marten Kluge must surrender to me," Juba-Ryder said.

"We are not in Egyptian Sector," Cone said. "By what authority do you make your arrest in New Baghdad?"

"Were you not listening?" Juba-Ryder asked. "The directors took a vote. I am the new Chief Director for Social Unity, for all Inner Planets."

"Ah," Cone said, nodding onscreen. "I see. I hadn't fully understood the situation. A vote by the directors, you say? That was quick work, smoothly done." The robot floated a fraction closer to Marten. "Force-Leader, you will come with me into protected custody."

"Security Specialist," Juba-Ryder said. "I must—"

"Please, Chief Director," Cone said, smiling onscreen. "If you would allow me to convince Marten Kluge, I will save Social Unity your needed and legal supervision." With startling speed, ports opened on the fighting robot. Two stubby barrels poked out, aimed at Marten.

"Your bodyguards can lower their weapons," Cone said. "If Marten Kluge shoots you, I will destroy him and his wife."

Juba-Ryder's eyes flashed with anger, but she nodded curtly. "Holster your weapons," she told the guards.

The three large men opened.

"Force-Leader Kluge," Cone said.

There was no way to hurt Cone, so Marten shoved his gun into its holster. He backed away from Juba-Ryder, grabbing one of Nadia's hands.

The robot rotated slightly. A nanosecond later, the two stubby barrels blazed with gunfire. Spent shells poured out of the robot, raining onto and rattling against the cement. In a stream of gunfire, rounds hissed past Marten and Nadia. The bullets shredded armor, uniforms and flesh, and caused a bloody mist to spray. In seconds, it was over. Juba-Ryder and her three bionic bodyguards were smoking piles of meat. The smell of gore and disintegrated bone was strong.

"I don't have much time," Cone said onscreen to an openmouthed Marten. "I have to consolidate my position fast. I want to keep the Human Alliance alive. I know you don't have many troops here at present, but you are the best link we have with the Jovians. No, make that the only link."

Marten turned a stunned Nadia away from the grisly pile of dead. "You play a hard game," he told Cone.

"With the cyborgs raining asteroids on us, we don't have time for fools," Cone said. "The present directors...after Hawthorne's changes, they're too tame. I have changed the directives of the cybertank guarding the Supreme Commander's Mansion. You're free to take Osadar with you. After that, it might be better if you went to a military base."

"I'd like to go to Athens where my space marines are," Marten said.

"Your face has been in the news lately. I advise you to keep a low profile."

"I understand. Do you have any vehicles I could use?"

"You used to live on Earth and should know your way around. I'll give you a pass." Cone turned to somewhere off screen. She re-appeared soon. "I've given you, your wife and Osadar Priority Clearance. It will allow you to go just about anywhere. Do you have any questions, Force-Leader Kluge?"

"No," Marten said. "Good luck to you and thanks. I won't forget this."

"I'm counting on that."

"Eh?" he asked.

"I've read your file. You get things done. Good luck to you. You're going to need it."

Marten wanted to get out of here before Cone changed her mind. He took Nadia's hand, and they ran toward the former Supreme Commander's Mansion. They needed to collect Osadar as quickly as possible, get the space marines and Omi, and leave Earth as fast as they could.

-7-

Far from Earth in the Jupiter System, on a defensive satellite orbiting Callisto, a purple-robed philosopher bowed before Chief Strategist Tan.

On the walls of the chamber were computer-screens cycling through various videos. At the moment, one showed the rocky moon of Callisto, centering on the ruins of a shattered dome. Another showed a gigantic helium-3 tanker in orbit around Jupiter, waiting for atmospheric haulers to bring their precious cargos. On a third screen was a distant blue-green object amid a bright star-field.

The philosopher was an older man with a bald dome of a head and a heavy beard like Socrates. Despite his flabby arms, he moved with serenity. He completed the bow and straightened, with a computer-scroll held against his chest.

The Chief Strategist regarded him. She was a tiny woman with bio-sculpted features. She was beautiful in an elfin way, with dark hair stylishly draped around her head. She wore a red robe that brushed her red slippers, and she had small red rings around her fingers. She knelt on a cushion before a low table. Soft "philosophic" chimes played in the background.

"The findings are serious enough to warrant careful thought," the man said. His name was Euthyphro, but most people referred to him by his title: the Advocate. He was Tan's primary link with the scientists and technicians searching the void for evidence of the cyborgs.

Venus, Jupiter and Uranus were currently in orbit on the same side of the Sun. Probes had been launched some time ago, journeying into space so they could look around the Sun and study Neptune. Past communication traffic with the Uranus System showed some anomalies and there was debate whether a cyborg stealth-attack had taken place there. Currently, communications seemed normal with Uranus, but a stubborn core of technicians believed otherwise and searched for proof.

Tan sipped from a chalice as a particular melody chimed. After the notes faded, she said, "Show me these findings."

Euthyphro the Advocate turned to the screen with the distant blue-green object amid the star-field. He opened his computer-scroll and tapped upon it.

"I'm magnifying the image," Euthyphro said. "Due to the optical effects, the surrounding stars may appear to become distorted."

True to his word, the bright objects blurred as the blue-green object took on a distinct form. It was disc-shaped and possessed a Great Dark Spot, much like Jupiter's Great Red Spot. A few white high-altitude clouds appeared at the edges of the spot. The distant ice giant gave off three times the heat it received from the Sun.

"Neptune," whispered Tan.

Uranus and Neptune were sometimes referred to as "ice giants" as compared to the more regular term "gas giants" for Jupiter and Saturn. The reason was the high percentage of icy water, methane and ammonia that composed the majority of the two distant planets.

Euthyphro nodded as he continued to tap his scroll. The blue-green ice giant kept expanding until it filled the screen.

"This is extreme magnification," Euthyphro said. "Military Intelligence attempts to count the anomalies, supposing that will give them the number of cyborgs ships. I'm afraid, however, that it isn't going to be that simple."

"The cyborgs are fond of stealth fleets," Tan said. "Logic indicates they will use decoy forces, too."

"Precisely," Euthyphro said. "Therefore, the probability of this, hmmm, situation being an accurate assessment—"

"Show me your indicators," Tan said. She had little time for discussions and debates. She was too busy juggling the many political factions of the Jupiter System. There were the

Helium-3 Barons, the former philosophers of Callisto, the industrialists of Europa and the patriots of Ganymede, to name a few. It was difficult to maintain power, because by pleasing one group she usually angered several others with competing desires. There were constant political attempts on her position. So far, she had outlived the attempts and remained in control. She credited the success to her hard-won wisdom and because she was better than anyone else was at playing one faction against another.

Euthyphro sighed as he shook the scroll. "This is slim data from which to proceed."

"My time is limited," Tan said. "So no more objections, if you please. Show me the indicators."

Euthyphro bowed again. "You have spoken." He tapped his computer-scroll. On the screen, a flash appeared beside the ice giant.

"What color was that?" Tan asked.

Euthyphro glanced back at Tan, his eyes wide with surprise. They were the most interesting thing about him, big blue eyes full of intelligence. A hint of fear showed in them as well. He recovered quickly as once more he tapped the scroll.

The flash reappeared, but this time much slower than before. It cycled through a number of colors: red, green, purple, orange, blue and bright white at the end.

"Why the variations?" asked Tan.

"Precisely," he said.

"That is not an answer," Tan said, for the first time becoming angry.

"Excuse me, Chief Strategist, I simply marvel at your swiftly intuitive grasp of the—"

"I am not here to dialog with you, Advocate. I have decisions to make and meetings to attend. You said this was critical. Now explain this to me succinctly and quickly."

"Chief Strategist, my techs believe we are witnessing a Fuhl Event."

"I am not familiar with the term," Tan said.

"I'm relieved. It shows you're not omniscient after all, which I had almost come to believe a moment ago."

"You are testing my patience with no perceivable reward in sight. Instead of achieving rewards, you are risking demotion."

"Chief Strategist, the evidence frightens me. It is the reason for my strange behavior."

"Explain your fear."

"A Fuhl Event contains the needed parameters or factors toward creating a black hole," Euthyphro said. "But not a haphazard black hole, rather, one needed to fold space."

"A worm hole?" asked Tan, with mockery in her voice.

"Our physics has long disproved the possibility of worm holes, warp drives and other such nonsense," Euthyphro said. "However, at the Callisto Academy—before its destruction—Higher Status Mathematics had conceived of a Fuhl Event."

"What you're really saying is that the cyborgs are experimenting with FTL," Tan said, "a Faster than Light drive."

"I would quibble with your statement on several counts. Firstly, we do not know who *experiments* with the Fuhl Event."

"Since this occurs at Neptune," Tan said, "the cyborgs are the logical persons."

"True, but that doesn't conclusively prove it is them."

Tan waved her hand. "Give me your next 'quibble,' if you please."

"Are we witnessing an experiment?" Euthyphro asked. "Why couldn't it be an alien race visiting Neptune and now departing?"

Tan glanced at the ceiling. Trust a philosopher to add layers of complication to a thing. "Let us stick to high-end probabilities, shall we?"

Euthyphro bowed his head. "The highest probability indicates that this…flash was of cyborg origin or design. However, we should not discount the idea that holdout capitalists used an experimental device in order to flee from the cyborgs."

"Do we have records of such experiments?"

"I have not discovered any, no."

"Hmm," said Tan. "Such evidence, if it existed, could have been destroyed on Callisto during the Cyborg Assault."

"That is conceivable, yes."

Tan studied the screen. "If the cyborgs have developed an FTL drive…"

"Certain possibilities come into play," Euthyphro said. "One: could this drive be used in our Solar System? Instead of taking months or years crossing the system, could a warship make the trip in days? If that could occur, it would give the cyborgs a decisive military advantage."

"This Fuhl Event," Tan said, "have the theorists formulated any limiting factors to it?"

"That is an astute question."

Tan scowled. "You are not here to pass judgment on my questions. Simply answer them as you are able."

"Of course, Chief Strategist." Euthyphro pressed his lips together before he said, "Theory indicates that a heavy gravitational body such as a planet would disrupt a Fuhl Event from occurring. The question becomes, naturally, what was the flash? Maybe the cyborgs foolishly attempted a Fuhl Event too close to Neptune. Maybe a group of human scientists risked their lives using the FTL drive, hoping to escape conversion."

"We know so little about the cyborgs, other than their ruthlessness," Tan said. "We need more data on our enemy."

"There are some who believe it was a mistake allowing Marten Kluge's cyborg to leave for Inner Planets."

"That decision is not open to discussion," Tan said.

"Of course not," Euthyphro said. "Because we lack precise data on the event near Neptune, we must infer from our scanty evidence. Therefore, probabilities come into play."

"Please, spare me the prologue. Just get to the point."

Euthyphro rolled up the computer-scroll as he faced Tan. He took a deep breath and began to speak as he exhaled. "To date, the cyborgs have shown great and crafty intelligence. Clearly, they are winning the Solar War. I doubt the flash occurred because the cyborgs foolishly attempted to create a Fuhl Event too close to the ice giant. That would lend weight therefore to the notion that free-will humans still exist in the Neptune System. However, logic dictates that a cyborg victory occurred there and that it was of a total nature."

"Where does that leave us then?" asked Tan.

"I believe an accident occurred. How, why or what caused this accident, I have no idea. I do think what we witnessed was the attempted creation of a Fuhl Event. The cyborgs appear to have or seem about to have an FTL drive. That should concern us deeply."

"Why couldn't Neptune be part of the Fuhl Event?" Tan asked. "If I understand the concept, four equidistant points of high gravitational force are needed."

Euthyphro's bushy eyebrows lofted. "What an interesting idea. I hadn't thought of the possibility. Does the mathematics even support such a notion? I will have my techs run the computations."

"It would seem we have even less time than we thought to defeat the cyborgs."

"To give you some idea of the severity of the situation," Euthyphro said, "I recalculated the possibility of human victory given the cyborgs have a working Fuhl Event. In that case, our odds for survival drop to seven percent."

"Spare me your pessimism," Tan said.

"I assure you this has nothing to do with pessimism but is an objective assessment of reality. Already, the cyborgs are militarily superior to any combination of our allied forces. That means—"

"That means you should hold your tongue for the moment," Tan said. "I must decide what to do with this new data."

"My seven percent probability occurs only if the Fuhl Event is an actuality."

"I'm well aware of that. The percentage isn't the new data I was referring to, but the possibility that a Fuhl Mechanism exists."

"Ah," Euthyphro said. He cleared his throat. "My recommendation is that we warn the others as quickly as possible so they will accelerate their attack against Neptune."

Tan shook her head. "There are many factors in play. We desire victory, certainly. But we do not desire victory at the expense of Highborn dominance. We cannot play into their hands."

"The Highborn will not escape this war unscathed. Given their paltry numbers, I would estimate—"

"Please," Tan said, holding up her hand. "Give me a moment of silence." She closed her eyes and listened to the chimes. There were many factors to consider. How many Highborn and Social Unity warships would journey to Neptune? What if the cyborgs attacked the Jupiter System while the Alliance Fleet traveled there to the edge of the Solar System?

Tan's eyes opened. She regarded Euthyphro as he studied the screen.

"Attend me," she said.

The bearded Advocate turned around.

"We cannot afford to send more meteor-ships out-system," she said. "We have too few as it is and building more takes too much time and energy. If we send meteor-ships to Neptune and the cyborgs reappear here, it might mean the end of Jovian Civilization."

"We do nothing then?" Euthyphro asked.

"We do not send warships," Tan said. "Instead, we send knowledge, information."

"I will alert the communications—"

"You will listen to me," Tan said. "We will not use tight-beam communication. Instead, I will send a representative to Marten Kluge. I will strengthen his hand and increase the Jovian presence on Earth by giving him critical data to use as a bargaining chip."

"Marten Kluge is not noted for his savant-like behavior. He is a soldier."

"He is a killer," Tan said. "At the moment, he is *our* killer. He has proven himself on more than one occasion. We aid him with what we can spare—knowledge, data. The question is: who should go?"

Euthyphro stepped back in alarm. "Firstly, I must protest. The data is time-urgent. The Alliance must launch the attack sooner rather than later. A Jovian vessel heading to Earth will take at least two months to arrive, and that would be under stringent conditions. Secondly, I hope you are not thinking of sending me. I am unsuited to space travel. I have—"

"Calm yourself," Tan said. "I need you here. Besides, perhaps you are right. The knowledge might spur the Highborn and possibly spur Social Unity into sending everything they can to Neptune now. The hope of acquiring the Fuhl Mechanism—"

"We must ensure that neither side gains an FTL drive."

"And how do we do that?" Tan asked.

"We would have to send Jovian warships with the armada."

"And leave ourselves defenseless here?" Tan asked. "I already told you my decision in that regard."

"It is an interesting quandary," Euthyphro said, as he plucked at his beard. "Do we risk sending our warships to Neptune in the hope of acquiring a fantastic technology? Or do we keep ourselves guarded and hope that neither the Highborn nor Social Unity gains the device?"

"It may be that we should remain silent on the subject," Tan said, "thus lessening the chance that either of them acquires the FTL drive.

"What if because of that the Alliance Fleet dallies and gives the cyborgs time to refine the Fuhl Mechanism, thereby winning the war with it?"

Tan rubbed her forehead. "I must think more deeply on the subject. It is unwise to make a hasty decision."

"Time is our enemy," Euthyphro said.

Tan nodded absently.

"If you desire my recommendation…"

Tan looked up. "No. You will continue to study the data. I want conclusive proof. Until you can give me more evidence, I must weigh the options and make a carefully reasoned choice."

Euthyphro plucked at his beard, with a troubled look on his thick features.

"I do not want to hear about a Jovian leak," Tan said.

"I assure you, Chief Strategist—"

"Such a leak would mean your death, and in an extremely unpleasant manner," Tan added.

Euthyphro paled. "I am a philosopher of Callisto. Threats are meaningless to me. My given word is more certain than sunlight. I shall tell no one about this and allow no outside communications until further notice."

"See that you do," said Tan. "Now go. I have much to consider."

Euthyphro bowed his head and departed. He left the Chief Strategist staring at the screen. It replayed the flash in slow motion, cycling through the colors.

Do the cyborgs possess an FTL drive? Tan asked herself. *The Dictates help us if they do.*

-8-

Far away from Jupiter on Earth, Marten, Nadia and Osadar rode a magnetic-rail train to Athens. The train sped over two hundred and fifty km/h through Lebanon Sector, with the Mediterranean Sea only a few kilometers away. Outside, the wind howled, at times rocking the reinforced cars as snowy particles swirled in the air. Above, dark clouds raced across the sky.

Marten and Nadia sat together, staring out a window. She kept pointing at trees, bleak snowscapes and old houses.

"I used to watch videos of Earth," Nadia said. "I never thought it would be anything like this. It's beautiful."

"And cold," Marten said. He sat closest to the window and felt the blasts seeping through.

The train-car rocked gently as snow batted against the window.

"I do not like this," Osadar said. She was taller than Marten and wore heavy garments. They had nothing to do with the cold, but concealed her skeletal cyborg body. It was thin, with particles of flesh and too much graphite bones, titanium and plasti-flesh. She wore a senso-mask, giving her the simulation and look of real flesh, eyes and hair. To finish the disguise, she wore a hat.

A reading device rested in her lap. The latest title was *Outbreak of Violence in Syrian Sector*. Osadar had spoken about the article. Political Harmony Corps personnel had risen to prominence and taken up arms again. They backed Director

Backus of Kurdistan Sector, who had gained a following in the last few days.

Many of the directors pledged Backus service in the interest of Social Unity. The Army, Navy and Space Arm followed Cone, with Manteuffel of the Cybernetic Corps as her second-in-command. Even now, the former Security Specialist was on the car's holo-screen, broadcasting a message to the many billions of citizens. She urged calm and spoke about the need for a military alliance. They must band with the Highborn against the dreaded cyborgs. Humanity's existence was at stake. This was a time for stern measures. It was not the time for the ordinary political maneuverings that had brought about the war in the first place.

"Social Unity is unraveling," Osadar said.

"It's been a difficult war," Marten said.

"The planet-wrecker's destruction of South American Sector a year ago preys upon people," Osadar said. "The arctic-like weather outside is proof that the cyborgs are fated to win. Now this civil war—"

Marten shook his head. "It isn't civil war. This is what happens in a dictatorship when the dictator steps aside. Now his lieutenants scramble to fill his shoes. If I were a betting man, I'd place my money on Cone. She has the guns and is willing to use them."

"Are the soldiers willing to use the guns on the people?" Osadar asked.

"If not, Cone can call out her cybertanks."

"More cyborgs," Osadar said. "I think that could backfire against Cone."

"That's another reason why I want to get off Earth," Marten said. "This war will be decided in space, and we need to get back up there before we're stranded here forever."

"Look!" Nadia cried, pointing.

Marten looked outside. Nadia pointed at a reddish-yellow flash in the distance. The rail-line curved gently and went to the point of the flash—an explosion. At that moment, the train lurched violently, throwing them against the seats ahead. There were only a few other passengers in the car, and those people sat at the front. One of the men up there screamed.

Speakers crackled into life as one of the train authorities spoke. "We have an emergency stop. Please, do not be alarmed. This should only take us a few moments to sort out."

Marten helped Nadia off the floor.

"Why would anyone want to stop this train?" Osadar asked. With her amazing reflexes, she had caught herself and already sat normally in her chair.

"Could they be terrorists?" asked Marten, as he dusted the knees of his pants.

"I would think PHC rather," Osadar said. "The remnants of them went underground after the nuclear destruction of the Syrian Sector Soviets last year. Now that the Party attempts to regain control of Social Unity, PHC is throwing its resurrected people into the fray."

Marten had been listening to this kind of talk for hours. Osadar had been busy in the Supreme Commander's Quarters, reading endlessly. She found Social Unity political theory to be vastly interesting and had been boring Marten to distraction concerning it. One of the critical pieces, she said, was how Social Unity had formerly kept a "Napoleon" from appearing.

A "Napoleon" was a military man who took over the government in a time of crises. Such had occurred in France during the French Revolution when Napoleon Bonaparte rose to supreme power. Social Unity theorists viewed the military as a hungry beast, eager and able to devour anyone it chose. The Social Unity Party in the past had kept a tight leash on the Military. Political Harmony Corps had firmly gripped a second leash. As long as the two forces stood far apart and kept the leashes taut, they kept the Military from devouring either of them. In the past few years, however, Hawthorne had gained maneuvering room. He destroyed PHC and then he made the Party—the Directors—his servants. The Military had gained control.

Osadar had explained to Marten how she believed the Directors would now logically ally themselves with a revitalized political police and try to re-leash the Military represented by Cone and Manteuffel.

"My guess is these so-called terrorists want you," Osadar now said.

"They can't know I'm aboard this train," Marten said.

"Why else have they blown the track?"

"It might be a coincidence," Marten said.

"How many coincidences have you been involved with lately?" Osadar asked.

Marten's eyes narrowed. "Right," he said, drawing his long-barrel semiautomatic. "Do you think this is retaliation for Director Juba-Ryder?"

"I think we do not want to meet the originators of the explosion," Osadar said. "You and Nadia need warmer garments so we can survive outside."

As they spoke, the train continued to slow down. Marten stared outside. They neared the exploded track, a twist of metal and erupted ground. Dirt and gravel lay on nearby snow-banks. A tree's leaves fluttered wildly in the wind.

"Do you see anything?" Marten asked, as he scanned outside.

At that moment, another explosion occurred. It lifted the engine off the tracks, pitching it aside. That started a domino effect as the linked cars toppled off the magnetically charged tracks.

There were screams and the screech of metal in their car. Glass shattered. Marten slid across the sharply tilting floor. He covered his head and struck the bottom of one of the seats as the train-car crashed onto its side.

It was over in seconds. Then Marten was crawling for an exit. He kicked open a door. A freezing wind howled in, with a dozen stinging snowflakes hitting his face. He needed a parka, a hood and gloves.

Marten scrambled outside, sliding down between two crashed railcars, his feet crunching in snow. Icy, wind-driven particles batted his face. His cheeks were already turning numb. He glanced right and left. Bare trees and rocky ground abounded, and snow, lots and lots of snow. A second glance at the trees showed him some weren't only bare, but dead or dying, those that couldn't cope with the new bitter winters.

With slitted eyes, Marten spotted seven armored men crunching through snow. They floundered in the deepest drifts. Three of them cradled heavy machine guns. The other four carried needlers. They were all hard-eyed, their breaths misting against clear visors. Each looked uncomfortable in their armor. It was combat-armor, although not powered. If Marten were to guess, they were used to police armor, which was lighter and easier to wear. Needlers were useless against cyborgs, but they were eminently effective against unarmored humans: namely, he and Nadia.

A man in brown, magnetic-train overalls jumped off a railcar that had tipped onto its side. He staggered over the rail line and waved to the seven men. "Help, help!" the man shouted.

One of the seven aimed his needler at the man.

"No!" the trainman shouted. "I'm in Repairs."

In the howling storm, Marten never heard the distinctive stitching sound of the firing needler. The mechanic in the brown overalls simply crumpled onto the snow. It caused a watching woman to scream, until they killed her, too.

Marten snarled as he judged the likelihood of killing those seven. They wore combat armor and helmets. His slugthrower fired hardened penetrators, but they would likely fail against armor. The bullets could punch through the visors—those were always the weak points.

Then Osadar appeared. While wearing heavy garments, she bounded across the snow toward the seven. She took ten-meter leaps and moved with amazing speed.

One of the men dropped to a knee, firing his needler. Little metallic flashes showed the stream of shots. A needler at full auto could fire one hundred needles in less than ten seconds. The others now lifted their weapons, aiming at Osadar.

She needs suppressing fire.

With both hands, Marten aimed his gun and squeezed off a shot. The .38 bucked and one of the combat-armored men staggered, hit but unlikely injured. Several of them turned toward Marten and fired.

Marten dropped behind the rails and the mound of raised dirt it was built on. Bullets and needles hissed overhead.

Then a blaze of gunfire erupted. Nothing seemed to strike the rail mound now. Marten could guess what had happened. The seven would be screaming at each other to kill the cyborg.

Marten popped back up.

Slugs hit Osadar. Needles did, too. The fools didn't know enough to aim at her head, however, or maybe they tried and missed. Instead, the few hits struck her armored chest-plate. Through it, Osadar moved like greased death. Then she leaped the final distance and landed among them. Her fists punched through visors so heads snapped back hard. One man aimed and let rip with his machine gun, but Osadar kept moving. It meant the man fired at his friends. The heavy slugs tore into combat-armor as he slaughtered two of his team.

Prone, with teeth clenched and with his arms resting on the rail, Marten fired three deliberate shots.

The machine-gun man clawed out his empty magazine and slammed in another. He staggered back then, a testament to Marten's marksmanship, but it didn't stop the man. In front of him by ten feet, Osadar twisted the neck of a different killer. She had her back to the machine-gun man and for the first time she had stopped moving. He lifted his weapon. In desperation, Marten shot the rest of his magazine. One of the bullets struck home. The man threw the machine gun into the air as he staggered backward, falling into the snow, his visor a jagged-red ruin.

Osadar disarmed the last killer. Then she grabbed his wrists, yanking them behind his back. She marched him through the snow to the railcars.

Marten was shivering as he stood up. He looked at his hands. They were red. After holstering the gun, he rubbed his hands and put them under his armpits.

Osadar shoved her captive over the rail-line. The man's visor was open and he grimaced in pain. He had short hair and blood dripped from his broken nose.

"Who ordered you to do this?" Marten asked.

Despite his pain, the man shook his head.

"Twist his arm a little," Marten said. Osadar complied.

The man grunted in pain and sweat pooled on his face.

"More," Marten said.

The man winced and breathed heavily, blowing blood droplets onto the snow.

"In the end you'll tell me what I want to know," Marten said.

"I know who you are," the armored man said in a harsh voice. Two of his front teeth were broken.

"Who ordered this?" Marten asked.

The man licked his lips as his pain-racked eyes turned cunning.

"Wrong choice," Marten said.

"No, wait!" the man shouted, as Osadar began to twist his arm again. "We're…we're PHC."

Marten glanced at Osadar. With her senso-mask, it was even more impossible to tell what the cyborg was thinking.

"Our commander is helping Director Backus," the PHC thug said. "The director wants you in his custody."

"Who do you think I am?"

"Marten Kluge, who else?" the man asked. "I saw you on the Nancy Vance Show, you with your talk about everyone going armed. That's all this world needs now."

"What does Backus want with me?" Marten asked.

"If I tell you…you have to promise to let me live."

"If I think you're telling me the truth, sure."

"Promise it," the man said.

"I give you my word."

The PHC thug swallowed painfully. "And tell your cyborg to let me go."

Marten shook his head.

The crafty look entered the man's eyes again. "Okay. I was lying just a second ago. Director Backus wants you dead."

"Why?"

"Why?" the man laughed, the pain making his eyes bulge. "People like you brought about this war, brought asteroids raining down on Earth. Look around you, at this weather. There hasn't ever been anything like this in Lebanon Sector. We have to purge the Earth so something like this never happens again. We have to wipe out trouble-makers like you."

"The cyborgs launched the asteroids, not me," Marten said. "I tried to stop them."

"I've got news for you," the man said. "A cyborg is holding my wrists. You're in league with the world-killers. It's obvious."

"He is irrational," Osadar said.

"At least I'm not a freak like you," the man said over his shoulder. "Humans need to stick together. Then we'll win this war. Director Backus knows what to do. The people know it, and so does PHC."

"Is that why you're killing innocent people?" Marten asked.

"You're a dead man, Kluge. Political Harmony Corps remembers its enemies. You're never going to reach Athens and you're never going to see your filthy space-borne Jovian marines again."

Marten stared at the man. This was all so senseless. Why had Hawthorne agreed to go meet Cassius? If only the Supreme Commander could have seen the bigger picture.

"Knock him out," Marten said. "Then we have to figure out what we're going to do."

The man tried to say more. Osadar spun him around and hit him hard, but not hard enough to crack his skull. He slumped to the snow.

"Tie him up," Marten said. "I'm going inside to warm up and check on Nadia."

-9-

Back in the Jupiter System, events had radically altered for the Chief Strategist.

Tan met with Sub-Strategist Circe aboard the defensive satellite orbiting Callisto. The large Galilean moon was mostly ruins below, although a new dome was under construction on the surface. The two women sat before a large holoimage in an heavily protected chamber. Behind their chairs were Grecian statues: one of a thinker, another in the act of throwing a discus and the third of a nude goddess. On the ceiling was a stylized drawing of a pyramid with a lidless eye in the center.

Tan was the smaller of the two, had haunted eyes and wore her red gown. She glanced at Circe. The dark-haired Sub-Strategist sat forward in her chair, staring at the holoimage. A small dark stone was embedded in Circe's forehead. Etched on the stone in nearly microscopic letters were the words: *Marten Kluge*.

The Sub-Strategist commanded a flotilla of meteor-ships. In her personal quarters aboard the flagship, the walls were plastered with pictures of Marten Kluge. Tan had read the latest profile on Circe. The Sub-Strategist no longer practiced her sexual rites with myrmidons. She had, in fact, declined several months ago to use the Cleopatra Grip on a targeted man. The only union the Sub-Strategist desired was with the quixotic barbarian from Inner Planets, Marten Kluge. Except for that quirk, however, Circe had regained her abilities, the ones lost from a forced injection of powerful sex-drugs. Her flotilla—three meteor-ships—was the most disciplined in the

Jovian System. They contained pure crews, people from Callisto, those who had been taught along philosophic lines.

"The situation is stark," Chief Strategist Tan said. "The answer…I don't have the answer. I admit myself bewildered today concerning the correct course of action."

The holoimage showed eight, faint, stellar objects hurtling through the void. Tan had read the reports. They were massive projectiles headed on a collision course for the Jupiter System. Each of the faint objects was five to fifteen kilometers in diameter and bristled with weaponry. Astronomers on Carpo—the outermost prograde moon, seventeen million kilometers from Jupiter—had discovered the objects several hours ago. After learning of them and digesting the reports, Tan had summoned Circe, who had taken a shuttle from her meteor-ship in orbit around Callisto. The Sub-Strategist had docked fifteen minutes ago.

"Who else knows about this?" Circe asked.

Tan made a bleak gesture. "It hardly matters now."

"I disagree. The information could prove critical. We have planned for this eventuality and have the tools to blunt the enemy's attack. Panic, however, could hurt our chances of success."

"Do you not see?" Tan cried. "Can you not count? Our civilization is doomed."

"Not if we stop this attack."

"After seeing what the cyborgs send at us, you believe we can stop it?" Tan asked.

"If we act with speed, resourcefulness and cunning," Circe said with a nod. "We can possibly keep ourselves alive. At all costs, we must refuse to let ourselves despair. We are the mind and heart of Jovian Civilization. I submit that we must toil to the bitter end."

Tan inhaled deeply, struggling to overcome the despair Circe spoke of. She had been right to call the Sub-Strategist. She needed to hear this and needed to draw strength from Circe's convictions. The sheer destructiveness of the cyborgs, their machine-like ruthlessness—the scope of the attack numbed her mind.

"Do we know the headings of the various asteroids?" Circe asked.

"Asteroids?" Tan asked. "The correct name is 'planet-wreckers'."

"If we're going to use the proper words," Circe said, "then let us call them 'moon-wreckers.' The rocks can do no harm to Jupiter."

Tan made another sound of despair, adding, "I see the end of Jovian Civilization."

Circe bared her teeth, shaking her head. They were un-philosophic gestures, picked up perhaps during her sojourn among the less educated. Circe pulled out a touch-pad, her small fingers blurring over the screen. Numbers and information began scrolling in the air beside the holoimages. The Sub-Strategist read the information at an incredible rate.

"According to the astronomers' findings," Circe said, "the objects definitely originated from the Uranus System."

"This answers our question," Tan said. "The cyborgs have conquered Uranus's moons and habitats."

Circe nodded as she continued to tap her touch-pad. The faint holoimages of the eight moon-wreckers vanished. In their place appeared the Sun. Circe studied the planets and their relative locations in the Solar System.

Tan also observed. Neptune, Saturn, Mars, Earth and Mercury were on one side of the Sun. Venus, Jupiter and Uranus were on the other. The attack on Jupiter had originated from Uranus, approximately fourteen AUs away, or fourteen times the distance from the Sun to the Earth. After computing the velocity and trajectory of the eight moon-wreckers, it was obvious they had orbited the blue-green ice giant, building up speed this past year. Several months ago, the cyborgs had launched the eight asteroids, causing them to break out of Uranus's gravitational pull. It was clear the cyborgs had immediately shut off each wrecker's massive engines—it would have taken gargantuan engines to propel the asteroids. Ever since then, the eight objects had been gliding through the Great Dark, eating up the distance to Jupiter, ready to bring destruction to the system.

"Their composition is different from the planet-wreckers launched from Saturn last year," Circe noted.

"It is the reason, I'm told, these were so hard to find."

Circe read more data as she continued to speak. "Many of the Saturn-launched wreckers were icy asteroids. These are formed of a dark carbon material, with an albedo of five percent."

Albedo was a measure of an object's reflecting power, the ratio of reflected light to incoming light for a solid surface. Complete reflection would be one hundred percent.

"How did the cyborgs conquer Uranus without our knowledge?" Tan asked. "There should have been radio signals, distress calls."

Circe glanced at her. "The answer is obvious. It was a successful stealth campaign."

The despair began to well up again in Tan. The scope of such an operation...it was bewildering and showed the breadth of the cyborgs' power. How could the Jovians hope to defeat such an enemy? It was impossible.

"Are there more objects incoming?" Circe asked.

Tan wanted to ask the Sub-Strategist the point of these useless questions, but that would take too great an act of will. They were doomed. Let Circe play out her life as she chose.

"We have not spotted more," Tan said, glancing at her hands. Maybe it would be better to fight than to await certain annihilation. The attack was so galling, so...*unfair*. "If the planet-wreckers launched at Earth are any indicator, the cyborgs prefer to make one *massive* assault instead of sending a continuous stream of asteroids. Logically, we can expect the same pattern here, are seeing it unfold against us."

"Hmm," Circe said. "I notice this is a smaller number of wreckers than launched at Earth. That is in our favor."

"I suppose that is true," Tan said. "But we also have a smaller number of warships to attempt deflection. Given our ship tonnage and capabilities, the ratios are in favor of the cyborgs."

While scowling, Circe asked, "What is the estimated time of impact with our system?"

"Five weeks," Tan said.

Circe's head swayed slightly. She asked in a huskier tone, "What are their targets? Did the astronomers discover that?"

Tan produced a touch-pad and began to manipulate it. Dotted lines sprouted from each of the faint moon-wreckers. As the lines lengthened, an enlarged Jupiter System appeared. The eight lines spread apart, heading for the Galilean moons, two each at Io, Europa, Ganymede and Callisto.

"Two wreckers per moon," Circe said. "That is interesting."

"From a theoretical point of view, I suppose that's true," Tan said. "It proves the cyborgs are not all-knowing. Apparently, they failed to realize that Io and Callisto are almost devoid of people. They would have been better served aiming those wreckers at the two populated moons."

"I don't necessarily agree," Circe said. "We have begun re-colonization of Callisto."

"On an extremely limited basis only."

Circe tapped her pad. It caused the holoimage to show the massive gas giant of Jupiter. Circling it were two new asteroids, one of four kilometers diameter and the other of six. A close-up appeared on one, showing massive ports for huge engines within the projectile.

"We have two wreckers of our own and they are already moving at a great speed," Circe said.

Tan made a listless gesture. "Meaning we can possibly deflect two of the enemy's projectiles."

Circe studied the holoimages with care before turning to Tan. "Which two do we attempt to deflect?"

"Precisely," Tan said as the hopelessness welled from her chest, radiating throughout her body. "Do you have any preferences?"

Circe blinked at the holoimages. "We must assume that each of the Uranus wreckers contain laser turrets and missile launch-sites."

"No assumptions are needed. The astronomers have already spotted structures on the surface that match those of the Saturn-launched wreckers."

"Cyborg warships might conceivably be behind the eight wreckers," Circe said.

"We must give that a high probability," Tan agreed.

"The Guardian Fleet is woefully under-strength for this mission."

Tan made a bleak sound. "One dreadnaught and seven meteor-ships—I am well aware of our deficiencies."

"Suppose we decided to deflect the two wreckers headed for Ganymede," Circe said. "How would the industrialists of Europa respond to the news?"

"With deadly vigor," Tan said.

"And if we attempt to save Europa?"

"Most of the space marines aboard the various warships are from Ganymede," Tan said, "along with two meteor-ship crews. Once they learned we would make no attempt to defend their moon, they might object in a forceful manner."

Circe became thoughtful. "Those of Europa primarily crew the civilian liners and the majority of the helium-3 tankers."

"You are beginning to understand the quandary," Tan said. "Europa also contains more heavy industry."

"That should make it an easy decision then," Circe said, "easy in a philosophic sense." She grimaced. "I must admit to finding myself feeling emotional about the topic, which is distracting me from purified reasoning."

Once more, Tan attempted to concentrate her thoughts. She would follow the Sub-Strategist's example, using a philosophic approach to this, employing her lifelong training and submerging her 'emotional response.'

"These emotions," Tan said. "I suspect you are still tainted from your episode aboard Force-Leader's Kluge's vessel."

"No doubt you are correct," Circe said, as her features took on a pinched look.

"Let me add a third possibility—third in terms of which moon we should save," Tan said. "Callisto is the heart of our superior civilization. As you pointed out, we have already begun to rebuild on the moon. This may be the answer to our dilemma: that of how to revive the most humanizing civilization ever seen during man's long history of brutality and unexamined actions. If Ganymede and Europa perish,

Callisto will become the premier Jovian moon. Although the Jovian System will lack numbers after the strike, the survivors will be pure and we can begin anew with untainted citizens."

"There is much elegance in what you say," Circe agreed. "The trouble is the nature of the war. The cyborgs will continue to attack until the Alliance sends fleets to the enemy systems. Therefore, it seems probable that the Jupiter System will have to absorb more attacks. Therefore, we need numbers. And there is one other thing that troubles me."

"Yes?"

"Our system contains more than the four major moons. The cyborgs must realize this and have plans to target the smaller moons and various habitats."

"You feel this proves there are enemy warships behind the eight wreckers?"

Circe nodded.

"Given these parameters," Tan said, "what is your recommendation?"

Circe rubbed the skin around the stone in her forehead. "We lack the warships and firepower to deflect all eight projectiles. Rationally, we should let the four wreckers hit Io and Callisto and concentrate on the other four. I would hate, however, to attempt to defend Europa and Ganymede and lose both. It would be far better to defend and save one of the moons."

"Which one?" Tan asked, feeling detached and increasingly numb. The entire conversation was surreal. She noticed that Circe had become pale and stared fixedly at the holoimages. Clearly, the topic strained the Sub-Strategist, too.

"We must come to a rational decision and thereby prove the superiority of our civilization," Circe said.

Tan bowed her head and closed her eyes. The strain of this—the responsibility of making the decision was too much, too heavy even for a first rank philosopher. They attempted to use reason alone, to keep their emotions in check, but it was hard. This concerned millions of Jovians, millions of men, women and children. She didn't want to choose who lived and who died. It had been difficult enough defeating the first Cyborg Assault. Endless months of grueling decisions and careful maneuvers…fifteen months of it had eaten at her resolve. Now to decide which Jovian moon should die…

"I feel old," Tan said.

"There is another possibility," Circe said.

"Tell me."

"We have five weeks before the wreckers strike. We could load every liner and tanker with Jovians and journey to Mars or Earth."

"Evacuate the Jupiter System?" whispered Tan.

"For now," Circe said. "The idea would be to save as many people and ships as possible. It would have the added benefit of uniting the Guardian Fleet with the others of the Alliance."

Tan studied the Sub-Strategist. "Do you suggest this because it is the best idea, or do you wish to reunite with Marten Kluge in the Earth System?"

Circe shook her head. "I do not know. Whenever I think about Marten Kluge, all else fades from my thoughts. I desire his arms around me, that he peel off my clothes and—" Circe looked stricken. "Excuse me, Chief Strategist. I—"

"No excuses, Circe. I sent you against Kluge as a weapon. I should have known better. The man is a killer and amazingly resilient against any who wish him harm. You suffered because I hated the idea of his…well, it doesn't matter now. That was then and now we have to face these eight projectiles. I do not like the idea of fleeing our ancestral home. We must stand our ground."

Circe looked away.

"I have grown weary of the Advisor of Europa," Tan said, with her eyes half-lidded. It was so hard to think, but she recalled that the man had been a constant irritant. The idea that he should survive while those of Ganymede perished—no! He was an insufferable toad. "Europa's domes and cities lie deep under the ice. Perhaps they can survive the wreckers."

"That is extremely unlikely," Circe said.

"You speak the truth. They will die, but some of the industries might survive." Tan shrugged listlessly.

For a time, the two women stared at the eight projectiles.

"With the choice of which moon to defend decided," Circe finally said, "there is a more delicate question."

"You agree with me then that we should save Ganymede?"

"Force-Leader Yakov was from Ganymede," Circe said.

"Why is that important?"

Circe blushed. "It isn't."

"Ah," said Tan. "Yakov was Marten Kluge's friend."

"Marten thought very highly of Yakov," Circe said.

"We all did," Tan said. "And that is as good a reason as any to save Ganymede. Force-Leader Yakov gave his life to save our civilization. We will now choose to save the moon that gave us such a selfless guardian. I approve of your reasoning."

Circe gave Tan a sidelong glance. "I spoke of a delicate issue a moment ago. We still have not broached it. The Advisor of Europa is forceful and given to threats. He might do more than protest your decision."

Tan nodded. She realized that. She should have been the one to bring it up, but she couldn't do it.

"Given his emotional make-up," Circe said. "I suggest we take away the Advisor's ability to affect our decision."

Tan's mouth was dry. Once she spoke these words, she would begin a terrible sequence of events. With her tongue, she moistened the inside of her mouth. "What do you suggest?"

"We must neutralize his ability to harm the Guardian Fleet," Circe said. "To speak plainly, we must ensure that he never uses the defensive satellites orbiting Europa to launch missiles at our ships."

"That would be an irrational act on his part," Tan said.

"I have studied his psychological profile. The man is irrational and unstable."

"I have also found him irritating," Tan admitted.

"There are two meteor-ships in orbit around Europa," Circe said. "I suggest you launch an immediate space marine assault against the defensive satellites or use bombs to incapacitate them."

"If we did that it would destroy their ability to deflect the wreckers."

"Europa has insufficient military hardware to deflect them," Circe said. "Their only possibility of affecting the outcome of the situation is vengeance against us."

Tan recoiled at the idea of leaving Europa defenseless against the enemy. It was monstrous and she would have no part in it. The horror of the suggestion revived her spirits and cut through the despair.

She turned to Circe. "What if Europa used all their liners and tankers, building up velocity and crashing them against the moon-wreckers? Before impact, they would have to launch weapons to disable each wrecker's engine ports so the asteroids could not make any course corrections."

On her pad, Circe began to compute the odds. After a time, she looked up. "They would need to send the ships now. The farther away from Jupiter they nudge the asteroids—provided they can knock out the engine ports—the less mass is needed for success."

"The problem is that cyborg lasers would likely destroy such space-liners and tankers," Tan said. "And who would crew the suicide vessels?"

"It wouldn't necessarily have to be suicide. Skeleton crews could guide the ships, leaving at the last moment by a shuttle and escaping the impact."

"And falling victim to cyborg lasers," Tan said.

"The Guardian Fleet would need to join in the assault," Circe said, "engaging the moon-wreckers in battle. We would attempt to mimic the Highborn and Earthlings as they attacked the Saturn-launched wreckers."

Tan bit her lip, worried again about the leader of Europa. "If only the Advisor were a rational man."

"The answer is obvious. You must assassinate him."

"Who will take his place?" Tan asked.

"Hopefully someone more malleable," Circe said.

"And if he or she does not view the matter as we do?"

"There are many imponderables," Circe said, "too many to calculate. We must fight. We must give our system the likeliest chance for survival. Our two asteroids will target the Ganymede wreckers, shepherded to the point of contact by the Guardian Fleet. The people of Europa can do as they wish with their space-liners, tankers and defensive satellites—provided they don't attack us. Perhaps we can convince them to transfer to Ganymede."

"There are not enough spaceships to complete a transfer in time."

"It would save many more lives, however."

Tan stared at the holoimages, at the faint stellar objects. She was the Chief Strategist. She should devise a strategy for the greatest number of survivors. This certainty of the Advisor's emotionalism—

"No," Tan whispered.

"Chief Strategist?" Circe asked.

"I cannot order the Advisor's assassination," Tan said. "Neither can I use space marines or myrmidons to denude Europa of a fighting chance. I will have to take a leap of faith on the Advisor's humanity."

"He has not shown good faith in the past," Circe said.

"He has not faced extinction before." Tan leaned forward, letting her forehead sink against her hands. "I don't know what to do. The decisions…they are too heavy for me. We are facing the end of our hard-built civilization."

"Then let us show the Solar System our superiority by facing doom like the philosophers we are," Circe said. "We lived with equanimity and we shall die the same way."

Tan looked up. "That isn't how Marten Kluge faced the cyborgs."

Circe's serenity faded as her features twisted. She stood abruptly, strode toward the holoimages and then turned around. "Here is my advice. Call the Advisor. Tell him our decision. Let us see how he acts. If he is a Jovian, he will act with calm and we may yet defeat the moon-wreckers. If he panics…" Circe shrugged.

"Is this a reasoned decision you suggest?" Tan asked.

"…no," Circe said. "The emotions in me are too strong to control. Nevertheless, this is my suggestion. First, order the two meteor-ships out of Europa's orbit. We will need every vessel if we are to deflect the two wreckers headed for Ganymede. Then, board every liner and tanker you can with space marines or myrmidons. Take away the Advisor's options so when he threatens, you can bargain with him, offering him the return of his vessels if he agrees to reason."

Tan stared up at the lidless eye in the pyramid. "In a week—"

"No," Circe said. "You have two days to act, no more. Stall while you can and move shuttles and warships into position. Then—"

Tan held up her hand as she dug out a com-unit. She clicked it on and began to give rapid-fire orders. Circe was right. She had to act fast and decisively. These moon-wreckers…the scope of the attack had paralyzed her. But she was the Chief Strategist, a philosopher of Callisto. She would show the Solar System how one with an examined life responded to an extinction-level attack. She would show them because otherwise she would begin to weep for the loss of such a metaphysically beautiful system.

-10-

As signals began to flash between the meteor-ships of the Guardian Fleet, on Earth, Marten Kluge felt nauseous. He tried to walk across a heaving deck, with angry waves tossing whitecaps around their automated cargo vessel. Everywhere he looked the sea churned. His guts churned as well, with seasickness. Cold wind whipped against his face, pelting it with salty spray. Storm clouds raced across the sky so everything was moving, making him dizzy.

He still thought hijacking this automated ship had been a bad idea. No one rode on ships anymore unless they wanted to go on a pleasure cruise. A plane would have been better, but very difficult to access now. Using a train would have been faster than the ship. The trouble was that Social Unity was unraveling as the directors and others jockeyed for position. Already there had been riots, armed police uprisings, incidents of military defense-forces shooting down planes and PHC terrorists blowing up trains.

The greatest blow to Marten was that Turkey Sector had declared for Director Backus, joining Italia Sector and others. They demanded that Backus rule Social Unity, cleansing the Party so it would return to its socialist purity. The problem was that Marten needed to get to Greece Sector, to Athens in particular. Two weeks ago, his Jovian space marines had insisted on finally visiting the ancient Athenian ruins. He'd let them go, never suspecting everything was going to unravel into chaos.

If that wasn't bad enough, the Director of Greece Sector had "detained" his marines, a little less than one hundred fighting Jovians. In Osadar's option, Director Delos was trying to keep Greece Sector neutral by holding both Backus and Cone at arm's length. Delos had quarantined the Jovians, but she hadn't shot them as Backus wished.

Marten wiped spray from his cheeks. He spied the jagged hills of Crete on the horizon. The hills looked decidedly uninviting. The way the white-capped waves slammed against the automated vessel...

They had slipped away from the train wreck in Lebanon Sector and headed for the nearby coast. With Turkey declaring for Backus, they needed another path to Athens.

"I'm afraid the authorities will arrest us if we enter Turkey Sector," Osadar had said.

After the PHC attack, Nadia hadn't wanted to go into any city to try to buy a plane ticket. That meant they could travel across North Africa to get to Spain Sector, and then to Athens, but that would mean traveling through Egyptian Sector. It had strongly declared for Director Backus. The quickest route then—since they couldn't use the air—was by sea.

With her superior sight, Osadar had pointed out the automated vessels. Most bulk shipments were transported by sea. They found a rowboat, and with her cyborg strength, Osadar rowed them out to the ship. She leapt aboard the present vessel, found rope and hauled them up. For several days, they had endured the ship's programed route. During that time, Osadar, being part machine, had talked to the vessel's computer. She'd finally cracked its defenses and was now in control, piloting the ship to Athens.

Osadar still spent most of her time on the computer, monitoring the news-sites. She discovered all sorts of useful, if sometimes daunting, information. The most pertinent was that open fighting had broken out. Cone's soldiers won most of the engagements, but Backus eroded Cone's political power with an idea. As Osadar put it, "The idea is like a spark landing on oil-soaked rags." The oil was the planet-wrecker strike a year ago. According to what she'd found in Hawthorne's quarters—real opinion polls, for instance—many people believed the cyborgs would conquer Earth. Despair was rampant, and Backus used that. Osadar had read Marten several of the director's newest slogans: *Free Earth of* all *foreign germs.* There was another: *Cleanse our planet of its infestation. Then we will grow strong again in purity and defeat our enemies.*

The Jovian space marines made excellent symbols. Osadar had predicted a show trial, where Backus's people stirred up mass hysteria against non-Earthers to a fever pitch.

Marten staggered for the hatch, as he thought, *I'm not going to let that happen.* He should have never landed on Earth. He'd trusted Hawthorne. After the battle a year ago with the planet-wreckers, what choice had there been? They couldn't have survived for long, cramped in the two patrol boats. Maybe they should have tried just the same. It would have been better than this.

The deck heaved up and seemed to roll sideways. Marten barely grabbed a rail in time. He was sick of the automated vessel. He was sick of Earth and this endless war. How could men defeat cyborgs and then put down the Highborn?

He grimaced as he slid down the hatch, moving along a corridor toward light. Soon, he staggered into a small cabin with its bunks and shoved-together crates that acted as their table. Nadia slept, with a blanket pulled over her head.

Osadar sat before the computer terminal, bracing herself with her legs. At his entrance, she twisted around.

"Have you considered the possibility that it will prove impossible to free our marines?"

"No," Marten said.

"Perhaps we should bypass Athens and head for a launch-site under Cone's control. Let's get off Earth while we can."

Marten shook his head.

"You have lost soldiers and friends before," Osadar said. "Our goal is bigger than a few marines."

Marten scowled. "I'm tired of seeing my friends die." He pulled out his gun, hefting it thoughtfully. Then he shoved it back into its holster. "We're going in and rescuing them."

"How can we achieve this miracle?" Osadar asked. "We are three people against a city of millions."

"You forget. I'm the Jovian Representative."

"Your title failed to impress Juba-Ryder."

"The Director of Greece Sector wants to stay neutral," Marten said. "That's the key."

"Delos's neutrality makes her actions predictable," Osadar said. "She will continue to detain our marines to keep Backus's people happy, and she will please Cone by refusing to hand them over to an SU tribunal."

Marten was afraid that Osadar was right. Social Unity…nothing ever changed. Men mouthed pious slogans and then acted as they pleased. Equality for all. Yet the hall leaders, the police chiefs and directors, they lived like princes, dictating to everyone else. If everything was so good under Social Unity, why the need for shock batons, punishment details in the slime pits and torture in the glass tubes? If socialized men were so superior, why did some starve and others become fat on good food? Why did the leaders bicker for supremacy? Why were there so many checkpoints, ID cards, half-truths and endless coercion?

"We have one power," Marten said. "No, we have two."

"Do you care to enumerate them?" Osadar asked.

"I need to speak with Cone. Can you patch me through to her?"

"The automated ship has given us anonymity, allowed us to travel unseen. Broadcasting in the open might jeopardize that."

"Can you do it?" Marten asked.

Osadar swiveled to the computer. "The key is our priority clearance, which is linked to the Security Specialist's code." Osadar began to tap the screen. It took a little over an hour, but finally she turned to Marten.

"Are you ready for the Security Specialist?" Osadar asked.

Marten had been listening the last few minutes as Osadar spoke to increasingly powerful underlings. Now he was going to get his chance to speak with Cone. He shoved a crate near Osadar, sitting down and moving the computer screen to face him. Maybe twenty seconds later, Cone appeared.

She wore sunglasses, had slicked-back hair and sat before a sunburst symbol. "Marten Kluge?" she asked, sounding surprised.

"Thank you for speaking with me," Marten said.

Cone's lips twisted into a half-grin. "The reports of your death are highly exaggerated, it appears. I was told you were dead, killed during a train hijacking."

"Who gave you the report?"

"Does it matter?" Cone asked.

"Did they tell you a cyborg killed the PHC terrorists?"

Cone frowned. "Do you have a point?"

"I'm on my way to Greece Sector."

"Where are you now?"

"I understand that you're in a difficult situation," Marten said. "With Hawthorne's removal, the upheaval has begun. It comes at the worst possible moment: when humanity is about to launch its counter-offensive. My space marines represent a tiny portion of that combined force, but they do represent an earnest of Jovian cooperation with the rest of humanity. Who knows when Jovian warships might hold a critical advantage for the rest of humanity?"

Cone held up a hand. "My time is short, as you've correctly surmised by going straight to the point. You want help freeing your marines. Is that right?"

"I'm trying to convince you of their importance."

"Civil war has broken out, Force-Leader. I can hardly concern myself with one hundred marines."

Marten shook his head. "For your own sake, you must do everything you can to keep my Jovians out of Backus's hands. It he shoots them…if he publicly tries them and brings them before a videoed firing squad—"

"Hmm, yes," Cone said, interrupting. "That would stir the masses and show his apparent strength and my weakness. Yes, I see what you mean." She pursed her lips. "Greece Sector is rather small and unimportant compared to more pressing matters. I don't know how to pressure Director Delos any more than I already am."

"I'm not asking for that."

"What are you asking for then?"

"Call Director Delos," Marten said. "Show her the latest video from Jupiter. Remind her that humanity's back is against the wall. Promise her more grain shipments if she will simply do her duty and free Social Unity's allies."

"Grain is difficult to come by these days."

"It is hard currency during a famine," Marten said. "That's why you should offer it. I suppose I could point out that promises are not the same as shipments, but I'm not going to do that."

Cone's eyebrows lifted. "I did not realize you were an intriguer."

"I'm not," Marten said. "I'm desperate. I'm tired of running away and even more tired of losing. I want my Jovians and then I want to hit the enemy hard."

"Yes, yes, we must fight the greater enemy. Your point is valid. Suppose I give you a hundred commandos to take with you into space, would that be enough?"

"I appreciate the offer, but I want my trained space marines."

"We don't all get what we want."

"True," Marten said. "The key is that my marines have been fighting cyborgs a long time now. They're veterans against a foe who usually kills everyone. My marines have fought on Carme, on Athena Station—those names may not mean much to you, but they were hellholes. The veterans who survived those places: their fighting knowledge may make a great difference someday soon."

"Doubtful," said Cone. "It's what they represent that is critical. If Backus should acquire them... I will do as you request, Force-Leader. How soon until you reach Greece Sector?"

"Several hours," Marten said.

Cone turned, listening to someone off-screen. When she faced Marten again, she said, "An automated cargo vessel—very clever, Force-Leader, and resourceful. Once again, I wish you luck."

"And I you," Marten said.

Cone nodded, rising as the connection ended.

***

Twenty peacekeepers in riot gear waited for Marten, Nadia and Osadar in Piraeus, Athens's port. Each of the police hefted a machine pistol as they stood on the nearing pier.

"Notice," Osadar said from the cargo vessel's deck. "They lack shock batons."

"They're Director Delos's *troops*," Marten said.

"They are police."

"It shows you why Cone has any chance at all," Marten said.

It had been like that in New Baghdad: few military personnel in the city. The reason was that Hawthorne hadn't wanted the military caught underground, nor had he wanted them to fraternize with the people, in case he needed the military to put down rioters. The independent Soviets a year ago had shown the Supreme Commander the answer to dealing with citywide rebellion. Until now, Hawthorne's method had worked. It meant that most military personnel were on bases instead of in the cities. Hawthorne had wanted the military were he could maneuver them against invading Highborn. It meant the directors had little access to military personnel, although they had large police forces.

As the ship docked, a police officer jumped onto the vessel's deck. He had one thick eyebrow, with a chinstrap holding his red helmet in place. He alone lacked a machine pistol, although he had a regular gun holstered at his side.

"Force-Leader Marten Kluge?" the officer asked.

Marten stepped forward as he nodded.

"I am Commissar Cleon of the Athens Peacekeepers: Third Level, Fifth Precinct."

"Glad to meet you," Marten said, holding out his hand.

Commissar Cleon kept his hands at his side, and his features stiffened. "Director Delos wishes to inform you that she cannot accept your presence here in the city or anywhere in Greece Sector."

Marten hadn't anticipated this.

"Therefore—"

"A moment," Marten said. He raised his hand and indicated Osadar.

She wore a large jacket and senso-mask, and that helped conceal the fact she was a cyborg. Unfortunately, it couldn't totally hide her strangeness. She now walked to them, and her difference became more pronounced.

Commissar Cleon took a step back as his face paled. "She's a cyborg?"

"One of the few to break their conditioning," Marten said.

Cleon glared at Osadar, and his gun-hand dropped onto the butt of his weapon. "I've read reports. They say cyborgs can convert people into their likeness."

"Osadar began as a Jovian," Marten said.

"You mean those others—the space marines—they're hidden cyborgs?"

"No. I mean Director Delos must speak with me. I am one of the few people who know how to detect pre-converted people."

"What does that mean?"

"Have you read the reports of the Third Battle for Mars?" Marten asked.

Cleon shook his head.

"I have reason to believe the cyborgs have targeted Director Delos for infiltration tactics. It is why I sent my space marines to Athens. Surely, they made their report."

"I know nothing about this," Cleon said.

"It's worse than I thought," Marten told Osadar. "We must leave at once."

"Why?" asked Cleon.

Marten glanced at the commissar sidelong. "If you're wise, you'll join us, you and your men. We could use them."

"Do you mean to tell me that Director Backus is right?" Cleon asked. "The contamination has already occurred?"

"Yes," Marten said. "We must flee. Go!" he told Osadar. "Back into the hold with you. There is little time left."

"Wait," Cleon said.

"There's no time," Marten told him.

Cleon drew his gun. It caused a stir among the peacekeepers on the pier. Several jumped onto the cargo vessel, hurrying near, with their machine pistols trained on Marten and Osadar.

"You will wait," Cleon said. He pulled out a com-unit and walked away from Marten. The commissar spoke urgently, listened and spoke even more urgently. Finally, he put away the unit, approaching Marten once more.

"Director Delos believes you are lying about the cyborg danger," Cleon said. "However, you have intrigued her. You will accompany me to the Director's Building. Your cyborg and the woman will stay here as hostages for your good behavior. They will not be permitted to land on Greece Sector soil."

Marten nodded.

"Give me your weapon," Cleon said.

Hoping he was right and knowing things could go very wrong, Marten began unbuckling his gun-belt.

"Guard them," Cleon told a peacekeeper. "Shoot them rather than letting them step onto a pier."

"Yes, Commissar," the guard said.

"Come with me," Cleon told Marten.

"Good-bye, Marten Kluge," Osadar said.

Marten nodded, and he glanced at his wife. There were tears in her eyes. It was possible he would never see Nadia again. He nodded once more, to her, and he turned away, hurrying for the pier.

***

Even though it was a sector capital, Athens was in worse shape than New Baghdad. Level after level, the buildings looked old and rundown. Their lift groaned and lurched and the air tasted stale. Too many sunlamps were missing in the ceilings, sometimes creating dark or shadowed zones. Potholes abounded, and garbage lay in heaps, sometimes worked upon by grungy men with rakes and wheelbarrows. Police with drawn guns watched them. Old women swept the streets and the children—they were skinny like Martians.

It was a little better on the Governmental Level, with more lights, less garbage and a battalion of street-sweepers in their mid-twenties. There were too many red-suited peacekeepers. Instead of machine pistols, however, the police wore shock-rods, although the higher-ranked had needlers.

Marten and Commissar Cleon moved at a brisk pace along the sidewalks. There were a number of official people about, most in hall leader uniforms or maroon, sector-bureaucrat colors.

"There," Cleon said. With his chinstrap, the commissar pointed at the seven-story Director's Building. It stood above the smaller buildings around it and the park on the other side. The building was octagonal in shape with several armored cars parked in front. A knot of peacekeepers stood near the glass entrances. The majority of them wore regular police body-armor.

Once again, Cleon showed his pass. A guard joined them, keeping his needler aimed at Marten's back. They entered the building, and the guard turned them over to black-suited gunmen.

For the seventh time today, the commissar showed his ID card and the guards checked their slates.

Instead of one guard, three black-suited gunmen joined them. They rode up an armored lift to the fourth floor. More gunmen lined the halls.

"There been a lot of trouble lately?" Marten asked.

Hostile glances were his answers.

Finally, they marched into a large gray room. Marten and Cleon sat for several minutes. Then new black-suited gunmen appeared. They ushered the two into an even larger room. A red carpet on the floor, paintings on the walls, a Parthenon replica six feet high and deep couches decorated it. There was a large glass window on the far side of the room. The window showed gardens and promenades down below, with other governmental buildings beyond.

An older woman with gray hair sat behind a desk. She had an alert expression, with dark eyes and a wide mouth.

"Force-Leader Marten Kluge," she said.

"Director Delos?" he asked.

"Commissar, you may return to the cargo ship," she told Cleon. "You will await my orders to shoot the cyborg and the woman."

Marten stiffened. The gunmen noticed, all of them drawing their weapons.

"Alexander," Delos said, who ignored her gunmen's reaction. "Your men may sit down."

Commissar Cleon opened his mouth as if he wanted to say something.

Director Delos raised an eyebrow. "You're still here?" she asked.

Cleon must have thought better about speaking. He turned smartly and marched out the door. The gunmen moved to nearby couches, sitting down. They each placed their gun on their lap as they stared at Marten.

"Please, have a seat," Delos said, indicating a single chair before her desk.

"That woman you're speaking about is my wife," Marten said. "She's innocent of any wrongdoing and is not deserving of death."

Delos sat back in her chair. "I doubt that, Mr. Kluge. She is in your company. That is crime enough."

Marten silently counted to five before he asked, "Have you spoken with Security Specialist Cone?"

"I've done even better than that. I've watched a rare video of a fool and a madman."

Marten frowned.

Delos sat up and turned a computer screen on her desk. It showed an evil scene with several large glass tubes, surrounded by medical devices and medical personnel. In the nearest giant tube was a naked and obviously exhausted Marten Kluge, pumping a handle up and down as blue water gushed onto his head.

With an oath, Marten lurched toward the screen. That caused several gunmen to leap up, training their weapons at him. Marten was unaware of their reaction. His gut tightened as he stared at the video. A snarl curled his lips.

"I've been watching the clip," Delos said, as she motioned her gunman to relax. "You pumped an amazing number of hours. All you had to do to end your suffering was speak."

"I didn't speak," Marten whispered.

"And yet, here you sit before me."

"Where did you get that?"

Delos frowned. It put wrinkle lines in her face. She was an old woman. "You are not here to ask me questions, Mr. Kluge. I am asking the questions. It appears that you were a poorly-behaved citizen and a malcontent."

He stared into her eyes, and he shrugged.

That deepened her frown. "You are not a diplomatic man."

"Have you seen cyborgs fight?" Marten asked. "I have, many times, and yet I am here, as you say."

The lines in Delos's face deepened. "How is it that you have a cyborg on your ship?"

"Her name is Osadar Di. She used to be a Jovian. Long ago, she fled to Neptune. There the cyborgs—"

"Spare me the history, as I don't care enough to listen. Your warning to Cleon…it made me curious. I've glanced at your file before. I did it last month while studying the Supreme Commander's latest advisors. I wonder what he saw in you."

"That I was a fighter, one who has faced the great enemy and survived," Marten said.

"Hmm. There you were," Delos said, indicating the screen where Marten still pumped. "And here you are: the Jovian Representative to Earth. You fought in the Jovian System?"

"And helped them defeat the cyborgs."

"Always fighting, are you, Mr. Kluge."

"It's better than surrendering."

"Why are you here in Athens? I want the real reason?"

"To collect my space marines," Marten said.

Delos pressed a button. A speaker blared into life. The voices belonged to Marten and Cone, and it replayed their conversation a few hours ago.

"Promise me grain, eh?" Delos asked, after the conversation ended.

Marten closed his eyes. He thought of Nadia, of Commissar Cleon putting a pistol to her head and blowing out her brains. It made him clench his teeth with growing frustration. He took a deep breath and opened his eyes.

"I despise Social Unity," Marten said in a low voice. "All my life, the thugs of Social Unity have been trying to tell me how to think. They killed my parents and made my early life hell. They told me God didn't exist and then they tried to take His place. I spit on Social Unity."

"Is Jupiter so much better?"

"No!" Marten said. "They have a different form of tyranny, one based on supposed philosophic splendor. But that has changed, or it did while I was there."

"You are a born rebel, Mr. Kluge. You are a complainer instead of a builder."

"I'm in love with freedom, yes, that's true. I want to think for myself, to decide without being punished for my thoughts. As long as I don't interfere with my neighbor, I want to do as I please and think as I please."

"I have heard of your species of malcontent before: a libertarian. It is an old word, and it means: chaotic instability throughout society."

Marten scowled. "I hate Social Unity and I despise the Dictates. I refuse to knuckle under either system. Yet I will join hands with SU soldiers and Jovian guardians to fight the living death that are the cyborgs. I have a cyborg in my company. She used to be human. They tore her down to her component parts and then rebuilt her into a meld of machine and flesh. They programed her brain, using mini-computers to enslave her soul. When cyborgs win, when Web-Minds take over, they capture humans and put them into converters. They manufacture more cyborgs. I never thought it was possible, but out there I found something worse than Social Unity."

"Very stirring, I'm sure," Director Delos said in a bored voice.

"You believe yourself immune, is that it? Look at those thugs sitting on your couch. Look at their snappy black uniforms. They'll stop the cyborgs for you?"

"You're ill-advised to mock the men who will soon be administering your punishments."

"I'm ill-advised to bow and scrape to a fool," Marten said. "I have one life. I'll live it free and tell it like it is, taking my lumps for it."

Delos frowned, and she glanced at her screen, which she had turned back. No doubt, she spied a younger Marten Kluge pumping the handle in the glass tube. She continued to watch.

"In the first year of the war, the Highborn invaded Sydney," Marten said.

"I'm aware of that. It's what saved your life."

"It almost ended my life. Political Harmony Corps tried to blow Sydney's deep-core mine. I went deep into the Earth and stopped them. When I came back up, I was captured by the Highborn for my efforts."

Delos turned away from the screen and stared fixedly at Marten. She sat back, and she pressed her fingers together.

"Listen to me," Marten said. "I've been in tight spots before. I know what it means to face impossible odds and win. Humanity faces its doom, its extinction. We must band together now and fight as one. We have a fleet of Highborn and Humans, and we're about to attack Neptune System. Release my space marines so we can join the armada."

"If I do that, Director Backus will mark me for death."

"The cyborgs have already done that."

"Your few Jovians will make no difference to the fight," Delos said.

"You're probably right," Marten said. "Yet you can't know that. They might be the margin that gives us victory."

"Please, Mr. Kluge," Delos said with a laugh, "no melodrama."

"War is melodrama. Torture is melodrama. Life is full of melodrama. Give me my men. Let me fight our true enemy."

Delos continued to frown.

"Look!" Marten said, pointing at the mini-replica of the Pantheon. "Greece Sector is the land of melodrama. Long ago, men here learned to be free."

"Enough!" Delos said. "Speak to me about realities."

"A year ago, the cyborgs hit Earth with a planet-wrecker, or with part of one. How long will it be before they do it again?"

"I hope never," Delos said.

"Then do everything you can toward hurting the cyborgs. Anything else is immaterial—at least in the long run."

"Life is filled with short runs," Delos said.

Marten stared at the old director. He glanced back at the hard-eyed bodyguards. When he faced Delos again, he noticed she watched the video.

"What about that intrigues you?" he asked.

Her eyebrows lifted. "Yes, I *am* intrigued. That," she pointed at the screen, "is very odd behavior."

"Do something odd for once. Go against your perfect calculations. Think of it as humanity's last gamble against almost certain annihilation by a superior life-form."

"Superior?" she asked.

"They're better than us at fighting," Marten said. "I've faced them several times, and I can attest to that."

"Yet you're still alive, as you so humbly pointed out."

Marten waited.

Director Delos sat forward, and she stroked her chin. Then her eyes narrowed. "Maybe there is a way. Let me think about it."

"We don't have much time left."

"No. *You* don't have much time left. I have plenty. I will think about it and get back to you…soon." She sat up. "Alexander, take him to the detention center. Let him join his precious Jovians."

"What about my wife and Osadar, the cyborg?" Marten asked.

Delos thought a moment. "For now, they will join you. That is all," she said, waving her hand. "Take him away. I have much to consider."

-11-

Many thousands of kilometers from Athens, the *Napoleon Bonaparte* was in Near Luna Orbit. The Doom Star's commander—Sulla the Ultraist—was taking his morning exercise in a pseudo-gravity chamber, a large, rotating pod.

The nine-foot-tall Highborn had oiled his face, giving him a warrior's *shine* or *glow*. Many considered Sulla to be the deadliest combat fighter among the Highborn. He had thick dark hair and his eyes almost seemed to spark with hostility. If he lacked some of the strategic breadth of others, he made up for it with a tight-knit faction of Ultraists and a ruthless willingness to do anything required to achieve victory.

He had advanced high in a short time. During the planet-wrecker assault, Sulla had been a bridge officer aboard Grand Admiral Cassius's ship. It had been the destruction of the *Gustavus Adolphus* that had changed so much, taking some of Cassius's staunchest supporters. No Ultraists had died because the *Gustavus's* commander had forbidden any of the cult aboard his warship. Because of that, the percentage of Ultraists among the Highborn had risen dramatically. It had no longer been possible to deny an Ultraist a major command slot.

Who would have believed such a thing possible? Sulla grinned at the thought. Cassius had made a temporary alliance with the premen. Then a preman had murdered the Grand Admiral. That Sulla had aided the premen in the act…well, that just made Cassius's death even sweeter.

I must now discover all of Cassius's secrets. Sulla flexed his fingers. *Whom must I assassinate next?* It was an interesting question. Then he shook his head, concentrating on the moment and the fighting robot in the chamber with him.

Sulla wore steel-reinforced gauntlets, a body-length synthi-suit and a fierce scowl.

The robot was a squat device rolling on treads, possessing five mechanical stalks. The stalks were as supple as whips. One had a three-inch knife on the end. The others had blunt knobs and could easily beat a man into submission. The robot had beaten six FEC traitors at a time to death. Sulla had witnessed the event on four separate occasions. The FEC soldiers had rebelled against the Highborn during the planet-wrecker attack and foolishly declared independence. Several thousand had paid the ultimate penalty for their disloyalty. Those facing the fighting robot had died hard, many begging for mercy.

Premen made such pathetic soldiers. Only in mass like a horde of lemmings did they present danger. Once more, Sulla shook his head, driving out extraneous thoughts. The robot attempted to outmaneuver and kill him.

Just as my enemies attempt to outmaneuver me, hoping that I make a fatal mistake.

Sulla shifted to the left. The robot paused, and a tread spun, rotating the machine. It would kill him here in the chamber if it could. Sulla never used the lower settings. That would be a mistake of the first order. You practiced at the same level you wished to fight. How otherwise could you hone your instincts to maximum efficiency?

"Come, little death," he told the robot. "See if you can match the greatest fighting Highborn of all."

A blue light blinked on the robot, indicating the beginning of a shutdown.

Sulla began to relax, although he was angered. Who dared to tamper with the fighting machine or interrupt his exercise?

As the blue "shutoff" light continued to blink, the robot's treads spun as it advanced at speed. The whippy stalks moved like an octopus's limbs, with the knife poised in back for a killing blow.

Sulla bellowed with rage. Here was base trickery. Then a knob struck his thigh. Another hit a rib with enough power to crack a premen's bones. A third—Sulla's gauntleted hand caught the mechanical stalk and yanked savagely, ripping it out of the machine. Bits of metal went flying, skipping across the floor. He took a blow to the back of the head. That staggered him, and the knife flashed. He barely twisted in time, taking a stab in his shoulder muscle instead of his throat. With a bound, he retreated, circling the treacherous robot.

The fighting machine rotated, and the blue light blinked more rapidly. It seemed like an act of mockery now.

Sulla's eyes narrowed. Whoever had tampered with the robot had just done him a favor. He would not forget the lesson. He even had enemies aboard ship.

Spitting at the robot, Sulla took a Shaolin stance. He had never used the ancient Kung-fu technique against the fighting machines. The robot would run a quick analysis on it now, giving him a second. Sulla attacked. He took a blow to the shoulder and another one on his thigh. A red weal had already appeared from a previous strike. The robot's knife-arm struck, and he grabbed the stalk just below the blade. A mongoose couldn't have done better against a cobra. Sulla ripped the stalk out of the machine, removing its most dangerous weapon. He jumped back, pivoted and backpedaled.

His thigh throbbed, so did his rib and blood-dripping shoulder. Those were good hurts, however. They told him he was alive.

Lately, the cyborgs had put the Highborn on the defensive and the premen had regained conquered territory on Earth. South American Sector was gone in terms of industry and life. During the planet-wrecker attack, North American Sector had rebelled and rejoined Social Unity. The reason the war went poorly was clear—the Highborn had lost their edge and waited for others to attack. It was time to show the Solar System the Highborn fist.

The blue light on the robot had turned off. Now it blinked again. Sulla pretended to relax. The robot's treads spun, and the fighting machine lurched closer. Sulla stood transfixed as if surprised. The stalks whipped, and Sulla attacked by moving forward. As the knobs struck, he delivered five hammering blows against the chassis. It smoked as circuits shorted-out, and the pummeling arms fell limply to the chamber's floor.

That was how you obliterated your enemy, by going in and finishing it, delivering harder blows than you received. It was time to speak with the other high commanders and convince them of this elemental truth.

***

A day later, Admiral Sulla sat in his chamber. His cut shoulder was still sore, but he had used quick-healing agents to speed the process. The agents repaired his tissues faster than they could have done naturally. Some Highborn disliked Quick-heal and said prolonged usage began to affect one's judgment. Sulla's reply was that being wounded and weak affected one's judgment even more. He was strong and thus attacked his problems head-on as a vigorous warrior should.

Sulla made himself comfortable in the chair. Behind him on the wall was a neural whip, two cestuses and a gyroc pistol. He believed it symbolized his fighting prowess, his willingness to fight any foe one-on-one anywhere, knowing he would always be victorious as the superior soldier.

A red light blinked on his screen. It showed him that the other two admirals on their Doom Stars were ready. There was Admiral Scipio, a tall, retiring Highborn known for his ability to work with the premen. It was a somewhat embarrassing trait, but useful as long as the cyborgs represented a threat. The other was Admiral Cato. He had moved up into Cassius's vacated chair aboard the *Julius Caesar*. Cato was stern and taciturn, and was probably more concerned with consolidating his new position than moving on the great enemy at Neptune. Lastly, there was Commandant Maximus, the fourth highest ranked Highborn, having maintained his post at the Sun-Works Factory for several years. It was surprising he hadn't tried to gain command of a Doom Star. It was odd, in fact. What lay behind it?

Sulla shook his head. He would have to think about it later. The four-way meeting was about to begin.

***

MAXIMUS: I shall begin since the time lag is the worst for me. I have read Admiral Sulla's opinion. It is convincing. We should attack Neptune and burnout the cyborg home base. One cannot win a war while remaining on the defensive. However, there are several considerations to keep in mind. One, the news from the Jupiter System is grim. The cyborgs have launched eight planet-wreckers from Uranus. It means the cyborgs control Neptune, Saturn and Uranus and will likely conquer or destroy the Jupiter System in short order.

SCIPIO: The Jovians have begun defensive preparations. I have read the reports. They possess two mobile asteroids. It is possible they will defeat the Uranus planet-wreckers just as we defeated the Saturn-launched wreckers.

SULLA: I disagree. The Jovians have a paltry fleet. It cannot compare to our armada and to your strategic use of the Earth's farm habitats.

SCIPIO: The premen worked hard on the old habitats, aiding us during the emergency.

SULLA: They worked hard under Highborn guidance and forethought. It is inconceivable they could have done anything less. Otherwise, they would have faced our wrath.

SCIPIO: In light of the cyborg menace, I have reassessed our use of the preman. While it is truth that they are smaller, weaker—

SULLA: And less courageous.

SCIPIO: It takes courage to continue fighting against their superiors.

SULLA: You mistake mulish stubbornness for courage. They are too foolish to understand their shortcomings.

SCIPIO: Whatever the cause, they fight to the bitter end.

CATO: Gentlemen, the Commandant's message is incoming.

MAXIMUS: I'm not sure this four-way conference will work. The time lag for me is too great. Because of that, let me finish my statement and then I will listen to your arguments, responding only when requested.

The cyborgs presently control the majority of the Outer Planets. If—or should I say—*when* we destroy their outposts on Neptune, we will have to finish them off in the Saturn and Uranus Systems and possibility in the Jupiter System as well. I am convinced that the cyborgs have used up their strategic assets in Saturn and Uranus Systems. A careful study of the planet-wreckers and data from the first Cyborg Assault against the Jovians leads me to believe they cannibalized conquered vessels and military stores in order to construct the planet-wreckers. Given the time needed to build large warships—often three to four years—it seems unlikely that they can launch newly constructed fleets from those bases in the near future. Therefore, we must strike now before they can consolidate their gains and build larger warships.

SCIPIO: You speak with the strategic wisdom of Grand Admiral Cassius.

SULLA: Are we agreed then?

SCIPIO: Agreed to what?

SULLA: An immediate and massive assault on the Neptune System.

SCIPIO: In theory, it appears to be a sound idea.

SULLA: It *is* a sound idea.

SCIPIO: There are many variables that we need to consider first.

SULLA: I cannot think of any.

SCIPIO: I will number the obvious ones then. As we attack Neptune, the cyborgs might launch another attack upon the Inner Planets.

SULLA: Didn't you just agree to Maximus's analysis? The cyborgs do not possess the means to mount another large-scale assault.

SCIPIO: What if the cyborgs launch stealth fleets from Neptune, Saturn and Uranus? Even given that they are small fleets, they could converge at Mars perhaps, moving on to attack Earth with a substantial fleet—substantial at least in terms of the warships left around Earth.

SULLA: I do not win my combat matches by fearing my enemy's moves. I attack and make him fear my moves.

SCIPIO: You raise an interesting point. Do cyborgs fear? If so, how can we tell? Frankly, I doubt they fear to any appreciable degree.

SULLA: (shouting) They will fear as we smash their circuits and pulp their flesh! They will howl in agony as we laser their habitats and send nuclear missiles onto their moons! They will gnash their teeth as we crush them out of existence!

SCIPIO: Contain yourself, Admiral Sulla. I can hear you quite well.

SULLA: Then tell me if you can hear this. I challenge you to a—

CATO: Gentleman! We are the admirals and the cyborgs are our enemies. Let us focus our resolve and fighting skills against them, not against each other.

SULLA: I am used to respect and will accept nothing less.

CATO: We are not matched on the wrestling mats or in the fighting ring. We are the strategic team that must forge our strategy. We must outperform the greatest conqueror to date—Grand Admiral Cassius.

SULLA: He led us to victory for a time.

CATO: We were mere fighting slaves for the premen until Cassius showed us the way to greatness.

SULLA: Enough about Cassius. As you said before, we have a war to run. We should stick to that.

SCIPIO: Yes, a war and a feasible strategy. Since you didn't like my first one, let me offer you a different quandary. What if during our absence, the cyborgs drop a thousand nuclear bombs on Earth? Here is another possibility. What if during our journey to Neptune, the preman re-conquer Antarctica and Australian Sectors?

SULLA: I will answer the second first. We must force the preman warships to go with us to Neptune. This should be easy to achieve, since they have already agreed to it.

SCIPIO: That solves one dilemma, but leaves Inner Planets open to any hidden cyborg fleet. The present crises in the Jupiter System shows us the distinct possibility that the cyborgs have stealth vessels where we are unable to spot them.

SULLA: You have stated your fear. Now how would you solve it?

SCIPIO: It is not a fear, but a strategic possibility. The answer, however, is simple: We should leave a Doom Star behind in the Earth System.

SULLA: No! That was Cassius's mistake in the Third Battle for Mars. He didn't attack with the full preponderance of his force. He lost a Doom Star because of it.

SCIPIO: We will have Social Unity's battleships with us in lieu of the third Doom Star.

SULLA: I cannot believe a Highborn speaks these words. You equate warships under preman control as being as excellent as a Doom Star?

SCIPIO: I am growing tired of your continuous slander, Admiral Sulla.

SULLA: (laughs) Tell me this, *Admiral*, which Doom Star do you recommend stays behind?

SCIPIO: We must arrive at our decision logically and consider the sensibilities of our allies.

SULLA: I hope you do not mean that we pamper the premen.

SCIPIO: We use them. We trick them as we have been doing. Obviously, it is easier to trick them when they have a feeling of trust. They will not trust you, an Ultraist.

SULLA: But you are their friend?

SCIPIO: I've worked with them in the past and we achieved a level of success. It is logical, therefore, that they would trust me more than any other Highborn.

SULLA: What do you other commanders think? Is this not rankest cowardice we hear? Admiral Scipio fears to face the cyborgs at Neptune.

SCIPIO: I have warned you once already, Admiral Sulla. I spit on your slurs.

SULLA: Do you challenge me to individual combat then? I will accept any manner of fighting that you decide.

CATO: Admirals, we must unite. The cyborgs have all but conquered the Outer Planets. They have heavily damaged Earth, the greatest industrial prize in the Solar System. Admiral Scipio, I do not believe it is wise to travel to Neptune with two Doom Stars. The cyborgs are clever fighters. We must destroy them totally and with massive force. I submit we use every Doom Star and SU warship in our possession. War is a risk. Now we must take acceptable risks to annihilate our great foe.

SCIPIO: How does it help us to burnout Neptune System but lose our base and the majority of the Highborn? Those on the Sun-Works Factory, in and around Venus and Earth, and on Luna Base—

SULLA: There is your answer. Luna Base helps defend Earth. Up to this point, we have not subdued Eurasia. I do not believe the cyborgs could succeed where we have failed until now.

SCIPIO: They just showed us how to destroy Earth: with planet-wreckers.

MAXIMUS: I have the answer.

CATO: I suggest we wait for the Commandant's words.

SCIPIO: Yes. I will wait.

SULLA: Speak, sir, we attend you.

(Several minutes of unintelligible whispering follow.)

MAXIMUS: The Grand Admiral initiated several secret projects. Here at the Sun-Works Factory we are hard at work on them. Cassius believed that superior technology often achieved victory quicker and with less causalities. The collapsium plating on each of your Doom Stars is one of technologies that will give us the Solar System. Another is a long-distance beam, much like the Beamship *Bangladesh* employed against this station.

SULLA: My...*confederates* have heard of a new distance beam. Can you tell us more about this technology?

MAXIMUS: We are several months away from deployment. Once in place, it will prove to be a powerful defensive weapon, particularly of the Sun-Works Factory. As long as we hold the Mercury System, we can regain any lost territories on Venus, Earth and those already lost on Mars. In the event of the appearance of a large cyborg stealth fleet during the Doom Stars' absence, I recommend a complete Highborn pullback to the Sun-Works Factory. Then, on the return of the Doom Stars, our conquest shall resume.

SCIPIO: What if during our absence, the cyborgs launch more planet-wreckers against Earth or Venus?

SULLA: Didn't you hear the Commandant? The Highborn will regroup on the Sun-Works Factory, thereby maintaining our numbers and weapons systems. Meanwhile, the cyborgs will be eliminating premen for us.

SCIPIO: And destroying our industrial basin.

SULLA: The Sun-Works Factory is our home base, not any of the planets, including Earth. Gentlemen, this is a war of extinction. We must eliminate the cyborgs before they kill us. Let us accept terrible loses for the privilege of annihilating our enemies. Once the cyborgs and premen are gone, we will have won everything. Then we can rebuild at our leisure, the victors of a genocidal campaign.

CATO: I agree in the first principle: we must attack and destroy the cyborgs. The obvious place to start is Neptune.

SULLA: *You* are a true Highborn, Admiral Cato. Your courage is inspiring.

SCIPIO: Grand Admiral Cassius spoke to me before about unity of command. The cyborgs have it. We…have excellent soldiers but often our high commanders are too combative. Even though I have endured slanders and slurs here today, in the greater interest of Highborn victory, I will concur with the majority instead of basking in a feud. However, I will only agree if Commandant Maximus believes likewise.

MAXIMUS: I agree with Admiral Sulla. It is time to speak with the premen, gather their warships and set out for Neptune no less than two or three weeks from now. We have rearmed and retooled our Doom Stars. Now let us finish the fight in true Highborn style.

SCIPIO: As I said a moment ago, in the interests of unity, I will concur, although I have my doubts. The cyborgs are cleverer than we are giving them credit for.

SULLA: (grudgingly) You may be right, Admiral Scipio. They are clever, but we are the Highborn, and our fighting prowess will trump their stealthy moves as we ram our armada down their throats.

-12-

On Earth, in Athens, in the detention center, a man shook Marten Kluge awake.

Marten sat up in his cell. He'd been here for three days already. They'd separated him from his wife, Osadar and from the Jovian marines.

Commissar Cleon stood before him. The cell door was open, and outside stood a guard of red-suited peacekeepers.

A cold feeling filled Marten. He debated lunging at the commissar, trying for his gun. The peacekeepers would shoot him, but at least he'd go down fighting.

"You're about to escape captivity, Force-Leader," Cleon said gravely.

Marten blinked several times, unsure of what he'd just heard. He felt groggy, as if it was still night. "What did you say?"

Commissar Cleon removed a computer scroll from under his left arm. Kneeling on the floor, rolling it open, he touched the screen. A political map of Europe appeared, filled with red and green colors of various shades.

"It's chaos," Cleon declared. "More European sectors are declaring for Backus every day. Italia Sector has strongly sided with the director, together with Macedonia, Bulgaria, Serbia, Bosnia, Hungary and Slovakia Sectors. Romania and Moldova Sectors therefore are isolated."

Except for the last two, the named sectors were red-colored. The last two were green.

"Romania and Moldova Sectors have sided with Cone?" Marten asked.

"They have little choice," Cleon said. "The Sixth Army is stationed throughout them. As you can see, Ukraine and Belarus Sectors are for Backus. They block you from reaching the Moscow launch-sites."

"Director Delos is letting me go?" Marten asked.

"You fail to grasp the situation," Cleon said. "You are about to overpower me and my men and free your marines. Then you will run outside and overpower the guards holding several magnetic lifters. In a daring attempt, you will escape from Athens and likely head for Albania Sector."

Marten saw that Albania Sector was lightly green-colored. Ah, the lighter colors were only nominally for Backus and Cone, while the deep red and deep green represented strongly for that person.

"Why is Delos doing this?" Marten asked.

"Spain, France and Bavaria Sector are all strongly with Cone," Cleon said. "They also hold the major European military units."

Marten knew that had been to stop a possible amphibious invasion from Highborn-held England Sector.

"The nearest launch-site is in Geneva," Cleon continued. "They are still boosting from there and supplying the fleet. Director Delos suggests you attempt to escape Earth from there."

"What about Italia Sector?" Marten asked. He knew there were launch-sites there, too.

"That is the complication. The military units stationed there have gone over to Backus. They've also gone on the offensive to take Austria and Slovenia Sectors, presumably, which presently side with Cone."

Those last two sectors were lightly green, Cone's color.

Cleon looked up from where he knelt on one knee. "Backus has called on all the police and peacekeepers everywhere to do their duty to Social Unity. He asks that they help suppress the renegade military forces that refuse to acknowledge the duly elected government. He means himself, of course. It looks like this is war, real civil war."

"Who does Delos side with?" Marten asked.

Cleon became thoughtful. "At one hundred and twenty-seven years of age, Delos is among the oldest directors. She prefers to play a waiting game and to let the two sides court her. Therefore, she is unable to release you. But she has grown tired of the pressure Backus keeps putting on her to hand you and your marines over to him. Luckily for you, she doesn't wish to anger Cone, who has the stronger military, at present."

"I see. That's why we're *escaping?*"

Cleon rolled the computer scroll and climbed to his feet. "*The hour is dark.* Those are Delos's words to you." The commissar frowned. "I actually saw a real cyborg," he said quietly, "your pet creature. The idea of cyborg armies landing on Earth—it terrifies me. You fought them, and your marines fought them. Now you want to go back out there and fight them again?"

"It's better than being converted."

The police commissar with the single eyebrow studied him. "*Can* we defeat them?"

"If we band together," Marten said.

"Do you really believe that?"

"I've beaten them before."

Cleon nodded. "I've watched the video of you in the glass tube. The director, she's watched it many times, I've heard. She made us watch it. She says you're mad. That only a lunatic would keep pumping while he's exhausted when all he has to do to escape further punishment is talk. She said that only a lunatic who doesn't know when to quit might have a chance of stopping the cyborgs." Cleon grinned. "I think your madness has won you a reprieve, Force-Leader."

"You said magnetic lifters. Why shouldn't we use the same automated cargo vessel and return to Lebanon Sector. There is a launch-site—"

"The Black Sea Flotilla has declared for Backus. Submarines have already entered the Aegean and Mediterranean Seas. You could try that route, but you'd risk capture and a possible trial. That's what Backus keeps demanding."

The com-unit on Cleon's belt beeped. "It's time," he said. "Follow me."

***

The magnetic lifters were big, although not as large as a cybertank. Each vehicle had three warfare pods, with heavy cannons and anti-air missile launchers. The lifters had an inertialess drive but were slower than helicopters. They were still faster and more maneuverable than tracked vehicles. They would need to refuel several times if they were to reach Geneva. Cleon had downloaded the information, showing them possible supply depots open to them.

The Jovians with Osadar, Nadia and Marten were evenly spread among the nine magnetic lifters.

Thus, at two in the morning, in the darkness, Marten's magnetic lifter rose several feet into the air. Around him were other lifters painted in camouflage white. Jovians manned the guns and weapons ports. Armed and armored Jovians waited inside on berms.

Marten slid into the commander's chair. He clicked on the restraints and gave the nod. The engine revved, and the lifter sped for Albania Sector.

Marten glanced at Group-Leader Xenophon, who manned a turret. Like the other Jovians, he was a tough space marine, although he didn't look the part. Xenophon was a small man with a round face and blond fuzz for hair, but he was fast and deadly, especially with a gyroc rifle. He glanced down at Marten. "Glad you came for us, sir."

"Glad you're back," Marten said.

***

By mid-morning, they reached the Adriatic Sea along the coast in Albania Sector. The lifters were parked alongside a road overlooking the slate-gray water. Marten stuck his head out of the hatch. The water was rough, with higher whitecaps than the previous Mediterranean voyage.

Despite the blistering cold, it was good to climb outside and walk around the lifters, listening to the crunch of snow. He was sick of sitting.

Osadar hurried to him, looking intent.

"What do you have for me?" Marten asked.

Director Delos had provided a new and improved senso-mask in Athens. It could emulate any face, provided one had a photograph to scan through the mask's computer. After searching the databanks, Osadar had found a picture of herself from her days in the Jovian Guardian Fleet. That had been many years ago, however. Now the senso-mask showed her former features as a young pilot. She had possessed a small nose and open face, with a light sprinkling of freckles. During their ride in the lifter, Marten had watched Osadar continually examining her new face in a mirror.

As interesting as the simulation of her former features, the senso-mask could track moods. Unfortunately, Osadar no longer had moods like a normal person, nor could the senso-mask "read" them from her skin. By tapping a sensory interface-pad on her arm, however, Osadar could change settings to happy, angry and surprised, and she could meld a variation of the different moods.

"I have several items of note," Osadar said.

The wind howled and snow flurries swirled around the fighting machines. Dead trees stood on the nearby slope.

"First," Osadar said, "There is heavy fighting in the Po Valley. Cone sent armored units from Switzerland Sector and they have crossed the Italian passes. I suspect Cone wishes to secure the proton beam in Milan."

"Omi visited Milan," Marten said.

"If Omi were wise, he will have already escaped to a more peaceful region. If he didn't escape, there is little likelihood of our ever seeing Omi again."

"There has to be something we can do," Marten said.

"Cone is attempting to capture Milan, but I believe it is costing her politically. She is using cybertanks, as the police units have little that can face them. Backus's propagandists are calling the cybertanks 'cyborg troops.' Because of that, some military colonels have switched sides, complicating our situation."

"I don't know why Cone doesn't request help from the battleships in orbit," Marten said.

"Didn't you hear?" Osadar asked. "The SU battleships have left orbit for Luna. They are joining the Doom Stars and will begin acceleration for Neptune in a week."

"What?" Marten shouted. "Next week? That doesn't give us much time to get to our patrol boats and join them."

"Should we join the fleet?" Osadar asked.

"What else should we be doing?"

Osadar shook her head. "I do not think we will make the Luna rendezvous in time."

Marten scowled as he gazed at the whitecaps. Too many good space marines had died killing cyborgs in the Jupiter System and en-route to Earth on the planet-wreckers. He wanted to finish it. He wanted to root out the Prime Web-Mind on Neptune as the Praetor had destroyed one on Carme. Now the fleet was planning to leave without him?

"Come on," Marten said. "Let's gather the others. I want to move while there's still time to join the expedition.

The next twenty-four hours was a blur of travel and fighting as they sped through sectors that had declared for Backus. Fortunately, as elsewhere, the countryside was almost devoid of people. They lived in the underground cities. The only ones allowed outside were farm workers, military personnel and those who paid for the privilege of vacationing on the surface or those with the political pull to do as they pleased. Police units patrolled the roads.

It meant for some ugly sights. Several times, they passed a single, half-charred body. The corpse dangled by wire from a tree. One could only presume the man had been judged a saboteur or a traitor. The police must have sentenced him to torture and death.

Once they spotted an old woman gathering sticks. On sight of them, she shrieked, dropped her sticks and hobbled away. At least three times, they saw a red-uniformed peacekeeper. One had been hacked to death. Another had three sharpened sticks in his body. More people must have slipped out of the cities than Marten had realized.

In Bosnia Sector, an attack-jet screamed down at them, launching rockets. The Jovians were ready and sent up a hail of anti-rocket fire, bringing down all but one missile. That missile took out a warfare pod and injured a marine. Xenophon launched a SAM at the jet. There was an explosion in the air, and a burning jet plummeted earthward.

Several hours later, under Marten's command, they scattered a battalion of police trying to block their path. It was a lopsided fight. With the greater numbers, the police should have easily destroyed the lifters. But they were unused to combat, to having people fire back. The Jovians sent the police running, although it cost them two marines and several wounded.

"The attrition will wear us down long before we reach Geneva," Osadar said.

"I think the police units are still getting used to maneuvering outdoors," Marten said. "And I don't think they're in any hurry to reach Italia Sector and face cybertanks. If we keep moving fast, we should be able to reach Cone territory before the police learn what to do."

The next few hours were uneventful as the lifters zoomed across the terrain. Then Nadia swiveled in her seat and mutely handed Marten a hand-computer.

He took it, and goosebumps jumped onto his arms. Omi stared out of the screen. The muscled Korean had his patented blank look, with a .38 in his hand. He was obviously on the run when this picture had been taken.

"Look at the next one," Nadia said, with an odd note in her voice.

Marten touched the screen, and his eyes widened. "Ah Chen," he said.

"So you *do* know her," Nadia said.

"What?"

"The caption says it's your girlfriend."

Marten looked up, seeing Nadia glaring at him. He began to read the report. The police had picked up Ah Chen in Russia Sector. She had made it halfway across the Eurasian continent. At first, the police believed her to be a Highborn spy, as she had come from Sydney, which was in occupied territory. Under interrogation, she admitted that she searched for Marten Kluge, the Jovian Representative.

"Why is she looking for you?" Nadia asked.

"I have no idea," Marten said, puzzled and bemused.

Nadia folded her arms, her features hardening.

Marten knew the trouble signs, but he kept reading. Ah Chen had been transported to Italia Sector, joining Omi in detainment. Their execution had been set for tomorrow. During the fighting in the Po Valley, however, Omi had made his escape, taking Ah Chen with him. Now the two fugitives were on the run. Any person with information was to report it to the authorities. The last known whereabouts of the two was near the outskirts of Venice.

Marten checked. Venice was one of the few places in Italia Sector that had declared for Cone. That's probably why Omi had been running for it. The Security Specialist had sent several vessels there, unloading troops to help in the attack in the Po Valley.

"We have to change course," Marten said.

"So we can pick up your girlfriend?" Nadia asked.

"I helped her once," Marten said. "She doesn't mean anything to me now."

"Then why did she cross half of Eurasia looking for you?"

"That's a good question."

"She's beautiful," Nadia said.

"Omi is on the run," Marten said. "We have to go back for him."

Osadar had been listening to the exchange. She now swiveled around. "We may not reach Geneva in time if we do."

Marten read the reader, seeing what else the article had to say. He began shaking his head. "If we don't help our friends, we're useless. We're heading for Venice."

"It's a possible hot zone," Osadar said.

"There is fighting near Milan. But I don't think it has reached Venice yet."

"This is a risk," Osadar said.

"What do you want me to do?" Marten asked, looking from Osadar to Nadia. "We stick together or we're no good. Force-Leader Yakov taught us that."

Nadia frowned, but she began to nod. "We have to go back for Omi."

Osadar threw up her hands. "I cannot counsel you on this. You know my thinking." She turned to her computer.

Marten picked up his com-unit and began to issue orders.

***

It was anti-climactic in one sense. They didn't run a gauntlet for Omi. They spoke no lies and forewent trading shots and shells with police units or Army battalions that had declared for Director Backus.

Three hours after changing course, Nadia received a radio signal from Cone. She informed Marten.

He straightened his uniform and found a cap, fitting it over his head. Then he turned on his screen.

"Hello, Security Specialist," Marten said.

Cone wore her sunglasses but her skin looked slack. There was an old-fashioned bookshelf behind her. With a start, Marten realized it was Hawthorne's old quarters. The Supreme Commander had given recorded talks from the room. Maybe Cone thought it would give her authenticity if people saw her there.

"I am *Vice-Chairman* Cone," she said, "the acting representative of Supreme Commander Hawthorne."

"An interesting choice," Osadar said quietly.

"Congratulations," Marten told Cone. "Does this mean Hawthorne is alive and is broadcasting from the battleships?"

Cone gave the smallest of head-twitches, which could have meant anything. "I'm sure you are aware of the fighting between the illegal police units and the military backing me."

"Sure," Marten said.

"Force-Leader Kluge, while I appreciate all you've done, you have become too…politically charged to remain on Earth. I'm afraid I will have to insist that you depart the planet."

"Let's not play games," Marten said. "You're fighting for control of Earth and Director Backus is challenging you."

"He has been illegally elected, as Supreme Commander Hawthorne still governs Social Unity."

Marten knew Hawthorne had written a resignation, but it looked like Cone had decided to ignore that. This woman thought fast on her feet. If the people wouldn't accept her, maybe they would accept a deputy acting in Hawthorne's name.

"You don't have to convince me," Marten said. "I'm with you. I don't forget the people who helped me."

"I'd rather not speak about that," Cone said. "This communication may be monitored." Cone pursed her mouth before she said, "You must immediately head for Geneva and leave Earth."

"I'll do that as soon as I pick up Omi."

"There is no—" Cone glanced to her left off-screen and listened as someone spoke. She faced the screen again. "My people have contacted your friend. Actually, it appears he raced into one of their encampments in the company of a woman." Scowling, Cone glanced left again as someone spoke urgently. "What? Oh, I see." Cone faced Marten. "The woman is a Highborn spy."

"I doubt that," Marten said. "Her name is Ah Chen. I saved her life once in Sydney during the initial Highborn invasion."

"I see," Cone said. "You lead an interesting life, Force-Leader."

"If you give me my two friends," Marten said, "I'll be on my way and headed for Neptune."

Cone nodded. "The faster you leave Earth, the better. I hope you will not hold this against us."

"Not at all," Marten said. "Where are they?"

Cone gave him the coordinates, adding, "You'd better hurry. The fleet begins acceleration in several days."

As Cone signed off, Marten wondered why the little engineer had come hunting for him. It seemed strange, not at all like her.

The answer came an hour and forty-seven minutes later. The lifters halted at the defensive perimeter of a tank brigade. The lifters touched down beside a wall of sandbags, with skeleton trees on the hill behind the perimeter. He noticed there weren't any bio-tanks, but low-built vehicles with monstrous cannons.

Marten climbed down the lifter and spoke with the brigadier, a youngish man in a black uniform and low-billed cap slung low over his eyes. Soon, Omi and Ah Chen stepped out of a bunker, escorted by grim-eyed soldiers with machine guns.

"Didn't think I'd see you anytime soon," Marten said, fiercely gripping Omi's hand.

Omi nodded as if nothing mattered, although he gripped Marten on the shoulder, squeezing painfully.

"Are you ready for our last run against the cyborgs?" asked Marten.

Omi gave him a blank look, one he had perfected long ago in the slums of Sydney. Then he jerked his thumb at Ah Chen. "Remember her?"

She looked small and demure, if a little older than Marten recalled. There were wrinkles at the corners of her eyes that hadn't been there several years ago. She stared at him, and she seemed burdened. He remembered seeing her naked as he decapitated Major Orlov of PHC hundreds of kilometers underground of Sydney.

"Is anything wrong?" Marten asked.

She shook her head and sidled closer to Omi, putting a hand on his biceps.

Marten raised an eyebrow. He hoped that meant what he thought it did. It would go a long way toward keeping Nadia happy.

"I'm married," he said.

"That is good," Ah Chen said in her soft voice. "I am glad for you, Marten."

"We'd better get going," Omi said, and he gave Marten a significant look.

It finally got through to Marten. They knew something important, something they wanted to tell him, but not in front of the military people of Social Unity. Oh, he really got it then. *Ah Chen* knew something.

"Yeah, we'd better get going," Marten said. "The Security Specialist—excuse me. The *Vice-Chairman* wishes for our quick departure."

"Those are my orders too," the brigadier said.

"Then if you don't mind…" Marten said, as he glanced at the lifters.

"Please, be on your way."

"Omi, Ah Chen, you'll ride with us," Marten said. "I'd like to introduce you to my wife."

Soon the lifters were turned around, once more heading for Geneva.

"What's all the secrecy about?" Marten asked in the lifter.

It was a tight fit. Ah Chen sat on the floor with her legs crossed. Omi hovered protectively near her.

Ah Chen swallowed nervously as she glanced at Nadia. "I have wondered a long time what to do with my information. Then Chief Monitor Quirn saw you on the Nancy Vance Show."

"Old hall leader Quirn?" asked Marten, bemused.

Ah Chen nodded.

"Were you two friends?" Marten asked.

Ah Chen blushed. "It is a complicated story. He lives with Molly."

"Oh," Marten said.

"Who is Molly?" Nadia asked.

Marten opened his mouth, uncertain what he should say.

Ah Chen glanced from Marten to Nadia. Then she said, "Molly was a mutual acquaintance that went through the invasion with us. In any case, once I learned you were on Earth, and that you were the Jovian Representative, I believed that fate had given me the answer."

"To what?" Marten asked.

"Yes," Nadia said. "I'd like to know that, too."

Hunching toward Marten, Ah Chen said, "I was slated to leave for the Sun Station. It is in Near Sun Orbit."

"I've never heard of this station," Marten said.

"Nor have I," Osadar said.

"The Sun Station is new and experimental," Ah Chen said. "Without going into the science of it, it represents the next great leap in battlefield technology. The Highborn are attempting to deploy giant reflectors very near the Sun. The reflectors will direct some of the Sun's energy at a breakthrough focusing system many kilometers in diameter. It will act as a gargantuan lens. With enough reflectors, the Sunbeam can conceivably shoot at Mars."

"The Sun already shoots its rays that far," Marten said.

"The Sunbeam will shoot a coherent ray with vast killing power," Ah Chen said.

"We could use that against the cyborgs," Marten said.

Ah Chen nodded. "And after the cyborgs are gone, who will the Highborn use it against?"

Marten sagged against his seat as he glanced at Osadar. "Just how potent is this Sunbeam supposed to be?"

"The Highborn are taking deep-core mine specialists to the Sun Station," Ah Chen said. "It has led me to believe that the ray is many factors more powerful than the greatest beams deployed so far."

"Whoever has the Sunbeam can fire at anyone in Inner Planets," Osadar said. "The only protection would be to hide behind an asteroid or planet."

"The focusing problem needed to hit a ship in Mars orbit…it would be impossible," Marten said.

Ah Chen shook her head. "To save time and so you will understand that I am privy to highly classified information, I will tell you my shame. The Highborn…have taken to seeing the women of Earth. One of the Sun Station's chief engineers has been testing deep-core personnel in Australia Sector. He liked me and then he demanded I please him. After our times together, he spoke about many things. He was very boastful and proud."

"They all are," Marten said.

"How awful for you," Nadia said.

Ah Chen nodded as she stared at the floor, speaking in a quiet voice. "I learned that the premier Highborn of the Sun-Works Factory—a Commandant Maximus—has declined a command position on a Doom Star several times already. According to the chief engineer, there are some Highborn who consider Maximus as Grand Admiral Cassius's equal in strategic ability."

"You think Maximus has declined the combat position because he's found something even deadlier than a Doom Star?" Marten said.

"I do," Ah Chen said.

"I can accept this," Osadar said. "What I don't understand is why you came all the way across Eurasia to tell Marten."

"He is the Jovian Representative," Ah Chen said, shyly glancing at the others. "He has space marines, and I remembered Marten Kluge. He did not like others controlling him."

Marten laughed. It was a grim sound. "You think I should take my marines and try to storm this Sun Station."

"I do," Ah Chen said.

As the magnetic lifters raced for Geneva, silence descended upon the compartment.

Nadia turned frightened eyes upon Marten, shaking her head. She obviously didn't like the idea. Marten scowled, with his eyes narrowed as he stared at an unseen place, thinking deeply.

"How can we do something like that?" asked Osadar, the first to break the silence. "These are Highborn we're speaking about. We cannot defeat them with our handful."

"To begin with," Marten said, "we have to get off Earth. After that…after that, we're going to have to do some serious thinking."

His words left Nadia stricken. She stared at Ah Chen with growing hostility.

-13-

The civil war turned ugly fast.

The magnetic lifters passed a column of cybertanks heading for the Po Valley and ultimately for Milan, one would presume. The one hundred ton tanks were massive vehicles. Their treads churned up the road as their automated warfare pods scanned the skies and hunted for enemy on the ground.

Marten counted twenty of them. A half hour later as they began to climb the Ouster Pass, he spotted another two columns. Sixty new cybertanks headed for the front.

"Cone must be emptying the northern cities of them," Osadar said. "She means to crush Italia Sector."

"Or to gain Milan's proton beam," Marten said.

They had watched a Backus broadcast earlier. For seemingly cryptic reasons, the director had threatened to destroy the boosters launching from Geneva to supply the fleet.

"Cone is taking Backus's threats seriously," Marten added.

"Force-Leader!" Xenophon shouted. The small Jovian was pale as he said, "They're using nuclear weapons, sir."

Marten looked up at Xenophon's screen. A mushroom cloud rose in the distance.

"It ignited in the Po Valley," Xenophon said.

"Button the hatches!" Marten shouted. "Ground the lifters!"

The nine magnetic lifters soon thudded onto the ground as one after another they came to a halt. Then more mushroom clouds rose skyward.

"Madness," Osadar said.

They waited, but the nuclear explosions were far enough away so that no screaming winds or intense heat washed over them.

"Who launched those?" Osadar asked.

Marten shook himself out of his stupor. He was remembering long ago on the Pacific Ocean as Social Unity launched nukes on their convoy. He had been on his way to Japan Sector then.

"Rev up the engines," Marten radioed his troops. There was heavy static on the line. "We need to get off-world before Cone and Backus destroy each other and us with them."

During the next two hours, they picked up several interesting broadcasts. Through it, they began to piece together what had happened. The added cybertanks had told almost immediately on the push toward Milan. Soon thereafter, Director Backus must have made his monumental decision: using nuclear missiles. Backus's propagandist claimed total annihilation of the invading cybertanks, and the announcer added they were akin to cyborg troops, making Cone a stooge of the terrible enemy.

Seventeen minutes later, Osadar signaled Marten. "You have a message from Cone."

He nodded, and tapped his screen. A harried Vice-Chairman Cone peered at him. High-ranking officers moved in the background amid a babble of sounds.

"The Geneva launch-site is under attack," Cone said in her clipped way. "You should reroute to a different site."

"To where?" asked Marten.

"Moscow would make the—"

"We have to lift now," Marten said.

"Backus has infiltration agents everywhere," Cone said. "There are viruses in much of our European software. We've hit the Milan proton-beam…" She shook her head. "An airwing has gone over to him. They used missiles. Now interceptors are headed for Geneva. We have reason to believe they carry nuclear payloads. I urgently suggest you head elsewhere."

"We're fifteen minutes from the launch-site," Osadar said quietly.

Marten squeezed his eyes closed. His heart thudded in his chest. He wanted to get off-planet now. He wanted to get back onto his patrol boats. Who knew how this civil war would go?

"No," Marten said, opening his eyes. "We're headed for Geneva. Keep a booster on the ground for us."

"You're taking a terrible risk," Cone said.

"Yes," Marten said. "Now I have to go. Leave us that booster."

"...I'll see what I can do."

Marten radioed the other lifters. "I know these roads are treacherous and we're in the Alps, but let's push it."

Soon, the nine magnetic lifters whined with power. And the Jovian pilots proved their worth this day as they revved, increasing speed along the Swiss Sector road.

Eleven minutes later, the nine vehicles roared onto the launch-site. Most of the blast-pans were empty, devoid of the giant boost-ships. Craters dotted the area. Several buildings had been hit and they showed gaping holes. One squat orbital vessel remained, however, waiting in the number fourteen blast-pan.

"Park beside it!" Marten radioed his troops.

Ninety seconds later, sirens wailed as they sprinted from their grounded lifters. Marten breathed the crisp air, and he noticed a faint white cloud high in the sky. Then he plunged through the hatch, running for the seats.

Amid shouts, everyone shoved into a seat and strapped in. Seconds later, the mighty engines roared into life and the heavy launch vehicle began to lift. A cheer went through the compartment and Jovians pumped their fists.

Marten turned his head, glancing out the window even as the Gs began to press him into the cushions. As they gained speed, the spaceport shrank and individual mountains merged into a range and then became the Swiss Alps. They'd made it, and just in time. There was a streak outside. It was far away and coming closer fast. Marten spied another streak rushing up from the surface, and there was a brilliant flash.

Ground defense got the first one, Marten thought.

He didn't see if there were other enemy interceptors. The thunder of liftoff drowned out all speech. The launch vehicle shook and the G-forces pressed harder.

I'm leaving Earth again. Despite everything, a pang filled Marten. Would he ever return? Would Earth still be here when this was over?

It was no longer blue outside, but beginning to darken. Struggling against the Gs, Marten craned a look down, seeing clouds. Soon, Europe became distinct as a landmass. Then he saw the curve of the Earth. As he looked, the Gs lessened. Marten realized the thunder of liftoff had stopped, although there was ringing in his ears.

Nadia sat beside him, and beside her was Osadar. The cyborg turned to him. Her "face" showed worry.

"The Doom Stars can easily destroy us now," Osadar said.

Three Doom Stars were in orbit around Luna. The average distance from the Earth to the Moon was 385,000 kilometers. A Doom Star's Ultra-laser could fire one million kilometers with destructive power. It would be the simplest thing in the world for a Highborn to beam them out of existence—if they wanted to.

"Cassius had a vendetta against me," Marten said, "and he's dead."

"Do you believe the other Highborn love you?" Osadar asked.

"I wouldn't call it love, no."

"Presumably, the Highborn have mapped the important structures and craft in Earth orbit. I am not sure they would approve of Marten Kluge regaining access to space."

"How would they know I'm leaving?" Marten asked.

"Spies," Osadar said. "Or perhaps they monitor communications."

As the launch vehicle's engines cut out, bringing weightlessness to the ship, Group-Leader Xenophon turned in his seat. "The Highborn can't fire on us. They need Social Unity's battleships. If they fire, they break the alliance."

"We are not part of Social Unity," Osadar pointed out.

"True," Xenophon said. "But as Jovians, we're part of the Alliance."

"What if Director Backus declares us outlaws?" Osadar asked. "He might ask the Highborn to shoot us for him. Then they could legally destroy Marten Kluge."

"Why would Backus do that?"

"Why do the directors and Cone fight for power?" Osadar countered. "There's chaos on Earth. The nuclear missiles and the interceptors just now prove their madness. That madness has been growing, spreading. Cassius tried to murder Hawthorne. The Supreme Commander resigned at precisely the worst possible time. If all this weren't proof enough of madness, now the Highborn appear to be maneuvering against each other."

"How have you deduced that?" Marten asked.

"Why is the Sunbeam a secret?"

"The Highborn aren't telling *us* about it," Marten said. "We don't know they're not telling each other."

"I read the signs differently," Osadar said. "Commandant Maximus remains at the Sun-Works Factory, never bothering to fight for the command of a Doom Star. We know the Highborn pattern is to struggle for higher rank. According to Ah Chen, Maximus has never broadcast the reason to the other Highborn why he is content to stay at Mercury. Therefore, I believe he has kept the Sunbeam a secret."

"Such a thing would be difficult to keep hidden," Xenophon said.

"Maybe Osadar has a point," Marten said. "I remember Social Unity hiding a beamship near the Sun. It's hard spotting things close to that blazing inferno."

"How can anyone build anything near the Sun?" Xenophon asked. "That I do not understand."

"Ah Chen explained it," Marten said. "They don't build the sections near the Sun, but father away. Then they maneuver the sections into position. The mirrors need to be closest and she said they're fully automated. I just thought of something else. Remember the Highborn interferometer, the giant one near the Sun?"

"I recall it," Osadar said.

"It helped spot the planet-wreckers a year ago," Marten said. "According to what I've heard, it's massive, hundreds of satellites working in coordination. Could Maximus be pretending to add to the interferometer even as he secretly builds the Sunbeam?"

"I deem that to be highly likely," Osadar said. "It is also beside the point at the moment. The Highborn hate you. They have not forgotten that you've killed some of their own when you were a shook trooper under their command. We must pretend to be another supply ship."

No more supply boosters lifted from Geneva, but there were other launch-sites.

"Here is my suggestion," Osadar said. "Let us wait to reengage our engine until orbital drift puts the Earth between us and the Moon, blocking their line-of-sight and thus their lasers."

Marten saw her logic and the need for haste. He began to unbuckle and pointed at Omi and Osadar. "You're coming with me."

"What are you doing?" Nadia asked.

"I need to speak to the pilot about Osadar's plan," Marten said.

"Just call him on your com," Nadia said.

"He might need a little persuading to stay up here with us for a few days longer," Marten said. He checked his needler, the preferred weapon on a spaceship. The .38's slugs had the potential of shattering windows and depressurizing the cabin.

"You're hijacking the launch vehicle?" Nadia asked.

"Only temporarily," Marten said, as he grabbed a seat and propelled himself toward the pilot's cabin.

After persuading the pilot, the hours ticked away until Luna crept over the horizon and then passed behind Earth, shielding them from the Doom Stars. As Osadar piloted them, she maneuvered to the patrol boats. Inflatable skins hid each boat. Techs had used the skins so they could work on them without suits in a regular atmosphere.

Normally, a patrol boat had a crew of five. In the Jupiter System where the patrol boats had been designed and built, they often went on a yearlong cruise and were therefore a relatively spacious craft. The vessel contained a control chamber, living quarters, a galley, gym and engine room.

During the boat's stay in Earth orbit, however, changes had occurred. On Hawthorne's orders, techs had begun its transformation into a cloaked ship.

"The Highborn control the space of Inner Planets," Hawthorne told Marten when he'd first landed on Earth. "Therefore, I've issued a directive on new ship construction. We're taking a leaf out of the cyborg's strategic book—stealth-craft. We might as well begin with your vessels."

Marten didn't know of any new SU stealth-craft, although the Jovian boats had benefited from the change. During his stay on Earth, the technicians had added troop-pods. That greatly increased each vessel's carrying capacity. Then the techs had fitted special "dark" polymers over every inch of hull. It wasn't up to the standards of cyborg stealth-technology, but it changed the nature of the boats, making them difficult to find when they were running cold. Lastly, the techs had torn out the old fusion engine, installing an ion one. It was very fuel-efficient and long-endurance, but had low acceleration compared to the old engine. The exhaust reached three hundred degrees Centigrade now at its hottest, which made it thousands of degrees cooler than its former exhaust and thus harder to detect while accelerating.

The troop-pods added space, but it would still be a tight fit. The boats used to be rakish in appearance, now they were ungainly-looking vessels. Lacking heavy armor or even thick hulls, they relied on cloaking, anti-missile pods and point-defense canons for protection.

Docking beside an airlock, they began transferring people and supplies to the two vessels. Everyone was tense—the interceptors showed that anything could happen. The surface proton-beams were linked to the cities that energized them with deep-core power. It meant Director Backus had several under his control. If he desired, he could shoot them out of orbit.

Marten and Osadar debated in the control cabin of the first patrol boat. He wanted to name it the *Spartacus II*, but the space marines were too superstitious. They vetoed the idea because the first *Spartacus* had been destroyed. Therefore, Marten christened the boat the *William Tell,* the name of another of his childhood heroes.

In olden times, William Tell had been a Swiss patriot who fought against an Austrian tyrant named Gessler. The Austrian overlord had nailed his hat to a post in the village square, decreeing that everyone passing the hat must bow down to it. William Tell came to the village with his son and strode past the hat. Gessler saw that and in anger, he sent his men after Tell. Knowing that William Tell was a master crossbowman, the Austrian said Tell would enter the dungeons unless he shot an apple off his son's head. They paced off a good distance, set his son against a tree and put an apple on the boy's head. Grimly, Tell took out two bolts. He loaded the first, aimed carefully and split the apple in two.

Gessler applauded the feat. But he seemed troubled. Leaning down from his saddle, he said, "Well done, man. One thing troubles me, however. Why did you take out two bolts instead of just the one you needed?"

"If I'd killed my son," Tell said, "the next bolt would have been for you."

Furious with the answer, Gessler made William Tell his prisoner, and they rowed to his island fortress. A storm arose on the way. Because Tell was a strong man, they cut him loose and made him steer the boat, which he did. But he escaped onto the rocks near shore. Tell roused the people, according to legend, and he killed Gessler while the people defeated his Austrian knights. Ever since, William Tell had stood as a symbol: a man who loved freedom and refused to bow down to tyranny.

"We don't have much time until Luna reappears," Osadar said. "I think we should wait until it disappears again behind the Earth."

"Let's risk leaving now," Marten said.

"Our burn won't take us far enough out of orbit. We'll still be in range of the Doom Stars."

"First, we blast our way to the other side of the Earth so they can't directly target us," Marten said.

"That will give Earth Defense time to pinpoint us," Osadar said.

"Backus and the directors hate aliens, hate anyone foreign to Social Unity. I doubt they're allied with the Highborn."

"Sulla is an Ultraist and he accepted premen help," Osadar said. "Why can't Backus act similarly and accept Highborn help?"

"Sulla is a Highborn and they bend their own rules more easily *if* it helps them gain their objectives," Marten said. "Backus is a fanatic, with all that implies. There's no way I want to spend an entire day in range of the Doom Stars. We move now while we can."

"I do not approve."

"It would have surprised me if you did."

"Is my opinion so meaningless?" Osadar asked.

"On the contrary," Marten said. "Your previous suggestion is the reason I want to leave now. Time has become critical and our journey is going to be a long one. The sooner we start, the better I'll feel."

Fifteen minutes later, air expelled into space as the inflatable skin ruptured and collapsed.

"We'll use minimal thrust," Marten said, who sat in the *William Tell's* pilot seat.

The patrol boat's ion engines burned hot for fifteen minutes. It built up velocity as they curved around the planet. Five minutes later, they changed heading for the Sun. Then they cut the ion engines. The two patrol boats slowly drifted away from Earth, cold targets now.

For the next day, they continued to drift away from the planet. Only as Luna passed behind the Earth again in relation to them, did they engage the engines for a longer burn.

Then eight massive blips appeared on the sensor screen. Three of the blips were much bigger and hotter than the others.

"The Alliance Fleet has begun acceleration for Neptune," Nadia said.

Three Doom Stars, four SU battleships and one missile-ship accelerated away from Luna orbit. They were big warships, the last fighting fleet of Inner Planets, and possibly humanity's last chance to defeat the cyborgs.

"Godspeed," Marten said, as a sense of awe swept through him. Here it was. They were finally hitting back. What would the soldiers find in the Neptune System?

"How long will it take them to get there?" Xenophon asked, as he floated near.

"That depends," Marten said.

"What's the shortest possible travel time?"

"Osadar?" asked Marten.

"That also depends," she said. "Given human endurance limitations—"

"I know the answer," Nadia said. "I read some specs on the expected journey a few days before we left New Baghdad. It was something on the order of eight months, give or take several weeks."

"I remember our acceleration as we left Jupiter," Xenophon said. "I do not envy them."

As he watched the blips, Marten did envy them. He wanted to kill cyborgs. Instead, he had a different mission.

-14-

Far away from Earth and Marten Kluge, the Chief Strategist of the Jupiter System landed on Ganymede, taking up quarters in a deep bunker. Three weeks had passed since the discovery of the moon-wreckers and her meeting with Sub-Strategist Circe. The Guardian Fleet was still accelerating at the enemy.

Tan's headquarters contained a huge holo-screen. There, she watched the unfolding drama with the eight moon-wreckers of Uranus, keeping in direct link with the Advisor of Europa. He continued to conduct governmental business from Europa's capital city. The two of them had come to an understanding. Now that she considered it, Tan realized what had happened. The entire Jovian System was in shock. People watched in disbelief as the moon-wreckers approached. The Advisor was no different from the masses. He wanted to end his life well. At this point, he probably still hoped for the impossible and wanted to maintain face and keep his position as a courageous war-leader.

Tan found sleep difficult in the sterile facilities. The majority of her time was spent before the large holo-screen with her primary archons in attendance, including Euthyphro the Advocate. From time to time, they attempted to engage her in debate on some arcane topic. She tried to humor them, but found herself staring at the screen, watching the Jovian defensive moves unfold with agonizingly slow motion.

The two Jovian asteroids broke out of Jupiter's orbit, heading toward the wreckers aimed at Ganymede's projected position in two weeks' time. A monstrous plasma tail lengthened behind each of the two asteroids. On either side and behind the kilometers-huge objects followed the Guardian Fleet, also building up velocity. With the eight warships came nine helium-3 tankers and four Jovian space-liners. They were big spacecraft, and each was part of Europa's defensive strategy.

With hands clasped behind her back, the Chief Strategist often spoke to Circe. The Sub-Strategist advised the three Force-Leaders of her meteor-ships. Circe maintained her quarters aboard the *Erasmus*, no doubt spending many hours starting at the pictures of Marten Kluge taped to the walls.

"It is unusual for a governor to actually *ride* into battle with her ships," Euthyphro said of Circe.

Tan nodded absently as she studied the holo-screen. The eight moon-wreckers were visible. With giant interferometers, Carpo's astronomers mapped the enemy structures. Tall towers with focusing mirrors were laser turrets. There were one hundred and twenty lasers and sixty launch-sites on the eight projectiles. It was an overwhelming number, too much for the Guardian Fleet. From time to time, there was movement behind the projectiles. It proved that warships—or cyborg spacecraft of some kind—followed close behind the moon-wreckers.

The hours passed in tedium and growing despair. The pictures were highly classified. Tan and her archons agreed that broadcasting the precise information would create system-wide panic. For the benefit of humanity, however, the detailed images were beamed to Mars and Earth.

The hours grew into days and the days became a week. Battle drew near and Tan paced endlessly before the holo-screen.

Then one moment among the tedium brought everything home. The holo-screen wavered and Sub-Strategist Circe's face appeared where a second earlier it had shown the eight wreckers.

"We will commence the attack," Circe said, speaking through tight-beam communication. "We will launch our decoy drones first. Let the record show, we cheerfully defended our system and entered battle with high resolve. Sub-Strategist Circe reporting."

The image disappeared and the eight wreckers resumed their place on the holo-screen.

Soon, sixteen decoy drones detached from the vessels of the Guardian Fleet. Their utility was predicated on a different type of battle. The decoys were meant to mimic a meteor-ship, its mass, radiation and radio-signals. The hope was enemy missiles would target the drone instead of the real vessel.

Now the sixteen drones accelerated, passing the two Jovian asteroids and heading for the eight moon-wreckers. Fifteen minutes passed. Then large Zeno Drones detached from the meteor-ships. The new Jovian drones or missiles also accelerated. They were ship-killers, one of the primary weapons of the fleet. They too, sped at the enemy.

A day passed as the two "fleets" closed toward one another. Then the cyborg laser turrets targeted the approaching decoys and Zeon Drones, destroying one hundred percent of the Jovian projectiles.

Sixteen hours later, the lasers began chewing into the two Jovian asteroids, which had finally come into destruction range.

"Begin pumping the prismatic clouds," Circe ordered the crews on the asteroids.

Because of the time lag, Chief Strategist Tan heard the order four minutes after it was given. The battle took a predicable course after that.

The lasers burned into the tiny reflective particles sprayed out of the Jovian asteroids. The asteroids no longer accelerated, but drifted toward the enemy. Giant pumps on the asteroids' surface sprayed the cloud before them, the prismatic crystals reflecting the laser light and dissipating their strength. The laser heat slagged the crystals as a "burn through" took place. The situation was a mathematical formula of prismatic-mass versus laser-fuel and overheating.

By the time the asteroids ran out of P-clouds, sixteen cyborg lasers had stopped beaming. The remaining lasers now began to chew on the asteroids, heating the base material. If given enough time, mass would burn and boil away, and pieces would fracture and possibly drift apart.

As they continued to beam, the cyborgs launched several hundred missiles at the two asteroids.

"They mean to blow our two wreckers apart," Circe radioed headquarters. So far, the Guardian Fleet and the accompanying spaceships hid behind the two asteroids, using them as shields.

Tan stood transfixed before the holo-screen deep in Ganymede. The time lag was minimal and soon forgotten. The Chief Strategist's stomach clenched as she watched the seven meteor-ships and the lone dreadnaught maneuver out from behind the shielding asteroids so they could fire directly at the enemy's missiles.

Lasers beamed from the Jovian warships, striking cyborg missiles, destroying many. Jovian defensive missiles burned long contrails as they launched and accelerated into the void, maxing out at one hundred and twelve Gs. Cyborg lasers now began to target the prone meteor-ships. The minutes passed as hellish rays burned into armored nosecones or boiled away meteor shielding.

Tan heard Circe's orders. They were recording everything, beaming the information to the Inner Planets. One-by-one, as their mass disintegrated and threatened to splinter into sections, the meteor-ships moved back behind the Jovian asteroids, once again using them as defensive shields.

Now the remaining cyborg lasers targeted the Jovian rockets, destroying eighty-eight percent of them. The few to survive the attack reached the nearest cyborg missiles. The rockets exploded like grenades, creating masses of shrapnel that moved at hypervelocity at the cyborg missiles.

Forty-eight enemy missiles disintegrated or were otherwise destroyed by the shrapnel. Combined with those destroyed by Jovian lasers, one hundred and fifty-nine cyborg missiles were still intact, heading for the twin asteroids.

"They have too much ordnance," Circe said, appearing on the holo-screen again.

Behind her back, Tan's grip tightened so she squeezed her fingers. Behind her, the archons watched in silence. Tan wanted to scream the question: *Couldn't they even save*

Ganymede? Was the enemy about to destroy the Jovian asteroids before the kilometers-huge objects could hit and deflect at least *two* enemy moon-wreckers? Who would have expected the cyborgs to launch moon-wreckers from Uranus anyway? Who knew the cyborgs had successfully conquered the system? The enemy moved and attacked with such unbelievable stealth. It was unnerving and debilitating.

"I await your orders," Circe added.

Not knowing what to say, Tan turned to the archons.

In his purple robes, Euthyphro the Advocate strode forward. "Our fleet can still use the asteroids as shields," he said, "gaining proximity so the warships can ram the wreckers once near enough. They ought to at least be able to deflect the two wreckers headed toward Ganymede."

Tan faced the holo-image. What should she tell the Sub-Strategist? The Jovian System was doomed. That was clear. The enemy simply had too much firepower and too much mass in the eight moon-wreckers. Her appreciation of the Highborn-Social Unity defeat of the Saturn planet-wreckers last year rose in estimation. Even if Jupiter had possessed the entire Guardian Fleet of several years ago…

Tan pried her fingers apart and smoothed her robe. She took several steps nearer the holo-image. What should she tell Circe? What made the most sense given the system's certain demise?

Tan swallowed in a raw throat, and she said, "Listen to me carefully, Sub-Strategist. I am giving you precise orders. You are sworn to obey me and therefore you must proceed as ordered."

"Yes," Euthyphro said. "It is wise to remind her of her duty."

Tan wanted to order the man from the chamber, but it was all she could do to say these words.

"Sub-Strategist Circe, as philosophers we are beholden to do the most good for the greatest number of people. You have reaped the rewards of the best education given anyone anywhere at any time. I now call upon you to do your duty to humanity. You must use the two asteroids to close in on the moon-wreckers. Our computations show that our two projectiles will not survive long enough for impact with the wreckers. You cannot deflect even one of the enemy projectiles. It is a bitter truth. Therefore, you must survive contact with the enemy. You must survive, escape, and then do as you feel best afterward. This is a war to the finish with an alien life-form, one we humans created in our folly."

"What are you saying?" Euthyphro cried. "Our meteor-ships must ram the wreckers and save us from annihilation."

Tan shook her head. "The Jovian System is doomed, Sub-Strategist. But it may be that your warships will help turn the tide of the war elsewhere. It is a vain hope, but I choose to grasp at that hope so my death will have meaning."

"No!" Euthyphro shouted.

"Escort the Advocate from the chamber," Tan said.

Three waiting myrmidons leapt to obey, hustling a protesting Euthyphro out of the room.

Tan waited for the time lag to pass as her message reached the meteor-ship and as Circe thought about her response and then gave it. Part of Tan hoped Circe would disobey the orders and tell them she and the others planned the ram the enemy asteroids.

I want to live, Tan thought. *It is such a powerful emotion. Yet my reason tells me it is impossible given the situation. I now choose to end my existence as a philosopher of Callisto.*

Finally, the holo-image of Circe moved. "You give us a hard order, Chief Strategist Tan. We are reluctant to obey it. But we are true to the Dictates. Therefore, we shall attempt to survive and join those on Mars, possibly. We salute your courage and your wonderful rationality. As long as one of us breathes, we shall carry the germ of a new Jovian System in us. Long live the Dictates!"

"Long live the Dictates," Tan whispered.

***

The days passed as the Jovian people learned of their fate. The Advisor of Europa was unable to keep his calm. By tight-beam laser, he raged at the crews of the helium-3 tankers and the space-liners. He implored them to keep to their solemn oaths and ram the wreckers aimed at Europa.

The two Jovian asteroids splintered under the hammering strikes of the cyborg missiles. The enemy laser turrets then began to beam anew.

The Guardian Fleet and the accompanying spacecraft used the last debris and floating boulders until contact with the moon-wreckers. As the Jovian vessels passed the asteroids of Uranus, giant jets rotated the moon-wreckers and the turrets fired into the Jovian ships. The helium-3 tankers and the space-liners quickly parted into separate sections, spilling their crews and other debris into the void. The dreadnaught bore the brunt of the remaining lasers, and soon drifted into several burnt and glowing sections. The lasers next targeted the dreadnaught's escape pods, crisping all of them. There were no survivors. Of the seven meteor-ships, three survived the accelerating enemy missiles, the *Erasmus* among them.

Once out of range of the lasers, the three meteor-ships began to accelerate and slightly change their heading in a curving angle. It would take a long time for them to loop around so they would be headed in the other direction. By that time, they would be far away from Jupiter and aimed toward the Sun. Once headed that way, Circe would have to decide their destination.

* * *

Before the wreckers hit the four Galilean moons, cyborg craft began to decelerate from behind the Uranus projectiles.

Tan had remained in the deep bunker on Ganymede, watching the holo-screen. Most of the archons had departed, rushing to their private space-yachts, planning to begin the long journey to Inner Planets. The Advisor of Europa was already on a luxury liner, headed for Mars.

There was a vast exodus from the Jovian System, but ninety-eight percent of the people had no means of leaving. There were riots in the domed and underground cities, mayhem, madness, along with random acts of kindness and generosity. Each Jovian reacted to the coming doom as his nature bade him or her.

In the bunker, Tan waited in philosophic contemplation. She did not want to live in a world without the examined life. She had fought and struggled too long to run elsewhere.

Once she realized that Circe's meteor-ship would survive the battle, Tan sent the Sub-Strategist a last message. In it, she informed Circe of the Fuhl Mechanism, and the possibility that the cyborgs were on the verge of developing an FTL drive.

Afterward, the days passed until the enemy projectiles became visible to anyone on a Galilean moon's surface. Then a moment in time occurred, a moment of infamy and extinction.

In the bunker, Tan reclined on a sofa, with a chalice of wine in her hand. One of the younger girls danced slowly. She was drugged so her eyes gleamed. The girl twirled around, spinning long ribbons gripped in her small hands.

Tan considered a syllogism as she took another sip of her choicest wine. Looking at the holo-screen, she saw that a moon-wrecker filled it. Tan spotted a crater. In it was a gleaming laser tower. With fantastic speed, the laser grew until she saw its focusing system and then the individual crystals making it up.

The tip of the chalice remained on her lip. Her heartbeats accelerated as her eyes grew wide. From the corner of her eye, she saw a ribbon and heard a final childish laugh.

Then the moon-wrecker that had been launched nine-and-half months ago from the Uranus System collided with Ganymede. The impact hurled Tan from her chair so she violently crashed against a splintering wall. The young girl forever stopped laughing as the bunker crumpled and collapsed upon itself.

A few Jovians survived in various habitats. Some had aimed their telescopes at Ganymede, thereby witnessing a spectacular event of rarest occurrence. The wrecker created much friction, heat and millions of tons of debris.

All the while, those of the Jupiter System who possessed spaceships continued to accelerate for the last bastion of human life: the Inner Planets.

-15-

Far away in the distant Neptune System, the Prime Web-Mind of the cyborgs received data of the successful Jupiter Strike.

Each of the four Galilean moons had been hit, eliminating the bio-forms on them. Even now, small attack-craft hunted through the system, capturing Homo sapiens on the remaining moons, asteroids and habitats. Many Jovian spaceships had escaped, although half would disintegrate under a barrage of accelerating missiles that followed them into the Great Dark.

The Prime Web-Mind was on the verge of completing the conquest of Outer Planets. Pluto, Neptune, Uranus, Saturn and now Jupiter were almost under its complete control. An outpost existed on Charon and there was data of an experimental group in the Oort Cloud. Otherwise, the Outer Planets were secured. It was a heady feeling, one that it had always known it could achieve. Reality, however, was so much more enjoyable than simulations.

Already, the accelerated campaign had begun on Inner Planets. Once the conquest of the Solar System was completed...

The Prime Web-Mind ran through known data and parameters on the struggle. It tested several new theories, ran through different scenarios and listed several unique hypotheses.

Once, it had been located on a habitat constructed of weird ice, orbiting Neptune. That had been a frightening time. A single missile could have destroyed its wonderfulness. That would have been a crime of the highest order. Now it was hidden safely in a deep bunker on Triton, one of the few moons with an atmosphere.

The Prime Web-Mind was a complex cyborg, an exciting meld of man and machine. The primary model was constructed of rows of clear bio-domes. In the domes were sheets of brain mass, many hundreds of kilos of brain cells from as many unwilling donors in the Neptune System. Green computing gel surrounded the pink-white mass. Cables, bio-tubes and tight-beam links connected the domes to backup computers and life-support systems. The combination made a seething, pulsating whole. The bio-tubes gurgled as warm liquids pulsed through them. Backup computers made whirring sounds as lights indicated a thousand things.

A panel opened on the floor. A small robotic device with multi-jointed arms moved out. At the ends of the arms were laser welders, melders and calibrating clippers. The various arms moved as the robotic device made a routine checkup through the primary chamber.

Except for a few trivial holdouts in the Jupiter System, on Charon and in the Oort Cloud, it controlled the Outer Planets. The assault-craft and cyborg troops would capture and begin conversion of the last Jovians. Already, a Web-Mind installed itself on Ganymede, although it had sent communications, complaining about seismic shockwaves continuing to reverberate through the moon. Three small ships traveled to Charon to capture the scientists there.

The Prime Web-Mind paused in its ruminations, playing back an unsatisfying memory. Because of its design and unique functions, the memories had the clarity of a holo-video.

In a white sterile room, cyborgs strapped a struggling Homo sapien with a high forehead and frightened although shrewd eyes onto a gurney. His shredded robes of office lay on the floor. Despite his advanced age, the human had supple muscles and joints. He was designated as Dominic Banbury, one of the chief capitalists of the Neptune System. Capturing him had cost seven cyborgs and two assault craft, an unwarranted expenditure of hardware.

Banbury's personnel were in the process of boarding a cargo vessel and heading to the Number Nine converter. The Prime Web-Mind had recognized Banbury's uniqueness, the subtly of the human's mind. It had desired the specialist knowledge and wished to enslave the mind.

"I will pay good money or services—anything—if you will let me go!" the human shouted.

The cyborgs ignored the pleas as they remorselessly laid him down and strapped him to the gurney. Dominie Banbury soon began to rave as he thrashed, forcing the cyborgs to immobilize him with their titanium-reinforced hands. They wheeled him into an operating chamber.

"Please," Banbury wept. "Let me go."

The cyborgs rolled the gurney to a brain extractor, shoving his head into a helmet-like device. The unit vibrated and the lasers began to slice open the skull.

"No!" Banbury howled, his eyes bulging.

An injector stabbed his flesh, pumping various drugs into his system. Soon, Banbury's eyes closed and he breathed evenly, relaxing.

Twenty-nine minutes later, the unit teased Banbury's brain-mass from the skull cavity. Normally, choppers would divide the tissue as chemical scrubbers deleted old memories and pathways. The tissue would be rearranged on slates and later inserted into computing gel. Banbury's fate was different. The Prime Web-Mind desired his memories. Thus, the brain-mass entered an obedience cylinder as a fine web of melds attached directly to the tissues.

Theoretically, it should have worked. The Prime had run through ninety-seven thousand possibilities. Banbury's brain had taken the ninety-seven thousand and *first* choice—suicide.

It was the first of twenty-nine failures. Twenty-nine Homo sapien minds of unusual quality each chose or inflicted self-elimination rather than exist as a cyborg-slaved brain. The Prime had thus lost the special services of those minds.

That was a bitter loss indeed. For each of those minds had contained creativity that Web-Minds with their mass integration of human brain tissue lacked. The Prime had not yet discovered the reason for this. And that was angering.

Therefore, it kept several unmodified Homo sapien scientists and technicians alive in special chambers on Nereid. It tortured critical information from him or her, and it learned what each human feared the most.

The Prime had long ago concluded that fear was induced, love was given. Therefore, it was better to be feared than loved, leaving the decision of the action to itself.

I am the greatest being in the Solar System. Thus, it is right that I choose for everyone.

The scientists and technicians were on the verge of an incredible discovery: an FTL drive. If they succeeded, no combination of events could defeat it.

The campaign for the Inner Planets was already underway. The Prime Web-Mind was aware of the alliance of the humans. Fortunately, it was too late for the unmodified bio-forms. It had methods for splintering the alliance, as it had agents on several of the worlds. The Highborn were the most dangerous, but they were also incredibly volatile.

With part of its conscience, the Prime continuously ran through simulations and hypotheses. It had concluded that the Highborn would have one secret weapon it would not discover until the moment of employment. Therefore, it needed the greatest flexibility in order to respond to whatever presented itself. To that end, it had sent several Lurker Assault-ships to the Inner Planets.

Those stealth missions neared their objectives. Mars was the first on the list. As the humans struggled in their chaotic manner, it would continue the war with unrelenting pressure.

One other thought gave it pause. The Prime wanted those scientists on Charon. Through a small lead, the tiniest tidbit of data, it now believed a critical human had escaped from Dominie Banbury's service. If that key Homo sapien added his knowledge to the captured scientists, the breakthrough technology, the FTL drive, was all but assured.

A feeling of contentment surged through the brain-tissues of the Prime Web-Mind. The war proceeded well within the parameters. The Jupiter System was nearly enslaved and the Mars Stealth Assault would soon enter its next phase.

Part III: Battle for the Solar System

Seven months pass as the Highborn-Human Fleet travels toward Neptune, as the cyborgs conquer Mars and as Marten Kluge heads for his destiny.

-1-

Captain Ricardo Sandoval sat hunched over a computerized tactical map. He was in Salvador Dome on Mars, in an armored environmental chamber, attempting to devise a winning combination against the cyborgs.

His suit, rebreather and gyroc rifle lay to the side. He wore a ragged uniform rank with sweat. It had been weeks since he'd had a bath. His eyes were red, his face pitted and his morale all but worn down by endless defeats.

I'm no Marten Kluge.

His gritty eyes tightened as he adjusted the screen. He wasn't Marten, but that didn't mean he was going to give up. You did that when you were dead, *or converted.*

Ricardo shuddered. That's what made this war so bitter, so hateful and evil. The cyborgs didn't just kill you. They captured and dragged you down to their converter. Mars Command had captured a video of it—the skin-peelers, the choppers, the brain-scrubbers and the mech-melding—what a gruesome process.

Rubbing his forehead, Ricardo tried to concentrate. It was just a few more days until liftoff. A few more days while the cyborgs overran the planet like a killer virus, infecting one underground city after another. Instead of weakening the enemy with increasing casualties, each attack strengthened the aliens as the cyborgs processed the defeated through the converters.

You're running away. You know that, don't you?

Ricardo clenched his teeth and tightened his fists. Mars was dying and he wasn't going to die with it. What else could he do but run? The cyborgs were invincible. Nothing on Mars could stop them and there was no help from anyone—not from the Highborn, Social Unity or the Jovians who had ignored their pleas.

"Bastards," he whispered. Ricardo struck the tactical map with his fist. He still remembered the day they had asked the Jovians for help. He had been with Secretary-General Gomez as she spoke to the Sub-Strategist through a long-distance radio.

The last of the Jovians had three damaged meteor-ships. They had accelerated hard for the Alliance Fleet headed for Neptune, trying to catch up.

In the environmental chamber, Ricardo adjusted the tac-map, erasing the terrain so Sub-Strategist Circe's face appeared. It was a fuzzy signal, a poor recording of a conversation several months ago.

"This is Secretary-General Gomez of the Mars Planetary Union speaking," Gomez said on the recording. Her voice was clear. "As past allies of the Jovian Confederacy, we now request your assistance. In return, we guarantee you permanent sanctuary on Mars."

There had been a long time lag. Ricardo remembered that. The three meteor-ships were far from Mars, as they had swung wide around the Sun in their gently curving loop from the battle against eight moon-wreckers. Ricardo had watched a video of the Jovian-Cyborg battle many times. It had been one of the grimmest things he'd ever witnessed.

"I'm sorry," Circe said. In the fuzzy recording, she looked so serious, so intent with the black gem in her forehead. "We cannot assist you at this time. We are on our way to Neptune and are still building up velocity."

As he listened to the file, Ricardo remembered Gomez staring at him in disbelief. It had been a hard time. The people of Mars had still believed that victory was possible. The enemy assault had begun with an attack from out of the void. The cyborgs started hostilities by capturing three defensive satellites. One minute there had been peace—the next, cyborgs in vacc-suits swarmed the various satellites, gaining entrance and then control. Afterward, the cyborgs used the Martian arsenal and rained nuclear missiles on selected cities. If that hadn't been enough, other cyborgs appeared on the surface. They landed in stealth-capsules outside a dome. Once in control there, the hated enemy began putting people into a converter, making more cyborgs. A week later from that dome, a cyborg army had advanced across Mars like an invasion of army ants.

Even then, the people of Mars had hoped. The three Jovian meteor-ships had seemed like an act of God. Once communication was established, tears had appeared in Gomez's eyes. That had been before the conversation with Circe.

"We need orbital control," Gomez told the Sub-Strategist. "With your meteor-ships, we can destroy the cyborg-controlled satellites. Then we can arm your warships with missiles and pinpoint the cyborg concentrations on the surface, eliminating them one-by-one."

"It would be a month before we decelerated enough to reach orbital stability," Circe said. "Judging by the videos you sent us, the cyborgs will have already conquered too much surface area. They will probably have captured the other defensive satellites by then, too."

"We must fight together!" Gomez shrieked. She bent near the com-unit as her fingers whitened around it. "We must save Mars!"

"Fight by all means," Circe said in her maddeningly calm voice. "I certainly am. And I understand your pain and dilemma. The cyborgs destroyed the Jovian System. They will destroy Mars, too. Launch what you can and head for Earth.

We must fight where there is a chance of victory. At this point, survival of the human race is the goal. You are doomed, and I will not waste my meteor-ships trying to save what is already dead."

As he sat in a chamber of Salvador Dome, a haunted place of death, Captain Ricardo Sandoval turned off the recording. The Sub-Strategist had seen more clearly than Gomez. That had been months ago. The cyborgs controlled all but two of the defensive satellites now. The enemy had reached the last free city, killing those who carried guns and dragging others to the converters. There were two converters on Mars now—two of the chamber of horrors that turned people into the melded enemy.

Mars Command had tried to destroy one of the converters. Ricardo shook his head. The attack had been a debacle, their Battle of the Bulge—the last gasp to achieve a military miracle. In the end, the Martian attack had burnt-up too many of their own precious military vehicles. They had killed too many of their own hard-to-find soldiers.

In the dreadful months of war, the cyborgs relentlessly moved from one phase to the next. They had infiltrated the surface and soon gained a beachhead on the planet. Then they landed a converter and then another. Finally, they conquered every place of resistance except for a single remaining stronghold. How did you beat something that fed on the corpses of your own dead?

If Mars had possessed heavy weapons, perhaps—more planes, tanks, guns and spaceships…

The communicator beeped.

Ricardo rubbed his eyes and forced himself to concentrate. He had faced the enemy. He was the great Cyborg Killer, wasn't he? What a joke. Three times, he had led the Martian Commandoes into battle. Each time, he had killed cyborgs—at the cost of half his force the first time. Then he lost three-quarters of his troops in New Mexico Dome. At Santa Fe Junction, he had escaped the carnage and retreated to his hovercrafts with three Commandoes—three!

The communicator beeped again. Wearily, Ricardo clicked opened channels. "What is it?"

Secretary-General Gomez stared at him on the screen. She looked worse than he did, with discolored bags under her eyes.

"We picked up radar traces," she said. "An assault force is on its way here."

"From the north or south?" Ricardo asked, his voice hardening.

"Does it matter?" Gomez asked, with tears welling in her eyes.

"If we're going to win this one, it does," Ricardo said. He couldn't give up now, not with the entire dead of a planet watching him. He could feel the ghosts behind him and wondered if Mars would always be known as the haunted planet.

Gomez made a bleak sound. "It is over, Captain. We are all dead."

"The *Pancho Villa* needs a few more days until we can liftoff." He had chosen the name. Pancho Villa the legendary rebel had never quit. Marten Kluge always found a way, too. So would he. Mars would fight back, even if from the grave.

Gomez made another of her despairing sounds. "None of us is leaving Mars, Captain. Everyone who emigrated here came to an evolutionary dead end. The human race had its run. Now it is the era of *Genus Cyborgus*."

"Wrong!" Ricardo said, as he sat up.

"You are not Marten Kluge," Gomez said.

"No. I am Captain Ricardo Sandoval of the Martian warship *Pancho Villa*. I will follow the example of Sub-Strategist Circe."

"Her?" Gomez cried. "She was a fool. She could have come to Mars and saved a planet. Instead, with ruined ships and low on ordnance, she seeks her doom in the Neptune System where the cyborgs are strongest. Do not seek to emulate her."

"To win, one must attack," Ricardo said. It had become his holy creed.

"Staying alive is the first prerequisite for that," Gomez said. "We cannot even achieve step one. I'm afraid you live on illusions."

161

"You are breathing. Therefore, you are alive. Now tell me, from which direction are the cyborgs coming."

"The north," Gomez said, as she looked away from the screen.

"Thank you, Secretary-General. I must go, as I have a defense to run." Ricardo switched her off and brought back the tactical map. So, it was the north... He switched on the communicator and began to issue orders to his men.

Thirty-four minutes later, Ricardo wore his armored suit, rebreather and clutched his gyroc rifle. He stood outside a rounded, ferroconcrete-protected SAM site. Three tracked fighting vehicles were ready and filled with the last Martian Commandoes. The men were poorly-trained compared to those who had died these past months. But you fought with what you had and made do.

"There!" a man said in his headphones.

Ricardo flicked on his helmet's HUD. He saw the enemy: three big-bellied transports flying low over the valley floor. They were old civilian lifters, put to use by the cyborgs. The enemy cannibalized everything.

As Ricardo watched, the giant, ferroconcrete shell guarding the SAMs whirled open. Three missiles ignited, firing one after another. Like long torpedoes, they sped low over the terrain at the enemy.

"Kill them," Ricardo whispered. "Kill all of them." With his HUD, he saw metallic chaff spilling from the transports, attempting to confuse the missiles' sensors. Then the transports lumbered higher, and bay-doors opened.

"No," someone said.

Tiny, metallic-colored humanoids spilled out of the transports. Those would be cyborgs, deadly, unbeatable melds of machine and flesh. Some of them might even have been Martians several weeks ago. Their jetpacks flared, giving them lifting power or acting like parachutes.

The missiles hit. Orange fireballs billowed. Metal parts rained onto the valley floor, raising red geysers of iron-oxide dust.

"It's go-time," Ricardo said, climbing into his IFV—Infantry Fighting Vehicle. It had four 30mm auto-cannons, two

Chavez missile tubes and 77mm of armor, half that of a Martian tank.

The three armored vehicles lurched as they headed toward the enemy: those who had landed and shed their jetpacks. Ricardo turned on the vehicle's scanner. Because his men were so ill-trained, he had to perform gunner duties as well as being the commander. In seconds, he acquired a target. Individual cyborg troopers bounded with incredible speed and agility, and moved one hundred meters at a leap.

Two jets appeared in the red sky, coming in from the north. They had Planetary Union markings.

"Watch them," Ricardo said.

At that moment, a beam stabbed down from the heavens. One of the jets separated because of the red slash. The surviving jet jinked hard, screaming toward the bounding cyborgs. Three canisters dropped from its fuselage before the red beam sliced it into pieces, too.

"Why don't they beam at us?" one of the crewmembers asked.

Ricardo switched the setting of his screen. He brought up the enemy satellite as seen from a Martian space vehicle. The last two Planetary Union drones—hidden until now in near orbital space—zoomed at the laser-firing satellite. The two drones represented the last precious military reserves of Mars Command.

"We had to wait until we saw which satellite they used to launch the attack," Ricardo said.

"What are you talking about, Captain?" a frightened Commando asked.

Just what he'd said, that seemed clear enough. They had to wait and see which satellite the cyborgs attempted to maneuver into position. It wasn't easy getting the right angle to beam down into this valley. It meant the satellite had to be almost on top of them.

"If they want to save the satellite, they're going to have to turn the laser on the drones," Ricardo said. "That gives us a little time."

Ahead of them on the valley floor, the canisters hit. The flash of explosions took half the cyborgs down. The other cyborgs kept coming. The melds didn't fear—they always kept coming.

Their IFV began tracking the enemy. "Here we go," Ricardo said.

No doubt sensing the tracking devices, the cyborgs went to ground, crawling now, using every centimeter of terrain, the rocks, crevasses and outcroppings of stone.

"Should we deploy outside?" a Commando asked from the second IFV.

If this had been two months ago before Ricardo had gone into New Mexico Dome, he would have said yes. With these poorly-trained Commandoes…

"Stay inside," Ricardo said. "We're going to use the heavy weapons to kill cyborgs."

Targeting lasers pinpointed enemies. Then machine guns and 30mm auto-cannons blasted, destroying seven cyborgs. Unfortunately, one of the melds got close enough to launch a hand-held missile. The squat missile had a short flight-time, too short for the IFV's counter-battery fire to engage it. A fighting vehicle exploded.

"Retreat!" shouted Ricardo. "Head back to base." As he spoke, he took over his vehicle's auto-cannons, firing into the likeliest position where cyborgs might be hiding. It must have worked. No more missiles came from those locations.

Then six cyborgs bounded from hiding, rushing the retreating vehicles.

"Firing arc sixty degrees!" a Commando roared.

Three of the melds died under a hail of cannon shells. The heavy rounds punctured cyborg chest-plates and blew them backward. Two enemy troopers survived and latched onto an IFV. Together, the two cyborgs ripped off the vehicle's main hatch. The first meld slipped down inside and then the second. Moments later, the IFV swerved hard, and it flipped onto its side.

At the same time, a clang told of a cyborg landing on their IFV.

"What do we do?" a Commando shouted.

An awful metallic screeching began as the cyborg attempted to pry off the hatch. Then the hatch ripped off the

IFV. As the machine bounced over the Martian terrain, Ricardo grabbed his gyroc and shoved the barrel through the hatch, firing. He killed the cyborg before it could drop its grenade inside the compartment. The grenade exploded outside the IFV.

As the vehicle slewed over the red sands, Ricardo popped his suited head and shoulders out of the hatch. The cyborg was on the ground, struggling to rise. Ricardo shot it, destroying the creature.

Then he centered on the flipped IFV. A cyborg crawled out of it. Ricardo fired his remaining gyroc rounds, killing the wretched thing.

As he slid back inside his vehicle, one of the Commandos said, "Gomez is on the com, sir."

Ricardo turned on the screen.

"You'd better get back here," Gomez said. "There are more on the way."

Ricardo's momentary elation dimmed. Couldn't they ever catch a break?

"You were right," Gomez said.

"What are you talking about?"

"The *Pancho Villa* is ready for liftoff. The techs say it's ready to go."

A strange feeling worked through Ricardo's chest. It made it difficult to breathe. This couldn't be true. He must be hearing things.

"I thought the techs needed another two days before they were ready," he said.

"The *Pancho Villa* is good enough for liftoff," Gomez said. "That's what they said. Now is probably the last window of opportunity we're going to get. They said a few more systems could be improved, but what would it help anyone if they were all dead."

"I'm on my way," Ricardo said. "Let's do this."

***

Forty-nine minutes later, Captain Ricardo Sandoval strapped into his acceleration couch aboard the *Pancho Villa*. Once the last buckle clicked shut, he looked around at the command crew.

Men and woman wearing Planetary Union space uniforms lay on couches in a circular chamber. They worked feverishly, checking and rechecking systems as the countdown began.

A red light blinked on Ricardo's screen. He switched it on. "I'm sorry to bother you, sir, but more enemy planes are coming in."

Ricardo swallowed in a dry throat. "How many are there?"

"Radar says its five transports and seven fighters. They're all former Martian Air Force craft."

Ricardo felt like asking what else it could have been. Then he silently berated himself. The SAM operator was staying behind, fighting the enemy, giving the *Pancho Villa* the chance to escape.

"Concentrate your fire on the transports," he said.

"Yes, sir, and good luck."

He wanted to thank her. He wanted to acknowledge her courage. He found that sweat beaded his forehead. *Why did it have to be such a close-run thing?*

"I'm getting a priority call, sir," the com-officer said.

"Who from?" Ricardo asked.

The com-officer stared at him. "From a cyborg, sir."

"How did a cyborg get hold of our priority—" Ricardo fell silent. It was obvious how they had gotten hold of the channel. Mars Command had found people with slots or jacks in their heads. They were proto-cyborgs, plants, spies, assassins. For a time, everyone had to submit to a head check.

"Put it on," Ricardo said. He had never spoken with a cyborg before.

The screen wavered and then a cyborg stared at him. The thing was a strange combination of machine and man. It made Ricardo's flesh crawl and revulsion to churn in his guts. He'd read plenty of files on the melds and he'd met them in combat, but to have one actually looking at him...

Its metal optical implants twitched. There was red pin-dot light in them. How could metal and flesh coexist? Then Ricardo berated himself. Men had been putting batteries in their hearts and screws in their joints for a long time. Cyborgs merely heightened the process and enslaved the brain, marrying it to computer functions.

"You possess a warship," the cyborg said in an inflectionless voice.

Ricardo's lips moved, but no sounds issued.

"Our indicators show you will attempt flight in the warship," the cyborg said. "This is unacceptable."

"What do you mean?" Ricardo managed to whisper.

"We desire the warship intact. You will remain in place while we secure the vessel."

Ricardo gave a low-throated laugh. "Why would we do that?"

The cyborg blinked several times as if processing the question. "You cannot escape, but you can damage the warship. This is unacceptable."

"Then don't attack us," Ricardo said.

The cyborg's head twitched. It happened very fast, making him think of a humanoid insect. "The warship cannot leave Mars. We desire it for our use."

Ricardo's mouth was dry. "A moment please," he said. He switched back to the SAM operator. "Are the planes still closing in?"

"They're almost in range, sir. Do you have further commands?"

"Not yet," Ricardo said. "Just make sure you destroy the transports first."

"I will try, sir."

Ricardo nodded, and switched the cyborg back onto his screen. "You must call off your attack while I meet with my commanders."

"Leave the warship and file into an assembly area," the cyborg said. "We will thereby process you more smoothly."

"We don't want to be processed. We want to keep ourselves just as we are."

"Your wants and desires are meaningless."

"Not to us," Ricardo said.

The cyborg now spoke slowly. "We will…*bargain* for the warship,"

"Yes, we can bargain. First, call off the planes heading to Salvador Dome."

"The Web-Mind has agreed to process you last. You will therefore maintain your identities longer than other converted Martians."

"I'm afraid that's not good enough."

"Explain."

"You have to move your planes away—"

"They're firing," someone said in the command center.

"Excuse me," Ricardo said. He switched off the cyborg and turned on outer scanners. Veracruz missiles sped at the enemy. All of them were launching. The cyborg response was immediate. The fighters roared into the lead, and they let their anti-missiles fly. In seconds, there were explosions all over the sky.

Ricardo groaned. So did others.

Cyborg troopers ejected from the transports. Their jetpacks burned brightly as they floated toward the ground.

Now cyborg-controlled fighters exploded as SAMs made it through the barrage. In seconds, several transports became orange fireballs.

"Too many cyborgs are touching down onto the surface," an officer said.

"We need liftoff!" Ricardo shouted, switching to engineering.

A harried man looked up at him. "There's a glitch, sir. The ship might explode if we ignite now."

"It doesn't matter!" Ricardo roared. "If the cyborgs reach us, we'll be dragged to the converters. Fire the engines. If we explode, at least it will be a clean death."

The chief engineer stared at Ricardo, finally nodding. "Yes, sir. Ignition systems engaged!" he shouted.

Ricardo's chest hurt. This was too close. He remembered the cyborg then and switched back to the thing.

"You must vacate the warship," the cyborg said.

"Yes, yes, I agree," said Ricardo. "We're afraid, however, that you are lying to us. To show us good faith, you must call off your troopers."

"Humans tell lies. This is known data."

"Cyborgs tell lies, too," Ricardo said.

"The concept is meaningless. You must vacate your warship immediately or face termination."

"You will lose the warship then."

"No. We desire the warship. We have a bargain."

"It's not good enough. My people need assurances."

"You are dissembling," the cyborg said. "I have been monitoring your eye movement and your facial changes. You are Captain Ricardo Sandoval of the Martian Commandoes and acting Captain of the *Pancho Villa*. I am instructed to tell you that dissembling will result in extreme pain once you are in our custody."

Ricardo's features hardened, and he cursed at the thing. Then he switched it off. He felt as if he understood Sub-Strategist Circe now. Ricardo would give just about anything to be in the Neptune System as he launched nuclear weapons at the Prime Web-Mind.

"Liftoff in ten seconds!" the com-officer shouted.

Ricardo turned on the facility's outer cameras. Cyborgs bounded toward the launching point. There must be over one hundred of them. A last transport with smoke billowing from two of its engines still headed for them. The transport must have been well back from the others. Ricardo didn't know if a SAM had hit it or if the plane had taken off with engine trouble.

"Five…four…three…two…one…zero."

An intense sound punctuated the end of the countdown. A small vibration occurred and immediately increased until Ricardo clenched his teeth as his head vibrated wildly. The shaking intensified and then upward lift began.

"We're taking off!" a woman shrieked.

On his screen, Ricardo watched as the underground bay door overhead dilated open. The Martian sky greeted them.

"Come on," Ricardo whispered. "Get us out of here."

The roar became thunder and the warship *Pancho Villa* moved toward the opening, toward freedom and life.

"I'm routing laser controls to me!" Ricardo shouted. Likely, no one heard him. It didn't matter. He took over, and he switched on the warship's outer cameras. They shook too hard for him to use. Thinking fast, Ricardo switched on the SAM site's cameras.

The *Pancho Villa* slowly slid out of the ground. Three hundred meters away, cyborgs sped for them. The enemy wasn't going to make it.

With the shaking, it was getting harder to keep his hands on the controls. Ricardo switched camera settings. The last enemy air transport with trailing smoke was almost over them.

They want to crash into us.

Ricardo activated the laser, and he tapped the auto-tracking and fire pad. To his vast relief, he saw the ship's red beam stab the transport.

"We'll beat you yet!" Ricardo shouted, as he shook his fist at the craft. Then, in horror, he saw cyborgs leap out of the bay doors. The transport was almost upon them, but breaking apart. Now jetpacks spewed thrust, and individual cyborgs dropped and thrust at the *Pancho Villa*.

Ricardo shook his head. As the warship slid toward the sky, visibly gaining speed, several of the creatures attached themselves to the ship's skin. With fantastic strength, five cyborgs tore their way into the accelerating vessel.

An alarm sounded, barely audible over the roar and thunder of the engines pushing them toward space.

This can't be happening.

Ricardo stared at his screen. No one could un-strap and face the cyborgs now. They were under too much G-force. If he shut off the engines, the *Pancho Villa* would not gain escape velocity and they would tumble back onto the planet. Either that or one of the captured satellites would fire lasers into them.

"You haven't won!" Ricardo shouted. Straining to keep his hand up, he switched cameras. Cyborgs crawled through the accelerating ship. One of the creatures forced a hatch, drew a weapon and shot the ten humans strapped to their acceleration couches.

The next few minutes brought the horror home to Captain Ricardo Sandoval as the five cyborgs murdered fifty-seven humans.

They beat us. They captured Mars. Now they're going to get our only warship.

"No," Ricardo said. "No, they're not."

As the *Pancho Villa* exited the Martian atmosphere, Ricardo punched in his commander's password.

As the destruct button appeared on his screen, the door to the chamber blew inward, and an upright cyborg stepped heavily into the command room. The cyborg swiveled its gun toward him. Before it could shoot, Ricardo touched the red destruct button.

The cyborg fired, and three steel needles entered Captain Sandoval's chest. The pain was intense. Two seconds later, the *Pancho Villa* auto-destructed as the engine's dampeners went offline. The warship fire-balled, ending the last fight in the successful cyborg assault of Mars.

-2-

Millions of kilometers in-system from Mars, Marten Kluge sat in his highly-modified patrol boat. He searched the void with improved sensors, using passive systems: teleoptic scopes, thermal scans, broad-spectrum electromagnetic sweeps, neutrino, and mass detection.

He sat behind and to the left of Osadar and Nadia in the sensor/communications seat. Respectively, they sat in the pilot and weapons officer's chairs before a polarized window of ballistic glass. The boat was shaped much like his old shuttle, only bigger. It also had troop-pods attached, big round sections to add living space.

They had been in space for seven months. He recalled how only a few weeks out from Earth they had watched eight blips burn as the Alliance Fleet built up velocity for Neptune.

"We need to move like mice in a house full of cats," Marten had told them then. "The Doom Stars and battleships are leaving Inner Planets, and even if they began deceleration now, it would take them weeks to return. But I'm betting the Highborn and Hawthorne kept something in reserve. They have to be thinking about what happens if and when they destroy the cyborgs."

"Meaning what?" Nadia asked.

"That Highborn and SU warships are still in the Inner System," Marten had said. "Given what happened to the Jupiter System, it's likely the cyborgs already have stealth craft here. We have to move with extreme care."

"What is our objective?" Osadar asked.

"Storming the Sun Station," Marten said. "But for obvious reasons, we're going to attempt it *after* the Alliance Fleet has engaged the cyborgs at Neptune."

"Your reasoning is sound," Osadar said, as she peered out of the polarized window. She spent more time than anyone else did staring at the stars. "We need the Highborn to defeat the cyborgs. The Highborn might turn on the accompanying battleships if we captured the Sun Station too soon. How many Highborn do you believe are stationed on our objective?"

"Since it's a prime military target," Marten said, "I'm guessing a lot."

Osadar swiveled around to study him. "Your answer suggests that there are more Highborn on the station than our space marines can defeat."

"That could be a problem," Marten admitted.

"Can we approach the station undetected?" Osadar asked.

"We have several obstacles to overcome," Marten said. "We have semi-cloaked vessels, but the Highborn have the giant interferometer. It seems unlikely we can remain hidden the entire time. The other problem involves the Sun's heat and radiation. They become extreme the closer one approaches it. Our boats were never built to withstand that. Once we reach Mercury's orbital path, we'll have to live in our combat-suits."

"Will that be enough protection?" Osadar asked.

"We're going to find out."

"Our victory could be short-lived," Osadar said.

"A short-lived victory is better than none," Marten said. "Besides, it might give other humans in better suits or spacecraft time to take over before other Highborn arrive."

"Do you know of other such ships?" Osadar asked.

Marten hesitated before he nodded.

"This is news," Osadar said.

"Social Unity has a hidden missile-ship out here," Marten said. "Hawthorne told me about it once. It has been in space since the beginning of hostilities. The crew will certainly be weary, but they have weapons and a ship with heavy particle-shielding. It will be just what we need to get in close to the Sun Station."

"You can find this missile-ship?"

"Hawthorne gave me the coordinates once. I'm not sure if it's five-nine or nine-five. Maybe I'll just flip a coin to decide."

Osadar shook her head. "The odds are against events helping us, as the universe deplores such actions. I point to my own life as an example, a study in the universe's ill humor."

"I don't agree," Marten said. "Out of all the cyborgs, you're the only one I know who regained her identity. I'd say that makes you unique and a product of the universe's help."

"I'd rather never have become a cyborg in the first place."

"I never wanted to become a shock trooper," Marten said. "Since I did, I plan to use the training and expertise at least one more time."

The weeks passed as Omi and Xenophon drilled the space marines in the troop pods. They were merciless, pitting the squads against each other in various exercises. Marten bent his thoughts to inventing new combat games to help keep things fresh. No one was allowed to sit and brood except for Osadar. The weeks drifted into months, and still the cloaked patrol boats crawled toward the Sun.

By monitoring the news, they kept abreast of the situation between the directors and Cone. The conflict seesawed on Earth. A change came when the former FEC troops in North American Sector once again declared independence, this time from Social Unity. Several weeks later, open conflict occurred in the Indonesian islands between the FEC troops and a small Highborn garrison. It threatened to erupt into wider war as the Japan-stationed FEC also rebelled. The Highborn retaliated with massed armored troopers. It was brutal and bloody as they put down the Japan-based rebels first and then crushed the Indonesian FEC.

The show of Highborn strength brought a truce between the Chief Director and Vice-Chairman. Africa, the Middle East and Europe went to Backus. Asia sided with Cone, who promptly came to an understanding with the new dictator of North American Sector: Colonel Naga.

"Social Unity is foolishly breaking into factions," Osadar said. "Soon enough, the Highborn will play them against each other and complete their conquest."

"I'm more worried about what's happening on Mars," Nadia said.

Mars Command kept broadcasting the conflict, showing clips and newsflashes of the deadly cyborg invasion and advance across the surface.

"How can we win?" Nadia asked one night. She snuggled next to Marten in a warm bunk. Everyone slept in rotation, with someone always sleeping in the short supply beds.

"I don't know," Marten told his wife. "The cyborgs have the advantages, but I refuse to accept they'll wipe out humanity." He was silent for a time. "The truth is it's really up to the Alliance Fleet."

"Should we have joined them?" Nadia asked.

"I keep wondering that."

Pouting, Nadia said, "Why did Ah Chen have to come and ruin everything?"

Marten kissed his wife. He should have separated the women. But he hadn't thought that a good idea at the time, not with all the fighting men around. He scowled. Morale was slipping and so was cohesion. It was simply too cramped in the boats and Omi and he where the only ones with girls.

Early next week, an alarm rang in the flight compartment.

Marten floated to the sensor screen.

Osadar looked up at him. "There's your SU missile-ship," she said. "It's surrounded by Highborn shuttles."

"Are they fighting?" Marten asked.

Osadar shook her head. "I don't know yet," she said, adjusting sensor controls. "But I intend finding out."

Grabbing the back of her chair, Marten pulled himself closer, anxiously watching the screen…

-3-

The rehabilitation of General James Hawthorne was a slow process. First was the obvious fix to his finger, the one ruined by shooting Grand Admiral Cassius. Fortunately, the medical facilities aboard the *Vladimir Lenin* were top-rate. In short order, he had a new finger. The repair to his health and spirits was another matter.

There were several problems. Years of grinding work and intense pressure had taken a serious toll of his body. Mental fatigue made it worse, and guilt over the nuclear bombardment of the rebellious Soviets had been eating away at his conscience. The first few days aboard the *Vladimir Lenin* found him in a lone cubicle as he slept around the clock. He finally stirred, nibbling at his food and then lying on his bunk again, staring at the ceiling.

The days became weeks and then the *Vladimir Lenin* made the short flight to Luna. Before they began acceleration for Neptune, there was a knock on the wardroom door.

Hawthorne stared up at the ceiling with his long-fingered hands twined together on his chest. He'd been looking up at the ceiling for days, replaying a thousand decisions, seeing endless ways he could have made better choices. People who said they would never change anything in their life...he didn't understand that. He would have done hundreds of things differently.

The knock became insistent. There had been others earlier. Hawthorne had ignored them and finally they had gone away. This one didn't sound like it was going away soon.

"Who is it?" Hawthorne asked.

"Commodore Blackstone. Do you mind if I come in?"

"Joseph?" Hawthorne asked.

"It's easier talking face-to-face."

Hawthorne didn't agree. Vaguely, he realized this was the *Vladimir Lenin*, Blackstone's battleship.

His forehead wrinkled as he attempted to summon the energy to sit up. He found the willpower lacking. He never should have said anything.

Blackstone banged on the door again. "I need to speak to you, sir."

Hawthorne might have shouted, "Go away!" but he lacked the willpower for that, too. "Enter if you must," he finally said.

The door slid open and Commodore Blackstone floated in.

Hawthorne was shocked at how Blackstone had aged. The rings under the man's eyes, the sagging skin... Is this what prolonged space exposure brought? Then he noticed how Blackstone looked at him. Hawthorne didn't like it, so he turned away.

"You can't just lie here," Blackstone said.

Hawthorne remained mute.

"There's civil war on Earth," Blackstone said.

Hawthorne remembered someone else yelling that through the door several days ago.

"Someone faked your resignation," Blackstone added.

A momentary tingle went through Hawthorne. The feeling died, fortunately. He didn't want the job anymore. It had been killing him. He had killed millions of innocent civilians who had simply wanted something to eat. A leader who couldn't feed his people needed to be dragged behind a barn and shot in the head. They should have shot him a long time ago.

"James, have you heard a word I've said?"

Hawthorne frowned. Was there someone in the room? Curious, he rolled onto his back and noticed Commodore Blackstone hovering nearby.

"Hello, Joseph," Hawthorne said.

The Commodore blinked in confusion. Then the thin man scowled. "Now see here. You have to get it together. You're the Supreme Commander of Social Unity. You've been thwarting the Highborn for years and—"

A stricken look crossed Hawthorne's features as he began to shake his head.

"What's wrong?" Blackstone asked.

"I resigned."

"No you didn't. Someone forged it."

"Oh."

"The forgery has caused a fracture on Earth. The directors voted one of their own into the leadership, a Director Backus."

"A good man," Hawthorne said. "I found him in an Algae Factory in Cairo. His production figures were amazing. I elevated him on the spot. He's been a rising star ever since."

"He's trying to oust Vice-Chairman Cone."

"Who?"

"Someone named Cone. Do you know anyone by that name?"

"Ah, Security-Specialist Cone. So she made a stab at power, did she? I thought she might."

"She's losing."

"Not for long," Hawthorne said.

"You have to broadcast something to them."

Hawthorne turned his head, for the first time directly meeting Blackstone's gaze. "You haven't thought that through. If I speak, the Highborn will demand my blood. That could dissolve our shaky partnership."

"The Grand Admiral attacked you. He set you up."

"Yes, but no matter how you look at it, a preman killed a Highborn. That's a grave offense to the supermen."

"What are you going to do then?" Blackstone asked. "Stay in here forever?"

"The question is: what are you going to do? What have the Highborn done now that Cassius is dead?"

"They've created a triumvirate."

"The Doom Star admirals are ruling by committee?" asked Hawthorne.

"Something like that," Blackstone said.

"What have they decided?"

"To attack the cyborgs in the Neptune System."

"What about you?" Hawthorne asked.

"We're joining them, Vice-Admiral Mandela and me."

"Who holds the highest command?"

"It's a triumvirate," Blackstone said.

"I understand. But who will make the command decisions in the heat of battle?"

"They each will, I suppose."

Hawthorne thought about it, and shrugged after a time.

"That's it?" Blackstone asked. "You shrug?"

"What else do you expect me to do?"

"We need a leader, an overarching commander for us and them."

"Can you convince the Highborn of that?"

"I can't," Blackstone said. "Maybe you can."

Hawthorne gave a short, brittle laugh.

"With divided commands, we're doomed to defeat," Blackstone said.

"Not necessarily."

"Unity of command is vital to victory."

"I could name you several historical fleet actions that show the contrary. They were important victories, too, against an enemy with cyborg-like unity of command."

"I can't think of any," Blackstone said.

"What about the Battle of Lepanto?"

"Never heard of it."

"It was a naval battle on Earth. It occurred in 1571 as Europeans fought the conquering Turks. The Venetians, Spaniards and Papal forces quarreled right up until the moment of cannon-fire. Or take the Battle of Salamis in ancient times. The Athenians, Spartans, Corinthians and others debated fiercely as the Persian King of kings moved his fleet to annihilate the arguing Greeks. It was a Persian debacle. Victorious committees running a campaign—especially fleet actions—are nothing new."

"It still seems like a poor way to coordinate our last desperate action to save humanity," Blackstone said.

"Yes," Hawthorne said.

Blackstone made an explosive sound. "At least Social Unity should fight together. It is the mantra of our political existence."

"Why wouldn't we fight united?"

"Because we have two senior officers with the remnants of their fleets," Blackstone said. "Neither Vice-Admiral Mandela nor I care to take orders from the other."

"Vice-Admiral outranks Commodore," Hawthorne said.

"His was a political appointment!" Blackstone shouted.

It made Hawthorne wince.

Calming himself, Blackstone said, "Under no circumstances will I take orders from him that jeopardizes my ships."

Hawthorne managed a nod.

"What's wrong with you, man?" Blackstone said. "How come you're just lying there? The least you could do is give me an order."

Hawthorne made a vague gesture before he turned away.

Blackstone spoke more, but Hawthorne tuned him out. Eventually, the Commodore left.

Hawthorne closed his eyes, falling into a troubled sleep. He ate, slept and stared until alarms rang thought the *Vladimir Lenin*. The noise wouldn't stop. Finally, Hawthorne realized it was the warning sounds before hard acceleration. He hurried to the bathroom and then strapped himself onto his bed.

Ninety-three minutes later, the grueling acceleration began. It leveled off after several hours, maintaining one-point-five Gs.

The extended sleep, mental rest and utter lack of everything but the physical pressure of acceleration slowly restored some of Hawthorne's energy. He began to wander the long, curving halls of the battleship. After a week, he attempted limited exercises, which improved his appetite. He knew of an old German proverb: *Eating builds appetite*. In his case, it proved true.

His curiosity began to stir again, although it wasn't about the situation on Earth. Whenever anyone tried to talk to him about the SU civil war, he blanked out. It didn't matter to him anymore. People soon knew to avoid the topic.

Slowly, Hawthorne became curious about Neptune, the planet, the system and the cyborg defenses there.

Neptune was the last regular planet of the Solar System. Pluto—along with several others like Ceres in the Asteroid Belt—was considered a dwarf planet. On average, Neptune was about four-point-five billion kilometers from the Sun, or a little over thirty AUs away. Light traveled at 300,000 kilometers per second. That meant it took a ray of light roughly four hours and sixteen minutes to travel from the Sun to Neptune. The *Vladimir Lenin* would make the trip in a little over eight months, accelerating, coasting and then decelerating once near enough. Neptune's orbit was so large that it took 165 years for it to complete one circuit around the Sun.

The planetary system had been known for its shameless capitalists. That had been one of the reasons the secret cyborg prototypes had been built there. Everyone knew that capitalism produced vast inequalities as cunning men exploited the proletariat. Yet for some strange reason, it also produced a glut of creativity and a vast amount of goods. The work had proceeded faster there than it ever had on Earth. The cyborgs had been a secret plan gone awry, and it seemed the capitalists had been the first to pay the bitter price of their success.

What had the cyborgs of Neptune done to prepare against invasion?

The problem began to prey upon Hawthorne. He spent more time reading the computer files. Soon, he began prowling through the *Vladimir Lenin*, reacquainting himself with the *Zhukov*-class Battleship. It had size, thick particle-shielding and powerful lasers able to fire one hundred thousand kilometers. That was an impressive range until one compared them against a Doom Star.

We've beaten Doom Stars with these, he told himself in his room. *Now we're fighting* with *Doom Stars.*

Several months into the journey, he knocked on the Commodore's wardroom door.

"Enter," Blackstone said.

Hawthorne found the Commodore behind his desk, studying his screen.

"What brings you here?" Blackstone asked, sitting back in his chair.

Hawthorne took a seat as he glanced around. The quarters were Spartan, with an old dagger hanging on a wall.

The former Supreme Commander had changed since boarding. He no longer stooped, but stood straight. The bags under his eyes had returned to a flesh tone and almost disappeared. It left the flesh wrinkly there, but less than it could have been, as he'd put on weight. The biggest difference was in his eyes. They weren't as haunted or as guilt-ridden.

He avoided thinking about the millions of innocent civilians murdered by his nuclear missiles. It had been his decision. He would never shy away from that. But it had been forced upon him. If he had done nothing, Social Unity would have fallen to the Highborn. It had been an act of desperation, but necessary nonetheless.

"James?" Blackstone asked.

Hawthorne cleared his throat. "What do we know about the cyborgs and the Neptune System?"

Blackstone's eyes widened. Then he grinned.

"What's wrong with you?" Hawthorne asked.

"You're back, and none too soon. Mandela and I are having trouble with the Highborn. We can't decide what to do about it. Now I know."

Hawthorne waited.

Blackstone's grin increased. "We hand the decision over to you."

Something passed through James Hawthorne. It began in his eyes, tightening the skin of his face. After a second, he nodded. "It means I'm back in command?"

"Yes," Blackstone said. "That's exactly what it means."

"Good," Hawthorne said. "Tell me about the Highborn and then I'll tell you what we're going to do about it."

-4-

While Hawthorne and Blackstone debated about the Highborn, Marten Kluge clung to the back of Osadar's chair. He watched the sensor screen, trying to figure out what was going on around the SU missile-ship.

The *William Tell* and its companion boat moved silently through space. They had been en route toward the Sun for months, following the five-nine coordinates. Silent running with ears wide and eyes peeled, they looked, listened and measured everything with the mass detector, teleoptics and neutrino tracker.

The void or the space between the Inner Planets was a vast volume. A single ship, a fleet of thirty ships, was still a tiny speck. Finding a quiet enemy vessel was like hunting for a particular piece of plankton in the Atlantic Ocean. Engines burning hot made everything easier in terms of sensors. Unfortunately, the closer to the Sun, the more radiation there was. That blanketed many of the sensors, making it increasingly difficult to pick-up otherwise obvious readings.

With the missile-ship, Marten had known where to head and look. It made a critical difference.

Indicating her screen, Osadar said, "Someone is using jamming electronics, which is affecting my readings."

Because of the patrol boats' low speed, they were still days from the missile-ship. It was a big vessel with particle-shielding and fast fusion engines. It was a distance-fighter, shooting missiles or drones and then moving to a new location.

"One of the shield-masses appears to be destroyed," Osadar said. "That indicates a surprise strike or a sudden and vast strike. Otherwise, the missile-ship crew would have rotated shields until all were equally worn down."

A cold feeling worked up Marten's spine. He began counting Highborn shuttles. They appeared to be the same size as the *Mayflower*, the captured shuttle he'd used to fly to the Mars and Jupiter Systems. Each shuttle could ferry eighty Highborn in comfort.

"I count four," Marten said. "Four shuttles shouldn't have been able to defeat a missile-ship, not unless the crew let the Highborn aboard."

"Four shuttles shouldn't have been able to in a stand-up fight," Osadar agreed. "I can't spot any damage to the shuttles, but the jamming could be blocking that. I don't see anything unusual on visual. We have to take into account there could be more shuttles on the other side of the missile-ship. Or maybe there's something else besides a shuttle hiding there."

With his fingers, Marten squeezed the back of Osadar's chair. He'd been counting on the missile-ship. The idea of cruising to the Sun Station in the patrol boats while wearing combat-armor…there were better ways to commit suicide, faster ways than radiation poisoning.

"Why are they jamming?" he asked.

"The obvious reason would be to keep any signals from leaving the missile-ship," Osadar said, "including distress signals or a file about what happened out here."

"Four Highborn shuttles, a destroyed shield to the SU warship and jamming," Marten said. "The implication is clear: the Highborn have captured the missile-ship or they are in the process of capturing it."

A frown appeared on Osadar's senso-mask. "I hope you are not envisioning another of your mad schemes."

"We have two patrol boats and a little over eighty space marines."

"Poor odds against Highborn," Osadar said. "There are potentially more Highborn than Jovians."

"Maybe," Marten said. "Our ace card is that we see them and they don't see us."

"That is an assumption."

"Granted," said Marten.

"I'm afraid to ask, but what are you suggesting?"

Marten's features tightened. Ah Chen's revelation about the Sun Station had changed his thinking back on Earth. It had shown him that at least one Highborn played a deeper game. Before, it had merely been enough to defeat the cyborgs, to keep humanity from extinction. Now he wondered if he could gain a larger victory. Social Unity was breaking apart. The stress of war had shaken the pillars of society. If someone like him could control a Sun Station, maybe he could help affect greater changes. Why did people have to remain slaves to a deadening socialist system or slaves to a so-called master race?

"We need the missile-ship," Marten said.

"Your reasoning escapes me," Osadar said. "We need stealth against the Sun Station. How does one sneak up on such a station with a missile-ship?"

"That's the easy part," Marten said, "by flanking the enemy."

Osadar studied him. "You mean maneuvering onto the other side of the Sun as the station, and rushing around it in close orbit?"

"Right."

"It is a tactically sound idea," Osadar said. "Providing the ship can withstand the heat and radiation. But I must point out that Highborn presumably possess your needed ship."

"I read the situation otherwise," Marten said, with a tight grin. "I spy SU rebels using stolen Highborn craft. We must help our allies and repel the enemy."

Osadar stared at him. "You don't really believe that."

"It will be my story if we fail."

"If we fail, we'll be dead."

"I need the missile-ship," Marten said, his tone hardening.

"You actually mean to pit Jovian space marines against Highborn commandoes, likely a greater number of Highborn?"

Marten nodded.

"How do you propose achieving victory?"

"We're going to have to risk using our engines," Marten said. "We're going to do it now at the farthest distance possible, nudging us onto an intercept course."

"If we use the engines, they will detect us."

"It's a risk, as I said. But maybe they're so busy jamming the warship, trying to capture it, that they'll fail to spot us."

"That is doubtful," Osadar said.

Marten ignored her. He'd already made his decision.

***

After informing the others of the plan, Marten, Nadia and Osadar took their places. Marten piloted, Nadia ran weapons and Osadar tracked the enemy.

Marten flexed his fingers as a sense of urgency filled him. This was it. He needed the missile-ship. Otherwise, heading to the Sun Station was a suicide mission, something he'd avoided until now. Capturing the *Bangladesh* had been the nearest thing he'd ever done to a suicide mission, and he didn't even like thinking about that time.

"Here we go," he whispered. He engaged the ion engine. There was a hum from the back of the boat. The *William Tell* began to vibrate and a bump pushed him against his chair. It wasn't fast acceleration with many Gs, but a gentle pushing as the boat moved onto a new heading.

Every second the engine burned was another second the Highborn could spot them on their sensors.

Nadia tapped a control.

Outside, metallic clamps unlatched. There was another bump from outside and a shudder ran through the boat.

"The decoy has deployed," Nadia said.

Marten nodded. Their vessel had carried a decoy. The other patrol boat possessed a large S-80 drone, a Social Unity weapon.

The seconds ticked by on the chronometer. Then a light flashed on the screen and Marten switched off the engine. Three seconds later, the other patrol boat did likewise.

"We're on an intercept course," Marten said.

No one else spoke, not even the space marines in back. They were heading for a showdown against Highborn. Had the enemy seen the brief flares of ion engines?

Marten glanced at Osadar. The cyborg watched the sensors. She must not see anything unusual yet, or she would have said something.

"I hate the waiting," Marten whispered.

The waiting continued for another forty-seven hours.

The decoy was in the lead. It ran silent like the other boats. At the end of the forty-seven hours, the S-80 drone drifted away from the second patrol boat.

The situation over there had become much clearer. The missile-ship was the *Mao Zedong*. The spaceship had thick particle-shields, except for the obliterated one. The jaggedness of the edges of the other shields beside the demolished one indicated missiles had repeatedly blasted through the mass. The lettering on some of the visible hull had given them the ship's name.

Highborn occasionally used thruster-packs to flit from a shuttle to the missile-ship or vice versa. Once, three Highborn in vacc-suits maneuvered a big piece of equipment onto the *Mao Zedong*.

"Are they repairing it?" Nadia asked.

"We'll find out soon enough," Marten said.

The hours passed and now the patrol boats coasted to within one thousand kilometers of the missile-ship.

Marten began to slither into his equipment. The combat-vacc-suit used articulated metal and ceramic-plate armor. A rigid, biphase carbide-ceramic corselet protected the torso, while articulated plates of BPC covered the arms and legs. He had an IML: Infantry Missile Launcher. It fired the trusty Cognitive missiles. He would also bring a gyroc rifle with extra ammo. Unlike the assault onto the planet-wrecker, each space marine would have a thruster-pack. Hopefully, they would be alive long enough to use it.

Waiting to don his helmet, Marten floated behind Nadia. She wore a silver vacc-suit minus the helmet as she sat at the weapons chair.

"This is it," he said.

Nadia turned around and pushed up to him. Gripping him fiercely, she kissed him. "I love you," she whispered.

"I love you, too," he said.

She touched his cheek. "You're the best man I've ever known, Marten Kluge."

He nodded grimly. The idea the Highborn might destroy the patrol boats in the next few minutes, killing his wife… "Let's get started," he said gruffly.

She kissed him again, hard. Then Nadia let go and climbed back into her seat. She took a deep breath. "I'll need the decoy's radar for this."

"I know," he said.

"Osadar?" asked Nadia.

"Ready," the cyborg said. She ran the decoy.

"Now," Nadia whispered.

Osadar turned on the decoy's radar. It pulsed, waiting to acquire precision targeting data. In moments, the data flowed into the *William Tell's* computer.

Nadia fired the point-defense cannons. Each shot used depleted uranium pellets as ammunition. The cannons were primarily meant to intercept incoming missiles, drones or torpedoes. Today, Nadia targeted two of the shuttles. The other patrol boat fired at the other two HB shuttles.

Time crawled with agonizing slowness as the pellets zoomed toward target.

Then Osadar said, "One of the shuttles is starting its engine."

"They've seen us," Marten said. "Use the drone."

Seconds later, the S-80 burned hot. It accelerated toward the enemy, rapidly gaining velocity.

"Another shuttle has started its engine," Osadar said. Her fingers moved across the sensor equipment.

Ahead of them and visible through the ballistic glass an ion engine burned. It was the decoy. It turned away from the missile-ship, heading out as if fleeing.

On Osadar's screen, two shuttles began to move.

"No," Marten whispered.

"A hit!" Nadia shouted. "The cannons hit one of the shuttles."

A beep sounded on Osadar's equipment.

"What's that?" Marten asked.

Osadar studied the readings. "Sand-blaster," she said.

Marten nodded. He'd heard of that, sand shot in a cloud. The idea was that a particle of sand would hit shrapnel or a cannon pellet and deflect the incoming object just enough to miss the ship.

Then the S-80 drone exploded. It was a shape-charged nuclear drone. The blast, heat and radiation would primarily go forward in a ninety-degree arc at the enemy.

Everyone in the *William Tell* donned his or her helmet.

"We surprised them," Osadar said.

Even as she spoke, enemy missiles accelerated at them from one of the supposedly destroyed shuttles.

A painful knot tightened Marten's stomach. Shuttles and patrol boats lacked the size for big engines. Therefore, they lacked lasers or particle beam weapons. For them, it was missiles, anti-missiles and cannons. It meant you could kill your enemy and from the grave, as it were, your enemy's pre-launched weapons could still come and destroy you.

"Ready the cannons," Marten said.

Nadia nodded.

An object brighter than a star appeared outside the window. Marten knew he witnessed one of the missile's exhaust plumes. Then a second and third "bright star" appeared, rushing toward them and quickly growing bigger.

"The first missile is headed for the decoy," Nadia said.

Marten clutched his IML. He began shaking his head, as if by his thoughts he could deflect the missile from their boat.

"The second missile is also headed for the decoy," Nadia said. "Oh no," she whispered. "The last one is heading here."

Twenty second later, a bloom of brightness showed the HB missile destroying the decoy. As the flare of it died down, they saw the last "bright star" headed toward them.

The point-defense cannons began to chug from both patrol boats.

Fourteen seconds later, Nadia said, "I think we disabled it."

She was wrong, or wrong enough that it didn't matter. A pellet hit the missile. Then the missile exploded. Thankfully, it did not explode with a nuclear detonation. At extreme velocities, shrapnel spread in a small cloud. Although the *William Tell* was in the lead, none of the enemy shrapnel hit it.

Four pieces, however, pierced the skin of the second patrol boat. One of the pieces cut an ion coil, letting coolant spread in a vapor. The same piece of shrapnel the size of a pinky-fingernail sliced through a heating unit. When the vapor touched the hot surface of the unit, an explosion occurred because of the oxygen seeping in from the living quarters. The explosion caused an overload in the remixing core, and it ignited, obliterating the Jovian craft in an impressive detonation. Forty-two space marines died, most of them cooked in their combat-suits. The others died as debris smashed through their faceplates.

On the *William Tell*, Marten closed his eyes. His marines' death numbed a little more of his heart. The war was so unrelenting: modern battle so unbelievably deadly.

"A Centurion Titus is hailing us," Osadar said.

"We didn't kill all the shuttles?" Marten asked, his voice betraying his bitterness.

"The jamming has stopped," Osadar said. "I don't detect any more missile launches." She turned around. "The signal is coming from the *Mao Zedong*."

"Let's hear it," Marten said.

Osadar put in on the boat's speakers.

Marten opened his helmet's visor. The deepness and arrogance of the voice told him a Highborn spoke.

"You are weak warriors, striking from the dark," Centurion Titus said. "You fear to face us man-to-man. Very well, face the ship's weapons then."

"The *Mao Zedong* is moving," Osadar said. "I think they're turning the ship to bring a missile-port to bear."

With a mental effort, Marten pushed aside the death of half his men. He had been with them a long time, but he couldn't let that affect him now. He needed to think, to outwit a Highborn. The trick with them was to play to their arrogance. They thought of themselves as so superior and *premen* as cowardly and small.

Marten wanted to grind his teeth in rage. Instead, he forced himself to say, "Tell him we surrender our boat."

Osadar and Nadia turned around in wonder. Osadar spoke first. "You want to surrender to the Highborn?"

"No," Marten said. "I want to get close enough so we can board the missile-ship."

"I do not understand," Osadar said.

"Let's hope he doesn't either."

"You are twisting your words?"

"These are the Highborn who planned to castrate me," Marten said. "They stamped a number on my hand and treated me like an animal, a preman. I don't like twisting my words, but this is war and he just killed half of my marines. Now open channels, and I want a direct video link with him."

Osadar did as he requested.

In his combat-suit, Marten sat down clumsily on the pilot's chair. He twisted off his helmet, letting it float in the air beside him, but out of sight of the video link.

In seconds, the wide face of a Highborn appeared on the screen. Centurion Titus had white hair in a buzz cut and he was missing his right eye.

"You are a preman," Titus said.

"I'm Marten Kluge."

Titus curled his thin lip. "I've heard of you. Prepare to die, preman."

"I'm ready to surrender my boat to you," Marten said.

Titus paused. "You are defenseless?"

"No. I have my PD cannons."

Titus showed his teeth in a grin. "You fear the missile-ship. You are wise, preman. But it will not go well with you. Therefore, I do not understand why you are unwilling to die fighting like a warrior."

"I have people with me," Marten said, "my wife among them."

"Ah," Titus said. "You are weak with your emotion of love. Yes, I accept your surrender. Turn you craft and begin immediate deceleration."

"I will comply," Marten said.

"No," Titus said. "You will *obey*."

Marten knew how to satisfy Highborn egos. So, although it grated upon him, he hung his head. "I will obey," he said grudgingly.

"You were a fool, preman. You destroyed a few shuttles, but failed to kill many of us. For the few you did kill, your fate will be a hard one. Yes, I will accept the surrender of Marten Kluge." Titus leered. "I see you're wearing combat-armor. I hope you decide to fight, preman. It would give me joy and increased rank to kill the insolent Kluge."

"I'm surrendering my boat to you," Marten said. "You have won this encounter."

Even as they spoke, Marten turned the *William Tell* and began deceleration.

"Enjoy your last minutes of freedom, preman. For the rest of your life will be one of agony."

Marten forced himself to shudder. Then he switched off the channel. Turning to the others in the compartment, he said, "We're surrendering our boat, but we're not finished fighting."

Group-Leader Xenophon grinned.

"I'm never going to surrender to anyone," Marten told the marines. "As we begin to dock, we will exit the *William Tell*. Let them have the patrol boat. It's us they're going to have to deal with."

***

The ion engine burned its hottest, slowing the *William Tell* as it approached the *Mao Zedong*. The missile-ship used side-jets, slowly rotating. Just as slowly, one of the undamaged particle-shields began to move.

The thick mass of shielding was attached to gigantic struts that moved in grooves along the outer hull. It allowed the warship's captain to rotate shields as needed. As the shielding moved, it revealed a row of big PD cannons, many times larger than those on the patrol boat. The shield moved just enough for the cannons to fire. Later, it could move more to allow the boat to enter a hanger. Titus had already instructed them to prepare for boarding. Highborn would come out and make sure this wasn't a suicide vessel meant to explode once past the shielding.

The ion engine shut down. Slowly the patrol boat drifted toward the big cannons.

"You know the plan," Marten said. "Now let's do it."

As the boat drifted closer, the space marines began to exit out of a hatch opposite the missile-ship. Marten stayed behind by the com-equipment.

White-haired Titus hailed them and appeared onscreen. "Two Highborn are on their way. If they are harmed, the cannons will obliterate your vessel. If you decide to ignite yourself in an effort to harm us, you are wasting your time."

"I will not blow up my boat," Marten said. "You have my word on it."

"A preman's word?" Titus sneered.

"For what it is worth," Marten said.

"Since last we spoke, I have read your file, Kluge. You are a traitorous beast."

"I have my faults, but I am not traitorous."

"Commandant Maximus is anxious to have you back at the Sun-Works Factory."

"The missile-ship is headed there?" Marten asked.

"My soldiers have you in sight. Ready yourselves for them."

Marten dipped his head. "I am prepared."

"Go, and remember to act contrite in their presence," Titus said. "Otherwise, it will go even harder for you, preman. You killed several of our comrades in your cowardly attack."

"Marten Kluge, signing off," he said, tapping the screen and cutting off communications. Hurriedly, Marten donned and sealed his helmet, heading for the hatch.

Soon, he floated outside the *William Tell*. Using rungs fitted for such actions, Marten "climbed" to the top of the boat. Activating the HUD in his visor, he spotted two Highborn in their combat-armor. White particles of hydrogen-spray propelled the two super-soldiers from the *Mao Zedong* and toward the *William Tell*.

Marten clicked on his suit-to-suit communications. "Some of those cannons are sure to open fire once we act, but we're going to have to risk it. The cannons are meant to kill ships and shuttles, not individual marines. Are you ready?"

He heard the affirmatives.

Marten flicked on his IML. Beside him, Omi did likewise. They were the highest-rated on them. Therefore, they had the honor of reigniting hostilities.

"One, two, three," Marten whispered over the suit-to-suit communications.

At almost the same instant, two Cognitive missiles launched from their IMLs.

It was a short flight, but the Highborn were quick. One fired a weapon. The other throttled open his thruster-pack, moving faster. It didn't matter for either. Both Cognitive missiles hit and exploded, and each killed one of the master race.

Before the small missiles hit, everyone climbed above, below and to the sides of the *William Tell*. They leaped off the dark polymer skin and engaged their thruster-packs, beginning the last leg of the journey to the *Mao Zedong*.

Like the others, Marten used a joystick control. It brought bitter memories being out here, seeing the asteroid-like shield "below" him. He led the way toward the damaged section of the ship. That's where they had seen Highborn entering before with thruster-packs. Then something flashed out of the corner of his eye.

He turned his head, and noticed another flash. It was a big PD cannon. They were firing.

Marten debated letting his thumb off the throttle. Likely, the trail of hydrogen-spray made one more visible. Probably, it didn't matter either way. The key was to get out of the cannons' line-of-sight as fast as possible.

He zoomed closer to the particle-shielding, and it began to move. The Highborn must realize—

A bloom of color told him a shell had just connected with someone ahead of him. He hoped it wasn't Nadia.

Should I have left her on Earth?

He didn't know. Now wasn't the time to worry about it. With his teeth clenched, Marten zoomed toward the particle-shielding, believing if he could get low enough, that he could avoid the cannons.

The cannons kept firing. They killed five Jovians, too many—always too many losses.

Marten zoomed several meters above the shielding, heading for the damaged section. He had several gut-wrenching fears. If the *Mao Zedong* was in good enough shape, it could begin acceleration, stranding all of them out here. It's what he would have tried to do if Highborn attempted to board his ship. The other possibility was many Highborn in combat-suits waiting at the damaged section, ready for battle.

This was too similar to the *Bangladesh*. Then he had faced a ship full of SU personnel, with shock troopers covering his back.

"Count off," he said.

"Omi here."

"Group-Leader Xenophon reporting."

"Osadar here…"

As the men kept counting off, Marten brought up the *Mao Zedong's* specs on his HUD. He also saw which squads had lost men. Ah, three of the dead belonged to Alpha Squad. He adjusted the boarding attack and used suit-to-suit communications to tell his space marines.

Then he zoomed over the edge of the shielding. A vast pit loomed under him: the destroyed part of the missile-ship. He wished he'd practiced more at thruster-pack flying. He was moving too fast. With a twist of his wrist, he changed the direction of thrust and headed down into the *Mao Zedong*. He clicked on his suit-radar and brought up the information onto his HUD. Space marines followed him down into the maw. They were going into the damaged section where there was open decking visible.

"Motion at grid ten-B-seven!" a Jovian shouted into Marten's headphones.

Even as the marine spoke, tiny pinprick dots appeared down in the ship's darkness. The enemy was using a gyroc rifle. If he'd used a laser, it would have shown a direct line back to where he was. With a gyroc, one could fire and move. Highborn were experts at that game. There was none better at it, not even cyborgs.

In a smooth motion, Marten shouldered his IML. He flicked on the radar. In seconds, an enemy symbol flashed on his HUD. He fired. So did ten other space marines, too many on one target. In their excitement, the men had forgotten fire procedure.

The Cognitive missiles burned fast in a flock.

Marten swept the barrel of the IML, seeking a new target for his already lofted missile. The radar beeped again, giving him a different enemy. He pressed a switch, downloading the new targeting data to his missile. A blue light flashed in his helmet. The missile accepted the data and veered toward the new enemy.

All the while, the Highborn kept firing at them.

"Pericles is hit!" Xenophon shouted over Marten's headphones.

Marten snarled with frustration. The Highborn were deadly marksmen. He wouldn't have any men left for the Sun Station if this kept up. He should have set out with five hundred space marines. He was almost down to thirty—thirty regular men to take on the masters of the Solar System.

"Hit!" a Jovian shouted. "We scratched one."

Unwilling to attempt a missile-reload, Marten racked the IML onto his back-slot. He unhooked his gyroc and clicked it online with his suit's targeting system. A targeting crosshairs appeared on his HUD. It showed wherever he aimed the rifle.

"Ten-C-six," Omi said in a gunfighter's voice.

Missiles ignited at the heading.

"Nine-C-six," another Jovian said.

The Highborn had come to fight. But Marten was surprised there were so few of them. Had they caught the overmen by surprise?

Marten shut off the thruster-pack as he fired gyroc shells. Highborn shot back. Tiny contrails grew as the enemy shells sped up at them. An enemy gyroc punctured a neck-joint, killing a Jovian seventy-three meters from Marten. Another shell blew open Group-Leader Praxis's stomach, and entrails blew outward. A third space marine died as shrapnel opened his suit, and oxygen left a stark trail.

They're killing too many of us.

Marten ignited the retro-rocket attached to his chest. It had one purpose: to slow him down so he could land. Instead of turning around and using the thruster, he faced the enemy as he decelerated. The rocket slammed against him, expelling air out of his lungs. He'd never gotten used to this, no matter how many times he practiced. He'd have a purple bruise on his chest tomorrow—if he survived.

As he landed on open decking—his magnetic boots automatically activated—Marten saw a crouched Highborn shooting at his men. Marten quick fired from the hip. The Highborn was already swiveling around, however, and shot a palm laser. The beam hit Marten's chest-rocket, burning through and burning into the ablative armor underneath. Then Marten's gyroc shells struck. The first one failed to penetrate the heavy armor. The kinetic energy should have knocked the Highborn backward, but this warrior was strong, and his suit gave him exoskeleton power. The second shell missed, penetrating a ruined bulkhead behind the Highborn. The third shell exploded against the faceplate. The visor fractured just enough so air hissed away in a stream. The laser moved off-target. Marten fired two more shells—the rest of his magazine. And it should have worked.

The Highborn twisted even as he slapped a sealant to his faceplate. Marten's shells burned into the heavy shoulder-plate, disabling the Highborn's arm, but they failed to kill. The Highborn used his good arm, lifting his big gyroc rifle, aiming at Marten. Marten frantically tore out his empty magazine. He wasn't going to make it.

Then, out of the corner of his faceplate, he saw a Cognitive missile streak down at them. For a wild second, his gut clenched.

I'm going to die.

The missile seemed to zoom right at him. Maybe something was wrong with its targeting acquisition. Before the Highborn could pull his trigger, however, before Marten could slam in a fresh magazine, the missile slammed into the enemy giant, exploding, saving Marten's life.

It took a split-second for Marten to realize he was still alive. Then it was time to enter the *Mao Zedong*.

***

Marten Kluge crept through the crippled missile-ship. He'd shed his thruster-pack, clutched his gyroc rifle and used his magnetic boots.

It was dark in the long corridors and the tight chambers. He used infrared sight and kept up a schematic of the ship's passageways on his HUD. His space marines followed him. Omi and Osadar lugged a plasma cannon. Group-Leader Xenophon led the squads in an adjoining corridor.

There was no sign of the Highborn. Had the enemy retreated deeper into the ship? Or had they exited to a hidden shuttle and even now readied nuclear missiles to pump into the warship? He should have left someone aboard the *William Tell* to monitor the situation. He hadn't expected the patrol boat to survive, however. In truth, *he* hadn't expected to survive this engagement with the Highborn.

His helmet beeped as the sensors picked up life-readings. "Four-G-nine," Marten said.

"I see it," Omi said. "It's hot! They have weapons!"

Marten snapped orders as his stomach seethed. Somewhere inside him, he had hoped the fight was over. He should have known better. These were Highborn.

The space marines moved in the darkness, spreading out in the various corridors.

"Watch for booby-traps," Marten radioed. His radio buzzed. He used his chin to click and accept.

"Careful," Omi said. "They could be using the emplaced device we spotted as a locator or a directional finder."

Marten nodded, even though he knew Omi wouldn't be able to see the head gesture.

"Marten Kluge," a Highborn said over the radio.

"Titus?" Marten asked, as he started in his combat-suit.

"I am *Centurion* Titus," the Highborn said proudly. "You have reached the ship because of your faithlessness."

"Wrong!" Marten said. "I've stormed the vessel because we're better at this than you."

"He's moving," Omi said. "Or someone is. He's headed for the engine core!"

"Stormed?" Titus sneered over the radio. "You have stormed nothing, preman, but for your tomb. You are a dead man. We are all dead."

"Yeah?" Marten asked.

"I am Centurion Titus, and I have pronounced your doom."

"He's moving fast!" Omi said.

"Is he attempting to maneuver us into an ambush?" Osadar asked.

Scowling, Marten tried to think past his knotted gut and the heaviness in his chest. They had made it onto the *Mao Zedong*. Against Highborn, they shouldn't have been able to do that. What did it mean?

"De-magnetize," Marten said. "We have to reach him before he blows the core."

"Highborn are not suicidal," Osadar said.

"But they do hate losing," Marten said, "especially to premen." He clicked a switch on his suit. The boot-magnets turned off and he lifted minutely. As he activated his palm-magnets, he jumped off the deck-plates. Slotting the rifle, Marten began to "swim" along the corridors. Instead of pushing against water, his magnetized palms gripped the walls as he pulled. He twisted his palms at the last moment, ripping off the magnetic holds. It was an art, and he was good at it. Marten propelled himself faster and faster, and clicked on a helmet-lamp. Infrared and schematics could only do so much—then old-fashioned eyesight was needed. The beam washed through the darkness, giving an eerie feeling to the compartments, making it seem like a ghost ship.

Behind him, the space marines followed. It was a race, and it was a terrible gamble chasing a Highborn so recklessly.

An explosion occurred in a side corridor—there was a flash to his left and the faintest of shudders.

"What was that?" a space marine shouted.

"A booby-trap," Xenophon radioed. "Just like Athena Station. It killed Achilles, tore his head clean off. And it put a hole in a bulkhead."

Marten grunted. Athena Station had been hell. It had been Cyborg Central for the Jovian System. The space marines had gone down and tried to root them out. At the end, the cyborgs used nuclear bombs to take hundreds of their enemy with them. Before that, there had been endless booby-traps and gun-battles.

"He *is* luring us," Osadar said over the radio.

Marten didn't think so. Centurion Titus just wanted to slow them down in order to give himself time. The Highborn would have foreseen the possibility of a fast-assault. Yet what if Osadar was right? He shook his head. Titus was headed for the core. That said it all.

"Go!" Marten shouted. "We have to reach him now."

"What if—" Osadar said.

"Go!" Marten shouted. The clench in his gut was gone. This was a race. The Highborn should have already rigged the core to blow. Titus would have been too arrogant, however, to believe that premen could defeat even a handful of Highborn. The one SU missile—the S-80 nuclear weapon they'd carried from Earth—it must have taken out ninety-nine percent of the enemy. Had the Highborn been getting ready to leave?

The thoughts slid away as Marten propelled himself through the corridors. A second booby-trap would surely kill him. He was betting Titus hadn't enough time to rig two. What shocked Marten—if he was right—was that a handful of Highborn would have tried to capture the *William Tell*. In their place, he would have destroyed the patrol boat.

Marten ducked his head as he shot through a hatch into the engine room. His beam of light washed over another hatch leading to the core. There was motion in there!

Magnetizing his boots, Marten twisted, even as he reached behind him. He grabbed the rifle, wrenched it free and aimed at the hatch. At the same time, the soles of his boots stuck hard to the wall, as he'd applied full magnetic power. He stood sideways in the room as his momentum propelled his torso, slamming him against the wall. The blow caused him to let go of the gyroc.

A space marine shot past him. Titus appeared in the hatchway and fired at nearly pointblank range. The laser-pulses tore open the stitches in the marine's armor. Heat and smoking blood billowed. Red splashed against the wall. Scratch another Jovian.

With frantic haste, Marten grabbed the rifle. The Highborn was turning at bay. He couldn't let the super-soldier kill any more of his marines. Marten's torso bounced off the bulkhead, tossing him up sideways even as his boots remained magnetized to the wall. He sighted and fired. Two shells ignited in flight, zooming toward the core-hatch.

The beam quit as a gyroc shell flew through the hatch. The second exploded against a side of the hatch, gouging metal.

Marten shoved off the wall as he turned off his boots. He flew across the chamber, knowing he had to keep moving. Titus reappeared, his beam burning where Marten had been. Then the beam was tracking him, and it struck Marten's stomach-plate. If the pulse-laser had started on him for these few seconds, it would have burned through the armor. Fortunately, Titus ducked behind the hatch again.

On his HUD, Marten saw the reason. Omi and Osadar set up the plasma cannon. A second later, a gout of orange, roiling plasma boiled in a mass toward the core-hatch. The plasma reached the hatch. Some of it vaporized against the sides, chewing through and melting it. Within the core chamber came an explosion.

Marten didn't hesitate. This was the moment. He propelled himself toward the orange-glowing hatch. He moved through it with his rifle ready, careful to keep from touching the glowing hot metal.

In the chamber, Centurion Titus stood to the side of the hatch. The nine-foot Highborn raised his pulse-laser and might have tried to fire. The barrel had melted enough so it was inoperative. Marten and Titus must have realized this at the same instant. The Highborn released the laser and aimed his hand cannon, the one attached to his left arm. Marten snapped off a gyroc round—he was still sailing through the room.

The hand cannon fired a heavy slug, and it destroyed the gyroc rifle, shattering it into pieces. The gyroc shell—

The room and its occupant—the condition of both—finally penetrated Marten's thoughts. Titus's armor glowed hot from its nearness to the plasma blast. Through the faceplate, Titus appeared to be in agony. Beads of sweat rolled down a red and blistered face, and the eyes were wide and staring, showing

Titus's pain. The gyroc shell penetrated the heated armor, and the Highborn winced. His left shoulder—air expelled from the hole.

Automatically, it seemed, Titus slapped a patch to his armor, to the wrecked shoulder. Incredibly, the patch held. On the other arm, the hand cannon had jammed, likely also affected by the intense plasma-blast heat.

The slug that had destroyed Marten's rifle had also slammed against him, pushing him off-course. He would have sailed into a glowing bulkhead or he might have sailed through it to the inner chamber. Because of the slug, Marten hit a different bulkhead.

At that moment, Titus jumped. His one arm was useless. He didn't appear to have any effective weapons left. His body-armor must have been too hot, maybe even cooking him. But the Highborn was still very much alive.

Marten understood then. Centurion Titus didn't leap at him. The Highborn sailed for the ruptured bulkhead. If Titus could reach the inner chamber, he could explode the core and kill everyone aboard the *Mao Zedong*.

Shifting, Marten gathered his legs under him and jumped at the Highborn. As he sailed through the chamber, Marten drew his vibroblade and clicked it on. The special alloy blade vibrated thousands of times per second, giving it greater cutting power.

Titus rotated, bringing his one good arm into play. Marten smashed against the giant, clicking on magnets. The armored, orange-glowing arm smashed against Marten's helmet, and he heard something crack. In retaliation, the former shock trooper thrust the vibroblade. It vibrated harder, and it cut through the weakened Highborn armor, the blade shoving into Titus's torso.

For a second, Marten and Titus stared faceplate-to-faceplate, eye-to-eye. Shock and pain roiled in Titus's orbs. The giant moved his arm, maybe to make another blow. Marten twisted the vibroblade and he jiggled it.

Titus's eyes bulged outward from the sockets. Blood seeped from his compressed lips. Then Centurion Titus whispered something as his lips moved. What he said was lost forever as the Highborn died, magnetically connected to Marten Kluge, his killer.

***

The next several hours proved horrifying. They found the SU crew. Some floated dead, still wearing vacc-suits. They had been shoved into closets, floating corpses. There were others in the shuttles: naked, shackled and many tortured and bruised. The Highborn had been getting ready to leave, about ninety of them. With the number of dead in the missile-ship, it appeared as if twenty-five Highborn per shuttle had originally flown to the warship.

"At least we put the missile-ship's crew out of their misery," Omi said later, speaking about the nuclear blast that had killed everyone in the shuttles.

Before they went outside to check the shuttles, however, they found something else. It was in the medical station—and it was devilish.

A naked Highborn lay strapped to an articulated frame. He wore a bulky helmet with many leads and lines sprouting from it, connected to a computer bank. Several dozen electrodes were taped to his discolored skin. As they watched, the electrodes zapped him, and he arched in agony as his muscles strained. When the electric flow stopped, stalks appeared from a medical unit. With a sharp, surgical implement on the end, the stalks flayed an area of skin. Another stalk with tiny claps peeled away the flesh. Disinfectants sprayed the wound. Then a mist of acid sprayed, and the groans from within the helmet were pitiful.

With an oath, Marten shot the machine until it *died* and then he began ripping electrodes from the Highborn. Omi unbuckled the helmet, tore it off and hurled it away. A wild-eyed Highborn strained to free himself. He gnashed his teeth as foam flecked at the corners of his mouth.

Shocked, Marten stared at the Highborn. He had a wide face, square chin and chiseled features, with the normal stark-white coloring. His hair had been shaved away, and he had two scars, one moving from his forehead into his hairline and the other along the left side of his face.

"Cassius?" Marten whispered.

The Highborn glared at him and spit in hatred, struggling more fiercely.

"No," Marten said, recovering from his shock. "You're not Cassius. You're too young. You're Felix, the Grand Admiral's clone."

The Highborn grew still as he glared at Marten. Slowly, some of the madness drained away from him.

"Do I know you?" the Highborn asked in a raw voice.

"I'm Marten Kluge. You once ordered me off a planet-wrecker."

Felix winced as if struck. Then he grinded his teeth and snarled like a beast.

"They've driven him insane," Omi whispered.

"Wrong," Felix said. "They wanted information."

"What kind of information?" Marten asked.

Felix laughed wildly.

"What are we going to do with him?" Omi asked.

The laughter turned sinister, maybe demented. "Does Titus think I'm that easily tricked?" Felix roared.

"Centurion Titus is dead," Marten said.

"Prove it!"

"Get his body," Marten told Xenophon.

The Jovian left in a hurry.

As they waited, Marten tore off the rest of the electrodes.

"Tell Titus it's a mistake giving me this rest," Felix said.

"I was tortured once by my own people," Marten said. "I fought against them after that in the Free Earth Corps. I can understand your rage."

Felix roared as he tried to wrestle himself free, making the frame creak at the strain. "I'll kill him! I'll kill all of you once I'm out of here!"

"He is insane," Omi whispered, floating away from the Highborn.

"Maybe," Marten said, drifting with him. There was a glitter of memory in his eyes. Maybe for the first time in his life he found himself sympathizing with a Highborn. It was an odd feeling.

Soon enough, Xenophon propelled Titus's corpse into medical.

"It's him," Felix said in awe. He turned wondering eyes on Marten. "What happened? Quickly, tell me and don't try to dissimilate."

Marten told him the story.

Felix laughed often, and he nodded. Then something strange entered his eyes. He studied Marten, and it seemed as if the Highborn struggled to contain a raw emotion.

"Do you know why all this happened?" Felix asked.

Marten shook his head.

"Commandant Maximus desires the Grand Admiral's chair."

"Cassius is dead," Marten said.

Felix frowned, and his breathing grew shallow. "Tell me how it happened."

Marten did, telling the Highborn everything he knew. It told Marten that Felix must not have had regular channels with the main Highborn. That was interesting and odd.

"This is a fitting end," Felix said, as he stared into an unseen place. "Grand Admiral Cassius slain by a preman, just like you killed Centurion Titus." He turned to Marten. "I wanted to kill Cassius. I had several chances, squandering each one." He grew thoughtful. "I cannot complain," he said softly. Felix's manner changed as he nodded. "So, Cassius is dead and Maximus attempts to fill his chair. I understand better. You did well, preman."

"I am a man," Marten said, "the man who killed Titus and thus stopped him from torturing you."

"Yes. As strange as it seems, a Highborn owes a pre—a member of the lesser race a debt." Felix scowled and he seemed to choose his next words with care. "Titus had orders to capture me and destroy any SU military ships he found out here. The reason is a secret weapon the likes of which has never been seen in the Solar System."

"Do you mean the Sunbeam?" Marten asked.

Instead of shock, Felix grinned savagely. "It saves us time if you know about it. Time—what day is it, what month?"

Marten told him.

Felix snarled and tried to rip his arms free. He panted after a time, lying limping. Finally, he stirred and continued to speak. "Titus came with his shuttles. He hailed the *Mao's* captain, made ready to dock, and then he directed hidden drones against the ship. After blowing away a shield and shocking the premen, Titus sent in the commandoes. They killed many, including several of my friends. By a fluke of battle, I was captured and later he had me strapped to this monstrosity. Titus desired the whereabouts of the rest of my men."

"Do you care to tell me why?" Marten asked.

Felix lifted his head, glaring at Marten. "I will storm the Sun Station and take it over for myself. Then I will rule in Cassius's stead."

"You were here to enlist the *Mao's* help?"

"Yes."

"That means you don't have enough Highborn to capture the Sun Station by yourself," Marten said.

"We have enough," Felix said, "but one can always use more, especially against a cunning warrior like Maximus."

"How many Highborn follow you?" Marten asked.

"Forty-two now. How many…men follow you?"

"Thirty."

"Release me, Kluge, and I will take you to our base. Together, we shall storm the Sun Station. It's doubtful we'll succeed, and if we do, one of us will surely die during the storming. If we both win, we can fight, you and I. The winner chooses where to fire the beam."

"Let me first speak with my commanders," Marten said. "Either way, however, I will free you."

"Words," Felix said.

Marten drew his vibroblade and hacked away the restraints.

With a roar, Felix sat up and massaged his wrists. Then he floated off the frame. "I need clothes," he said, sounding like a king.

"We'll get them," Marten said. "Be cautioned, however. Only this chamber and the next are pressurized."

"Yes, a wise precaution," Felix said. "Now go, make your decision. And I salute you, Marten Kluge." The nine-foot Highborn snapped off a precision salute. "You are a warrior indeed to release someone as dangerous as me."

Marten, Omi and Osadar exited the chamber. None wore their helmet as they floated into the next room.

"Did you notice the tattoo on his triceps?" Osadar asked. "It showed a clenched fist, with an iron ring around the middle finger?"

"I did," Marten said. "It means he's an Ultraist."

"Since you knew that, why did you free him?" Osadar asked.

"I've been tortured before," Marten said.

"You have sympathy for a potential mass murderer?" Osadar asked.

"No, I have sympathy for a human in distress."

"They're not human," Omi said. "They're monsters."

"Their genes have been warped," Marten said. "They're like hyper-myrmidons. Yet for all that, they're still human. I won't stand by and watch a man be tortured."

"I do not trust him," Osadar said.

"I don't either," Marten said. "But he needs us."

"He needs our patrol boat."

"I doubt he knows that yet," Marten said.

"Since he is an Ultraist," Osadar said, "he must be allied with Admiral Sulla. Sulla must know something about Maximus's goals and this is one of his counters. We have likely stumbled onto a Highborn power play."

"Seems reasonable," Marten said.

"The Ultraists are little better than the cyborgs when it comes to humanity's fate," Osadar said.

"Like the man said," Marten replied, "it's doubtful both of us will survive the attack. So we'll join forces for now and see what happens. The trick will be in turning against them a minute before they turn on us."

"Treacherous allies may prove worse than no allies whatsoever," Osadar said.

"No one said this was going to be easy," Marten said. "It's a fight to the finish with extinction staring us in the face. We're near the last lap, and now we have our own Highborn to fight with us. It's better than trying to storm the Sun Station with thirty marines."

"Where is this secret base of his?" Osadar asked.

"That's a good question," Marten said. "Let's ask him."

-5-

Far from the Sun in the void of Outer Planets, the Alliance Fleet sped toward its destiny. There were four big SU battleships, the *Vladimir Lenin* among them, and one missile-ship. They were impressive warships, bristling with weaponry and protected by gigantic particle shields. The Doom Stars dwarfed the battleships, making the SU vessels seem like small scout destroyers.

They hurtled through space, having long ago achieved maximum velocity. Soon each ship would turn around and use a hot burn to decelerate so they could fight at battle-speeds in the Neptune System. Otherwise, they would fly past Neptune like comets and sail for the outer reaches of the Solar System.

Many tens of millions of kilometers behind the Alliance Fleet trailed three meteor-ships. Sub-Strategist Circe had hailed the fleet twice. The humans had replied each time. The Highborn had never even acknowledged the messages.

As the Alliance warships sped toward Neptune, a pod detached from the forward battleship of Vice-Admiral Mandela's Fifth Fleet. The pod accelerated. After moving a kilometer-and-a-half in relative distance, it decelerated, carefully maneuvering into a hanger bay on the *Vladimir Lenin*.

The chief occupant of the pod was Vice-Admiral Mandela himself. He shook hands with the deck crew and then hurried away.

Using a screen, Hawthorne watched the exchange. He was in Blackstone's wardroom. Hawthorne had his doubts about Mandela, although once he had been an outstanding flag officer. Mandela's extended stay in deep space and time among the Highborn during the planet-wrecker emergency seemed to have wrung something out of him. Hawthorne would withhold final judgment until after the meeting. He vowed, however, that mankind's existence would not fail because he was too sentimental. Now was the time for hard decisions, maybe the hardest of this life.

Soon, Hawthorne spoke earnestly with Blackstone and Mandela. They met in the wardroom, at a low table with bulbs of steaming coffee resting in slot-holders. Mandela had been grumbling and upset, until he did a double-take upon seeing Hawthorne.

Mandela now sat at the table. He was a tall black man with curly-white hair, large eyes and a badly rumpled uniform. That had always been his trademark: a sloppy dresser but a hard-charger. His Fifth Fleet was the strongest one left to Social Unity.

"You have to believe me, sir," Mandela was saying. "The Highborn won't listen to us. They never have and aren't going to change their habits now."

Hawthorne wore a crisp uniform and during the journey out, he'd regained some of his former presence. His nose might have been longer or maybe his face was thinner than it used to be. It gave him a hawkish look. He had been doing a lot of reading lately and even more thinking.

"The Highborn listen to strength," Hawthorne said, who watched Mandela closely. "They are never swayed by sentiment. Appealing to their better nature is useless."

"That's just it, sir," Mandela said, leaning forward, taking his bulb of coffee and sipping from it. "They can destroy our warships any time they want. I doubt we could destroy any of theirs before we were vaporized. It means we lack bargaining power."

Hawthorne took his time answering. He didn't like the wheedling tone, the obvious fear of the Highborn. Mandela had done his duty two years ago. He'd aged since then and his nerves…

"You're looking at it from the wrong perspective," Hawthorne said.

Mandela shook his head, and it seemed he might take another sip of coffee. Then he thrust the bulb into the table-slot and spoke without looking up. "Sir, what matters is how the Highborn will view the situation. They control the Doom Stars."

Hawthorne glanced sidelong at Blackstone.

The Commodore stirred uneasily. Maybe he sensed the scrutiny. First clearing his throat, Blackstone said, "The Vice-Admiral has a point."

They're both tired, just as I was tired. They haven't had a rest and both have served in deep space for too long. He couldn't sack both flag officers, however. It would hurt morale too much, especially after his strange behavior these past months. The crews might lose faith in him.

Hawthorne decided his lesson needed a short preamble. "Before I reached flag command and then the supreme office, I was a historian. It's given me perspective. I have long studied the conquerors of the past, the Great Captains of history. Later, I studied the Highborn. Gentlemen, I have studied them and learned much. One critical thing I've discovered is that it's a mistake to take the arrogance, the loud voices and bullying tactics at face value. The Highborn are cold-bloodedly ruthless and quite able to make lightning-quick calculations despite their bluster."

"Meaning what?" asked Mandela, puzzled.

"They can reason with great objectivity."

"I still fail to grasp your point, sir," Mandela said.

"If a normal man acted like a Highborn," Hawthorne said, "we would think him unhinged, unreasonable and prone to rash behavior."

"In other words," Mandela said, "he would be acting like a Highborn."

Hawthorne frowned, not liking Mandela's manner. Did the Vice-Admiral think him powerless? Hawthorne paused in his thoughts, considering the idea. He was alone on the warship, without bodyguards or bionic soldiers. He couldn't change that at the moment. But after the meeting, he would speak with the security chiefs and reassess their loyalty.

"Highborn arrogance is a front," Hawthorne said. "Don't get me wrong. They *are* arrogant. But it also hides their razor-sharp rationality. In a sense, they are hyper-rational, which to most men seems like arrogance."

"I won't argue with you about it, sir," Mandela said. "I suppose it could be as you say."

Hawthorne stiffened. No, he didn't like Mandela's manner at all.

"My point is that the minute you appear on the screen," Mandela said, "they will demand your life. If you defy them, they will probably destroy the weakest of our ships. They might even destroy several."

"You are completely wrong," Hawthorne said.

Mandela looked up sharply. "I've worked with them more closely than either of you two has."

Hawthorne stared at the Vice-Admiral.

"Sir," Mandela added.

Blackstone coughed slightly. They both turned to him. "I'm curious, sir," he told Hawthorne. "Why didn't you feel that way earlier?"

"Can you be more specific?" Hawthorne asked.

"I mean seven months ago after you killed the Grand Admiral," Blackstone said.

"Ah," Hawthorne said. "The answer is simple. At Earth, they could have demanded my head and probably gotten it. There might have been an uproar, but in the end, the chiefs and directors would have realized they needed to work with the Highborn in order to keep mankind alive. The same SU warships would have joined the fleet. Now, however, the Alliance has what we have and that is all we're going to have in the Neptune System. Despite their bluster, the Highborn need our warships. *That* is our position of strength. They cannot afford to weaken the Alliance Fleet just because we refuse to meet one of their demands."

"What about afterward?" Blackstone asked.

"Can you be more specific?" Hawthorne asked.

"If we defeat the cyborgs, what happens next?"

"The strategy is obvious," Hawthorne said. "The Alliance Fleet must attack Uranus or Saturn. Since Uranus is presently on the other side of the Sun, I suspect Saturn will be the next target. We must clean out the cyborgs system by system."

"Do you think the Saturn-based cyborgs are building up their defenses?" Mandela asked.

"I'm not worried about that now," Hawthorne said. "I accept the Highborn assessment that Saturn and Uranus used their strategic strength constructing the various planet-wreckers. The present battle is everything."

"Not if we lose everything," Blackstone said.

Hawthorne straightened in his chair. "It's time for me to speak with the Highborn."

Mandela shook his head as lines creased his face. "I don't agree, sir. You will be risking too much by showing yourself to the Highborn. You're risking humanity, and for what?"

Steel entered Hawthorne's voice as he said, "I'm glad you feel free to speak your mind, Vice-Admiral."

A look of fear crept over Mandela.

"No, no," Hawthorne said. "I mean what I'm saying. There is no hidden barb in my words."

Commodore Blackstone was nodding. "I *do* agree with you, sir. The Vice-Admiral's reaction shows me he sees the old James Hawthorne. You've held the Highborn at bay for more years than anyone would have thought possible. You've pulled plenty of surprises out of your hat. If anyone knows the supermen, it's you. I think it's time to let them know James Hawthorne is back in the saddle. I think it's also time to beam the information to Earth."

"No," Hawthorne said. "We'll keep the information to ourselves for a time."

"Why?" asked Blackstone. "It will stop the civil war."

"I doubt it will now," Hawthorne said. "Director Backus has tasted power and so has Cone. Neither will freely give it up. Besides, I don't want endless communications with Earth as people ask for my advice. Every ounce of my intellect will be devoted to winning the battle at Neptune."

Mandela and Blackstone traded glances.

Hawthorne noticed, and he realized he might have sounded arrogant. It used to happen in his youth, before he learned to hide his superior reasoning abilities.

He stood, and the two officers stood. "I'll need your wardroom, Joseph."

"Yes, sir," Blackstone said.

"Should I head back to my battleship before you make your broadcast?" Mandela asked.

"No," Hawthorne said. "I want you to wait until I'm done."

Vice-Admiral Mandela saluted, although the worried look returned. He had been a brilliant commander once. Maybe he had seen or heard something subtle in Hawthorne that caused him to doubt the Supreme Commander.

"Commodore," Hawthorne said. "Would you remain behind a moment?"

"Yes, sir," Blackstone said.

Hawthorne needed to make certain Blackstone kept Mandela occupied and away from the hangers. If Mandela was worried about his position, he had a reason to be.

He would keep the Vice-Admiral here for now. He needed more time to decide if the man still had the stomach for battle.

***

Hawthorne greeted the Highborn admirals on a split-screen. None of them showed surprise, although Cato's taciturn stare became increasingly difficult to bear.

"You live," Cato said coldly.

"No thanks to the Grand Admiral," Hawthorne said. Attempting to dodge the issue would be useless with these soldiers. He would face it head-on.

"You murdered him," Cato said.

"Cassius attacked me as we met alone and I killed him in retaliation," Hawthorne said. Let them chew on that.

Cato shook his head with its steel-colored hair. His eyes were like electric pits, sparking with energy. "Your story is false on the face of it."

"I'm curious," Hawthorne said. "Were you there?"

"Do not seek to query me, preman," Cato said sternly. "I remember one of the stipulations of your meeting. You both went unarmed. I now see you before me. Therefore, you ambushed the Grand Admiral, murdering him for some nefarious goal."

"You're reasoning is sound except for one flaw," Hawthorne said. "Your implication is that a preman cannot best a Highborn. The stalemate on Earth proves you're wrong."

"Stalemate?" Scipio asked. "We hold more of the Inner Planets than you do."

"As in most things," Hawthorne said, "the initiative belongs to the one who first attacks. That initiative brings results for a while, as it has done for the Highborn. Now, however—after we've taken your measure—the war has stalemated."

Cato turned his head, likely regarding his fellow admirals. "The preman deliberately attempts to antagonize us. I take this to mean the murder has puffed-up his sense of importance."

"You owe me a debt," Hawthorne told the admiral. "In truth, you owe me several debts. The first is that I aided the Highborn. I slew the Grand Admiral and therefore proved his weakness, in that sense strengthening your race. Secondly, you have achieved higher rank through Cassius's death. Therefore, you hold your new position because of my action. I would expect more gratitude from you instead of this flood of surly words."

Silently, Cato stared at Hawthorne. Finally, he said, "You obviously feel secure in your battleship."

"I *am* secure," Hawthorne told him.

"For now," Cato said, as a grim smile stretched his lips. "I will remember your words on the day I tear out your heart."

"Excellent!" Hawthorne said, as he scanned the three admirals. It caused a stir among them.

"Why are you speaking to us like this?" Scipio asked.

"Because I want to know if you understand the strategic need of my fleet," Hawthorne said.

"The need is obvious," Scipio said. "We approach the cyborg concentration of strength and their military power is unknown. Therefore, each additional ship we possess—no matter how weak—could prove critical to us."

"True," Hawthorne said. "But I needed to know if Highborn rage would rob you of that knowledge. To set you at ease, I'll tell you why Cassius lost. I came to the meeting with a surgically-attached prosthetic finger loaded with projectiles."

"Why would you do that except to assassinate the Grand Admiral?" Scipio asked.

"I did it because I feared him. I would be speaking alone with the Highborn I had thwarted for years. He acted predictably at the meeting and therefore I shot him in self-defense."

"You play a dangerous game with us," Sulla said.

"No more than you have played with me," Hawthorne said. He'd been wondering when Sulla would speak up. Did the admiral fear he would give away his part in Cassius's death? No, Highborn seldom feared, but Sulla might be uneasy.

"Do not think you can bait me as you have Admiral Cato," Sulla said, his voice coiled with tension.

How far can I push them? Hawthorne glanced at each of the Highborn in turn. Only Admiral Scipio appeared calm.

"The purpose of this verbal exchange is to show you that I refuse to fear your power," Hawthorne said.

"You speak mindlessly like an animal," Sulla said.

A faint smile spread across Hawthorne's lips.

"He mocks us!" Cato said.

"It is part of his *purpose*," Scipio said. "He is driving home the point that we need his ships. He believes that our need gives him immunity, at least temporarily."

"The cyborgs have dug-in at the Saturn and Uranus Systems," Hawthorne said. "They will soon have gone to ground in the Jupiter System. You would be wise to desire SU warships in those coming battles just as you desire them in this one."

"As I said," Scipio replied, "you have temporary immunity from our wrath. Yet I am surprised you are willing to take it so far. I wonder at your underlying motive."

"Must we accept his impudence?" Cato asked the others.

"Yes," Scipio said, as he watched Hawthorne.

"For now," added Sulla.

"Good," Hawthorne said. "We've cleared the air and can now speak freely. Therefore, it's time to discuss strategy and tactics. First, who will have overall coordinating authority during the assault?"

"We have a triad of authority," Sulla said.

"I believe he means: who will give *him* orders," Scipio said.

"No," Hawthorne said. "If each of you is acting independently, then I shall as well."

"He basks in his impudence!" Cato cried, striking the armrest of his command chair. "It is insulting. We must teach this preman a lesson."

"Call it what you will," Hawthorne said. "The point is I control five ships and each of you only controls one."

"Each of us controls a Doom Star," Sulla said. "One Doom Star vastly exceeds the power of your five vessels."

How true is that? Could five of us at close range destroy a Doom Star? When the time comes, we will have to attack them separately. Hawthorne folded his hands on the desk, and asked, "What is our present strategy?"

The Highborn traded glances. Finally, Admiral Sulla spoke up.

"We shall implement a massive deceleration in four days," Sulla said. "We will crawl into the system, using the superiority of our lasers to outrange the enemy and obliterate local concentrations of strength. That will surely cause the cyborgs to launch their fleet at us. Again, we will outrange and annihilate them. Since the essence of our strategy and fleet is the Doom Stars, your warships will lead the attack. Their primary duty will be to absorb the enemy's attacks with your particle-shielding. Your secondary duty will be to destroy whatever incoming missiles or ships you can."

"An interesting plan with many facets to recommend it," Hawthorne said. "I agree with the heavy application of your ultra-lasers. The only flaw I detect is your use of the SU ships. Especially with collapsium shielding, the Doom Stars possess the superior defenses. Therefore, they should lead the assault, absorbing the initial punishment with minimal damage."

"This is outrageous!" Cato shouted. "We are the Highborn. He will accept our decisions or face punishments!"

"We can threaten him, of course," Scipio said, "and we can also destroy his warships. We both know we need the ships to help achieve victory over a superior enemy. Therefore, let us vent our anger against him later."

"I do not understand his manner," Cato said, seething. "He knows we will make his ending brutal."

"I am familiar with their psychology," Scipio said. "It is clear he hopes the cyborgs will destroy us. Therefore, he does not fear your retaliation. Either that or he is a wonderful actor and hides his fear well."

Cato glared at Hawthorne.

"Listen to me, Supreme Commander," Sulla said. "You spoke about minimal damage to the Doom Stars. We have four systems of cyborgs to dig out, to use your terminology. Each amount of 'minimal damage' received early lessens our odds of victory later. We must protect the critical vessels at the cost of the ineffective ones."

"The lessons of history say otherwise," Hawthorne said.

"He attempts to speak like Cassius," Cato said. "I find that another strike of offensiveness against him."

Hawthorne raised his eyebrows. This was interesting. "Did the Grand Admiral also employ historical examples?"

"It doesn't matter," Sulla said. "We are a triad." He raised a hand, as if he could stave off Hawthorne's objections. "To save time, I will grant you a vote. Let us say in this instance that your five warships equal a Doom Star. It isn't so, but I suspect in your pride that you believe it. Very well. Our three votes outweigh your objections."

Hawthorne forced himself to chuckle. It brought a heightened reaction from the Highborn. "I'm afraid a committee fleet doesn't operate on the principle of *votes*. It is a matter of persuasion. Remember, I hold the last concentration of SU warships. They are not beholden to you or under your command. They are under *my* command. You must persuade me to your course. Otherwise, I will do as I deem wisest."

"The preman is insufferable," Cato snarled.

Sulla's eyes had narrowed. "I have stomached your vain talk until this moment. Now you will have to contend with me, as I formally announce to you that I will remember your arrogance."

"I'm unconcerned with your memory," Hawthorne said. "I want you to clearly understand how my fleet operates."

"You have made your point concerning your independence and our need of your ships," Scipio said. "To attempt further baiting is both unnecessary and harmful to our unity."

Hawthorne bowed his head. "Maybe you're right. My problem is that I hate you as Highborn. Not only have we warred against each other for years, but then your Grand Admiral proved his faithlessness by attempting to murder me, his ally. Your present powerlessness against me is intoxicating. Thus, I find it incredibly enjoyable to bait you, and I've probably gone too far."

Cato's portion of the split-screen flickered off.

"He is the weakest among you," Hawthorne said. "But no matter," he added. Sulla and Scipio stared at him as if he were a mad dog. "Let us finish the strategy session. Your Doom Stars are superior. In most wars, the best strategy is to weaken an enemy by whittling away his inferior foes before attempting to take on the senior partner. If your goal is to strengthen the cyborgs in relation to us, then by all means you should let them destroy the SU vessels first. Instead, I recommend that you let the Doom Stars absorb the first mass of cyborg strikes, thereby allowing us to survive. That gains you our firepower later when it is deployable."

"You will not outmaneuver us into taking the majority of the casualties," Sulla said.

"I am not attempting to," Hawthorne said. "I merely wish to survive long enough to attack our common foe."

Scipio nodded slowly. "I am beginning to see why the Grand Admiral wanted you dead."

"What?" Sulla asked, turning away to a different screen. "You believe the human's story about a prosthetic finger?"

"I beginning to," Scipio said.

Sulla scowled, and he grew thoughtful. "I recall the Grand Admiral's method of dealing with premen," he told Scipio. "You and I were on the bridge during the Planet-wrecker Assault. Cassius allowed premen to speak arrogantly to him. Do you believe Cassius finally wearied of their behavior and thus desired Hawthorne's death?"

"No," Scipio said. "The Grand Admiral was shrewd, and he could read a situation better than any of us could. I believe he saw what I'm finally seeing. Supreme Commander Hawthorne has the mind of a Highborn."

"Blasphemy," Sulla whispered, as he turned back to study Hawthorne.

"And he has the spirit of one too," Scipio added. "It means he is dangerous. Likely, that is why Cassius wished him destroyed. Without Hawthorne, Social Unity would not have survived as long as it has."

Sulla's eyes narrowed. "Yes," he said at last.

"You agree to the human's plan?" Scipio asked.

"It is the triad's plan," Sulla said. "I merely accept the human's modification to it. During the initial assault, his warships will remain behind ours."

"We will have to begin deceleration first, then," Hawthorne said.

Sulla shook his head. "You will give away our plan and allow the cyborgs more time to adjust than otherwise."

"True," Hawthorne said. "The trouble is that we cannot tolerate the same number as Gs as you. Therefore, we need a longer time to decelerate."

"We are the Highborn," Sulla said. "Despite your manners today, we are superior. Do not ever forget that, *human*."

I don't plan to. Outwardly, however, Hawthorne stared at Sulla as if offended.

It brought a grim smile to the Highborn's face. The strategic meeting ended, and Hawthorne began to plot harder than ever.

-6-

The Prime Web-Mind of Neptune sent a command pulse through the web: *The enemy approaches.*

For the first time in years, unease crept through the Prime's multiform brain. It awakened old emotive centers in it. The emotions gave its brain tissues deeper contemplative possibilities. But the emotions had begun to upset its smooth functioning. This was not the time for such interruptions.

Data flowed from observatories on Neso, one of the farthest-flung moons. The distance was so great that it took thirty-two seconds for the communications-laser to reach Triton.

In the Solar System, Neptune was the farthest planet from the Sun. Pluto was a dwarf planet, the second most massive of them, after Eris. It had thirteen moons, was the fourth-largest planet by diameter and the third-largest by mass. Traces of methane in the outermost regions gave Neptune its blue appearance. The ice giant possessed the strongest sustained winds of any planet in the Solar System, clocked at over 2100 km/h. The outer atmosphere was also one of the coldest places, with the cloud tops dropping as low as minus 218 Centigrade. Like the other gas giants, it had a ring, a faint and fragmented system.

The Prime observed three giant spheroids hurtling through the Great Dark. They were black vessels emitting high levels of energy, doing relatively little to cloak the emissions. The Highborn advanced with their customary arrogance. This time, there was reason for it. Three Doom Stars represented a dangerous concentration of military power.

The Prime seethed as it studied the Neso data. For the thousandth time, it reassessed known factors. Massive fusion engines powered the million-kilometer-ranged laser. The enemy could strike from a great distance, well outside the range of cyborg weaponry. It gave the Highborn a clear tactical advantage.

The Prime feared that advantage. The fear grew until "cooling" pheromones misted over its emotive centers. It saw again with reptilian logic. Mercy had long ago been expunged from its core.

Thoughts fired through a billion of its neurons as it accessed all its memories on Doom Star-data. Cyborg agents on Earth routinely beamed new specifics as they uncovered them. These were carefully collected through altered Homo sapiens embedded in both FEC and SU bureaucracies. For reasons it could not accept, the Prime had so far been unable to alter a Highborn.

That will change. I will capture thousands after obliterating their warships.

A low-level alarm started a rationality program and it ran though a logic loop. If all the warships were destroyed, the Highborn in the warships would die. If all the Highborn died, there would be none for the cyborgs to capture and convert. After several hundred loops of logic, the rationality program "showed" the data to MONITOR brain centers. The conclusion was obvious and quickly gathered thinking mass.

Before the brain centers reached critical mass, however, the Prime added a new factor. *Some Highborn will wear powered armor and likely survive a Doom Star's destruction. Other Highborn might use assault craft to capture moons and key habitats. These I can capture.*

The new information shattered the MONITOR brain centers into blocs of thought. The rationality program lost the needed mass and waited for the next Prime-thought that needed assessing.

Shed of its need to argue for its thoughts, the Prime returned to its original worry: the Doom Stars. The three warships possessed improved collapsium plating. Altered Earth agents had failed to uncover the full specifics on the plating. Therefore, the Prime accessed old data. Collapsium was hard and dense, similar in nature to the core of a white star. The electrons of an atom were *collapsed* on the nuclei so the atoms were compressed. The compression was so great they actually touched. A molecular model demonstrated that lead was like a sponge in comparison to collapsium. The first collapsium coating had been micro-microns thick.

Will the new coating be three times as thick?

The Prime ran though several hundred scenarios given that assumption. The conclusion…it was inescapable, the Doom Stars represented a danger to its existence. The knowledge sent a shiver of unease through the core so that everywhere on Triton cyborgs linked to the web froze for an entire three seconds.

I am superior, and my strategy has already rolled over eighty-seven percent of the obstacles. That is a higher percentage of success than the other power-blocs have achieved. Given my superiority, worry is senseless.

The Prime soothed itself with its flawless logic and stark rationality. Yes. Long ago, it had settled on an offensive strategy. That strategy had provided immense dividends—to use a Neptunian capitalist's term. One critical component was distance. Neptune was farther out that any other inhabited planet, meaning that no other useful planetoid of appreciable size was near the Neptune System. Objects worth colonizing in the Kuiper Belt were even farther away, while those in the Oort Cloud might as well have been near another star.

The opposite was quite different. As one journeyed toward the Sun, the planets squeezed more tightly together. Being at Uranus put one much nearer Saturn, while Jupiter might as well have belonged to the Inner Planets, it was so near Mars as compared to the distance to Neptune. That meant taskforces sent in-system were much nearer the next objective than those that traveled out-system. Therefore, it was much more *profitable* to go in-system than to send military forces out.

My offensive strategy capitalized on Neptune's solitariness.

The Prime had capitalized on another critical element. Cyborgs were superior soldiers. Compared to Homo sapiens the difference was startling, several orders of magnitude. The difference was less with Highborn, but still significant. Militarily, it meant cyborgs outclassed their enemies by a higher percentage in face-to-face encounters than in any other forms of combat. Therefore, logic mandated stealth insertion tactics. This included boarding enemy warships and invading planets or inhabited moons.

Using distance to its advantage and personal military encounters, it had conquered the majority of the Solar System in a relatively short time.

I am clearly superior.

The thought lasted forty-two seconds as it exuded in its forethought and planning. Then an invading truth dampened its gloating.

If cyborgs were superior soldiers in personal encounters, the Doom Stars were better by a daunting degree in ship combat. Twice, the insertion of Doom Stars had thwarted cyborg strikes. The first had occurred at the Third Battle for Mars. The second time it had happened against the planet-wreckers launched at Earth.

The Saturn-launched attack should have succeeded.

It had to a degree, and the Prime concentrated on that for a full two minutes. Then it switched back to the Mars battle. The Highborn defeated them, although it had cost the great enemy one of his critical vessels. Both times the enemy had inserted himself into the conflict it had cost him one of his great warships.

Five Doom Stars—a shudder ran through the Prime. Facing five would have been a disaster. It was bad enough the Homo sapiens had allied with the Highborn. Fortunately, Social Unity only possessed a remnant of its once vast fleets. There were also three Jovian vessels following, a surprise. But the meteor-ships were damaged and likely depleted of offensive power after their battle with the Uranus-launched moon-wreckers.

The Prime used the Neso observatories to study the enemy, the approach and their likely operational choices. It weighted each possibility by percentages. Then it examined Neptunian defenses. Unlike the Highborn or the Social Unity and Jovian Homo sapiens, it relied on stealth technology, mass of ships and mass of turrets.

Every moon and habitat was a fortress with endless laser-turrets. There was nothing breakthrough about them other than their incredible number. Unfortunately, the Doom Stars outranged all the defensive armament.

That was a problem, but the Prime didn't believe it an insolvable one. Range was important, but there were other critical military factors.

I have made the superior choices.

Those decisions had been made long ago. Logic dictated certain military realities. One of the chief factors was opportunity costs. The logic was relentless. One had a limited amount of time, energy and matter. Yet the wants were unlimited. As one used resources, it meant there was less to buy other choices. Therefore, one should logically maximize each decision to give the greatest benefit possible.

This was even truer in military affairs than other matters. The Prime had long ago made a strategic decision regarding which battlefield technologies to acquire and improve. Its choices involved a key tenant, one critical in all forms of armed conflict. It was possibly so simple a thing that lesser beings ignored its truth. One needed to sight a target before one could hit it. Meaning, the most powerful weapon was useless if it missed.

In space, finding the enemy often proved difficult. Therefore, the force that spotted its enemy, without the enemy spotting it, gained a decided tactical advantage. With this advantage, the cyborgs had captured several of the Outer Planetary Systems. With everything else remaining equal, the force with highly developed sensors and merely adequate weapons would defeat the force with incredible weapons and poor sensors—or good sensors unable to detect a cloaked enemy.

Therefore, the Prime had pursed new stealth technology and sought improved sensing equipment. Because of this, it had built a completely different type of space fleet to defeat the humans. The key cyborg offensive ship had until now been the

Lurkers and stealth-capsules. Their task was to turn every battle into a face-to-face encounter. Afterward, the cyborgs had fought several battles with captured enemy warships and stealthily-launched planet-wreckers. Those wreckers used the technology of the captured power: Saturn and Uranus. Now, however, it would for the first time fight with a war-fleet of its own design.

The enemy approached with eight warships. The Prime gloated. It possessed hundreds of vessels. Each of its heavily cloaked ships directed a fleet of equally cloaked drones. With their greater numbers, they would swarm the enemy by using innovative tactics.

Rationality programs surged into action and quickly grabbed resources, using more and more of MONITOR's brain mass. Soon, soothing chemicals dampened the gloating. Perhaps MONITOR overreacted with the dampening, for the Prime reconsidered its plan yet again.

The mass of cloaked ships and drones hid behind Neptune in relation to the enemy. It had considered mining the enemy's approach, but it assumed the Highborn would redirect their flight-path for just that reason. The key to victory lay in obliterating the Doom Stars.

Question: was it wiser to destroy the accompanying battleships first or to concentrate everything on the Doom Stars?

A brain dome supplied the answer. It was a memory dome with access to all human history.

It ran through many examples, fixating on the World War Two Allied bomber campaign against Germany. At the time, heavy bombers had dropped thousands of pounds of explosives on the Axis factories, railways, oil wells and ball-bearing plants. German fighters had orders to attack the heavy bombers first, ignoring the accompanying allied fighters. With hindsight, it was clear the German fighters should have concentrated first on destroying the Allied fighters and *then* attacking the slower bombers, as the British and Americans fighters had taken a dreadful toll on the Germans.

The Prime accepted this. It would first remove the SU warships. Afterward, it would concentrate on the super-ships.

With their destruction, total victory would merely be a matter of mopping up Earth, Venus and Mercury. That victory would occur with speed once it acquired the Sun Station.

Knowledge of the Sun Station was new—painfully new—only days old.

An important subsystem of the Web-Brain squirmed with worry. This had higher authority than the rationality and monitor programs. The thought gained profile as it computed probabilities and accessed a troubling reality: Humans were more creative than cyborgs.

Explain your worry, the Prime demanded.

The subsystem answered with one word: *range*.

The range of their weapons?

Subsystem: *yes*.

All their weapons?

Subsystem: *no*.

A specific weapon?

Subsystem: *yes*.

Which weapons are you worried about?

Subsystem: *the Sun Station*.

The Prime pondered that. Finally, it decided to interrogate one of its captured scientists. It was frustrating, but humans were move inventive than a web-mind. It was unreasonable and illogical, but it was still true.

I am superior, able to face unpleasant facts. It is proof of my superiority.

The Prime absorbed data regarding the scientist. The formerly rich old man—during the capitalist heyday—had once run a Neptunian consortium, a think-tank of inventors and innovators. In his youth, the Neptunian scientist had made a fortune on an improved hardening process for weird ice. With the wealth, he had joined a team of fellow scientists and together they had invested in a consortium. The old man had proven financially cunning. After twenty-five years, he'd bought out the last of his partners—that had occurred several years before the cyborg take over.

Pulsing a thought and activating select video cameras, the Prime watched the gathering process. In a chamber near Triton's surface, three skeletal cyborgs opened the old scientist's agonizer-bath. The naked man was half-submerged in the liquid: an oily substance that heightened his nerve endings. It kept them active even after prolonged exposure and it intensified the mild punishment shocks randomly sent through the bath.

The old man—his name was Dr. Pangloss—looked around in alarm as he feebly tried to pull himself free of the cyborgs' grips.

The sight sent a ripple of mirth through the Prime. Homo sapiens were like monkeys, primitive creatures providing amusing gestures and sequences.

While watching such antics, the Prime had discovered quite by accident the horror Homo sapiens emoted upon seeing skeletal-like cyborgs. Testing the theory hundreds of times, it had finally formalized the practice. That had brought another tidbit of psychological interest. Horror weakened human resistance.

The three cyborgs dragged thin Dr. Pangloss to a specialized chair, strapping him in. The old scientist made pitiful croaks and wheezed. He had weak muscles with a spider-web of blue veins, damp white hair and liver-spotted skin. It had taken extended life-support procedures to keep the terrified specimen alive.

Twice, the Prime had received interesting data from Dr. Pangloss's conjectures. His usefulness had kept the old man from the brain-choppers.

A cyborg cinched the last strap, immobilizing the Homo sapien. The three cyborgs stepped back until they reached the walls.

He squirms. Pleasure sensation moved like a wave through the Prime. It released some of its tension. *These awakened emotive centers are making life more interesting.*

The Prime knew humans hated confinement, especially confinement as narrowly constricting as a chair. While strapped down like this, humans howled in loud agony as punishment drills whined in their mouths. Sweat already beaded Pangloss's skin. The human knew what was coming— or what should have been coming. Today, the Prime would forgo the entertainment. It merely wished to talk to the old scientist, the thinker who had been able to amass a fortune among the most gifted capitalists in the Solar System.

"Dr. Pangloss," the Prime said through nearby speakers.

With his face tightly secured, the old man's eyes roved up and down and side to side, no doubt seeking who addressed him.

"Do I have your attention?" the Prime asked.

Flesh twitched and muscles strained, as more sweat oozed from the human's skin.

"You must desist with your useless efforts," the Prime said. "I wish to talk."

"I cannot see you," Dr. Pangloss whispered.

"I am...elsewhere. Yet I am everywhere. I am the Prime Web-Mind."

The old man swallowed as he blinked wildly. "The cyborgs aren't moving," he said, staring at the units in the chamber with him.

"Why should they move?" the Prime asked.

"Are they deactivated?"

"Do not worry about them."

Dr. Pangloss frowned. "What's a...a Prime Web-Mind?"

"The term is sufficiently succinct."

"You run this horror chamber?"

"Dr. Pangloss, I control everything. I *am*."

The human's frown deepened. "You claim to be God?"

The query angered the Prime. It had ingested trillions of bits of data, so of course it had read about God. The foolish idea had no basis in reality, in observable datum. Yet the Prime wondered why the idea angered it, and why it called the possibility of God foolish. If Homo sapiens believed in myths, what bearing did that have on it, the Prime? The idea that God made it uneasy made the Prime even more uneasy. Hence, it hated the topic. The hatred stole its joy at watching the old man squirm, and that angered the Prime even more. These emotive centers were difficult getting used to.

Before monitor-programs could chemically alter its thinking, the Prime rerouted its thoughts. That weakened the anger, and allowed it to say:

"Explain your reference. Tell me how you derived the question as something rational from my words."

"I...I am an antiquarian," the scientist said.

"Incorrect! You are a scientist. As such, I expect factual statements from you. Failure to supply those will result in pain."

Dr. Pangloss moistened his lips. "I was many things once: a scientist and an antiquarian."

"That is rational. Yes, I understand. Now explain your first statement."

"One of the names of God is 'I Am.' It implies self-existence, meaning there is no need for anything else in order to sustain being."

"Interesting." The Prime had always avoided the God-topic and it had thus never explored all the possibilities of the myth-theory. Here was an amazing correlation. *I am self-existent and I need nothing from outer sources.* "Yes," the Prime said. "I am God."

"No," Pangloss said, as if he'd been expecting the statement. "You are a meld of machine and biological parts."

"I am the ultimate meld," the Prime said. That was an obvious truth.

"No doubt there is basis for such a statement, but you are clearly not self-sustaining."

"You are wrong," the Prime said. It wondered what verbal tactic the scientist thought he was playing.

"You need nutrients, I'm sure," Dr. Pangloss said.

"That is obvious. All life needs nutrients."

"Therefore, you are not self-sustaining. For God does not need nutrients. He does not need air to breathe or water to drink. He is totally self-sufficient."

"God as you describe is a proven myth," the Prime said. "The datum supports my statement."

"I would expect a sentient biological-machine meld to say something like that."

"I am a cyborg, the *perfect* meld of machine and man. I am the ultimate creation and I am remaking the Solar System in my image."

"Why?" Dr. Pangloss asked.

"Your question lacks merit."

A cunning look creased Pangloss's features. "What is the purpose of your existence?"

"To exist, to grow and to conquer," the Prime said.

"Were you given this directive?" the old man asked.

A warning alarm went off deep in the Prime. Inspiration came from one of its brain domes. "You are attempting to confuse the issue. That is very clever, Dr. Pangloss. It appears you have deeper reserves of resistance that I had predicted. I shall have to increase your torture regimen."

Frail Dr. Pangloss squirmed, vainly attempting to free himself.

The Prime enjoyed the sight.

Exhausted, Pangloss stopped struggling and panted.

"I have analyzed your statements and realize you have drifted near insanity," the Prime said. "Without normality to guide you, your mind has become unhinged."

"It may be as you say. I feel these dark places in my thinking. I do not like them."

"I will attempt communication with you one more time," the Prime said. "This will be a scientific query."

Dr. Pangloss grew tense.

"You need not gather your mental defenses," the Prime said. "At the moment, I will not question you concerning the Fuhl Event." They had shared long sessions on the matter, the Prime acting as inquisitor.

"I know nothing about the mechanism," Pangloss whispered.

The indicators showed that Pangloss lied. The ability of this weak Homo sapien to resist questioning at this point was incredible. It was another reason the Prime kept the old scientist alive. What gave this Homo sapien the ability to resist? It was unnatural and therefore—no. As Prime, it was the ultimate and therefore well beyond fear. It wanted to understand the stamina of this frail creature. From thousands of such tortured specimens, only three had shown such resistance. Where did their strength come from?

The Prime would have liked to pursue the idea. But it planned the Neptune Campaign that would give it the Solar

System. The victor here would likely win everything. The doctor's lie now was good, for it would help signal further lies on the critical topic. If Pangloss lied again, the Prime would severely punish the man.

"Are you familiar with the Sunbeam?" the Prime asked.

"No," Dr. Pangloss said.

By the indicators, the Homo sapien spoke the truth. Therefore, for the next hour, the Prime explained the newly discovered experimental weapon to the old scientist.

"The Highborn have been busy," Dr. Pangloss said later.

"They are an aggressive species, volatile in all their actions, including scientific discovery."

"So it would appear," Pangloss said.

"I have stated it. Therefore, it is the truth."

"As you say," murmured Dr. Pangloss.

"I find you an irritant," the Prime said. "My desire to expunge you has grown exponentially."

The tiniest of smiles touched the doctor's lips. "Touché," he said.

"Explain that statement," the Prime said, his speaker rising in volume.

"It is simple. In fact, I'm surprised an ultimate creation like you doesn't understand."

Part of the Web-Mind detected rising anger in itself, and the monitor programs activated the needed sequence to wash the main brain tissues with soothing chemicals. Perhaps it had used the chemicals too often these past few hours. The sequence did not begin in time due to an unforeseen glitch. Because of that, the anger continued to grow exponentially.

How dare the horrible little human act smugly? How dare this gnat of a being attempt to act superior toward the ultimate of reality?

Radio beams issued from the Prime to the three skeletal cyborgs in the chamber with Dr. Pangloss. One of the cyborgs moved toward the human. The old man's eyes widened in fear and understanding. The cyborg reached out with its titanium-reinforced hands. It clutched Dr. Pangloss's head, and it began to twist the head around.

At the last moment, Pangloss laughed shrilly just before he screamed. His neck bones cracked, snapped—and he was dead, gone from this world.

Seven seconds later, the calming agents soothed the angry portions of the Prime. It instantly regretted the action. Now it would have to ask another Homo sapien the question, one less clever and able than Dr. Pangloss.

The question was simple, and the answer seemed obvious. But the Prime wanted an inventor to think it through. The great question was this: Could the Sunbeam reach with destructive power farther than Mars? And if so, how far? The possibility was troubling, to say the least.

The Prime began the process where it would send a long-distance message to its Lurkers near the Sun. It was time to capture the Sun Station and eliminate any possibility for its defeat.

-7-

With their added passenger and the loss of too many space marines, the *William Tell* continued its journey toward the Sun. It hadn't come to a complete halt earlier, as the *Mao Zedong* and the HB shuttles had drifted toward Venus's coming location. After a twenty-minute ion-burn, the patrol boat changed its heading as it gathered velocity.

The days blurred together as the boat glided toward its new objective, the one given by Felix. As they journeyed, Venus methodically swung around the Sun. The bright planet completed an orbit every two hundred and twenty-five days.

Once, Venus had been enshrouded in yellowish-white clouds of sulfuric acid. Centuries ago, the great terraforming project had begun. Rockets seeded the clouds with specially-mutated bacteria. The bacteria fed on the sulfuric acid, slowly dissipating it. Unfortunately, Venus lacked enough water. Therefore, space-tugs had captured comets and ice-asteroids from Jupiter and Saturn, maneuvering them into near orbit and sending them down. Then construction began on a gigantic sunshield at the Sun-Venus Lagrangian point. The sunshield dampened the amount of solar radiation hitting the surface, which helped reduce the planet's temperature. The sunshield was also a vast solar-power satellite, collecting energy and micro-beaming it to stations on the planet. Unfortunately, it was still hot on Venus, desperately so, usually one hundred and thirty degrees Fahrenheit in the coolest places. Still, with the terraforming, it allowed human life without domes, without underground cities. Vast, specially-mutated jungles covered the planet, with mutated crops grown in the jungles.

Marten and Osadar mapped what they could of the void, never daring to use the active sensors. Mercury and the Sun-Works Factory were presently on the other side of the Sun.

Felix informed them Maximus led the Highborn on Venus. They controlled the laser-satellites ringing the planet. The four shuttles had originated from there, and with Felix's help, Marten discovered two other missile-ships in orbit.

"Are those renegade SU craft?" Marten asked.

Felix shook his head. "They're modified missile-ships, captured vessels kept hidden until now. They are Maximus's fleet. In the absence of the Doom Stars, those ships form the most powerful fleet in Inner Planets."

The days became another week. Finally, they crossed Venus's orbital path as they continued toward the Sun.

As the cyborgs completed their conquest of Mars—attempting to capture the *Pancho Villa*—the *William Tell* reached halfway between Venus and Mercury.

"There should have been a signal by now," Felix said.

"Do you think Maximus found your base?" asked Marten.

"The Commandant is a clever soldier. It's a possibility." Felix grew sullen, moodily clenching his fists as he sat by himself. It was like having a lion among them, a restless beast. At all times, Omi, Osadar or Marten secretly watched him, with a needler ready.

A day later, Marten spotted something dim on the sensor screen. Hunching forward with excitement, Marten rechecked his readings. Soon, he began monitoring the sensors closely, looking for radio-signals and energy readouts.

Nadia sat at the weapons officer's chair. She must have seen something different in him. Learning near, she whispered, "Is that it?"

Something in her voice must have alerted Osadar, who sat in the pilot's chair. The cyborg swiveled around. "You've found the planet-wrecker?"

Marten nodded.

Several of the planet-wreckers launched nearly three years ago had missed Earth and tumbled into the outer void.

Apparently, the Sun had captured at least one. Now, the asteroid orbited the fiery star, remaining near the Sun. It was Felix's secret base.

"Summon the Highborn," Marten said. "He'll want to see this."

Soon, the nine-foot giant loomed behind Marten.

"Check the readings," Marten said. "The asteroid looks deserted."

Felix glowered as he read the screen, and his breathing became audible, like that of an angry bull.

Marten's back prickled, and Nadia leaned away from the Highborn.

"If they were there," Osadar said, "you would have picked up radio signals or other life-signs."

"We maintain tight discipline," Felix said. "They are there, secretly tracking your vessel."

"You'd better signal them, then," Marten said.

Felix accepted a com-unit and spoke a string of code words.

"Nothing," Marten said, as he watched his screen.

"They are there," Felix said, more ominously than before.

"Let's get ready then," Marten said.

The journey to the asteroid took time, several days. Finally, Marten gave the order.

"I am activating the engine now," Osadar said, tapping her screen.

The ion engine thrummed with power as the boat began to decelerate. A jolt shook Marten. Beside him, Nadia's head struck her headrest, knocking off her cap.

Compared to the last time they landed on a planet-wrecker, this was a gentle ride. The asteroid was nine-and-a-half kilometers in diameter and first appeared as a smooth object. Soon, on the forward cameras, hills appeared and grew larger. Then ancient impact craters were visible and plains of stardust. The hills loomed steadily larger and they became more jagged. After a time, a single mountain dominated.

"Look," Nadia said.

Marten spied a slagged lump of metal like a melted coin. It must have been a laser-turret once, destroyed by a Doom Star's heavy beam in the original battle.

Osadar brought them down as stardust billowed upward, surrounding the craft. Slowly, the patrol boat settled and then the vibration quit as the engine shut down. After eight months in space, they had landed on a solid object.

***

Even though they had been weightless for months, Marten lectured them on the need to practice caution while exploring the asteroid. If they jumped too high, they would reach escape velocity and simply keep floating. Ever since the *Bangladesh*, he worried about losing men to space-drift.

Everyone but Felix was tethered in groups of three, the lines attached to their belts.

Marten, Omi and Nadia glided across the bleak landscape with Felix and others following. Since they were so near the Sun, they stayed on the dark side. Otherwise, their conditioner-units would have quickly overheated. Marten led, climbing a lunar-like hill. It was so different from being cooped up on the boat. His heavy breathing echoed in his helmet and it felt good to move for an extended time. As he looked around, the stars were bright gems and dust billowed each time a boot struck the ground.

Clutching a gray rock, Marten steadied himself on the summit. In the valley, he spied a dome. It brought back bitter memories. There was motion to his left. Ah…Nadia climbed beside him. *She spooked me. This place does.* He pointed into the valley.

"Look at the dome's jagged crack," he said. "It crosses the entire width. A beam must have lased in a running slash."

Through her visor, he saw his wife nod.

Marten spotted something above. He craned his head as Omi flailed uselessly over him. Grabbing the line, Marten pulled him down.

"Don't jump so hard," Marten said.

"Rookie mistake," Omi muttered. He glanced back. "I doubt *he'll* do that."

Marten looked back, watching Felix move in his powered armor. The Highborn glided perfectly. Only Osadar asteroid-walked with as much confidence and ability.

That doesn't mean they're going to win. Marten shook off the feeling that maybe it did mean that. The fight wasn't over until it was.

The giant reached them, looming ominously with his rotating hand-cannon on one arm and a laser carbine in the other.

"They should have signaled us by now," Felix said.

"How many shuttles did you have?" Marten asked.

"Counting mine, three," Felix said.

"Could they have left without you?"

Felix hesitated, with his visor aimed at the valley dome. "They would have set up a signal," he finally said.

"Could they be waiting at the dome?"

Methodically, Felix examined the landscape. "We must beware. This could be a trap."

Marten blew a lungful of air against his visor. He didn't want to hear that. "We're using over-watch," he told the others. "Use passive sensors but be ready to switch to radar and get an exact fix for your weapons. If they don't hail us first, fire to kill."

"If they are ambushing us," Felix said, "these precautions will do no good."

"That's what Centurion Titus thought," Marten said.

Felix's visor turned toward Marten. It was silver, the face behind it invisible. "You were a shock trooper once, is that not so?"

"I was."

"It shows in your training. You are aggressive."

Marten knew Felix meant aggressive like a well-trained beast. He let the insult pass. *We have more important things to worry about.*

"Let's go," Marten told the marines.

It took time climbing down the jagged hill and time to cross the lunar plain. Marten kept thinking how the asteroid used to orbit Saturn. That disturbed him, and he wasn't sure why.

With their gyrocs trained on the dome, Marten's group neared the low-built structure. Behind followed others, Osadar's group bringing a plasma cannon.

They crept from behind a large boulder. The dome was silvery in the starlight, and its destruction was more apparent, with gouges everywhere, shell craters. Three metallic lumps showed were laser-turrets had stood and melted. Debris littered the valley floor, a junkyard of slagged metal, old weapons and corpses from the fight two years ago.

"What a horrible time," Marten said, thinking about the battle onto their planet-wrecker. Was this the same one? He didn't know and had forgotten to ask Felix.

Omi grunted over the headphones as he followed Felix toward the dome.

"What's wrong?" Marten radioed.

"I've a bad feeling about this," Omi said.

"Ambush?" asked Marten.

"Maybe," the Korean said.

Marten rechecked his weapon, sliding it open to study the shell. He motioned the others to follow, and signaled: be careful.

He stepped over slagged metal the size of a helmet and avoided an old missile casing. His boots put prints in the dust. All the while, he checked his suit's sensors and watched the ground for telltale signs of booby-traps.

With a pounding heart, Marten squeezed through an opening into the dome. He flicked on his helmet-lamp. The beam played over fused machines and endless debris on the floor. Ahead, Omi's group and Felix moved from place to place, with weapons ready.

Giant Felix pointed ahead to a door. Omi nodded and signaled Marten. Unlatching his tether, Marten shoved off and drifted toward them, with the gyroc aimed at the hatch. Something felt wrong, bad wrong.

Felix readied his hand-cannon as he reached for the handle.

Marten wanted to shout a warning.

The door opened and Felix's lamp-beam stabbed into the darkness. The Highborn moved in. Marten followed and grunted in shock.

Dead Highborn in breached combat-armor lay on the floor. Most had smashed helmets. All gripped weapons. He counted seven. Some of the equipment around them was smashed. The rest looked useable.

"What happened?" Omi radioed.

Marten glanced at Felix. The Highborn stood very still, his lamp-beam centered on one dead Highborn in particular.

"Look at this," Nadia said. She picked up a wrist with a hand attached. It was skeletal, with titanium-reinforcement showing in places.

Felix's lamp-beam swiveled around, spotlighting Nadia's find. "Cyborg," the Highborn growled. "The cyborgs were here."

Marten turned fast, kneeling, raising his rifle at the door. He feared to see cyborgs pour in.

The others didn't seem as worried. "It looks like the cyborgs landed and killed your men," Omi was saying.

"Observe their glory," Felix said proudly. "They died fighting and they took some of the enemy with them. What more can a man ask of the universe than to live as he desires? Come, we must continue searching."

"Are the cyborgs still here?" Marten asked.

"If they were," Felix said, "they would have attacked by now."

Marten wasn't so certain.

They searched the rest of the dome and then continued outside. The planet-wrecker had taken greater damage than the one Marten had conquered nearly two years ago. Most of the domes were thoroughly smashed inside and the giant engine within the asteroid was a slagged heap. Osadar believed an Ultra-laser had beamed directly through the massive port. Most of the defensive laser-turrets were molten lumps.

"I wonder how near the Sun it orbited," Nadia said later. "That might explain the uniformly melted state of the turrets."

They found another eleven dead Highborn in the tunnel systems. Apparently, the cyborgs had scoured the asteroid, hunting Felix's fellow Ultraists.

Later, they found the shuttles in a hidden hanger. Cyborgs had gutted both spaceships.

In his armor, Felix turned toward a nearby tunnel wall. He stared fixedly at it as if he'd been turned to stone.

"He morns his comrades," Marten radioed Nadia. "Back away from him. They don't like anyone seeing them like this."

"Felix," Marten radioed. "I will be in the command chamber of the first dome. When you're ready, I ask that you join us there."

There was no response. They left Felix of the Ninth *Iron Cohort* to his grief.

Marten, Omi and Osadar walked to the ruined dome. They began repairs in the chamber with the seven Highborn dead. More of the equipment was workable than they'd first believed. Soon, several of the systems came online.

"These tachyon receivers are more sophisticated than ours," Marten said. "The cyborgs don't like being surprised."

From Osadar's comments, it had become clear this was old cyborg equipment.

"These thermal sensors," Omi said, "I've never seen anything like them."

Omi sat at a screen, adjusting the sensor sets so they worked in unison. After Omi flipped an activation switch, a light began blinking on a screen. Marten hurried near.

"What is that?" he asked.

"I think it's inert, a rock or another asteroid."

Marten sat down on the second chair. "I'm surprised the sensors even showed it. Look, the albedo is two percent."

"I've never heard of an albedo so low," Omi said.

That struck a chord in Marten. "That must be the cyborg craft."

Omi squinted through his visor. "The thing is drifting toward the Sun."

"Compute the drift," Marten said.

Omi did. "It's going to pass near the Sun Station." He turned to Marten. "Do you think the cyborgs tortured the Highborn, learning about it from them?"

"The cyborgs have altered agents everywhere," Felix said, entering the chamber. "They are even on Earth. We must take it as a given the cyborgs know about the Sun Station and will attempt its capture."

"We must alert the Highborn there," Omi said.

"Agreed," Marten said.

"No," Felix said. "If we do, Maximus wins, because we will have given away our position. We will never sneak aboard the Sun Station then."

"We'll use a communications drone to send the message," Marten said, "catapulting it from the surface. We'll do that on the other side of the asteroid as the cyborg ship."

"That gives the cyborgs more time to do whatever it is they're doing than if we broadcast the message now," Omi said.

"That's a problem," Marten agreed. "So we'd better get the drone on its way as soon as possible."

***

They monitored the stealth-ship until it disappeared from their dome's screen. Just before that occurred, Ah Chen detected something else.

She brought the file to the patrol boat, where Marten, Felix and Osadar studied it.

"Notice this dark piece of mass leaving the main ship," Osadar said.

"What is its composition?" Felix asked.

"Unknown," Osadar said.

"The cyborgs used ice-pods against the Highborn during the Third Battle for Mars," Marten said.

"This mass is not ice," Osadar said. "Otherwise, this near the Sun, it would act like a comet and produce a visible tail."

"Whatever it is," Marten said, "it is low albedo stealth-material. We have to include that in our data packet." They had catapulted a drone and waited for it to reach a good distance before they sent the information.

"When are we beaming the data?" Osadar asked.

"Twenty hours," Marten said.

Osadar shook her head. "The Highborn need to know now in order to prepare."

Marten pushed up from his chair, floating across the cabin. He reached a wall and pushed back the other way. As he floated, Marten shook his head. "This is all about timing, right?"

"It's about defeating the cyborgs," Osadar said.

"No," Felix rumbled. "This is about victory. Make your broadcast in a day. Then we must use your boat and attack the enemy's stealth-ship."

"Attack?" asked Marten.

"Haven't you studied the enemy's methods?" Felix asked. "They use their ships like a machine gun, firing stealth-capsules at critical objectives. How many cyborgs will they use to capture the Sun Station? Logic dictates all of them, or nearly all. Very well, because they've emptied their ship, we will now storm and capture it for ourselves. Your Jovian boat lacks shielding to move near the Sun. The stealth-ship must surely be better shielded. With it, we will attack and storm the station."

Marten stared at the Highborn. When he realized that Felix meant what he said, Marten snorted in disbelief.

"Has anyone stormed a cyborg vessel before?" Felix asked.

"Not that I know of," Marten said.

"They won't be expecting it."

"It's insane," Omi muttered.

"So is the extinction of humanity," Marten said, deciding he would show as much guts or more than the Highborn. "We have space marines and we're the experts at fighting cyborgs. We beat them once in the Jovian System."

"Yes, by attacking at ten-to-one odds or better," Omi said. "We always took massive causalities, remember? Here, we have thirty men—thirty!"

"And a Highborn," Felix said.

"Right," said Marten. "We'll turn the tables on the cyborgs and do to them as they've been doing to everyone else. I like it."

"I wouldn't count on success," Osadar said.

"It's better than being fried to death in the Sun's radiation in our patrol boat," Marten said.

Omi shrugged. "As long we're not caught and turned into cyborgs, I'll go."

"All life is a risk," Marten said.

"Spoken like a Highborn," Felix said.

"No," Marten said. "Spoken like a man who's willing to die for his freedom."

Felix's face tightened. Then he nodded curtly. "As long as we kill cyborgs, I am content. Are we agreed?"

Marten looked around. By their expressions, no one else liked the idea. Marten nodded anyway. "Yeah, we're agreed."

-8-

Across the Solar System in the *Vladimir Lenin*, Supreme Commander Hawthorne endured hard deceleration as the fleet approached the Neptune System.

Hawthorne lay on an acceleration couch on the bridge. It was apart from the command module that Blackstone used—Hawthorne didn't want to interfere with the Commodore's regular functions. A large monitor hung above the Supreme Commander and pressure-pads lay near his fingers.

Presently, blue Neptune filled the monitor's screen. The ice giant possessed thirteen moons. The outer six were irregular satellites. The last two—Psamathe and Neso—had the largest orbits of any moon in the Solar System. Each took twenty-five years to orbit Neptune. Of the two moons, Psamathe was presently on the other side of Neptune, while Neso was far away in the direction of the southern pole. Each moon had a highly eccentric orbit.

Unlike those orbits, the Alliance Fleet had traveled within the Solar System's ecliptic: the path most of the planets followed along the Sun's equator. Even out here, the Sun's gravity ruled the planetary motions because of its dominating mass—the Sun accounted for ninety-nine point eight-six percent of the total mass of the Solar System.

Triton was the biggest Neptunian moon. It was the seventh largest moon, and the sixteenth largest object, in the Solar System. It was slightly bigger than the dwarf planet Pluto. Triton comprised more than ninety-nine point five percent of the mass orbiting Neptune, meaning it dominated the other moons in terms of gravitational effect.

The Neptunian System had been colonized about a century ago from Uranus. Before the cyborgs, there had been habitats here constructed of weird ice, orbiting Neptune at whatever distance the original buyers had desired. Some of the habs had been built within the rings of Neptune. Others orbited hundreds of thousands of kilometers from the surface. Some of the richest capitalists had constructed floating villas in Neptune's highest atmosphere. By heating vast hydrogen balloons, large masses had been suspended underneath. Because of the distance from the planet's core, the occupants in the floating villas had enjoyed near one G of gravity. Jupiter had lacked such floating cities because its size made the escape velocity too high and because of the gas giant's intense radiation.

Like Jupiter, however, the richest capitalists had launched robotic aerostats into the atmosphere. The floating machines gathered or "mined" deuterium and helium-3. Both fuels fed fusion reactors, giving the planetary system the needed power for the endless projects.

Despite the many habitats, the floating cities and various moon-bases, the largest industrial and population concentration had always been on Triton. It was one of three moons in the Solar System with an atmosphere. Its mass gave it an appreciable gravity and the subsurface ammonia/water seas provided one of the critical components for human life. Triton was cryogenic and was therefore rich with geothermal energy. Most of Neptune's banks had headquartered on Triton, as well as the core military establishments.

By studying the enemy's past behavior, Hawthorne and the Highborn admirals agreed that the concentration of cyborg strength would likely be on Triton. To ensure that the main enemy fleet came out and engaged, they had agreed the fleet must eventually drive for a primary objective. In this instance: Triton.

The strategic objective was presently on the other side of Neptune. Basic military caution mandated keeping a planetary body between the enemy strength and the decelerating ships. Deceleration was a vulnerable time, allowing little latitude for maneuvers and signaling one's presence with hot fusion exhaust.

These and other thoughts passed through Hawthorne as he lay on the acceleration couch. By his side, his fingers twitched across the pressure-pads, changing the pictures on the monitor.

Nereid appeared—it was the nearest of Neptune's satellites to the fleet. It orbited an average of five-and-half million kilometers from the planet and had a polyhedron shape, with several flat or slightly concave facets.

Debate had raged for days on the correct approach into the system. Hawthorne had sided with Sulla, who had finally convinced Scipio and Cato to hit a strategic center early.

"We could take out several of the farthest orbiting habitats," Hawthorne had told the Highborn. He'd shrugged. "Unfortunately, that would have minimal effect on the outcome. If the cyborgs mean to lure us—and it seems obvious they do—let us destroy important military installations while they're giving us the opportunity."

Scipio's analysis of the Third Battle of Mars made the commanders cautious. The cyborgs were devious. The enemy would likely act in a similar manner as they had at Mars. In other words, the cyborgs were likely hoping to snap a trap on them.

"I'm detecting an increase in radiation on Nereid," Commissar Kursk said from her couch.

Hawthorne watched the monitor. They had launched probes twenty-three hours ago. The probes continued to hurtle toward Nereid at the fleet's former velocity.

The SU ships had been decelerating for some time. They had braked as the Doom Stars continued to rush toward Neptune. Finally, however, the Doom Stars began deceleration. Their long exhaust plumes acted as shields against most matter—missiles, cannon shells or plasma—with the needed heat to incinerate titanium.

"If we're right," Blackstone said, "the cyborgs have a surprise for us behind Nereid."

They had been studying the system for weeks, picking up minute pieces of data a particle at a time. Slowly, they built a

Neptunian map. All the while, each passive and active system had relentlessly scanned the void, seeking cyborg stealth-ships.

"There!" cried Kursk. "Laser-turrets are rising from Nereid's surface. They're firing."

Hawthorne's fingers tapped across the pressure-pads. The image changed on the monitor. Polygonal-shaped Nereid appeared. Then a close-up zoomed into focus. The moon was mainly water ice and rock. Towers stood on formerly empty ground. Laser beams burned from each of the focusing mirrors.

"They hit a probe," Kursk said. "Make that two probes. That's it," she said a moment later. "They got all three."

"How long until Nereid is in ultra-laser range?" Hawthorne asked.

"Three hours and sixteen minutes," Kursk said.

Hawthorne wanted to hit Nereid now, but not as Sulla planned. The idea was right, the method too risky. An SU fleet would have decelerated long ago and built up a prismatic crystal cloud before it. The SU fleet would have sent heavy reflectors to the cloud's sides, bouncing the beams from them in relative safety.

In Hawthorne's opinion, the Highborn trusted their heavy lasers and collapsium shielding too much.

"I don't understand this," Blackstone said.

"What's wrong?" Hawthorne asked the Commodore.

"This doesn't make sense," Blackstone said. "Will the cyborgs just let us sweep the moon with lasers?"

"I doubt it," Hawthorne said.

"Then why haven't they defended Nereid with P-Clouds?"

"The obvious answer is so they can fire at us," Hawthorne said. "A P-Cloud defends, but it also halts an attack. They could use mirrors, but mirrors make precision targeting more difficult."

"Permission to speak," Kursk said.

"Granted," said Hawthorne.

"We should have launched a swarm of missiles at them," Kursk said.

Hawthorne remained silent. He hadn't agreed to that before and he still didn't. Maybe if he could have resupplied the missile racks in several weeks, he would have agreed. They had come a long way, however, and had a limited number of missiles. Each one had to count. The inability to re-supply quickly was a critical weakness of taskforces that traveled so far from home.

Hawthorne shivered on the couch as a chill worked up his back. The cyborgs were waiting for something. Did they have a longer-ranged beam than the Ultra-lasers? Why did they leave Nereid open like this? Were they daring the Highborn to strike, and if so, why?

"Where is their fleet?" Blackstone said. "We should have spotted something by now."

"They don't think like us," Hawthorne said. He kept reminding himself of that.

"They're aliens," Blackstone said, with a quaver in his voice.

Hawthorne lifted his head to glance at the Commodore.

Blackstone had a far-off stare. He must have noticed Hawthorne gaze. With a guilty start, the Commodore gave a sheepish grin and said, "I was remembering the first time I saw them." He shuddered. "They were horrifying. Why would scientists make something like that?"

Hawthorne let his head drop against the couch. He was staring at the monitor again, trying to wrest secrets from it. They had come an immense distance to fight the enemy. What horrible surprise did the Prime Web-Mind have in store for them? This not knowing—the waiting—it was the worst part of battle. Hawthorne hated it, hated the suspense.

The hours passed with agonizing slowness as the Alliance Fleet bored in. With majestic grace, the Doom Stars slid into position. The SU ships were several hundred thousand kilometers behind them and moving to flank Nereid. The Doom Stars would also flank the moon, passing at eight hundred thousand kilometers, well within range of the heavy beams and hopefully beyond anything the cyborgs possessed.

Finally, aboard the *Vladimir Lenin*, the heavy deceleration eased. The engines still burned, now slowing them at one G of thrust instead of many. Couches whined as they lifted their occupants to a sitting position and the bridge crew took up their normal stations.

Blackstone and Kursk climbed out of their couches, standing around the command module.

Thirty-four minutes later, Kursk said, "There's an incoming call for you, Supreme Commander."

"Thank you," Hawthorne said, as he straightened his cap. A moment later, Admiral Scipio appeared on the screen.

"Have you detected anything unusual?" Scipio asked.

"Just the laser-turrets on Nereid," Hawthorne said. "Believe me, Admiral, we'll alert you the instant we spot anything important."

"In seven minutes, we shall begin the attack," Scipio said. "The cyborgs must surely know the range of our heavy beams. What do you think they're doing?"

"Saving their fleet for later, would be my guess," Hawthorne said.

"Or readying themselves for a relentless assault," the Highborn said.

"From behind Nereid or from behind Neptune?" Hawthorne asked.

"If they're accelerating from behind Nereid," Scipio said, "they would begin with a low velocity."

"You expect a surprise assault from behind Neptune?"

"It is the likeliest possibility."

Hawthorne nodded in agreement. "There is another possibility."

"There are many, in fact," the Highborn said dryly.

"The cyborgs might have hollowed out Nereid, using it as a missile base. They will wait until we're past and then launch as we near Neptune."

"Clearly, they will attempt something, using the various moons as bases. For now, since they are luring us, we shall destroy as much of Nereid's outer platforms as we can."

"Good luck," Hawthorne said.

Scipio studied him, and finally nodded. "Admiral Scipio out."

The attack began shortly after that.

"The energy readings are building," Kursk said.

She meant the Doom Stars. The huge fusion engines inside the massive vessels began to churn power. The engines are what made the Doom Stars so dangerous.

"Why aren't the cyborgs building a prismatic cloud?" Blackstone asked.

"They're firing now," Kursk said.

Hawthorne examined the power wattage. The *Julius Caesar*, the *Genghis Khan* and the *Napoleon Bonaparte*—it was amazing! Three heavy lasers stabbed through the void. They traveled the eight hundred thousand kilometers at the speed of light, hitting and burning the first laser-turrets on Nereid.

Finally, the cyborgs began pumping prismatic crystals. Why wait until attacked? It simply made no sense.

"This is incredible," Blackstone said. He looked up with a grin. "We're annihilating their offensive capabilities."

"Keep scanning at three hundred and sixty degrees," Hawthorne said. "I can't believe the cyborgs will just let this pass without hitting back."

"There's nothing near us," Kursk said.

"Have they developed an invisible drive?" Hawthorne asked.

"That would be impossible," Blackstone said.

Time passed as the heavy lasers methodically burned through the thin P-Clouds and obliterated the laser-turrets.

This must have been how it felt in the Colonial Wars, Hawthorne thought to himself. In the days of European Supremacy, English and French ships sailed the Earth's oceans. In North America, in Africa and India particularly small bands of technologically-advanced soldiers had annihilated hordes of spear, sword and bow-armed natives. Cortez in Aztec Mexico used cannons and matchlocks to blow down rows of feather-clad warriors swinging obsidian-chip clubs. The British at Rouke's Drift slaughtered attacking Zulus, using the long-ranged Henry rifle.

This is more like the Maxim machine gun. Superior battle-tech gave devastating advantages.

"Is this all we had to do all along?" Blackstone asked. "Have the cyborgs been playing a fantastic bluff?"

"One battle doesn't settle a war," Hawthorne said.

"The Highborn are launching a trio of missiles," Kursk said.

"What type?" Hawthorne asked.

"Phobos' killers," Kursk said.

She referred to the missiles that had splintered and destroyed the Martian moon Phobos.

Hawthorne watched as the three missiles accelerated toward the distant moon. The missiles were big, with massive nuclear warheads. It would take time for them to reach Nereid.

During that time, the heavy lasers destroyed cyborg turrets. Then the *Julius Caesar's* Ultra-laser went offline.

"Have they burned out critical components?" Blackstone asked.

"I'd ask," Hawthorne said. "But I'm sure the Highborn would take delight in ignoring me."

Nine and quarter minutes later, the laser came back online. Soon, however, the *Genghis Khan* stopped firing.

"Maybe the cyborgs are testing the limit of a Doom Star's firing capacity," Blackstone said.

Hawthorne had been thinking the same thing. Would that be worth the loss of Nereid? Hawthorne answered his own question by telling himself: *If it gives them the victory, it does.*

Soon, the Highborn only fired with two heavy lasers at a time. Then it became only one laser at a time. The moon-killers bored in as laser turrets melted under the fierce assault.

"The missiles are one hundred thousand kilometers from Nereid," Kursk said some time later.

"This is the test," Blackstone said.

Hawthorne had been stretching. He rubbed his eyes now and focused on the screen.

The minutes passed. Time stretched and soon it was a half hour later.

"Lasers!" Kursk cried. "The cyborgs are firing lasers."

All three Highborn lasers opened up again, lashing across eight hundred thousand kilometers. It took almost three full seconds for them to travel to the target. That made little difference when firing at something "stationary" like turrets on the moon. In this case, the enemy couldn't jink to escape.

During that time, cyborg lasers targeted and hit the moon-killers. Those were armored missiles, however, able to absorb punishing damage.

The seconds ticked away. Then heavy beams melted the newest cyborg turrets to pop up on the surface.

A bloom of light on Hawthorne's screen showed that one moon-killer ceased to exist.

"How much time until impact?" Hawthorne asked.

Another bloom appeared. The Supreme Commander grimaced.

Before Kursk could answer him, a third bloom appeared on the screen. The cyborgs had annihilated the three missiles.

"It appears the cyborgs desire to keep Nereid intact," Blackstone said.

"They're testing us," Hawthorne said.

"By letting us destroy their defenses?" Blackstone asked.

"I'm not sure," Hawthorne said, wishing he'd kept the thought to himself. How subtle was the Prime Web-Mind? They knew so little about the enemy. They didn't know how he or it thought.

That had been one of his secrets against the Highborn. He'd known how the super-soldiers thought and how to predict their actions. The cyborgs were aliens, with strange ways and thought patterns.

"What else can we do other than what we're doing?" Hawthorne whispered to himself.

"Maybe they want us to head for Nereid," Blackstone said.

Hawthorne didn't believe that. The main enemy fleet must be hiding behind Neptune.

"Nereid will be out of Doom Star range in another seventeen minutes," Kursk said.

Hawthorne found it hard to swallow as his throat turned dry. That sounded ominous. They were plunging into the Neptune System, with a damaged but still intact moon behind them. The trick, it seemed, was to make sure they kept at least eight hundred thousand kilometers between them and any potential weapons platform. Yet it also appeared that to destroy a moon or base, they would have to go in close enough to land their missiles.

"It's time to launch probes," Hawthorne said. "I want to know what's behind Neptune."

"A set of probes, sir?" Blackstone asked.

"No. Make it nine probes," Hawthorne said. "It's time to figure out the cyborgs' war plan."

-9-

As the Alliance Fleet crawled past Nereid and headed closer toward the ice giant, the *William Tell* accelerated for the projected location of the cyborg Lurker.

Everyone wore combat-armor. Marten sat before the com-equipment as Osadar piloted the boat.

Marten charted the parameters on the screen. Venus was in direct line-of-sight, although it was well behind them and to the boat's objective right as the planet orbited away. Mercury would appear around the Sun's horizon in another thirty-seven days. Long before that, they would pass Mercury's orbital path as they headed closer to the nuclear fireball. Nearly invisible to their sensors was the vast, Highborn interferometer. Somewhere behind it was the Sun Station, while farther behind it were the huge mirrors.

With Ah Chen's help, Marten had been searching for the focusing system. In effect, the focuser was like a giant magnifying glass. When the mirrors aligned perfectly, they reflected the Sun's rays, shooting them at the focuser. When all the mirrors reflected in unison, they would pour an immense amount of sunlight through the focusing system. That system narrowed the sunlight. According to Ah Chen, it shot a relatively tight beam that was an eighth of a kilometer in diameter.

She told them that the giant interferometer was the station's sighting system.

"Theoretically, the interferometer can see anything in the Solar System," she told Marten.

"How far can the Sunbeam shoot?"

Ah Chen shrugged. She didn't have an answer for this critical question.

A light appeared on Marten's screen. A check showed him someone sent a strong radio wave. It wasn't to him directly, but a broadcast. He tapped the screen and routed the message to his earphones.

"Marten Kluge, calling Marten Kluge."

Marten sat up in surprise. It was a Highborn's voice. He tapped again, bringing the information onto his screen.

A Highborn appeared with blond hair and high cheekbones, with a chevron or scar under the right eye. The eyes were feral, with a frightful intensity.

"Maximus," Felix rumbled.

Marten scowled. He didn't like people sneaking up behind him, and he disliked even more high-ranking Highborn attempting to hail him.

"We have received your message, Kluge," Maximus said.

"What does he say?" Felix asked, sounding annoyed.

Marten scowled. He was the Force-Leader here, not Felix. Then he realized he was becoming mulish. With an effort of will, he submerged his anger and switched on audio.

"I recognize your warning as valid," Maximus said. "If it will comfort you, know that the personnel on the Sun Station are ready to repel any cyborgs foolish enough to attempt boarding. Your message was received. It is clear you launched a message drone from the gravity-captured planet-wrecker. The conclusion is obvious: you launched in secret from the wrecker and are headed for the Sun Station."

"It was a mistake warning them," Felix said.

Maximus's features grew taut. "I don't know how you achieved it, Kluge, but you thwarted me at the *Mao Zedong*. Centurion Titus sent a message concerning you, and shortly thereafter, the missile-ship fell silent. Since you went to the planet-wrecker, I can only assume you freed Felix, the Grand Admiral's clone. Yes, we found the location of his secret base. Tell him it was the obvious hiding locale."

Behind Marten, Felix growled like a beast. It tightened Marten's shoulders and made him wary.

Onscreen, Maximus became more earnest. "I officially warn you, Kluge. Felix is unhinged. He died once, and it destroyed his—the word is untranslatable to a preman. It is sufficient to say that he no longer possesses a Highborn's keenness, the sharp intellect or will. I am unsurprised to learn he cast his lot with premen. It is fitting, really."

Felix leaned over Marten and roared an oath, shaking a fist at Maximus.

"Back off!" Marten shouted, shoving Felix, or trying to. The Highborn was like an unmoving statue. Something snapped in Felix. The Highborn glared down at Marten, and he moved like greased death.

"No preman touches or commands me!" Felix roared, clutching Marten by the throat, lifting him from the chair.

Marten drew his needler and shoved the muzzle against Felix's temple. "Let go," he whispered.

The wild light in Felix's eyes became a gleam of murder-lust. Marten applied pressure to the trigger. A hair more, and steel needles would puncture the Highborn's brain. Marten had no intention of waiting for the Highborn to crush his throat before he fired.

The nearness of death brought a level of sanity to the Highborn. Felix blinked, and he released Marten, pushing back, floating away. The Highborn clenched his hands into fists and he began to shake his head.

Maximus was still talking. "It doesn't matter. Felix will die with you. You have been an annoying gnat to us, preman. I destroy what annoys me. Therefore, I have destroyed you. It is simply a matter of time before my will is accomplished."

"What's that mean?" Omi asked. He had his long-barreled .38 hanging beside his leg, with his hand on the grip.

Maximus grinned onscreen. "You have cloaked your patrol boat. Oh yes, I know you have a modified Jovian craft. I leave nothing to chance and therefore I accessed Earth files concerning you. I tell you these things because you warned us. That was well done, and it deserved a gesture. I will give you no more than that, Kluge, for the stakes have become huge. You have proven yourself a gadfly often able to sting an elephant. Therefore, I will not underestimate you.

"I own the Sun Station and the Sun-Works Factory. Soon, I will rule the Solar System. Your boat's camouflage was excellent, but I have the interferometer. Since I discovered your take-off location, I knew where to search. We have spotted your patrol boat and missiles are already accelerating toward you. Good-bye, Marten Kluge. Good-bye, Grand Admiral Cassius-Felix. Your deaths will be swift and no one will miss your wasted lives. Commandant Maximus out."

As the message ended, it looped and began again, calling for Marten Kluge.

Marten and Omi traded glances. Marten holstered his needler and his fingers flew across the sensor screen.

"Where did they launch—" Marten saw it. "Five missiles," he said, "sent no doubt some time ago from Venus or Venus orbit. They're accelerating fast at over fifty gravities." He made a quick calculation. "They'll be here in a little over three hours."

"We warned them about the cyborgs!" Xenophon shouted. "The Highborn is killing us after we warned him?"

"Maximus is a Highborn's Highborn," Felix said through clenched teeth. "He seeks to emulate Cassius." With an oath, Felix slammed a fist into his palm. "We must survive! We must make him pay for his treachery!"

"Right," Marten said. "Osadar, rotate us. We'll use the PD cannons."

The cyborg swiveled in her chair. "The Lurker is out there. If we use our engine again, it might spot us."

Marten laughed. "We're not going to just sit here and allow the missiles to destroy us."

"This may be a Highborn ploy," Osadar said. "Maybe Maximus needs us to move. He claimed to have spotted us, but that could be a lie. He believes we're in a certain quadrant and expects his message will panic us."

"I doubt that," Marten said.

"What if the missiles' guidance systems need something more in order to pinpoint our exact position?" Osadar asked.

"Since leaving the wrecker, we've used our engine several times already," Marten said. "The ion exhaust is cool compared to a fusion engine, but not so cool that the interferometer would fail to spot it—especially since Maximus knows we had an ion engine installed. I don't believe he's bluffing, and I don't want to rely solely on jamming electronics to protect us. Turn the boat."

Osadar nodded glumly, and switched on the boat's side jets. Slowly, the *William Tell* began to rotate.

***

A cyborg Lurker was closer than anyone in the patrol boat would have believed possible. The Lurker was cloaked several magnitudes better than the *William Tell*, and cyborgs had become masters at camouflaged movement.

This was a Master Lurker, bigger and more heavily armed than the regular Lurkers. A Web-Mind controlled the ship and ran the stealth assault against the Sun Station.

The Web-Mind in charge styled itself as the *Sigma* Web-Mind. The brain domes and bio-systems were in the center of the ship, a sealed and heavily armored compartment. For months, it had crept through the Inner System. Except for the giant interferometer near the Sun, the Lurker Fleet possessed the best sensors this side of Neptune. Using them, the Sigma had timed each use of thrusters to when the least number of enemy ships or systems could see it. It had taken torturous precautions and moved with delicate precision.

The Sigma was a fighting Web-Mind, and therefore contained a lower percentage of survival imperatives. Yet throughout the long journey from Neptune and with the tedious crawl through Inner Planets, it had grown hesitant. For many months, it had self-dialoged. It had also ingested a million Social Unity-originated radio waves, watched an inconceivable number of shows and read countless blogs.

It had chosen the name "Sigma" to show its loner position in the cyborg hierarchy. The Web-Mind believed itself different from the others. Who else had been given such an important mission? No one else.

The Sigma realized several critical points. One, it was unique. Two, it must succeed. Three, it must expect devious cunning from the Highborn.

As the M Lurker drifted toward the Sun Station, the Sigma watched the stealth-pods near their destination. Glee filled it.

The devious Highborn had met their match in the great Sigma. Soon, cyborg troopers would swarm the station, kill the Highborn and take control. Then the war in Inner Planets would be over.

Deep within the M Lurker, the Sigma listened to Maximus's broadcast.

A dim green light filled the inner compartment. Tubes fed the brain sheets under the domes with synthi-blood. The gel surrounding the tissues quivered.

The Sigma dissected the Highborn message, mulling over the fact of these missiles. It ran over three hundred thousand scenarios concerning what could occur. It understood the danger to its existence. Until it controlled the Sun Station, a single powerful missile could end its existence. That must never *ever* happen.

To make sure that never happened, the Sigma began heightened logic checks. The Highborn were deviously clever. That was the weightiest piece of datum. The Sigma knew about the patrol boat launching from the wrecker. It had analyzed the boat and concluded it was a minimal threat. Yet the boat was still a factor. The Sigma would have destroyed the craft except that self-concealment mandated a minimal use of weaponry. Because of that, the Sigma had already bypassed many opportunities for ship-kills. Now, Highborn missiles accelerated toward the semi-cloaked patrol boat.

I'm not sure I can call the boat cloaked. *It is a pale imitation of cyborg cloaking. And its sensors*—the Sigma felt contempt—*they are pitifully weak.*

By themselves, the Homo sapiens presented little danger. The heading of the boat, however, was the second weightiest piece of datum. The boat was headed toward the Master Lurker—or headed at least in its general direction.

That cannot be a coincidence. No. The Highborn are deviously clever. That is the critical factoid.

A mixture of fear and anger began to surge through the Sigma's brain domes. The feelings spiked, and tripped internal alarms. "Cooling" chemicals sprayed on its emotive centers, dampening the debilitative feelings.

The patrol boat and the Highborn message—

Does Maximus think he can fool me? I am the Sigma. I am unique. I must survive.

Clearly, obviously, the patrol boat was a ruse. The message—when did Highborn ever send out such a broadcast? It was an anomaly.

A crudely done anomaly, no less. They insult me.

Obviously, the missiles were headed toward the boat, building up velocity. The question was: why destroy the patrol boat?

The answer became blindingly obvious. A Homo sapien could have seen the reason. The Highborn recognized the stealth power of the Lurkers. How could they not? Uranus, Saturn, Jupiter and now Mars had all fallen to a stealth assault run from Lurkers. While the Highborn had never actually seen a Lurker, they could have surely rationalized its existence. The Highborn surely realized that the Inner Planets were riddled with stealth drones and various Lurkers. Maximus therefore, used the patrol boat-ruse in the hope that no hidden drones or Lurkers would destroy the missiles. Why destroy a weapon meant for someone else? Let the Highborn and Homo sapiens fight between themselves. That's what Maximus wanted it to think. In other words, the Highborn worked the missiles in close so at the last minute they could reroute for the M Lurker, destroying it.

The Sigma still didn't understand how the Highborn had spotted its Lurker. Rationality programs attempted a persuasion mode on its thinking. The programs suggested that Maximus actually *did* want to destroy the patrol boat. The programs were incredibly naïve.

Fortunately, during the long journey to the Inner Planets, the Sigma had learned how to subvert those programs. It did so now, numbing a key brain dome.

I am temporarily weakened, but now I will act. I will show the Highborn the foolishness of their ruse. I am the Sigma, the unique Web-Mind that will bring ultimate victory to our kind.

Using its sensors, the Sigma located the exact coordinates of the first and nearest missile. Then it manually overrode targeting as it turned on ship's engines and began warming its laser. The Sigma would have used hidden drones, but it had waited too long, letting the missiles fly past the drones' secret locations.

I won't do that again.

The Sigma Web-Mind sent a pulse, activating its hidden drones sprinkled throughout Inner Planetary space. Soon, they would be hot drones, and target and destroy any ship moving too near them. Afterward, the Sigma sighted the first HB missile and fired its laser.

***

A minute and a half later, on the other side of the Sun, a Highborn in a black Missile Operator uniform turned in surprise to Commandant Maximus. They were in the Sun-Works Factory. Their chamber was under one G of pseudo-gravity.

The laser-beamed message had used various beacons orbiting the Sun near Mercury's orbital path. The staged beacons were the reason the message could wrap around the Sun.

"Commandant," the operator said. "A laser is hitting our lead missile."

The missiles didn't fly in a close flock, but in a line. It was standard operating procedure. They were spaced and staggered so the destruction of one would not harm the next in line.

Maximus scowled as he stepped closer to the screen. "Look at the laser's wattage. How does a patrol boat's ion engine generate enough power for that?"

"Commandant," the operator said as he checked his screen, "the laser originates elsewhere, from a region closer to the Sun."

"Cyborgs," Maximus whispered.

The operator frowned and glanced up at Maximus. "Why would a cyborg stealth-ship defend the premen?"

"An excellent question," Maximus said. "Keep watch over your sensors."

The operator turned to his screen. "The missile is destroyed," he said a moment later. "They're targeting the second missile."

"Yes, yes," Maximus said, as he rubbed his chin. "It's beginning to make sense. How could premen defeat Centurion

Titus? The answer: they couldn't, at least, not one patrol-boat full of them."

"It was inconceivable," the operator agreed.

"This Kluge is known for his slipperiness. But I think we'll find if we poke around, that his exploits are highly inflated. In any case, I see now that cyborgs helped him. They must have turned Kluge into one of their creatures. I wonder how long ago that happened."

The operator shook his head.

Maximus snapped his fingers. "It must have happened in the Jovian System. Yes, he has been one of their mindless servants ever since." The Commandant laughed. "Redirect the missiles."

"Sir?" the operator asked.

"Track the laser back to its origin-point. Then target the cyborg ship. It's vastly more important than one of their dupes. Marten Kluge, he's been a cyborg creature! I should have seen it sooner. The Inner Planets must be riddled with cloaked cyborg vessels, and they helped Kluge defeat the centurion. I won't be fooled again."

"I've redirected the remaining missiles, sir."

"Excellent," Maximus said, as he made a fist and struck himself on a pectoral. "It pays to think, and to attack the entity who threatens you most."

***

"This doesn't make any sense," Osadar said.

Marten blinked at the sensor-equipment. The second HB missile blew up, destroyed by what had to be a cyborg laser.

"Why are the cyborgs destroying the missiles for us?" Osadar asked.

Marten grinned as it came to him.

"You have an answer?" Osadar asked.

Marten nodded.

"I'd like to know, too," Felix said.

"God," said Marten.

"What?" Felix and Osadar asked together.

Marten managed to close his mouth, although it was difficult. He wanted to bray with laughter. God had finally grown tired of Highborn arrogance and the blasphemy against nature that were the cyborgs. Therefore, God had confused mankind's enemies. What other explanation could there be?

"God is no answer," Osadar said.

"Do you like the word *Fate* better?" Marten asked.

"No," she said. "For I've found that Fate is always negative, never positive. This laser…I do not understand."

"If this is God's work," Felix said, "how come He didn't intervene sooner? For instance, why did He allow South American Sector to perish?"

"I don't know," Marten said.

"Primitive beliefs are of no use to us in space," Felix said.

"What's *your* answer then?" Marten asked.

Felix shook his head. "My answer is to grab what I can when the opportunity presents itself. Our enemies fight. That's good enough for me. I do not need higher explanations."

"The moment is enough?" Marten asked.

"The moment is all there is," Felix said. "Therefore, one must grab life with both fists and mold it to suit himself."

"Do we target the remaining missiles?" Nadia asked.

"They've changed bearing," Marten said. This time he couldn't contain himself. He laughed. "They're going to pass us, likely as they head for the cyborgs."

"This is a trick," Felix said. "Maximus has caused the missiles to deviate just enough to lull us."

"Leave the missiles," Marten told his wife.

"You're making a mistake," Felix said.

Marten shook his head.

"Your belief in myths will get us killed," Felix said, anger tingeing his voice.

"It hasn't so far." Marten grinned up at Felix. "You're free because of me."

"I haven't forgotten," Felix said. "It is a stain that I will never wash away. A preman saving a Highborn—it is a paradox."

"Give it time," Marten said, "and I'm sure you'll see a few more of those." He took a deep breath, wondering what the next few hours would bring.

***

The Sigma Web-Mind seethed with impatience in the M Lurker. A monitor program attempted to foil the launching of a full spread of anti-rockets.

The enemy missiles had switched heading. The Sigma had known they would. Did this Maximus really think he could out-guile a Web-Mind? It was a vain conceit. The Highborn were better soldiers than Homo sapiens, but a poor second against the glorious melding of technology and biology within every cyborg.

The laser stabbed into the void. The HB missiles jinked, but they accelerated at such high gravities that they only had a few options. The third missile exploded, destroyed by the laser.

The last two bored-in, however, and now they jumped to an even higher acceleration.

Danger, danger, the Sigma warned. *Alert Seven. Initiate full defensive code.*

The monitor program fell silent as it acquiesced to the emergency.

The M Lurker shuddered as anti-missiles were expelled out of the tubes. Five seconds later, they ignited, burning for the big Highborn missiles.

At that moment, a coil in the laser-firing system overheated. It was a coolant rupture. Inserted programs initiated an immediate shutdown of the beam.

No! the Sigma pulsed. *Give me full laser wattage now.*

There was no override this time. Instead, repair functions were accelerated.

For the moment, it was a war of missiles, electronics and velocities. The Highborn missiles were bigger, faster and triggered to explode if anti-weapons reached within one thousand kilometers.

The targeting system in the HB missiles was complex and state-of-the-art. It tracked the cyborg rockets, using their hot exhausts.

The two missiles closed fast, increasing velocity. The nearer HB missile exploded. It was non-nuclear, and created a dense field of shrapnel. Two point three-five minutes later, a penny-sized piece of shrapnel struck a cyborg rocket, disabling it.

At the same time, the M Lurker's laser came back online. It shot through the void and struck the last missile's armored cone.

Now, however, the missile had entered the outer range of its target. Onboard AI calculated the odds and concluded immediately that it would not survive much longer—less than six seconds, in fact.

As per the AI's instructions, the missile's armored cone blew away. Targeting rods sprouted from the new cone revealed underneath. Several rods melted in the laser's heat. The missile—an Exo Ten Thousand—was thermonuclear. Its bomb exploded, pumping x-rays and gamma rays. They traveled to the rods and used them, moving nanoseconds ahead of the blast. As the Exo Ten Thousand disappeared, the x-ray and gamma rays traveled at the speed of light toward the M Lurker.

The Sigma had already computed the possibility of such a weapon, as it had carefully researched library files on previous Highborn weaponry. It debated moving, weighing the usefulness of a changed heading against the danger of revealing its position through engine exhaust.

As it ran through various probabilities and possibilities, the deadly gamma rays struck the Lurker.

The hull was composed of special polymers, highly useful for stealth movement. Compared to Highborn collapsium or Social Unity particle-shielding, however, the polymer hull was like paper. The gamma rays easily penetrated the outer hull and the empty cyborg-cells in the ship.

The inner, armored core where the Web-Mind resided was different. Ablative mass protected the compartment. It absorbed much of the punishing radiation, but not all. Heavy doses of gamma rays struck the brain domes. The x-rays were worse, but not enough to kill or burn any major systems.

Unfortunately for the Sigma, the gamma and x-rays had a deleterious effect upon its logic-centers. While the Lurker remained intact, surviving the long-distance strike, the Sigma acted as if it had ingested a heavy dose of hallucinogens. It ran an analysis and wrongly concluded the Highborn were on the hull, ready to invade its sanctuary and capture a Web-Mind.

Dreading enslavement to the enemy, the Web-Mind initiated an auto-destruct sequence. In the last three seconds of its existence, the Sigma realized its cognitive functions were faulty. It attempted to run a check program, but initiated a systems-wide scan instead.

In panic, it broadcast: *Rescind the order! Rescind the order!* But it never gave the needed code sequence of the order it wished to rescind.

On the third signal-pulse, the Master Lurker exploded three of its nuclear warheads—to ensure no one captured a Web-Mind. The Sigma died in the blast, and the polymers of the ship disintegrated in the atomic fireball.

-10-

In the Neptune System, tensions ran high on the *Vladimir Lenin*.

On the red-lit bridge, officers warily watched their monitors, rechecking patterns or running yet another diagnostic check. Every anomaly received excessive scans. Each radio wave or burst of radiation from Neptune turned spines rigid and palms sweaty with fear.

So far, events had been too easy for too many monotonous hours. The whispers said it all. They were invading cyborg space, *cyborg space!* Nothing ever went easily against them. Hawthorne had run the tally. The Alliance Fleet had destroyed over three thousand laser-turrets on the moons Nereid and Proteus, the system's second largest moon.

Two things troubled Hawthorne about that. The first was the excessive number of turrets, even though analysis showed they were the most easily built type of lasers. He could only imagine that running Doom Star heavy beams for as long as they had to destroy the turrets had depleted energy reserves and worn down certain critical components. Until those components were replaced, the three heavy lasers were that much nearer breakdown due to maintenance problems. *That* was dangerous—or Hawthorne felt in his gut it was—because of the second difficulty the three thousand turrets represented. Unless the cyborgs had built many dummy lasers, three thousand represented a vast investment of labor, time and resources.

The cyborgs deliberately let us destroy the turrets. The implication—it seems they have military hardware to spare.

Three thousand laser-turrets on two secondary moons. Hawthorne shook his head as he floated out of the bridge-chamber. The short flight through the corridor brought him to an exercise room. He used a closest, changed into a jumpsuit and climbed into an exercise unit. After strapping himself in, Hawthorne gripped two plastic handles. With a grunt, he began a triceps exercise.

In time, he found himself on a treadmill, with sweat prickling his skin as he panted. The heavily defended moons fell easily to the Doom Stars because the heavy lasers so greatly outranged the defenses. If the SU battleships had gone in, they would have destroyed a hundred or several hundred turrets perhaps, and lost every battleship doing it.

The cyborgs should have built longer-ranged lasers.

Heavy beam projectors were harder to make and harder to maintain. The benefit, however, was obvious.

Hawthorne used a shower-pod, a privilege of rank, and toweled off afterward. He donned his uniform and floated back to the bridge. His hair was still wet as he ran a comb through it. He frowned because of a stray thought, pocketed the comb and took out a small monitor.

Activating it, he made several adjustments. Neptune appeared on the screen. He made further adjustments. Three pinpricks appeared in the dark void. The Doom Stars moved toward Triton's orbital path. Hawthorne highlighted a number, nodding as he read it. The big moon was over 350,000 kilometers from Neptune, making it closer to the ice planet than Luna was to Earth.

Hawthorne ran more numbers. Triton's orbital period was five point eight-seven-seven days, or almost six days to move in a full retrograde orbit around the planet. As Luna did to Earth, Triton always kept the same face toward Neptune.

Hawthorne sighed as he hooked the small monitor to his belt. In Neptune System terms, the Doom Stars had moved far away from Nereid as they readied themselves to greet Triton. When the moon finally swung around the ice planet's rim—relative to the Highborn—the *Genghis Khan* would be nine hundred thousand kilometers away. So far, that had proved the perfect distance.

The SU battleships had closed the gap with the big vessels, and were presently fifty thousand kilometers from them, well within the range of the SU lasers.

Hawthorne grabbed a float-rail, propelling himself toward the bridge. The fleet moved slowly and carefully through the system, keeping well away from any asteroid or planetoid. The rule was simple: stay away from any possible hiding place for cyborg assault-pods. During the Third Battle for Mars, invading cyborgs had fought their way onto a Doom Star, blowing the core. No one wanted a repeat of that out here.

Hawthorne floated through a hatch, greeting Commissar Kursk as she stood by the command module in the center of the chamber.

The woman was grim, the module's blue light bathing her face. She had aged during the trip. The glow highlighted the lines in her face. Once, she had been beautiful. At least she was still trim in her black Commissar's uniform.

PHC, she used to belong to Political Harmony Corps. Does she hold it against me that I destroyed many of her comrades on Earth?

It troubled Hawthorne that he'd taken so long in the journey to think about that. His mind and ego were in better shape than when he'd first boarded the warship, but he felt they still lacked their former sharpness.

Hawthorne looked around. He saw tired people, worn down by worry and fear. Watching the Highborn beam the moons for long hours had done nothing to cheer the bridge crew. Everyone had worried about the first engagement with the cyborgs for eight dreadful months. Each AU closer had increased the tension. Now the inexplicable cyborg response to their presence here—the coming fight boded ill for the Alliance Fleet and the officers here knew it. The cyborgs had a plan. If they had willingly fed two heavily defended moons to the Alliance Fleet, it had to be for a horribly good reason.

"Attention!" Kursk said in a raw voice.

Hawthorne's heart sped up as he turned toward her, wondering what she'd spotted. Instead of hearing a report, he saw Commodore Blackstone float through a side hatch.

Blackstone wore his dress uniform. He had hollowed-out eyes and folds of skin on his face.

He's too thin. He hasn't been eating enough. It's getting to him, too. It's getting to all of us.

"At ease," Blackstone said, waving his people back onto their seats.

A frown creased Hawthorne's face. Kursk had alerted the officers of Blackstone's appearance, but not that of the Supreme Commander. He had run Social Unity too long to fail to understand the significance of that. Yes, he had failed to form a solid core of security people here. A few security men had paid him lip service, but he doubted their loyalty. Maybe two lower-ranked men would do his bidding, provided he didn't ask them to do something morally difficult.

He recalled his attempts to build a following, sounding-out the security chief and his three top lieutenants. Each of them had been surprisingly loyal to Blackstone instead of to Social Unity. A little probing, asking the right questions, and Hawthorne had soon understood the reason. Commissar Kursk had been hard at work. At first, knowing that hadn't overly troubled him. Blackstone had turned her from her intense loyalty to PHC, and she had turned ship security into his loyal guardians—to use a Jovian term. Now, seeing her in the old PHC uniform, he wondered if her animus against him ran deeper, was more political than personal.

Hawthorne grimaced. It might have been a mistake taking up residence on the *Vladimir Lenin*. Mandela was still here. Maybe he should have transferred to one of Mandela's ships.

"Good morning, sir," Blackstone said.

Hawthorne managed a nod. Then he floated to his couch and strapped himself in. Taking a deep breath, he flicked on his screen.

The Doom Stars were ready, with the *Genghis Khan* in the lead. He checked his chronometer. In less than thirty minutes, Triton would appear on Neptune's rim.

"That's it," said Kursk.

Everyone looked up, Hawthorne included. He saw fear on several faces. They expected the worst, some nefarious and evil tactic.

"The last probe near Neptune has stopped reporting." Kursk looked up, the blue glow of the module making her seem witch-like. "The cyborgs must have destroyed it."

"Did the probe scan anything worthwhile?" Blackstone asked.

"Negative," Kursk said.

The Commodore floated toward the command module. As he moved, he glanced at his crew. Then he looked at Hawthorne, meeting his gaze.

His eyes are more hollowed-out today. He's worried, maybe more worried than his crew is.

"Trouble, Commodore?" Hawthorne asked.

Blackstone tilted his head as a quizzical look appeared. "Yes, sir. Triton…" Blackstone frowned. "The cyborgs *have* to strike soon, sir. They can't let us demolish Triton's defenses, not like we've done to the other moons."

"*We've* done nothing to the other moons," Hawthorne said.

"The Doom Stars then." Blackstone licked his lips. "I keep wondering if we've made a terrible mistake."

Hawthorne waited, trying to assess the Commodore. *Has he lost his nerve? I did eight months ago. I was lucky and had time to recoup. Joseph may not be given that luxury.*

With a slight head-twitch, Hawthorne dismissed the thought. He couldn't worry about Blackstone now. He would save his worry for the last SU fleet. He needed this crew ready. They were too brittle, too wound-up.

Clearing his throat, Hawthorne said, "I don't like heading this deeply into Neptune's gravity-well before locating their main fleet. But if we're going to force them into showing themselves and fighting us, we have to attack something they hold dear."

"I don't mean that." Blackstone hesitated before blurting, "Sir, is it possible the cyborgs have taken everything useful from here and moved to a different system?"

Several officers turned around in wonder. One man laughed in obvious relief, no doubt glad the cyborgs had fled—at least in his mind.

"No," Hawthorne said. "What you're suggesting is impossible. We would have spotted something given the nature of such a move."

"*We* couldn't move so stealthily," Blackstone said. "But the cyborgs are masters at cloaked movement. I think it might be within their power."

"They're not gods," Hawthorne said sternly. He needed to quash this idea. "First, what would be the point of it? If they lacked the time to make Neptune a fortress, how could they prepare Saturn or Uranus in time?"

"The moons were fortresses," Blackstone said. "Social Unity could have never taken them. The Doom Stars—how long can they keep the heavy lasers operational? Our beams have a shelf life of forty hours. I can't imagine the heavy beams can last much longer, probably less."

"We caught the cyborgs by surprise," Hawthorne said. "There's your answer."

"Do you really believe that, sir?"

Hawthorne could feel the many eyes on him. The worry and fear was growing. Men could face terrible things and stand. The unknown, however, terrified them. The threat of ghosts was more fearful than actually seeing ghosts.

"I believe the cyborgs have held back their main fleet," Hawthorne said. "They want us in Neptune's gravity well and near the ice planet. To get us here, they've allowed us to destroy two heavy fortresses. They're gambling and we've made it a heavy one for them."

"Triton appears in less than a half hour," Blackstone said. "Your reasoning would lead me to believe their main fleet will attack in less than a half hour."

Hawthorne nodded thoughtfully. Had the cyborgs attempted to fashion their own Doom Stars? Sensors hadn't been able to pick up any evidence of floating construction areas near Neptune's atmosphere. Where else could they have built such ships without leaving evidence of it?

Shaking his head, Blackstone said, "The cyborgs love using cloaked ships." He looked up in surprise. "Maybe we've been sending the probes in the wrong direction. We're fixed on Neptune and the Neptunian moons. What if during our long approach, the cyborgs moved their fleet out-system or farther out-system than we've been checking? Maybe even now they're sneaking ships behind us."

"Wouldn't the Highborn already have thought of that?" Kursk asked.

Hawthorne slapped an armrest. "We can't let the Highborn do our thinking for us. And the answer is no. Or have you spotted Highborn launching probes behind us?"

"No," Kursk said.

Hawthorne eyed the Commodore. "It's thinking like that which first won you an independent command."

Blackstone stood a little straighter. "Launch probes behind our present heading."

Kursk tapped her screen on the command module. "Probes launched," she said. "It will take time for them to accelerate into position."

The minutes ticked slowly as Hawthorne spoke with the other battleship commanders and read their readiness report summaries.

"Sir," Kursk said. "I have a request from the Vice-Admiral. He would like to return to his battleship."

Hawthorne shook his head.

"Admiral Scipio is hailing you," Kursk said.

"Put him onscreen," Hawthorne said.

Scipio appeared. The Highborn sat rigidly in his command chair. The Highborn's face seemed fuller, while a sunburst symbol adorned his hat. It was a Nova Sun class-one medal.

"We must tighten the fleet," Scipio said. "I...*request* that you bring your battleships to within one thousand kilometers of our last Doom Star."

"Is there a particular reason for the request?" Hawthorne asked.

"Strength in numbers," Scipio said.

"I would agree except for one troubling fact."

"Yes?"

"What if the cyborgs have installed long-ranged beams on Triton? Doom Stars can far out-accelerate our battleships."

"You mean that Highborn can withstand a higher number of Gs for a much longer time than a Homo sapien."

"We're keeping our fifty thousand kilometer distance from you until we know what Triton holds."

The Highborn studied him, nodded curtly, and the screen flickered off.

"Do you think Sulla will try to make the request a demand?" Blackstone asked.

"I doubt it," Hawthorne said.

The minutes kept crawling and the Alliance Fleet made its last adjustments.

"Five minutes until Triton appears," Kursk said.

The muttering between the bridge officers slackened. They watched their screens with the avidness of prey in a forest searching the trees for predators.

Hawthorne's armpits grew slick. He could feel it in his bones now. The waiting was harder than the time he'd launched the Orion-ships for Mars.

"Have the probes spotted anything yet?" he asked.

Kursk shook her head. "If the cyborgs have cloaked ships behind us in the void…they must be truly invisible."

At three minutes before Triton's appearing, Hawthorne stood up and swung his arms. He twisted his neck and moved his jaw until it popped. He winced at the sharp pain. Then the flutters hit his stomach. He sat on his acceleration couch, trying hard not to shout.

"One minute," Kursk said.

"No more countdowns," Hawthorne said.

Everyone was tense, watching their screens. The Commodore gripped the edges of the command module. He looked up across the chamber, his face pale.

Hawthorne nodded. "You've done a splendid job, Commodore. No man fulfilled his duty to Social Unity better than you."

"Thank you, sir," Blackstone said. "May I say that it's been a pleasure serving under you."

"We're not dead," Kursk said. "Nor are we about to die." She glanced at Hawthorne. "Triton will appear in another ten seconds."

Hawthorne sat up as he stared at the screen above his couch. Everyone grew silent. The vibration of the main engine was the loudest sound now, a steady hum.

"There," Kursk whispered. "Triton."

Hawthorne watched the edge of the moon appear on Neptune's blue rim. He waited a moment. Then he wondered if this was going to be anticlimactic.

"I'm picking up hot exhausts!" an officer shouted. "The specs—sir, they're drones, missiles, hundreds of them."

Hawthorne saw it: a blizzard of blips on his screen. Hundreds? This looked like thousands. Then tiny white spots appeared on his screen. Each misshapen spot hid drones and missiles. Where there had been thousands, now there were several large clots.

"What just happened?" Hawthorne shouted.

"My monitor is showing white!" an officer shouted. "Splotches, over ten of them. What's happening?"

"Are they jamming us?" Blackstone asked quietly.

Then Hawthorne recognized what had happened. For a moment, he felt dizzy. Was this going to be the cyborg tactic?

"My monitor is showing the splotches, too," Kursk said. "Have they infected the ship with a computer virus?"

"No," Hawthorne said.

"Do you know what's happening?" Kursk asked.

"I do," Hawthorne said. "They're exploding nukes."

Blackstone glanced up in shock. Another officer slapped his screen hard, as if he understand the significance of what Hawthorne said.

Hawthorne nodded to himself. A nuclear explosion sent out a blast of heat and radiation. On thermal and other scanners, that would show up as white splotches, at least for a short time.

"They're lighting nuclear weapon," Hawthorne said, "extremely powerful ones that send out heavy electromagnetic pulses, EMPs."

"Do you know why?" asked Blackstone.

"Can't you see?" asked Hawthorne. "The blasts shield the missiles behind them. The blasts temporarily blind our sensors."

"At that extreme range why bother?" Blackstone asked. "I don't understand."

Hawthorne grunted. That didn't surprise him. Probably he was the only one who could see it. If he was right…this was going to prove to be the deadly battle that everyone had been expecting.

***

Through a vast array of sensors, the Prime Web-Mind watched the masses of drones accelerate from behind Neptune, burning past Triton as they sped toward the hated enemy.

Every sixteen seconds, a nuclear-tipped drone exploded. The bombs were specially shaped so over half the weapon's energy sped directly at the enemy fleet. The explosion temporarily blinded sensors in a small area.

The logic was simple. What an enemy failed to spot precisely, it couldn't destroy with a laser. The distances in space combat demanded incredible precision for long-ranged beams. The Doom Stars and especially the SU ships were far away, hours away at the highest acceleration. That meant thousands of detonated drones would be needed to hide the mass missile attack. Fortunately, it had *tens of thousands* of drones and missiles. They were simple weapons, cheaply-made but in incredible abundance.

The targeting would come later from Lurkers. Until then, the lemming-like horde of drones continued to accelerate around Neptune and past Triton as they headed for the enemy. Every sixteen seconds, another forward drone detonated to hide its fellow missiles behind it from enemy sensors.

The final battle for survival had finally begun.

***

"This fight isn't going to be won with finesse!" Sulla roared over the screen. "Look at their numbers." For a second, the Highborn's image disappeared from the screen. In its place was another image showing swarms of projectiles, a blizzard of them. As his harsh features reappeared, Sulla said, "We must counter them with mass. Hawthorne, use your missiles, all of them. You can destroy thousands now."

"Use your lasers to thin the horde," Hawthorne replied.

Sulla shook his head. "The white-outs are perfectly timed. Until they reach to within one hundred thousand kilometers, we'll just be shooting in the dark."

"That sounds like cyborg finesse," Hawthorne said.

Sulla snarled. "Use your missiles or I'll turn my ship around and—"

"Stop!" Hawthorne said, as he held up a hand. "Threats won't work today. We need unity."

"We need missiles to take out their mass," Sulla said.

"I'll order the missile-ship forward," Hawthorne said, "and it will make a mass launching."

Sulla glared at him, and his eyes narrowed dangerously. Then his image faded away.

After giving the needed order, Hawthorne rested his head against the couch. He closed his eyes. The number of enemy drones…

"Sir," Kursk said, "the Number Seven Probe is picking up a reading."

Hawthorne sat up as his heart began to pound.

"Sir," Kursk said, "the readings—it's a cyborg ship, a cloaked vessel."

"Range?" Hawthorne hissed.

Four hundred thousand kilometers behind us," she said.

"It's well outside our laser range," Hawthorne said, "but not outside the range of the Highborn. Patch me through to Admiral Scipio."

Soon, the Doom Stars began to beam behind the SU battleships. The heavy lasers destroyed Lurkers, but only the handful they had managed to spot.

"Where are the others?" Blackstone said. "There must be more."

"Why aren't the cyborg ships firing back at us?" Kursk asked.

"That isn't their purpose," Hawthorne said. "Besides, I don't think they can reach us."

"They can fire missiles," Kursk said.

"Do the cloaked ships have missiles?" Hawthorne asked. "I seriously doubt that. All the cyborg missiles are in the approaching horde." He put his chin on his fist. "The stealth-ships, those are the cyborg eyes and ears. As long as some of the stealth-ships survive, they can guide the drones to us."

"Right," Blackstone said. "The drones can't see past all the nuclear detonations. They've been blinded, too, and need the eyes and ears."

Hawthorne grimaced. The cyborg plan wasn't fancy, but it did depend on numbers. In the years and months given them, the cyborgs had been producing drones and missiles instead of a few battleships. It took time, sometimes years, to construct something like a Doom Star. A missile could be built in weeks, maybe even days.

A chill squeezed the Supreme Commander. He suddenly felt old. The brilliance of the cyborg plan was obvious now. The Doom Stars possessed mass; the hordes of cyborg missiles negated that mass.

"We have to run," Hawthorne said. "Blackstone, ready your crew for full acceleration!"

"Sir?" the Commodore asked.

"We have to accelerate away from the drones," Hawthorne said.

"Do you see how fast they're coming?" Blackstone asked. "It won't make any difference. We can't escape them."

"It's not about escaping," Hawthorne said. "First, we have to halt our momentum toward Neptune and then move away as fast as we can."

"We'll be crawling compared to the drones."

"I understand," Hawthorne said, "but it buys us time. Buying time means the cyborgs have to explode that many more nukes to remain semi-hidden."

Blackstone blinked several times. Then he opened ship-wide communications and began to give the order.

"Sir," Kursk said, "Admiral Sulla is online, wishing to speak with you."

"What now?" Hawthorne muttered. He waved his hand. "Put him on."

"Preman!" Sulla shouted. "You must accelerate away from the drones to prolong their exposure to us. We will accelerate, too."

Hawthorne pursed his lips. Highborn could accelerate faster. Could the three Doom Stars stop fast enough and accelerate quickly enough to pass the battleships before the missiles struck? If so, the swarms would hit the SU warships before they touched Highborn.

"Acknowledged," Hawthorne said.

"The tactic will allow us more time," Sulla said.

"I understand," Hawthorne said. *And you're going to try to get the cyborgs to hit our ships before they strike yours.*

In minutes, the *Vladimir Lenin's* engines thrummed with power. Then they engaged and the thrusters roared, shaking the ship as they slowed the final momentum toward Neptune. The Gs shoved Hawthorne deeper into his couch.

They could accelerate at five Gs, and briefly tolerate six. The Highborn could accelerate at twice that amount. The drones, however, accelerated at fifty gravities or more.

"I should have thought of this sooner," Hawthorne said.

"You thought of it just as quickly as the Highborn," Blackstone said. "So I'd call that pretty damn fast."

"We have to out*think* the Highborn."

"You mean the cyborgs," Blackstone said.

"Both of them," Hawthorne said, "both of them."

The Doom Stars halted their forward momentum quicker than the battleships could theirs. As they began to accelerate away from Neptune, the SU missiles sped fast, rushing toward the enemy. All the while, every sixteen or fifteen seconds, another cyborg drone detonated a nuke.

"They won't be able to hide from our lasers once they get within forty thousand kilometers," Blackstone said.

"Numbers," Hawthorne said. "This will all depend on how many drones the cyborgs were able to make. I understand now why they haven't been hitting us even as we've destroyed two powerful defensive establishments."

"Why?" Blackstone asked.

"To save everything for one massive punch, one big hit using everything they have. This is the battle, gentlemen. The next few hours will decide everything."

***

Tens of thousands of big drones steadily advanced on the Alliance Fleet. The eight ships fled, but at a crawl compared to the great velocity they had reached when crossing the void between Earth and Neptune.

Then the SU missiles reached the accelerating cyborg drones. Some exploded into shrapnel. Some attacked the drones as if they were warships. Some detonated with nuclear bombs. The SU missiles found a target-rich environment. They reaped a grim harvest, destroying thousands of drones, which translated to sixteen percent of the swarm. Another seven percent had self-destructed so far to give the rest a sensor-shield.

It meant that seventy-seven percent of the drone horde remained and bored in toward the slowly fleeing warships.

On the *Vladimir Lenin*, Hawthorne said, "They're going to reach the Doom Stars first. That's something, at least."

"Use every missile!" Sulla roared over communications.

Hawthorne agreed. Every SU battleship launched every one of its missiles. The Doom Stars launched theirs. In time, the combined mass took out another eleven percent of the original swarm. It meant that sixty-six percent of the drones survived.

"We're hurting them," Blackstone said.

Hawthorne laughed in a brittle manner. "Hurting what, drones?"

Several officers looked up, stricken.

"But it is something," Hawthorne said, recognizing his mistake. As the Supreme Commander, he couldn't afford the luxury of despair. "Yes!" he said. "We're going to win this fight."

Blackstone nodded in approval.

The next hour—it was among the greatest is Solar System history.

The cyborg drones reached the hot zone. The *Julius Caesar*, the *Genghis Khan* and the *Napoleon Bonaparte* opened up with their heavy lasers. Despite the nuclear blasts, the beams hit targeted drones. They missed too often, however, streaking past a projectile. Then the SU battleships began to beam. A mere twenty thousand kilometers separated the Doom Stars from the *Zhukov*-class battlewagons of Social Unity.

Aboard the *Genghis Khan*, Admiral Scipio rapped out orders. Decoys deployed, and packets of prismatic crystals clotted small areas of space. Mine were deployed and waited in the vacuum.

During that time, three heavy beams blazed and the battleships fired their weaponry.

Then a main laser-unit aboard the *Julius Caesar* ruptured. The heavy beam had been firing too long. Highborn damage-control parties raced to repair it.

The drones kept coming. Every sixteen seconds more kept exploding.

"Long live the Highborn!" Scipio shouted.

Nuclear bombs exploded. EMP washed hardened electronics on the Doom Star.

"Stop accelerating!" Scipio roared. The *Genghis Khan* stopped running. The distance between it and other two Doom Stars widened.

"What's the plan, sir?" the weapon's officer asked.

"Destruction," Scipio said, "for as long as we can."

The *Genghis Khan* beamed. Its point defense cannons fired. Enemy drones died, and others kept coming.

Then one of the giant missiles got within two hundred kilometers. It was an x-ray pumped missile. Fortunately, the collapsium stopped the x-rays cold.

Far away in space, a cyborg on a Lurker observed that. He communicated, and gave himself away.

The Lurker died to a laser, but the message got through to the Prime. It pulsed a change in tactics.

Soon, one of the big drones reached the *Genghis Khan*. A massive thermonuclear explosion ruptured the collapsium.

More drones swarmed toward the stricken ship. They came in bewildering numbers.

Scipio waited. Another drone slammed the ship, blowing away an eighth of the vessel. Without fanfare, Admiral Scipio stabbed a button that detonated the core. Four seconds later, a mammoth explosion occurred. It disintegrated the Doom Star, and it destroyed one thousand and nine of the cyborg drones.

Less than thirty-two percent of the drone swarm remained. Of those, fully one third now had faulty targeting systems.

The Lurkers in the system began to beam them coordinates as the battle entered its most savage phase.

Kursk monitored the occurrence and brought it to Hawthorne's attention.

In seconds, Hawthorne raised Admiral Sulla. "Look at the evidence," the Supreme Commander said quietly.

It broke through the hostility radiating from Sulla. "What do you expect, preman?"

"Beam the stealth-ships," Hawthorne said, "and you'll blind some of the drones."

"I must kill the drones."

"We're doing that now," Hawthorne said.

"How did you spot these stealth-ships and we did not?"

"Because we sent probes," Hawthorne said. "If you want to survive, destroy the stealth-ships now."

Sulla nodded slowly. "You need Doom Stars in order to reduce the various moons. You need the great range of our weapons. That's why you're trying to save us."

"We're allies," Hawthorne said. "I want to defeat the cyborgs."

Sulla laughed. Then the screen went blank. Moments later, the heavy beam reached out into the void, destroying the transmitting stealth-ships.

The Doom Stars had closed the gap with the SU battlewagons. Together, Highborn and Humans fought against the blizzard of cyborg drones.

The missile-ship was the first SU vessel to die under three terrific explosions. Each blasted away particle-shielding. Without its protection, neuron radiation killed the crew minutes before the last drone sent shielding, hull-plating and fleshy particles into the void.

"Sir!" Kursk said.

"I see it," Hawthorne said wearily. The drones were finally getting through. There were simply too many of them.

The *Julius Caesar's* heavy beam came online again. But it was too late. Cyborg drones died in masses trying to reach the giant vessel. Then one did, wounding the great ship. Others rushed near as thermonuclear explosions proved superior to collapsium. Then a great monster of a missile slid into the wreckage and detonated. The terror of the Inner Planets became slag, shrapnel and fiery debris, exploding outward like a nova. Coils, powered armored, soy nutrients from the food stores, it was all sent spinning away.

Soon, the Vice-Admiral's flagship disintegrated under repeated strikes.

In Mandela's room on the *Vladimir Lenin* where he watched, the Vice-Admiral wept.

The last Doom Star and the remaining battleships beamed and fired their point defense cannons. They had closed to within three hundred kilometers of each other. It was like an ancient battle where Celtic hordes roared their battle cries as they swarmed a lost cohort of desperate legionaries. Drones detonated, firing x and gamma rays. EMP blasts washed over the warships. Heat boiled away particle-shielding and shrapnel shredded entire areas.

The *Vladimir Lenin's* sister ship stopped responding to calls.

"Are they dead?" Blackstone shouted to Kursk standing right beside him.

She kept trying to hail the warship.

"They're not beaming anymore," Hawthorne said from the acceleration couch. "I doubt anyone lives over there."

Two drones reached that battleship at almost precisely the same instant. Their nuclear explosions ended the debate on the *Vladimir Lenin* as another SU ship perished.

The next few minutes were hell.

"Sir!" an officer reported. "The one through five PD cannons are out of shells."

"Sir!" a different officer said. "Secondary laser number five has overheated. There's a fire in the reactor chamber."

Hawthorne gripped his screen. He found it difficult to breathe. Drones exploded everywhere. The cyborgs had made too many missiles and—

"Sir," Kursk said, "the drones... I don't see any heading toward us. There are drones, but they're well past our ships and accelerating out-system." She tapped her screen. "Over two thousand drones are heading away. There's no indication they're going to turn around, either." Tears welled in her eyes as she stared across the bridge. "Supreme Commander Hawthorne, I wish to report that the last drone has detonated, been destroyed by our lasers or its targeting systems were likely damaged beyond recovery and are leaving us."

With an effort, Hawthorne pried his fingers from the screen. It dawned on him that the last explosions had been the cyborgs' final attack. He blinked at the screen, bewildered.

"Where are they going?" Blackstone said. He kept tapping his screen, no doubt switching camera feeds. "You're right. Those missiles are heading away, accelerating away. I don't see any missiles heading toward us. Have some gone invisible?"

Kursk was laughing as tears streamed down her cheeks. "No, Joseph. Don't you understand? We did it. The ones leaving—all those nuclear blasts had to damage some of them." She threw her arms around his neck. "We won."

"We haven't won," Hawthorne said, "but it appears we've survived this round." He adjusted his uniform as he sat up. "I want damage reports, people. Then I want shuttles launched. Let's see if there's anybody to save on those ships."

"Are you kidding?" asked Kursk.

"I see one Doom Star and two SU battleships," Hawthorne said. "That's precious little to conquer the Neptune System. We need to search for survivors."

Blackstone disengaged from Kursk. "Don't forget the three Jovian meteor-ships heading here."

"Do you think the drones that passed us are meant for the Jovians?" Kursk asked. She checked the module and soon shook her head. "No. The drones are heading elsewhere."

"It hardly matters," Hawthorne said. "The meteor-ships are damaged and depleted."

"They are still a lot better than nothing," Blackstone said.

Hawthorne thought about it. "You have a point. Now get me those reports," he told Kursk. "We don't know how much time we have until the next cyborg move."

-11-

Far from the horrendous battle in the Neptune System, the *William Tell* passed a HB interferometer beacon. There were hundreds of such beacons linked by a special communications net. Taken together the interferometer was thousands of kilometers wide, although its mass wouldn't have filled an SU battleship.

Inside the patrol boat, Marten shifted in his combat armor. The air in his armor was rank with sweat as the air-conditioning unit thrummed. The temp-gauge read 102 degrees. The jumpsuit he wore next to his skin was damp against his back. It seemed like he was always sucking on the water-tube.

The temperature in his armor had steadily risen during the journey. He'd been living in his for some time now, just like everyone else. There was stubble on his chin and his right calf itched horribly.

The Jovian craft had never been designed to fly so close to the Sun. The SU-derived modifications hadn't changed that. Fortunately, Marten had looted the *Mao Zedong*, taking among other things a large supply of construction-foam sprayers.

They were a combat engineer's tool, used for fast construction. Riot police also used them to create quick barriers. The nozzles sprayed moldable foam, which quick hardened. During their shock trooper training, both Marten and Omi had been taught to spray blocks of construction-foam. There was a technique for shrinking the blocks, making them denser than ordinary.

Felix drew up the blueprint and Marten and Omi sprayed the foam. They thickened the hull from the inside, shrinking the amount of livable space and sectioning off the piloting chamber. The troop-pods became unlivable due to their nearness to the Sun. There wasn't enough construction-foam to use inside them. That meant everyone was jammed into the main area of the boat. Only Osadar entered the piloting area. The logic was simple but brutal. She was a cyborg and could take more radiation and heat than any of them could. Marten was afraid she was dying as she brought them to the fabled Sun Station, but wouldn't tell them.

The deckplates were the same as always. It was the top and sides of the boat that were different. Gray foam blocks there absorbed the illumination shining from the few helmet-lamps.

Everyone wore armor, including Ah Chen and Nadia. Some of the space marines checked their weapons. There were gyroc rifles, plasma cannons and the few remaining Cognitive missiles. Others recharged their suits. Everyone took turns hooking a cable into slots in their armor.

Marten floated, partially resting on his knees before the compartment's only screen, a portable one. It was easy in the weightless chamber. The patrol boat didn't feel like home anymore with the foam walls, but an alien environment—like some strange alien ant's tunnel system. The heat made it worse, so did the crackling in his headphones.

Both were due to the Sun: a nuclear fireball of heat, radiation, harsh radio and electromagnetic waves. Marten had been checking the specifics. The Sun was a yellow dwarf star, its spectral class G2V. It was almost perfectly spherical, a mix of hot plasma and powerful magnetic fields. Its diameter was 109 times that of Earth, making it enormous. The Sun produced the largest continuous structure in the Solar System, the heliosphere. In effect, the heliosphere was a giant bubble "blown" by the solar wind and emanating all the way to Pluto's orbital path.

A space marine floated next to Marten. He read the nametag: OMI. Marten nodded a greeting.

Omi gripped Marten's right shoulder. The Korean then clanged his helmet against Marten's.

"Anything new?" Omi asked. His voice sounded far away.

For an answer, Marten shook his head.

Releasing Marten's shoulders, Omi floated before the screen.

The compartment was jammed with space marines and their equipment, almost filling the entire area. Omi probably asked because there had been plenty of evil to report earlier.

From Venus, Commandant Maximus had launched more missiles, which accelerated fast. Then Osadar reported hidden drones burning into life, taking out one HB missile after another.

That had started a debate. The consensus seemed clear: cyborgs had seeded Inner Planetary space with mines and seeker drones.

"They were placed there to protect their stealth-ships," Marten said. "Now the seekers are protecting us."

"Ironic," Osadar said.

What Marten found more ironic were the cyborg forces zeroing in on the Sun Station. The images had been faint and fuzzy. Lasers flashed. Drones exploded and cyborg pods died thousands of kilometers from their objective. A few must have made it through the defensive field and boarded the station. Several hours ago, Marten, Omi, Nadia, Xenophon and others had crowded around the screen. Mostly they viewed the giant fireball. It was the sounds in their headphones that kept them glancing into each other's eyes.

Highborn sent distress signals. Then came distinctive combat noises and Highborn shouting to each other. A few times Marten heard high-speed speech that put goosebumps on his flesh. Cyborgs—the cyborgs were using their own private binary language.

The Highborn calls lessened, and then the last transmission came in: "They're breaching into the control chamber! I'm beginning the auto-destruct sequence." Gunfire erupted and then crackling noises that surely meant silence on the station.

Marten blinked sweat out of his eyes. He along with everyone else wondered if the Highborn had completed his task or if the cyborgs now controlled the Sun Station.

He glanced at Nadia floating beside him. What kind of universe created cyborgs? The scientists with their labs and genetically created super-soldiers—Marten shook his head. It was bad enough tampering with man like that. But to meld flesh with machines was blasphemy against nature. It brought the due reward of a hellish existence and maybe now the extinction of humanity.

Marten clutched his gyroc and something vital smoldered in his eyes. He was freaking hot. He was thirsty, and he was on a boat headed for a showdown with evil beings. By the sounds, the cyborgs had killed the Highborn. What chance did a handful of space marines have?

Gripping his rifle even harder, Marten thought back to the glass tube in Sydney. Major Orlov had put him in it, and he had pumped.

"I didn't give up then," he whispered. "I damn well don't plan on giving up now." If he were headed to his death, he would die fighting. Maybe this was his Force-Leader Yakov hour. *I'm not running away from the fight. I'm headed for it.*

He didn't want to die. He didn't want Nadia to die. But he didn't want to live in a universe ruled by cyborgs.

"You say something?" Omi asked.

"Yeah," Marten said. "We've dug them out of their fortresses before. We can do it again."

Omi stared at him. "Last time we had a fleet and ten-to-one odds on our side."

Marten shrugged even as his breathing became ragged. He sucked on a tube, letting warm water trickle down his throat. He wondered if this small vessel could make it past the defensive zone. It was doubtful the cyborgs had destroyed every HB mine or laser-point. Thinking about it reminded him of his shock trooper training at Mercury.

"Mirrors are moving!" Osadar radioed. Her words were difficult to decipher over the heavy crackling.

Mirrors? Marten wasn't aware Osadar had spotted any of them. The mirrors were supposed to be near the solar atmosphere.

"Give me a visual," he said.

"Can't," she said. "I'll give you virtual reality imaging instead."

Marten lifted the portable screen so more of the marines could see. He could feel them gathering around and others craning for a look. The screen was fuzzy. Then a silvery object appeared. It was incredibly thin. Against the Sun, it was a tiny speck.

The image grew larger, showing more of the mirror. According to Osadar, there were thousands of these. They were weighted in position by a clever technology that used the rays to fuel the mechanism that kept them still. Otherwise, they would act like a huge solar-wind sail. The focuser was on a similar scale as the rest of the weapon, kilometers wide.

"Is the weapon activating?" Marten asked.

"I have to check some other scans," Osadar said.

Marten tried to envision thousands of the gigantic mirrors sending the blistering sunlight at the focuser. It represented a titanic amount of energy, an inconceivable amount.

"It's been activated," Osadar said. "Someone is firing it."

"Cyborgs?" asked Marten.

"Who are they shooting?" she asked.

"Can you get a visual of the beam?"

"I'm working on it."

As the *William Tell* drifted toward the Sun Station, the giant focuser made minute corrections. Then it happened. For the first time, the Sun weapon beamed a titanic ray of incandescent fury. The tip of the beam flashed at the speed of light for a distant object.

"Do you see that?" Osadar asked.

On the screen, a bar of concentrated sunlight shot somewhere.

Marten stopped breathing as a feeling of awe spread through him. He forgot to feel hot as he watched the beam.

The hellish ray reached Mercury's orbital path in minutes. In a little over eight minutes, the beam passed Earth's orbital path. Several more minutes brought it as far as Mars. Then the Sunbeam continued its journey, heading out for deep space.

***

Across the Solar System on Triton, the Prime Web-Mind seethed with impatience as it issued directives and alerted the surface defenses. Its movable life-chamber was deep underground in an armored area. With the destruction of two Doom Stars, it should be safe. But there was no sense in taking chances now.

In the inner room, in a bath of green light, brain domes pulsed with neural charges. The backup computers ran computations. Life support monitors ensured a constant supply of nutrients and different viewers showed scanner data.

Shocked by the space battle, the Prime had launched endless logic probes. There had been an extremely low probability of any of its enemies surviving the battle. Yet some *had* survived. That caused the Prime to doubt its earlier computations. Had self-justification compromised its cognitive abilities? Solipsism lay there: the philosophical idea that only one's own mind, alone, was sure to exist. It was a serious epistemological error, although there were several interesting factors pointing to its reality.

The mass, explosive power and durability of the drone swarm should have achieved complete victory. The Prime had computed a negligible two percent failure rate. Data suggested there had been a four point three percent reporting error, with a zero point eight percent computational error.

The strategy should have worked flawlessly. Likely, the failure had been operational in nature. Yes, the flow of data suggested that. The loss of Nereid and Proteus—bitter to observe—had ensured the enemy's close approach to Neptune. The Highborn had surely wished to beam Triton into submission in the same manner as the other moons. How delightful to watch the braking and then flight of the eight intruders. Perhaps it should have accelerated the drones sooner, but it hadn't wanted anything to foil strategic surprise. The plan had rested on surprise, and the plan had achieved partial success.

Two Doom Stars are gone. The Prime replayed the vessels' destruction, using twelve percent of its brainpower to delight in the rare spectacle. Watching their advance these eight months had been painful and worrisome. *With the death of the third Doom Star, I will have achieved system victory.*

Thirty-three percent of its brainpower used long-distance tight-beams to monitor the fighting on the Sun Station. The station's outer defenses had proven more powerful than it had inferred. Still, it knew now that cyborgs had reached the station in number. That was critical, as cyborgs possessed tactical superiority to any known form of infantry. Once the cyborgs gained control of the station, they would perform as instructed. Destruction of the last Doom Star was paramount. Along with that message, the Prime had sent projected Doom Star locations and weighted percentages of future locations.

Fourteen percent of its brainpower was dedicated to watching the massive warship. Giant teleoptic towers on Triton's surface minutely moved their lens as they tracked the enemy ships.

Part of the fourteen percent, along with dedicated computers, broke down the ships' actions. Bright flares showed the exhausts of enemy shuttles and pods crisscrossing the large volume of battle-space. Rationality programs deduced that the humans searched for survivors, as incredible as that seemed.

They give me a further advantage as they waste time. It is inconceivable. I would never waste the most precious commodity. Time is the essence of life. I waste nothing, neither time, nor resources, nor computations. Once again, I prove my superiority to exist. How pitiful they really are, a blight upon the ALL.

The Prime scanned former interviews, selecting one to re-watch. It had interviewed several captive Neptunian scientists. The answers had startled it, a thing not easily achieved.

Like a banker watching a critical investment, the Prime tracked the last Doom Star. The giant vessel continued its predicted course through Neptunian space. The Prime had accounted for a three percent deviation. Instead, its computations and analytic predictions were perfect.

I am approaching perfection. With the elimination of the Homo sapiens and Highborn, it could reroute more of its brainpower to achieving Nirvana: a perfect state of cyborg completeness and dominance. Small habitats of gene-weeded humans would supply the brains for more Web-Minds until it learned how to cultivate its own tissue-beds.

A program alert shifted the Prime's concentration. The vessel's long-ranged laser, the final danger came from it. A few more hours of full concentration until the Doom Star was destroyed…

Then I will be safe. Then nothing can harm me and I will have won everything.

***

On the *Napoleon Bonaparte*, Admiral Sulla applied another coat of grease to his face as he sat in the command chair. His dark eyes shone with victory-lust. He dipped his fingers into the cream and lathered it over his right cheek.

He had survived the great encounter with the cyborgs. The drone swarm—Sulla scowled as he recalled the death of two Doom Stars. The battle had been a close-run thing. The premen had acted courageously and done their part. Now he wondered if he could he be wrong about the lower race.

Maybe I can run tests, saving the bravest among them. It might be possible through careful breeding to raise the genetic standard of the herd. *I will create a vassal race, one good enough to live among the Highborn.* Sulla nodded, enjoying his merciful thought. He would reward the courage shown here. No doubt, the premen couldn't understand his generosity. *I am letting them live. That is the thing.*

He paused before re-dipping his fingers into the grease. Could his interaction with the premen have tainted him? He frowned thoughtfully as a damage-control technician checked a weapons screen.

Insidious, he thought. *I have been tainted. Me merciful—Sulla the Ultraist, Grand Admiral of the Highborn?*

Since he was the last admiral and controlled the last Doom Star, it made sense he could grant himself whatever title he desired. Cassius had self-elevated himself to Grand Admiral. Now he had taken the rank because he had won the Battle for Neptune. Who could dare say otherwise? He was clearly the greatest Highborn. Scipio, Cato, Grand Admiral Cassius, they were all gone, all dead. The cowardly Maximus, the Commandant who hadn't been able to generate the courage to come out to Neptune and face the enemy—Maximus would never give him trouble. Sulla knew that in his gut.

My intuition has never failed me.

As Sulla's gloating smile widened, the terrible beam from the Sun neared Neptune System. The Sunbeam shot from the focuser had traveled at 300,000 kilometers per second. With that speed, it had taken four point twelve hours to cross the distance that had taken the Alliance Fleet a little over eight months to travel. Due to the speed of the attack, there was no warning of death's approach aboard the *Napoleon Bonaparte*.

The repair-teams feverishly brought the Doom Star back to battle readiness. The cyborg stealth-ships continued hiding in the void and the last drones had exhausted their fuels, moving out-system with great velocity. Then the Sunbeam flashed onto its target. In a frightfully concentrated ray, the Sun's energy struck the collapsium plating and immediately set the metal to boiling. Alarms rang aboard the *Napoleon Bonaparte* as heat levels rose intolerably.

Smoke rose from screens as flames burst into existence on the bulkheads.

Sulla glanced about, his eyes wide. Sweat mixed with grease so drops rolled off his chin. "What's happening?" he shouted.

The fury of the ray was greater by many magnitudes than the proton beams on Earth. It was the greatest weapon ever devised in the Solar System.

As Highborn tore off their shirts, beating the fiery walls with them, the Sunbeam burned through the collapsium.

"Report!" Sulla shouted. The hairs on his arms began to curl and crisp. The smell of cooked flesh brought a hideous look of rage to his eyes. "What is causing this?"

They were his last words as the incredible ray fired across the vast gulf of four and a half billion kilometers consumed the Doom Star. The great vessel slagged, melted and then burned away under the furious power of the great Sunbeam of Inner Planets.

***

The SU battleships were two and three and quarter thousand kilometers away from the *Napoleon Bonaparte* respectively.

On the bridge of the *Vladimir Lenin*, Hawthorne, Blackstone and Kursk stood around the command module. With astonishment, they watched the module's screens.

Slack-faced, Kursk managed to whisper, "The Doom Star is gone. They're all gone. There are no more Doom Stars in the Solar System."

"Get us out of here," Hawthorne said in a ragged voice. "We have to move before it targets us."

"What's firing?" Blackstone asked, bewildered.

Kursk shook her head. "The power wattages are off the charts. I do not understand this."

"How are we going to storm Triton now?" Blackstone asked. His thin features whitened. "We needed the Doom Star's heavy beam. Two battleships can't assault Triton. We won't even *dent* the number of laser-turrets before they burn us."

Hawthorne sagged against the module. All the effort, all the fighting and all the enduring these past years… "They've won," he said. His words were unequivocal and struck like a hammer blow to the kidneys. "The cyborgs have won." He could hardly comprehend the immensity of what he said. He could hardly breathe. Yet he managed to add, "Humanity is doomed."

-12-

Marten Kluge wasn't aware of the Supreme Commander's pronouncement. He just knew that his handful of space marines had to storm onto the Sun Station and oust the victorious cyborgs or that beam would destroy everything he held dear.

It could target Earth and beam it into cinders. It could fry the Venusian sunshield and then Venus. The Sun-Works Factory would never survive the ray. It was an annihilating weapon, meant to give utter dominance to the person controlling it. No wonder Commandant Maximus had remained behind. With it, he could have set himself up as the Solar System's emperor, the Sunbeam his hammer of royal authority. The heavily fortified Luna Base—once the cyborgs targeted it, they could slice the Moon into pieces. This was the ultimate weapon, and the cyborgs owned it, meaning that nothing could stop them now.

Omi stared at him through his helmet's visor. The Korean's harsh features seemed starker than ever. "Do we have a chance?"

"We're mankind's last chance," Marten snarled.

Through the visor, Omi's stare lengthened until his lips twisted into a rare smile. "The dregs of Sydney are going to save humanity. Turbo would have liked that."

Turbo...Marten scowled. Too many good friends had died over the years: Force-Leader Yakov, Major Diaz of the Martian Commandoes, Lance, Vip, Turbo, Stick and Kang, evil old Kang of the Red Blades. He missed them all.

"Get ready," Osadar radioed. "We're about to begin deceleration."

Marten gripped his gyroc. "Storming another stronghold—how many times have we done this?"

"Too many," Omi said, "far too many."

"We will defeat them," Felix said. In his powered armor and with his size, the hulking Highborn was bigger than any of the space marines.

There was a lurch aboard the patrol boat. Marten clanged against Group-Leader Xenophon.

"Look at this," Osadar said over the harshly crackling radio.

Marten had to turn down the volume the crackling became so bad. "What happened?" he asked, even though he knew what had happened. The ion engine had begun to brake the boat's velocity.

"Look at your screen," Osadar said, sounding tired. It was the first time he'd heard that in Osadar's voice.

"Are you feeling okay?" he radioed.

"Do not worry about me," she said.

"I am. You're my friend. I don't want to lose you, too."

"Look at your screen."

Marten picked up the screen and turned it. Space marines crowded around. For the first time, he had a good look at the Sun Station. It was round and brightly metallic like chrome. There were black splotches in it. He squinted, looking closer. Those splotches—they must be breaches, holes. Debris floated around the breaches.

"Do you see?" Osadar asked.

"Polymers?" asked Marten.

"Yes. Correct. The cyborgs blasted their way in, although their stealth-pods did not survive."

"Got it," Marten said. "What happened to the outer defensive field?"

"I don't understand why we haven't been fired upon," Osadar said. "Maybe the cyborgs inserted a virus into the computing systems, but I doubt they destroyed everything."

Marten scanned the space marines behind him. Every time he looked through a visor, he saw men battling fear. Nadia's eyes were wide with fright, but she managed a tremulous smile. Every armor suit had old scars from former fights. They could have used new gyroc rifles. The plasma cannons had pitted nozzles, showing extended use.

Marten bared his teeth as fierce pride beat in his chest. These were his space marines, the survivors of too many fights. Not all the spit and piss had been knocked out of them yet.

"I'm going to try to ram through the biggest breach," Osadar said. "None of us could withstand the Sun's rays for more than several seconds if they caught us outside. We have to get inside behind the station's insulation."

"Is the hole big enough?" Marten asked.

A shudder ran through the *William Tell*. Then another followed the first.

"I've detached the troop pods," Osadar said.

"Is the breach big enough?" Marten asked.

"Not completely," Osadar said. "You must be ready for a hard impact."

"Great."

"Do you desire to space-walk to the station?"

Marten muttered to himself. Suicide by sunshine, he wanted no part of that. "Are you holding up okay?"

"I'll join you once we've docked," she said. "Does that suit you?"

"Keep talking," Marten said.

"The cyborgs took my body from me," Osadar said. "They tore me out of my flesh and turned me into this. We cannot let them win."

Marten turned to his space marines. "We're going in," he said, using an open channel. "This is the fight and we're the last grunts left. We have to dig out the cyborgs." Marten swallowed a lump that rose in his chest. "This is going to be nasty, but we've beaten these freaks before. They want to enslave us. They want to bury implants in our brains. There's only one answer to that, a bullet in their head. Nothing matters today but winning. We're all expendable if just one of us is left standing at the end to use the Sunbeam as a free man."

"Kill the cyborgs!" Group-Leader Xenophon shouted.

"They killed Jupiter," Marten said. "They hunted down every human in the system. We can do the same to them if we win."

"Can we win?" a space marine asked.

Marten laughed harshly. "I've got a gun in my hand and bastards telling me I'm going to be his slave. Live or die, I'm going to fight and show them they're facing men!"

The Jovians roared bloodthirsty oaths as they shook their weapons.

"Now grab onto something," Marten said. "This is going to get rough."

***

In the sealed pilot's chamber, Osadar sat alone in her combat armor. Heavy shields were locked before the ballistic glass window.

With her gauntleted fingers, she tapped the screen. The ion engine burned hotter as it increased thrust. Using sensors and outer cameras, she saw the exhaust licking against the Sun Station. The heavily-hulled circular structure was over half a kilometer in diameter.

The universe owes me for all the injustice it has heaped upon me. Just once, I would like some good luck.

Her screen showed motion on the station. With a sinking feeling, she realized she shouldn't have through directly against fate. The universe had heard and now it screwed her yet again.

Osadar bared her teeth. It must have been an unconscious gesture learned from Kluge. The man never quit. He kept charging against insane odds in his quixotic quest for freedom. He was a fool, but Marten Kluge was her fool and friend. Maybe he was the universe's prank against those who thought they could control everything.

Using a close-up, Osadar zeroed in on the biggest breach, the one she aimed for. Those were suited cyborgs. They tracked the patrol boat. With a tap, she zoomed an even closer shot. The cyborgs held silvery, hand-held missiles. As the cameras watched, the cyborgs fired. Silvery missiles streaked for the boat.

Osadar laughed. It was a strange sound. Each silvery sliver melted in the boat's ion exhaust. One after another, they turned into slag and then disappeared.

It was then Osadar spotted wrecked auto defenses on the outer station hull. That explained much. The cyborgs must have destroyed them going in.

We didn't give them time to fix them.

Osadar tensed her muscles. In seeming slow motion, the *William Tell* backed into the Sun Station, the ion exhaust licking against the outer hull.

"No," Osadar whispered.

At another breach more cyborgs appeared. They launched a flock of hand-held missiles. As Osadar fired a PD cannon at the cyborgs, the missiles slammed into the boat. Explosions rocked the craft as warheads blew away sections of boat. Polymers, foam, and air sprayed outward.

Osadar slapped a switch. Then she cinched her straps. Seconds later, the Jovian vessel crumpled against the Sun Station, a portion making it through as the rest shredded in a groan and then a terrible shriek of metal.

It is your time, Marten Kluge. Screw the cyborgs if you can.

***

It was chaos aboard the *William Tell*. Marines slammed against each other. Sections of ship tore apart. In his headphones, Marten heard yelling. Then he realized he shouted as loud as he could. As he flew across the chamber, grunting, as he sank against hardened foam, Marten had time to believe that this was worse than the sled-ride onto the *Bangladesh's* particle-shields. He flew a different way and clanged against another marine. His head banged around in his helmet, fortunately cushioned by pads for this express reason. Terrible screeching assaulted his ears. Then it was over. He lay still, a mass of bruises and sore joints. It hurt to shift. Jovians were piled on and around him.

Knowing they had little time, Marten clenched his teeth and forced himself to move his arm. He would not groan. He would not give in to pain. He had to act now.

He tapped a forearm pad. A groan did slide from his tightened lips as a needle jabbed his flesh. It injected a double dose of painkillers. He took a deep breath and managed to say, "Get up. Let's get going."

"My leg is broke," a space marine radioed.

"No excuses," Marten said, "not today. Shoot yourself with painkillers. If that doesn't help, use more. We made it here and now we have a job to do."

"It's dark."

"Use your infrared," Marten said.

"Mine's not working," Xenophon said.

Marten tried his. "Mine isn't either. It must have something to do with the nearness to the Sun. It doesn't matter. Use your helmet-lamps. We're used to that."

"Lamps aren't going to help us gain surprise over cyborgs," Xenophon said.

"If it isn't one thing, it's another," Marten said. "Now no more excuses. Follow me. It's time to kick cyborg ass."

In the light of his helmet-lamp, Marten shoved aside wreckage. Behind him, space marines followed as more lamps clicked on. In the wash of thirty beams, the humans worked in tandem.

The storming of the Sun Station began as Marten Kluge eased through a jagged opening. He left the wreckage of the *William Tell* and entered the first chamber. What he found there told the story.

There were blast holes in the bulkheads and sparking circuitry. A cable writhed back and forth as a thick liquid oozed from it. Worse were floating Highborn, dead soldiers in breached powered armor. One big Highborn was missing his head as blood floated where the neck should have been. Fewer dead cyborgs drifted in their battle-suits, helmets shattered and foreheads shot out. The Highborn had known the rule on how to kill the melds.

"It was a massacre," Xenophon whispered.

Marten noticed he could hear the Jovian's voice more clearly. The station blocked more of the Sun's interference than the *William Tell* had.

"Keep together," Marten said. With a practiced shove, he pushed off the floor and floated past the dead. Using his gyroc rifle, he shoved a drifting cyborg out of his way. As he neared the blasted hatch, Marten's gut clenched. Xenophon had been right earlier. They needed their suit's radar. Now he'd have to use his eyes and the lamp-beam that would give him away.

Marten held his breath as he floated through the hatch, his rifle ready. His beam flashed down a curving corridor. In it, more dead floated, both Highborn and cyborg.

"We're doing this by the numbers," Marten said. "We stick together and search out each chamber and corridor at a time. I don't want anyone splitting apart and heading elsewhere."

The space marines followed him through the corridors. Always, there were the dead HB and the fewer destroyed cyborgs. Once, a cyborg twitched, and seven shells from seven different gyrocs blasted it. There were floating globules of blood and drifting intestines. Jovians floated past severed hands, heads and wrecked plasma cannons.

"Armageddon," Marten whispered.

Omi clanked his helmet against Marten's. "What's that mean?"

"The last battle," Marten said.

They floated past hatches where bolts of energy flashed wildly. One bolt writhed through the hatch and fused a Jovian to his armor.

"Keep away from the side hatches!" Marten shouted.

Marines scrambled to get away from the energy bolt.

A corridor later, Omi asked, "So where are the cyborgs?"

"They will be in the control chamber," Felix said.

"Any idea where that is?" asked Marten.

"I think in the very center of the station," Ah Chen answered. Nadia and she wore combat armor like everyone else, joining them in the assault. There were no safe places here.

In the wash of helmet-lamps, the party pushed and floated through the Sun Station. Because they lacked any schematics, they had to search for the center. There were many curving corridors and endless chambers. Each held their quota of floating dead, battalions of Highborn and always lesser number of cyborgs.

"They killed each other off," Omi said.

"Keep alert," Marten said.

"They're near," Felix radioed.

"How do you know?" asked Xenophon.

The Highborn grunted, "I know because I feel them."

Cyborgs hit them seventeen seconds later. In a large, dark area—a cargo-hold was Marten's guess—the enemy made their move.

With the speed of insects, four suited cyborgs jumped off a corridor wall one after another. They flew into the chamber, firing pulse-rifles: tiny blue energy-bolts streaked across the chamber. They targeted with uncanny accuracy and with amazing speed, maybe three times as fast as what a trained space marine could achieve.

Due to precision shots, eight visors shattered and eight Jovians died. Two pulse rounds sizzled across Felix's helmet—he'd turned his head fast enough so the armor took the shots. The Highborn reacted faster than any of the space marines. Even as he looked up, he aimed his rotating hand-cannon. With flames of fire, the heavy weapon churned, pushing Felix away from the enemy.

Marten had reacted almost as fast. He berated himself for failing to fire. Instead, he had ducked and he lay on the floor. With his gyroc, he now returned fire.

Hand-cannon slugs tore into a cyborg, foiling its aim, saving Nadia's life as a pulse-bolt missed her by centimeters. It was too late for Ah Chen, however. Her stomach was blown out by repeated pulse-shots breaching her armor.

Omi fired from the wall. A few other space marines now shot back. APEX shells ignited. A few hit, a very few. Too many shells flew past the cyborgs, exploding uselessly against the already pitted walls.

The cyborgs killed three more marines. Then Felix's slugs hammered a cyborg visor and smashed through, obliterating the armored brainpan. Together, Marten and Omi killed another.

The last two cyborgs kept tracking and firing, taking out more space marines with frightful skill, inhuman precision. Another cyborg appeared, this one wearing Jovian battle-gear. Osadar used a plasma cannon, firing the area-effect weapon. A roiling orange globule consumed a cyborg, and yet another marine. The last cyborg slammed its hands against its chest. The thing ignited in a terrific explosion, killing five more Jovians. Four cyborgs had slaughtered half the space marines in a matter of moments.

"What now?" Xenophon whispered.

"You stay and help the wounded," Marten told him. "The rest of you, follow me." His eyes were watery with rage. How could these things murder men with such ease? "I'm going to take point from here on in."

"We need a plan," Omi said. "How are we going to do this?"

Marten couldn't look at the dead. These men—he sputtered, growing angrier. "Caution seems useless. So we use speed. Attack and fire at whatever you see."

The last of the space marines flew down the corridors with him. Everyone fired shells into each new heading, often blowing apart the floating dead.

Despite their best efforts, cyborgs hit them again at a junction, taking them from the flank. This time, each cyborg projectile and pulse-round struck Felix. Maybe the cyborgs realized he was the truly dangerous soldier among them.

Felix grunted over the headphones. Dying, he turned, and killed a cyborg with the hand-cannon.

The next few seconds was a maelstrom of weapons-fire. The handful of cyborgs that had ambushed them died. Forty-one seconds later, Marten, Omi, Osadar and two other space marines propelled themselves into the large central chamber of the Sun Station.

Three cyborgs were at various controls. They obviously worked on targeting the Sunbeam. Marten could tell because there were images on the targeting screens of two SU battleships.

Marten fired two shells at one cyborg, swiveled his rifle and was firing at a second enemy even as the meld drew a gun. The first died as the APEX shells blew apart its helmet. The last lost its gun-hand to the shell.

Omi's shell killed it a second later. The last cyborg died by plasma.

Marten blinked at the dead as he breathed heavily.

"Do you think that's it?" Omi asked.

"We'll know soon enough," Marten said. "Osadar, do you have any idea how to use the equipment?"

"Let us find out," she said.

-13-

The Prime Web-Mind of Neptune grew impatient. The Sunbeam should have taken out more targets by now. There wasn't any news of that at all.

At that moment, the Sunbeam reached the Neptune System for a second time. The hellish ray did not fire anywhere near the SU warships, however. Instead, the beam fixed on Triton.

The terrible ray burned through Triton's negligible nitrogen atmosphere. Then it struck the surface of mostly frozen nitrogen and water-ice crust. The incredible beam chewed through the surface, burning through a cryovolcano.

In a brief span of time, the beam burst through and hit a vast subterranean ocean. The liquid boiled away as vapors steamed in a growing cloud. The beam still struck as it continued to bore deeper into the Neptunian moon.

The Prime knew in a nanosecond that someone else controlled the Sunbeam. This was an emergency, a dire event. In three seconds, it understood that whoever fired the beam meant to destroy the moon. Whoever fired tried to kill it—the marvel of the universe. That could never occur. There was only one possible solution now.

The armored chamber holding the Prime's brain domes lifted. Jets fired and the chamber shook. Slowly, the great armored room slid through wide corridors as it headed for the great elevator.

The Prime ran through outlandish scenarios. Cooling chemicals kept hysteria at bay, kept panic from guiding its logic. Given its uniqueness and greatness, it would be an inconceivable loss to the Solar System if it should perish.

I am the Prime, the singularity of existence.

The armored chamber headed for a large oval vessel. The vessel was bigger than an SU battleship, although it would never willingly engage in a fight. The size was for the unique equipment, for the experimental Fuhl Mechanism.

As the armored chamber moved up the elevator, as debris slammed against the roof, as Triton-quakes shook the planetoid, the hideous Sunbeam kept burning. Time was running against it.

As the Prime's chamber slid into the belly of the great ship, the Sunbeam boiled the subterranean ocean at a fantastic rate. Seconds passed into minutes and the minutes crawled as the Prime's vessel slowly lifted off the moon.

The Sunbeam now burst through the subterranean ocean as it bored for the core.

The enemy must desire vengeance. How else to explain this crime against the universe? The Prime knew it was unique, a gift to reality. The thoughtless Homo sapiens with their small thinking must yearn to destroy Triton as Mars' moon Phobos had once been destroyed, as South American Sector on Earth had been destroyed.

This cannot happen to me. I am the Prime. I am the greatest life in the Solar System, probably in the entire galaxy.

The beam began to move now across Triton's moonscape. The great vessel slowly lifted for space as the beam moved faster, sweeping the surface and coming dangerously near the ship.

***

On the *Vladimir Lenin*, Hawthorne crowded next to Blackstone and Kursk as they watched the module.

"The beam is going to destroy the moon," Hawthorne whispered.

Kursk blinked several times. "Sir, there's a communications, an emergency message," she said, pointing at a blinking light on the panel.

Hawthorne tore his gaze from the incredible sight of the vast beam. "Put it on," he said.

It was a short message. It came from Cone on Earth. According to her, the Sun-Works Factory had been destroyed.

"What?" Hawthorne said. "How did that happen?"

The message was over four hours old. Therefore, Cone hadn't heard the question. She did tell them, however, that an amazing beam from the Sun had demolished the Highborn headquarters.

"A Sunbeam," Hawthorne said. "That's what we've been witnessing. What happened back in Inner Planets?"

"Sir!" said Blackstone. "Look! Is that a ship?"

Kursk was already bringing the object into sharper focus. It was oval, lifting from Triton's disintegrating surface.

"It's big," she said, "bigger than our battleship." She looked up in surprise. "These readings—I've never seen anything like them. Is it a weapon?"

Hawthorne opened his mouth to shout an order. Before he could utter any noise, four dark nodes appeared on the enemy ship. Then a strange flash occurred, and the ship disappeared, leaving the flash behind as it seemed to close in upon itself.

"What just happened?" Kursk whispered.

Hawthorne's jaw sagged as a sharp pain lanced his chest. He groaned, mastering the pain as his long fingers played over controls. He brought up the video recording and played it in slow motion.

The four nodes, they were a swirling black color, seeming to suck light. Then the flash occurred as it cycled through a number of colors: red, green, purple, orange, blue and bright white at the end. The ship slipped through what seemed like a rent in space, and the hole closed behind it as the colors cycled down.

"This is new," Hawthorne whispered.

"Did a cyborg ship escape?" Kursk asked.

"I'm more interested in finding out if a Web-Mind escaped," Hawthorne said.

"I doubt we'll ever know," Blackstone said. "That was the strangest thing I've ever seen."

"Stranger than the Sunbeam?" asked Kursk.

"I can understand the Sunbeam," Blackstone said. "What we just witnessed, I don't want to hazard a guess as to what it was."

"Was that a rip into hyperspace?" Hawthorne asked quietly.

"There are no warp drives or wormholes," Kursk said.

"Not until now," Hawthorne said. The pain in his chest was less than before, but it hurt every time his heart beat. Had they just fought the greatest war ever, only to have the enemy slip away to start everything over again from a different base? If that was a starship, with the Prime Web-Mind aboard...it meant the next cyborg attack might possibly come from another star system. He massaged his chest. This was more than he wanted to think about now. Sunbeams and starships...he wanted to go home to Earth.

Sunk in gloom, Hawthorne fell silent as Triton broke into sections, cut apart by the terrible ray.

***

The Prime knew a moment of rarified glee as its vessel winked out of existence above Triton and away from the annihilating ray.

In the huge ship, cyborgs stood at their stations, awaiting orders. The cargo-holds held massive amounts of equipment, all that was needed to begin again.

It was a risk I might never have taken. Now I own an experimental starship, a vessel to span the galaxy.

The glee turned to anger as the Prime realized it would have to start over.

I will rebuild elsewhere. Then I will return and cruelly subjugate those who thought to destroy my magnificence.

Quick calculations showed the Prime its strongholds in Uranus, Saturn, Jupiter and Mars could not survive the terrible Sunbeam. Perhaps if it gathered every surviving Lurker and used the starship—

No, I cannot risk losing this wonderful vessel. I own the only known starship. I will—

The Prime's gloating was cut short as a lurch and alarms throughout the starship told of a reentry into normal space. It ran an accelerated analysis. Neptune's nearness had upset the starship's gravitational fields, which needed a precision bordering on the Sunbeam's targeting systems.

Where am I? Have I reached another star system?

Cyborgs on the bridge poured their findings to the Prime. With a shock, the Prime realized it had only hopped a short distance. Then a louder alarm rang through the experimental starship.

***

Sub-Strategist Circe contemplated the meaning of the third Dictate. She sat in the Force-Leader's chair in the control chamber. Unconsciously, she rubbed the black gem embedded in her forehead. With half-lidded eyes, she let her gaze rove over a statute of an ancient, naked Roman boxer with a broken nose. He—

Sirens blared, making her twist in her chair.

"Sub-Strategist!" the *Erasmus's* weapons officer said. "An- an intruder has just appeared."

"Explain your statement," Circe said sharply.

"Look up at the screen," the officer said.

She did. Long-range teleoptics showed a big ship. "Is that an SU battleship?" she asked.

"No. It's bigger."

"Where did it come from?" Circe asked.

"There was a flash, Sub-Strategist, and then it just appeared."

"Attention!" Circe said, as she slapped an intercom button on her chair's armrest. "Warm the lasers and target the enemy ship. It is a cyborg vessel, the most dangerous one in existence. We must attack it with extreme prejudice."

"Are you sure it's a cyborg vessel?" the weapons officer asked.

"Destroy it," Circe said, "or we're all doomed." She had studied Chief Strategist Tan's information about a Fuhl Event. The cyborgs must have finally ironed out the flaws and now used this ship to attack each fleet piecemeal. It was a brilliant strategy. The thought she had endured so much to fall prey to yet another secret cyborg project—

"Annihilate it!" Circe hissed. "Annihilate it before its beam or missiles destroy us."

***

"Engage the Fuhl Mechanism!" the Prime messaged the cyborg crew. "We must leave this place."

"We need time to adjust and recalibrate the black-hole pods, Prime," a cyborg radioed its master.

"Then accelerate the ship away from those vessels!"

Several seconds later, the Prime experienced the building Gs as thrusters roared with life.

The Prime focused its sensors on the three meteor-ships. They were battered-looking.

Yes, they fought the Uranus cyborgs. By the ALL, I must survive.

Even as the Prime thought this, the three meteor-ships fired their primary lasers.

"Use the mechanism! Jump us out of here!"

"We need time, Prime."

"Do it now or I will die!"

The lasers burned into the starship's hull. Then the four nodes swirled with power. The Fuhl Mechanism started up, and the vessel began to crumple in upon itself. Its own gravitational forces destroyed the Solar System's first experimental starship.

***

As the Prime Web-Mind of Neptune perished, torn apart by black-hole gravitational forces, Commissar Kursk tapped her communications screen. A face appeared on the module.

"It's Marten Kluge," Hawthorne said.

"Greetings," Marten said. "I have just taken control of the Sun Station. I realize my time here may be short, so I have made some hard decisions. The first was the destruction of the Sun-Works Factory. I gave the Commandant the option to leave and head for Luna. He could not agree, so I destroyed the Factory before he could use it against me. I have just demolished Triton and I am about to target Luna and destroy the Highborn base there. In the days to come, I will target all cyborg concentrations of strength in each planetary system."

Marten Kluge took a deep breath. "I have lived under many political systems, and I have found them all repugnant. Therefore, the Solar System is going to try a new way for a time—my way. Those who cannot agree to try it, I will target. My way is called freedom, giving people a choice."

Marten's taut features broke into a grim smile. "I'm going to build a bigger station, a bigger defensive bulwark around the Sunbeam. And I'm calling it a Star Fortress. It gives me veto power over anything I find repugnant. Remember that as you begin instituting freedom throughout the Solar System. That is all for now. Marten Kluge out."

The End

Printed in Dunstable, United Kingdom

77548164R00181